Dancing
to
Her Own Tune

Sheila Hunter
&
Sara Powter

Bible Quotes from King James Version

ISBN: 9780645110715
Paperback edition

Pacific Wanderland Publications
Kincumber NSW 2251

saragpowter@gmail.com
www.sarapowter.com.au

1st edition 2021 printed by Kindle, an Amazon Company;
available on Kindle Unlimited & KDP
2nd 2021 Paperback Edition - Amazon
New cover 2024 - amazon
3rd 2023 Hardback Edition - Amazon

To Sheila Hunter, you inspire me still,
even though you're
no longer with me,
Thanks, mum.

This manuscript had only 30k words,
but she had written herself into a corner.
Sheila Hunter died in 2002.
I wanted to finish it, so I did.
Sara

Cover Painting
by Joseph Lycett (Cropped) - In Public Domain

TITLE: North View of Sydney ,New South Wales / taken from the North Shore
View_of_Sydney_Cove_from_Dawes_Point.png
(630 × 425 pixels, file size: 552 KB,)

From Dixson Galleries, State Library of New South Wales
DG V1 / 78   IE NUMBER: IE3198807   FILE NUMBER: FL3198817
FILE TITLE:
North View of Sydney, New South Wales

Cover Inset
A Young Beauty
Gustave Jacquet (1846 – 1909)
In Public Domain

How our ancestors coped as convicts still leaves me in awe!
They each had scars on their hearts.

To all those who have gone before us,
thank you!

Thanks to Alpha Male, my husband,
Steve, for all his support in my writing.
He's my Alpha reader.

Australian Historical Novels
(All stand-alone books)

A First Fleet Stories (1788+)

Gentle Annie Soames
Paternity Unknown (2026)

The Hunter to Macquarie Collection (1795-1822)

When Upon Life's Billows (2025)
Saddler's Song (2025)
Tuppence to Pass (2025)
His Majesty's Pageboy (2025)
Fist Full of Holey Dollars (2026)
Far From the Whispering Sheoaks (2026)
Bound Down in Iron Chains (2026)

Unlikely Convict Ladies Trilogy (1792-1840s)

Dancing to her Own Tune
(co-authored by Sheila Hunter & Sara Powter)
Amelia's Tears
A Lady in Irons

The Lockleys of Parramatta (1800-1901)

Unshackled Lives - *Prequel novella - free with newsletter signup*
Hands Upon the Anvil
Out Where the Brolgas Dance
Diamonds in the Dirt
The Earl's Shadow
Once a Jolly Swagman
Jonty's Journey

The Convict Birthstain Collection (1820-1840s)

No More, My Love
The Vine Weaver
Scotch at The Rocks
Waiting at the Sliprails
Convict Shadows of the Past
In Defence of Her Honour
I Can't Stop Tomorrow *(2024)*
Madeline's Boy *(2024)*
Jam or Marmalade for Tea *(2025)*

Shelia Hunter's
Australian Colonial Trilogy (1840-1850s)

Mattie
Ricky
The Heather to the Hawkesbury

To my patient and ever-loving husband, Stephen.
Thanks for doing the initial read-through.

To Roby Aiken
for your patience in correcting my punctuation
and to my Beta readers
Noreen Robertson and Linda Upcroft
for doing the final read-throughs,
and to Dasha Brandt for the corrections in the final copy.

& Anna Marie Leffew for the wonderful advertising she does for me.
And…

Rebekah Robinson for redoing the covers
Cover by Beckon Creative
beck@beckoncreative.biz

Acknowledgement of Country:
In the spirit of reconciliation, I acknowledge the Traditional Custodians of country throughout Australia and their connections to land, sea and community. We pay our respect to their Elders, past and present, and extend that respect to all Aboriginal and Torres Strait Islander peoples today.

Table of Contents

*The grammar and language in this book are
Australian English spelling.*

Character list at back of the book

KEY
~ - Time passing in the same locality

- Different locality/country

Chapter 1   Annie

*A*nnie White was unhappy. She had arrived on the *Pitt* in 1792 with the Third Fleet and was almost immediately assigned to a Mrs Tremaine. The Tremaine's were some of the relatively few free settlers. Mrs Tremaine had arrived with her husband. They had come here to seek a new life, thinking that they would better themselves. Mrs Tremaine's family had been tin miners in Cornwall, and she and her husband hoped to get a farm of their own and carry on in the traditional way of farming they had left. But the land was not as lush and green as their native Cornwall, and they found the going difficult. They were allocated plenty of convict help for their little farm out towards Parramatta, but they found them most inefficient. The going was tough, for the soil was not easy, and the rainfall somewhat haphazard. However, with the doggedness of their Cornish heritage, they kept going and did make something of their life, but it certainly was not one of ease. They had a dairy herd and grew vegetables for the population of Sydney Town.

Mr Tremaine had told Annie to work on the farm, but Mrs Tremaine found she was not the usual type of harsh, rough convict and had taken the girl into the kitchen to help. It was there that Annie found the kindness that she had not known for some years.

Annie was now in her late twenties. A rather tall, stately woman with fair curly hair, which she found hard to keep tidy. She was well built, not pretty, for her life had made her bitter, and it showed on her face. She was not chatty but always most helpful and was willing to learn from her mistress, a grand cook. This kind little Cornish woman taught Annie to cook and she was, soon after her arrival on the farm, able to cook most of the meals that Mrs Tremaine wanted. She even claimed that Annie's Cornish pasties were as good as her own.

Annie did not look for happiness, for she had learned that one could not expect fairness in life, and righteousness should bring some joy. Perhaps some people find that elusive commodity, but certainly not those of her order. She had known some happiness in her life, but it had lasted such a short time. It was now gone forever. Annie had no idea what she would do when she left the kindness found with Mrs Tremaine. She had almost served her seven years; she knew that she would have to go and start another life. There seemed little future in this harsh brown and hot land. She longed for the green fields of home but at the same time knowing that there was no life for her there, as she had no family. There was no reason to go back to England. No, she would just have to find some position where she could feel a modicum of safety. She wished she could stay with Mrs Tremaine, but that dear lady had told her she could not afford to have paid servants, so Annie would have to find her place in life.

"Annie," said Mrs Tremaine one morning, "Have you thought what you would do when you leave here?" The farmer's wife was a tiny dark woman who bustled everywhere. Annie always admired the way her mistress fussed. She was like a little doll on wheels as her little legs moved very fast under her long skirts.

"No, ma'am," answered Annie. "At least I've thought about it, but I have no idea what I will do. I will have to find somewhere, Mrs Tremaine. I am sure I will."

"Where will you go until you find a position?" her mistress asked.

"That I don't know, ma'am, but I daresay I will be able to find a room or something."

"Well, Mr Tremaine and I are giving you a small amount of money, Annie, as you have been a very good, helpful girl, and we will write a letter telling your next employer what a good girl you are."

"Oh, ma'am, thank you so. It will make all the difference. Ma'am, I'm very grateful," said Annie. "It will set me up for a position easily with a reference."

"Annie, there is one thing I want to know, and I know you will tell me the truth; you were sent out here for stealing, weren't you?"

"Yes, ma'am, I was."

"Did you steal, Annie? I have never asked you." Mrs Tremaine looked directly at her gauging her reaction.

"Ma'am, you know what is on my papers," Annie said.

"Yes, Annie, I do. But I am asking you, did you steal?"

Annie looked straight back at the woman and said, "No, ma'am, I did not, and I do not understand why I was accused as I was. It has always puzzled me."

"I thought so, lass, for you could have stolen while you were here, and you never have," Mrs Tremaine said, smiling as she said it. "When you leave here tomorrow," she continued, "I want you to go to Mistress Frame's lodging house in the main street. You will find a room has been arranged for you and payment has been made for one week. In that time, you will probably have found a new position or some such. Will you do this?"

"Ma'am, you are so good. Why are you doing this? There is no need, for I do hope to find employment," exclaimed Annie, wondering why her employer was so generous, and if she had found her so valuable why she was letting her go.

"You just be a good girl and do as I say," was all the woman would say. Then she added, "Alf is taking the cart into town tomorrow, and you can go with him."

"Thank you, ma'am; I was wondering how I would manage it," said Annie thoughtfully.

The next morning, Alf, the driver, put her bag among the vegetables he was taking to town. "Free, lass?" he asked.

"Yes, I don't really believe it. I think I am. At least I have my papers."

"What yer gonna do?" the man asked.

"I am going to a room that Mrs Tremaine arranged for me. She is very kind."

"Must think a lot o' yer," Alf said.

"Yes, they were very good to me," said Annie, still bewildered about her leave-taking. For Mrs Tremaine sent her away with food for several days in a basket that she could keep. She also gave her some money for clothes so she would not have to wear Government issue clothing.

"I put a box on the tray for yer to lean on," said Alf. "Long way ter Sydney Town. Slow trip," he added tersely.

Annie gratefully sat upon the vehicle, leaning her back against the box that the man had placed for her. She was interested to see the development of the settlements along the road from Sydney Town to Parramatta. Five years before, when she had gone to Tremaine's farm, there was little along this road but bush, but now there were farms and some bigger houses. "Soon," mused Annie. "It will be a new century. I wonder what a new century will bring. Can I ever like it in this place?" At the same time, worrying about what would be her life ahead was frightening. There were so many pitfalls for a single woman, and she had heard terrible tales even in the protection of Tremaine's farm. She had never had to plan her future before; her position as a maid in England had always been security. Even as a convict, she had protection of a sort. At least she had never had to think, just be obedient.

After several hours they reached Sydney, and she had to find the lodging house that Mrs Tremaine had arranged for her. She got down from the cart and looked around her, wondering which way to go. Alf hadn't waited for long, giving her a surly, "Good luck."

"Want some company, love?" asked a gruff voice beside her. It was a man who was eying her over.

"No, thank you," she replied in as haughty a voice as she could muster and headed along a track near a creek. She just wanted to get away from the man. So clutching her basket and her bundle in which carried her few clothes, she hurried along. She could hear the voice calling after her, but she took no notice.

There were tiny houses and shacks along this way; some places were reminiscent of an English village, giving little protection from the glaring summer sun. At last, she saw a woman sweeping the front steps of her small cottage. She was hot and somewhat frightened, for she didn't know which way to go and was hesitant about asking. "Could you tell me where I will find Mistress Frame's lodging house, please?" she asked.

"Yus, luv, yer going the wrong ways. Go back there to thet track and turn up to thet way. Then turn thet way again, and yer'll see it in the next road. Two story place it are." The toothless lady said lispingly.

Annie thanked her, and, following the directions given by the woman's expressive hands, she turned left and then right and found herself on a more significant road with better houses, and there she found her goal. It was a much larger building than the houses she had passed, it was two stories high, and it looked as though it could be three rooms wide. Annie knocked, and a rather large woman came to the door. "Yus?" she asked.

"I believe there is a room booked for me; my name is White," Annie asked nervously

"Yus, I wus wonderin' when yer'd come. Come in," invited the woman, who eyed Annie so carefully that she felt very awkward. "Me name's Frame. Yer room's up there. I won't go up them stairs agin' so yer'll find it just at the top of the stairs — the one with the door open to air. Yer'll find everythin' yer want. Clean linen I 'ave, an' ther'll be supper when I ring ther gong, in about two hours."

"Thank you, Mrs Frame, I will find my way all right," said Annie, still startled at the turn of events. On reaching the head of the stairs, she found a room with the door ajar as instructed. She pushed the door wide and looked at the neat, clean room. There was a large iron bedstead with a white cotton quilt on it. The room also had a washstand with a bowl and jug of water and a chair. There was a curtain across one corner behind which she could hang her clothes. She put her few things down and sat on the chair, looking around her. What was she to do? Where was she to go? Where was she to begin? She walked to the washstand and poured some water into the bowl; she sluiced her face with the cool water and took a towel to dry herself. She heard puffing and then a voice calling her. She opened her door and looked over the stairs.

"There's a gentleman to see yer, luv. Yer kin come to my sitting room, if yer, please, there ain't nobody in there," Mrs Frame called to her.

"A gentleman?" queried Annie, "But I don't know a gentleman."

"Well, 'e's 'ere, yer better come down. An' honey, he be a true gentleman, not some trumped-up dandy." Mrs Frame said proudly.

Annie was suddenly frightened, "I don't know any gentleman. What sort of place is this?" she asked fearfully.

"I'll have yer know it's a decent place. I don't 'ave nothin' else. I don't know 'oo the gentleman is, but 'e is 'ere an' he's aksed ever so nicely for you, so you come on down," The large woman said indignantly, then turned to go down. "The 'ide o' some people," she said.

Annie ran down and caught up with the woman. She put her hand on her shoulder and said, "I'm sorry, Mrs Frame. I really am sorry, but I am so terrified. I'm all alone and have no one to look out for me. I don't know the way of the world, and please don't go far. I might need you. Please forgive me."

"Orright, luv, I daresay I wus a mite 'asty. But I'm decent I am an' I run a decent 'ouse." Mrs Frame told Annie which room she'd left the man in. "An' I put 'im in the best drawin' room too. You mind yourselves."

"Thank you, I am sure we will," said Annie. She went down expecting it to be some mistake. On reaching the sitting room, she saw a young gentleman dressed in a stylish mode. He was tall and good looking, and as he turned around, she gasped, "Master Tim? Master Tim, is it you? Why are you not in England?"

"Yes, Annie, come here. I am glad to see you." He took her hands in his and looked at her. "You look in fine fettle, Annie. Is everything all right? Is the room suitable?"

Mrs Frame saw that he was respectful to Annie and that she did indeed know him. Annie turned to her and smiled a thank you. So Mrs Frame was content to leave them alone.

"Oh, Master Tim, did you arrange it? Is this all your doing?"

"Yes, Annie, with Mrs Tremaine's assistance, but come and sit down and let me tell you all about it." He led her to a chair.

"Master Tim, Sir Cecil?" she asked anxiously.

"I am sorry, Annie, but Uncle died nearly five years ago."

"Oh, I thought he must have, or I would have heard from him," she said despondently.

"It is because of him that I am here, Annie. He was much upset to find what had happened when he returned from the Far East. By that time, you had come out here, and his hands were tied. He wanted to move heaven and earth to get you back, but then he fell ill with a stroke and couldn't."

Annie looked at the man, "Oh," was all she said. "I do wish I'd known," she said softly after a while.

Tim continued with the story, "As soon as he could, he sent for me and told me your story. This meeting happened just after his seizure. He commissioned me to seek you out if I could and tell you what had happened and help you. He died soon after. I knew that it would not be possible to do anything while your sentence was upon you. I took the things he wanted you to have and put them in safekeeping at my place. So I got a friend who came here as an officer to find out about you, where you were and how you were doing, and when you would be free. So when I had that information, I arranged to come out here as an emissary to the Governor so I could be here to help you when it came time for your release. I did not contact you before as I had already spoken to Mrs Tremaine, and I knew you were safe, and well looked after, also she knew I was watching over you."

"Oh, Master Tim, that was kind of you. Did you arrange the room here and everything with Mrs Tremaine? The money and stuff?"

"Yes, Annie, I did. Although she said, she had some for you too. It was hard to give her an explanation as to why I was doing this, so I didn't give one. I just said it was from my family in England. I didn't specify whose family." He chuckled. "She appears to be a kind-hearted woman and did not ask for more information. She was fond of you and wished to help you. She was quite ready to fall in with my plans. I must tell you what I have done for, sadly, I will be returning to England as soon as the Governor has his papers ready, and I was worried that I wouldn't be able to see you before I left."

"What a task Sir Cecil gave you, Master Tim, and to think you did all this for me."

"Annie, Uncle Cecil was very fond of you. He knew the great wrong done to you. He made me promise to do what he asked and to say nothing to anyone at all, so I haven't. He trusted me to do this for him. Who am I to refuse to see that a man's dying wish is carried out?" Tim smiled wickedly at her, then chuckled. "You should have seen their faces when a large cart arrived, and on his instruction, various items of furniture were removed from the Hall and sent to me."

"But coming out here must have cost a lot of money?"

Tim grinned at her. "No, not a cent, for I came as a Government messenger, and so I am engaged by them, you see. Remember I was working with Uncle Cec? I'm in the same job. I have been back and forwards often over the past years. Uncle wanted to send a lot of money out for you, but he couldn't work out how. Uncle spoke to me; he had no means of procuring it, so he gave me all he had at the time. Lady Broome-Hall had for some reason left £250 in cash with him, so he gave me that for you. Now let me tell you what I have done."

"Yes, sir, but I am staggered at this, for I thought all this time that I was alone. Oh, Master Tim, this is wonderful. Just to think you have done this." Annie wept; she was so stunned. He cared; they both did.

"But you don't know what I have done yet. Listen. I have leased some land, which I hope will soon be permanent, for they don't give titles to land yet. It isn't far from here, and I think you will like it. It is in your name, and I have had a small cottage built on it and a shed. Knowing you were working on a farm whilst here, I presumed you have learnt how to grow things and probably grow vegetables or something and keep yourself. What do you say?"

Annie laughed, still teary. "Some land, you say and a house of my own? I can't believe it. But I must tell you that I know very little about growing things, for I mostly worked in the kitchen. Master Tim, if anyone can grow vegetables on that land, I will and be very grateful. A house? It seems like a dream, after all these years." Annie looked up and straight at him. Tears were rolling down her cheeks. "And I thought all this time he had forgotten me. I loved him so much, he was so kind and gentle to me, and I was wondering if he'd just used me, Master Tim."

"He didn't forget you, Annie. His last words were, 'Tell Annie I love her'. I know because Betsy told me. Do you remember Betsy? She stayed with him until he died, then returned to Lady Broome-Hall. Her mother, Sarah, was her maid, you know. She knew he trusted me and that I had his confidence."

It was enough for Annie. Those few words healed so many hurts in the small world. She sobbed. After some time, when she regained her composure, she said, "Yes, Betsy was kind. She was my only friend. She must have been a few years older than me, but she was always protecting me. I loved her so much, and she was my only friend. Cec was so good to all his staff. What of the family, Master Tim?" Annie enquired.

"Just the same, Annie," Tim smiled down at her. "Now come along, let's go and look at this estate of yours." Then stopping as he turned around. "Annie, it isn't very big, you know, but it is something to start with."

"Can we go now? I can't believe that I have some land. Any size will be fine; I am just so grateful; I can't believe it," she repeated.

"Run up and get your hat, and we'll go." Annie went quickly to her room, washed her face, grabbed her hat and ran downstairs. She called Mrs Frame to tell her she would be gone for a while but would be back for the meal, but that everything was all right and she knew Mr Timothy Styles from England. Tim had a gig at the door, and soon they were bowling along the rutted road with a modicum of speed.

Looking around at everything, Annie said, "I suppose I will know every bit of this place before long, but at the moment, it is all so strange. I have looked at the one piece of scenery for five years, Master Tim."

"Was it very hard, Annie? Was it very bad?" Tim felt so sorry for her.

"It was at first. It was terrible in gaol. Betsy visited me once and brought a coat and my blanket. She had managed to put some coins in one of the coat pockets, and they certainly helped. The horror of being accused and shamed; the prison was bad enough, but then there was the terrible ship. Oh, Master Tim, that was horrible, the dirt, the hunger and the stench. But when I got to Mrs Tremaine, it was wonderful in comparison. She is a very good woman, and she taught me a great deal. She was kind and even loving. I'd see her looking at me, and she'd shake her head with pity. I didn't stay in the fields for long; she took me into the kitchen and taught me to cook. She'd come across one of the other convicts trying to attack me. I was outside in the sun weeding. She took me under her wing, so to speak, Master Tim. She arrived in time and looked after me from then on, and she taught me to cook. Maybe that is what I can do; maybe I can cook and bake things and sell them. I'll have to earn some money somehow. But you'll see, Master Tim, I'll make a good thing of it. You'll see," she assured him.

Tim had a lump in his throat! He took a deep breath before saying, "I hope you can, Annie. I know the soil isn't good in the town, but I thought you could manage better here than out in the country. I didn't like to think of your being away from the population. The farms next door are the Church Glebe."

The horse slowed to a walk as they negotiated a rise. The place was not very hilly but high enough to be interesting. The very first thing Annie saw was a gargantuan rock in the front yard that dwarfed a lovely cottage, and it was at this building that Tim pulled up. The enormous rock was almost the same size as the cottage itself, and it took up the entire corner of a fenced-in area of land, with a small house at the opposite corner to the rock. It even formed part of the fenced area. Near it was a wide gate that had good strong fasteners on it.

Tim helped Annie down and tied the reins to the fence post. He opened the gate and called her in, saying, "Welcome, Mistress White, to your new home."

Annie stood and looked around her. She could see that Tim had planned it all well. The house was white-washed and painted with dark-green trim on the windows and door edges with a white door. The roof was of shingle. Very fancy in comparison to the houses she had seen in the town. It even had a tiny verandah out the front. There was a shed against the back fence. Part of the land had recently been dug over so that her garden had a start already. She looked at the large plot and wondered whether it was indeed hers. It seemed too good to be true and blessed Sir Cecil and his messenger.

"Oh, Master Tim," she was too awestruck even to cry.

"Come on, Annie, come and see your new home," called Tim, who was fumbling with a big key at the door. She joined him and went into the house across the verandah. There were only three rooms, the kitchen, a small sitting room, and a bedroom, but Annie thought it was superb. The main door opened to an area where one could sit in the evenings; this led to the kitchen where Annie exclaimed over what she saw. "Oh, Master Tim, an enclosed stove. I can't believe it. Now I really will be able to cook and sell food."

"I brought it out from England, Annie, for I hoped I would be able to do this for you, and my sister tells me that they are all the rage. Do you like it?"

"Oh, yes, it is wonderful. You've got furniture too." There was a table and four chairs and a dresser with cutlery and crockery, pots and pans and a kettle and everything one could need. "But how did you know what to have?" she asked. Then she saw a low bookshelf, "Aren't these from Sir Cecil's sitting room?"

Tim nodded. "These are the ones he wished you to have. This furniture is the table where you learned to read with him. He chose each item especially for you. The bed is new, though." He smiled at the astonished look on her face. "I asked my sister's housekeeper. She thought I was mad, but made a list out for me. As I heard that you couldn't get anything out here, I had them pack these and I brought them with me. The bed, too, and all the things for it and sheets and things. Did I do all right?" Tim looked somewhat worried.

"How can you ask? I think it is a dream; it must be. Nothing like this could happen to me." She walked into the bedroom and looked at the bed, chair, and washstand that was not unlike those in Mrs Frame's house. But the bed had a horsehair mattress, it was bare, but there were piled up sheets and blankets on the chair. There were mats on the wooden floor and a drape at the corner for hanging clothes. "Master Tim, a real bed, not a pallet," she cried with joy. "Sir Cecil didn't tell you to do all this, did he? He wouldn't have known."

"Well, he told me he wanted to have a place ready for you, and so I found out how. I've learned a lot in doing it. Some of the furniture is from Uncle's room. Now I will have to return you to Mrs Frame's for I have to dine out tonight. So think about it all and decide what else you want and we can purchase it tomorrow. You will need food and things, and we must stock up before I have to leave you to it. Do you like it, Annie? Will it do?" The look on his face showed concern.

She just turned around and looked at him with a wide smile. "It certainly will do, Master Tim. Thank you. I hate to leave it; I would like to move in quickly, in case it disappears during the night. I still can't believe you have done all this." She looked around again. "Mister Tim, can I hug you?"

He opened his arms to her, and she went into them and embraced him. She wept onto his shoulder. It was just so much to take in.

"Well, I have done it, and I must say I like it too. I think this land has potential, Annie. You never know, I might come and live here in this country myself," Tim said when she'd pulled away.

"That would be grand. Then I could look after you." She brightened with that thought.

"No, you have to make a life of your own and have lots of friends." He looked a little anxious. Not wanting to offend her, but not wanting to encourage her either.

Crestfallen, she said, "I have lost the way of making friends, and now, I am my own self nowadays. I think I have talked more today than I have in the seven years since I was arrested." She answered so softly he hardly heard her.

"You will settle in, Annie; I am sure you will make friends again."

She spoke softly, "I've lost my courage, though, that's the thing. I don't want to trust anyone ever again." She still felt betrayed.

"You trust me, don't you?" Tim asked anxiously.

"Yes, I do, but you belong to the 'good past'. To the only time I was ever happy, and I belonged to someone who loved me. You belong to the dream. I feel I will wake up and find it isn't here at all." She wiped a tear from her cheek with the back of her hand.

"Yes, you won't wake, though, as it's all real. Come on, or we will be late." She nodded and walked out to the gig. He took her back to Mrs Frame's house.

The following day when Annie woke up, she looked around, feeling that she was in a strange place. Then she realised where she was; she was still in Mrs Frame's bare little room. "Is it all true?" she asked herself. "Is all that happened yesterday true?" She dressed and made her way to the dining room, where she was served with thick and creamy oat porridge by a small girl in a clean overall. She sniffed as she moved around the table, where four others were sitting. Annie looked around her and smiled at the three men and a woman. She only got half-smiles back. There was little said but the necessary conversation in such a situation, such as "pass the salt" or "sugar please".

This was a town where curiosity was not encouraged. Many citizens had much to hide, and those who could wanted to begin a new life. Most found that the best way to get on in this colony was to get on with your own life and keep your nose out of everyone else's. There were too many hurt feelings to take on friends very lightly. Last night's meal had been silent, too, until Mrs Frame had appeared. She began an innocuous conversation that relieved the monotony of the meal but would never fill the feeling of wanting to be conversant with the life around her, as Annie felt.

Annie had been willing to chat to her, as the conversation was not something she'd even been encouraged to indulge. So she was in a state of pure joy, knowing that she had something to live for and something that she could look forward to doing and that she did not need to find a job. At the back of her mind, she had a desperate feeling that she would not be able to make the most of this incredible gift that was now hers, but her happiness would not let her look at this, and so stowed it away until she had to face it. She had no qualms in accepting it. For she knew it was given with love.

As planned, Timothy Styles came for her mid-morning. He took her up in the gig and then to Campbell's Store where she made purchases with the £10 he gave her. It was an absolute fortune, more than a year's wages, and she felt guilty in spending any of it, but she needed clothes and food. She also needed a good hat. Then they went to her house where she was able to look at things better than she had the day before, for she had been so stunned that she hadn't taken it all in.

"Did you sleep well last night, Annie?" asked Tim.

"Not really, Master Tim," she answered. "I was too dazzled. I kept thinking of your kindness."

"Not mine, Annie," Tim protested.

"Yes, yours, Master Tim, for you could have found lots of excuses not to come. Not to do what he wished. Not many would have done all you have done for a convict girl with my background, Master Tim. In a way, you lived your life for this."

"Well, if I did, I am glad. Come on; we didn't see everything yesterday." Tim hitched the horse to the rail near the rock again and opened a small gate in the brush fence. "See, you have another gate, Annie, for when you have a horse and gig of your own. This one is not big enough to let one through. Let's look around the place before we go into the house. I should have shown you the most important thing of all." He led Annie round the far side of the house.

Tim threw his arms wide. "See ... a tank," Tim said, "You can catch rain from the shingle roof, and it will drain into the water tank. It isn't very big but will give you nice water to drink." Then he led her down to the bottom of the slope, below the turned soil of the garden. "Behold, a well," he said dramatically. "See, it even has a windlass on it and a light wooden bucket. The man who dug it tells me it is good drinking, too. The tank will save you going down to the Tank Stream, as that water is now often contaminated; if there is any water there are all."

"Oh, Master Tim, that's wonderful," she stood clapping her hands together with glee. "I never thought of water, and I should have, for I know how precious it is in this place," she exclaimed. "Maybe I could even sell that."

He smiled. "Now for the shed," he said, "I don't think we looked at it yesterday."

Annie thought the man was like a small boy showing off his new Christmas toys. He was so excited about what he was showing her. It indeed was like Christmas for Annie. They looked at the tools and even a small hand cart in the shed. It had shelves for storage, and Tim assured her it was a very snug, dry shed that she could use as a storeroom. Then on to the house where he was determined to set the fire going so they could cook their first meal in the new home. Annie made straight for a chair when he opened the door, and sitting at the table, she burst into tears.

"Annie, whatever is the matter?" he asked.

"I'm just so happy. I can't believe it. Oh, Master Tim, after everything that's happened, I can't believe it," she wept.

He was squatting in front of her. "When Uncle Cecil told me what you meant to him, I admit I was astounded. I thought that it was just an older man having a good time with a young girl. I'd seen you around and knew you to be a nice girl who was always smiling. But as you know, we never spoke much. Annie, in these last two days, I now see what he meant." He paused, thinking. "Annie, you really did love him, didn't you? Weren't you in this for the money? You really are astounded with all this." He smiled at her.

She nodded. "I loved Cec, Master Tim, but what is more he loved me, and he was the only one to do so." She sounded so despondent.

"Come on, Annie, that's not the way for a new settler to act." Tim tried to cheer her up.

"You mean me?" she asked, stunned.

"Yes, Annie, I mean you. You're free, Annie. An emancipist, and this is the beginning of a new life for you." Tim stood then patted her on her shoulder gently. "Come on, my girl. I'll light the fire, and you get the things unpacked and let's eat our first meal in your new house."

Tim found he was not very proficient in lighting the stove, so Annie took over that job while he brought the shopping in from the gig.

"Firewood, Master Tim? I daresay I will have to find where I can get some," said Annie. "But I can take the little pull cart in the shed out and pick up sticks from the bush."

"Well, no, I've found that the bush is pretty well cleaned out of sticks around here, Annie, so I got a fellow with a cart named Bert Todd to bring a load. It was quite cheap, and he will call again to ask when you want more. He's piled the wood at the back of the house for you."

"You think of everything," Annie said.

"I must admit that there is much more to setting up a house than I ever thought, Annie. I've learnt such a lot and wouldn't have achieved much without Willy Knight's help. He built the cottage and lives just down the road from here. He has a wife and seven children, all born here. He's a pretty rough looking chap but nice. I am sure they will be good neighbours. I'm pleased about that, for I have been worried about your living here alone when I'm gone."

A look of horror crossed her face, "Master Tim, when will that be?" asked Annie fearfully.

"Next week, I am sorry, Annie. I learnt last night that the dispatches would be ready for me to sail on the *Roslyn Castle*. I'll probably be back in a year or so. So you got your freedom just in time, Annie. I tried to delay my going but must obey orders," said Tim miserably. "I'd hoped to see you settled, Annie, but I suppose I'll just have to be satisfied that I was able to do what I did in the time I've had. I'll come and visit on my return."

Annie looked as though she was going to cry again, but then took a deep breath and said, "Master Tim, I'm going to miss you badly and really can't believe you are here anyway, and now you are going. For that matter, I still find it hard to believe all this is even here, either. But I won't let you down ..."

"Or Uncle Cecil ..." put in Tim.

"Yes, Master Tim, or Cec either, I won't let either of you down. I'll try to do what I can and make a living from the place, but if I can't, I will find a job, I promise you." She lifted her chin in a very determined way.

He smiled at her determined attitude. "I'm sure you won't let yourself down, Annie, and that's the most important thing now. By the way, I must tell you about the money."

"What money?" gasped Annie.

"I told you he gave me what he had on him. Well, that was £250. All this, including the cottage, was less than £50. So, Annie, there is ample money left over. I wondered what I would do with it, for you will need some to live on until you get settled and also when you can buy the land you will have to pay for this. I am informed it should only be about £15 to buy outright, but I've included that in the £50 I said was 'spent'. So I asked the Governor who I could leave it with, and he put me on to Fraser Finley and Co. He has your money and will give you what you need when you need it. I will take you to meet him, and you will find you can trust him. He will help you and advise you, too." Tim smiled at her stunned expression.

"Is there much money?" she asked hesitantly.

"Not what I would call much. Just enough to buy this and then a bit over £200 for your needs."

"Oh, glory be, Master Tim. I would call that a lot, sir," she exclaimed.

"It isn't really. Everything is so expensive here. There would not be much left if I had bought everything here, Annie. It was just as well. I was advised to bring all I could. Thankfully I have some useful friends."

"Master Tim, £10 was more than a year's wage for me in England, so for me to have that much and own this. Sir, I'm rich beyond my wildest dreams. You have certainly been busy on my behalf." She was star-struck. "That's twenty years wages for me, sir, and I don't even have to pay rent from it." The sign of contentment she expelled was one of delight. "I could have saved a lot even on £10 a year." A slow smile crept across her face. Her eyes twinkled with joy.

"I am glad I have had the adventure of coming here and seeing the place. I like it, Annie. This trip is my fourth one. It is so, well, raw, but there's something about the place that I like." Tim stood looking out the front door. The view from the cottage verandah was a delight. He could see down into the edges of Sydney Town. "I will try to come back often. But one day, I might even stay for a while next trip."

Annie placed a basket on the table behind him. She stood unpacking the contents on the clean red gingham tablecloth. She didn't answer him as she didn't know what to say. He turned and asked what she had in the basket. She looked up at him and grinned. "It was a parting gift from the farm. Let us see what Mrs Tremaine gave us to eat. She gave me this basket of food as I was leaving. I wondered why I'd need preserves and cheeses and the like, but now I know she knew about this place; it makes sense. She is very kind." They had a cob loaf with pickles, corned beef, cheese and thick creamy butter. Mrs Tremaine added a jar of her delicious thick apple flavoured, lilli pilli jelly to eat with more bread and butter. They sat down at the table with the door still open and enjoyed their sumptuous feast.

Chapter 2   Rip and Sam

*A*nnie found that life after Tim's departure was quite grim. She positively dithered. She was frightened to go about by herself and got lonely staying home. Then taking herself to task, she set to getting herself sorted out. Her clothing amounted to very little, as did her entire cottage contents. She found it hard going.

Most of her neighbours distrusted her, for they knew she had the sponsorship of a gentleman, and that did not endear her to them. She certainly had no intentions of explaining what that entailed. Most were working people who had come to the colony as convicts, and they all thought the worst of everyone. They did not take kindly to either authority or nobility and were uncomfortable in her presence, thinking she had 'authority' behind her. They knew Mister Tim worked for the Government. Unfortunately, he'd told Willy Knight that himself. Some thought she was just a paid woman or loose lady of the night and looked down on her. So it was some time before she could make headway with them, and then only a little.

She was lonely, so very lonely.

Annie gardened whenever she could. She had planted the vegetables she needed to make Cornish pasties, namely carrots, onions and potatoes, green peas, and beans. At first, Annie could interest no one in her fresh-baked wares, but Mrs Frame took some regularly, and the two of the hotels started ordering some. At times she ate very little except the crumbs of the pasties she had cooked that day, but at other times she had so many over that they went off before she could eat them. Willy Knight was often given some for all his children.

She put a large sign on both sides of the big rock in the front yard.

The new sign picked up business considerably. So she decided to name her business *The Rock*. Her new sign read, *The Rock Bakery – orders taken.*

Her first six months were the worst, for she had had to buy all her vegetables and meat and eke out her limited supply of cash on hand. She was horrified when she found she had spent over £1 on these precious supplies. She had no intention of dipping into her capital funds. However, she found she could buy a large section of kangaroo tail and dice the meat so finely that it was as good as putting it through the mincer. She had to add butter, though, as it was very lean meat. She wondered whether she would ever make her project work.

At the first signs of winter, things looked up somewhat. She hit on the idea of producing large quantities of thick vegetable broth with some barley in it, and she soon found that the nearby workmen would come and buy a bowl for their midday meal. She even added a long bench seat on the verandah for them to sit on. She displayed her pasties, and when she could afford the meat, pies, and bit by bit, her beautifully cooked foods were becoming better known. "Comfort foods," she called them.

She went to Mr Finley and asked him whether she should take some of her precious money and make a shop-type serving window on her verandah. Not precisely understanding what she meant, he elected to come to a look for himself. He was pleased with her efforts and was suitably impressed with the soup and pasties she provided for him. He could see that she could easily have a serving hatch put into the kitchen facing onto the verandah so she could serve people while they were undercover and at the same time keep them from coming right into the house. He could see that she would be better protected from the populace, and he thought that was a good thing. So he suggested that she go ahead and get the window put in. She was pleased to find that it only cost her £2.

She became a commercial proposition from then on, for she also had another sign put up at the window telling people what she had for sale that day. At the same time, she was selling more and more to hotels and inns. She did not have the time to deliver them herself as she had been doing. She employed Billy, one of Willy Knight's boys, to collect them each morning and deliver them to her customers.

She had neither the time nor the inclination for social interaction. She worked from before dawn each morning making her daily goods, and when her selling job was over for the day, she worked in the garden until she could not see any more. She loved her tiny home. However, it was sweltering in the summer, for she had to keep her stove going for long hours, but this, in turn, was a comfort in the cold weather when she was snug and warm in the chill breezes.

She saw more of Bert Todd than anyone, for he delivered copious loads of wood to her very regularly as her stove was constantly on. Bert was always full of news of the town. So she learned more of the town doings than she had thought possible.

Billy brought her news; so even though she saw even less of the place, she still knew the town's happenings. She still had to go to Campbell's Store for supplies to the markets for perishables from time to time but was usually in such a hurry that she could not spend time chatting even if she found anyone to talk to or was willing to speak to her.

So life went on this way for Annie. The first unhappy days turned into productive weeks, and she was stunned to one day find that she'd been in the cottage for over two years. Sometimes she felt pleased about her life and what she was achieving, but she was profoundly lonely and longed for companionship with others.

Bert appeared one day with a half-grown mongrel dog and asked her if she would like it. It was a miserable specimen of an animal, of medium-sized that looked as though it had been starving for a long time. It possibly was just at the gangly half-grown stage. It had a whiskery sort of hair that was quite unkempt and was quite filthy at the time of its arrival.

"Jest thought yer'd like summat ter talk to of a noight, missus. It ain't much, but I reckon better'n some. It were makin' a nuisance of it down at the barracks, and they reckon ter shoot the mongrel. I thunked a' yer and thunked it were a good place ter keep it on account of yer fence. Wot do yer thunk, Missus?"

"Oh, Bert, I don't know. It looks like a miserable specimen. Do you think it would be healthy?" She'd had nothing to do with animals except Cecil's gun dog, Scram.

"Oi reckon so, missus. It be a good forager. Oi reckon it'd do real good on yer pasties and scraps," he added with a wheezy guffaw.

"It was kind of you to think of me, Bert, but ..." Just then, the dog looked up at her and sort of smiled. It wagged its tail, and its tongue lolled out the side of its mouth and smiled right at her, then turned round in a circle and lay at her feet. "Oh, you poor thing, I think you need company as much as I do."

"Yer better take 'im, missus. Oi reckon yer'd like 'im. Give 'im a try, missus. If yer don' like 'im oi'll take 'im away then." He handed the string he had tied around the dog's neck to her and headed for the gate.

Annie called, "I suppose I will thank you, Bert, but at the moment, I wonder whether I should."

Bert waved his hand and shut the gate. "Oh, don't feed it, onion Missus. It makes 'em sick."

Annie looked down at the dog. "Well, do we feed you or clean you first?" she asked it. "Feed, I think, then you might be more inclined to being washed. I'll have to think up a name for you. I wonder if you will be a good watchdog. At the moment, you don't look as though you are good for anything, and if you dig up my garden, I'll get rid of you, quick."

The dog was more than happy to eat some leftover kangaroo tail bones after she'd removed the meat. He also ate carrot tops and pea pods. One she had on for stock, but this one didn't fit in her pan. Annie expected it to gobble its food, but she was surprised to find that it was quite a dainty eater. "That's one thing in your favour," said Annie. "I never could abide a dog that gobbled everything." She untied the string and took him to the pump, where she tried to wash some of the dirt from its coat.

Dog didn't like this at all and protested by shaking itself repeatedly all over Annie, but she hung on to the scruff of its neck and scrubbed with a bar of rough yellow soap until she thought he was clean enough. There were bubbles everywhere before she rinsed him off. She rubbed him down with a clean rag, and so that he wouldn't roll in the dirt and destroy her handiwork, she left him tied up onto the verandah to lick his wounded spirit after such indignities. She thought he looked quite reasonable after all this, but "dog" didn't think so, for he gave her a disdainful look and a yelp, then stretched himself and sighed a deep sigh and went to sleep to recover.

"Dog," filled a niche.

Annie couldn't think of a proper name and thought she would leave it until one came to her. He was a very companionable chap, quite content to sit beside her in the evenings and content to spend most of his days on the verandah sniffing out the delivery boy and the customers. Dog also cleaned up the scraps she dropped while cooking. Annie didn't think he would be much of a watchdog, but he somehow distrusted Willy's poor boy and always greeted him with a growl.

She found that Dog rapidly had classed himself as her protector. One day a rough fellow arrived at the shop window and demanded more from her than he was willing to pay. Within a moment, Dog had ripped from where he was sleeping and attached himself to the man's leg. The man left the place quickly when he found a dog wishing to clamp his teeth into his bony shin for a second taste.

Annie called him off, and Dog then relieved himself by madly barking as he accompanied the intruder to the gate, which the rude customer then slammed in the dog's face. Annie thought this an excellent time to name her now useful companion and called him "Rip".

Annie felt that her life had considerably improved now she had Rip to talk to. Occasionally she wished she had someone to answer her, but Rip would look at her with his big brown liquid amber eyes and smile, so she didn't mind that much that he didn't speak. He'd also filled out from the walking skeleton he'd been on arrival.

"I wish I had someone to read with," said Annie one night. She thought back to the day that Tim had shown her the cupboard from Cec's bedside. She hadn't noticed it at first, and then it had suddenly hit her. That was the cupboard that Sir Cecil kept by his bed. So she had walked to it and run her hands over the carvings around the door. The wood felt alive, and she said, "Ahh." A few tears fell again at the happy memories she'd known with Cec.

"You recognise it, Annie?" Tim had asked.

"Yes," she nodded, with tears still filling her eyes, "He had it beside his bed, and he kept our favourite books in it."

"Open it," she was instructed.

Annie had opened the door of the bedside cupboard; there were six leather-bound volumes. Before taking them out, she knew what they were; they was Cec's Bible, three volumes of Shakespeare, a book of verse by John Donne, and Samuel Pepys' Diary. Her fist went to her mouth, and she gasped, "Oh, Ceccy." Annie had sat down on the floor, taking them out one by one and lovingly feeling the soft leather bindings. She turned to him, looking up, "Are they mine? Are they mine to keep, Master Tim?"

"Yes, Annie, they are yours to keep. I hope you will enjoy them. He said you'd love them, and they each meant something to you both."

"But, how did you know?" She had looked up at Tim dreamily with tears filling her eyes. She brushed them away angrily.

"He told me you learned to read from these, Annie. He wanted you to have them. And look, did you know about this?" Tim knelt beside her and put his hand into the back of the cupboard. "Did you know there is a secret place here?"

"No, I didn't. Show me, please."

She watched as he pushed a small motif. "Well, you move this little flower." Tim pushed at a carved flower on the border. "It is a bit hard, but that is its safety. You push it this way; then, you draw out this bar that nestles behind it and releases the back panel. You can get your hand in it now. You can safely keep your money here or other valuables. I don't think anyone will find it."

Annie put her hand in the aperture and felt around. Tim observed her and saw her expression change. "There is something here."

"Yes, Annie, he wrote you a letter. Uncle said it is for you to read alone. Read it when you are all by yourself."

She took the letter out and turned it over. It was closed with a wax seal; she knew Cec's handwriting even though it looked shaky. She looked mutely at the man, tears pouring down her cheeks.

Tim stood up and said, "Read it now if you like; I'll wait outside."

She nodded. Annie looked down at Rip, thinking of that precious time where she was cared for and cherished. She didn't realise that the tears were falling again. "I am very fortunate, Rip. Though I have lost a special friend, now I have you."

She read it. The letter poured out his love and passion for her. It's all she had to cling to in her loneliness. He also stated his anger at his family at what had occurred to her after he left. He so wished he'd taken her with him; however, he also knew that to be impossible. He told her to continue to trust him. She'd had to stop reading a few times as she read the depth of his feelings for her. She kept the now well-read letter in Cec's safe place, only now her convict release papers were with it.

Rip seemed to think that Annie expected something of him, so he stood, stretched, and then came to her, leaning against her chair and put his head up to be patted. He became more and more important to Annie. She was rarely about without him. He trotted behind her when she went to town and even disdained to smell out other dogs when he was her companion. He wasn't always good, though. He loved to slip out through the gate to explore and go about doggie business. He would return and sit at the gate, giving one short sharp bark and wait until she let him in. She, of course, never knew what he got up to, for sometimes, he would come back looking sheepish. Still, at others, he came back looking very cocky and very pleased with himself, and it was after these latter excursions that he would flop down in the shade, or the sun, depending on the weather, and sleep an exhausted sleep for hours.

The colony was growing all this time as the century came to its close, the town was getting more and more free settlers, and the town was growing. Some better houses were being built now, and Willy Knight, the builder, was quite busy. He was not very experienced in building large homes, but there were few carpenters to choose from, so he instead had free rein.

Annie's business grew, too, and by the time New Year 1800 came, she was a well-known businesswoman with nearly three years experience under her belt. And her baking was much sought after. Little had changed in the years she had been in her house. She was still a lonely woman with only superficial contact with her customers and other passing people. She didn't socialise, and she had no friends but Bert and Willy.

On a very wet day, Bert Todd pushed open the gate and called to her. "Hoy, missus, Oi say, missus, be you there?"

Annie came from the house onto the verandah to find Bert holding another man in soaked clothing. The puddle around them was growing larger by the moment.

"Who is that, Bert?" she asked. "Come in; you'll both be soaked."

"We are now, missus. I wus passin' an' oi see'd 'im settin' there agin the big rock. He be real wet, Missus. He looks crook, but he's not drunk, no smell of grog," Bert said. "W'at more I see'd him get turfed from th' horspital as they needed 'is bed. I hears they got lice down ther', 'n they got something called typhus. So they turfed out everyone they culd."

"What can I do with him, Bert? Who is he? Do you know?" Annie did not want a stranger anywhere near her. Being alone was bad enough when strangers passed by; for one to stay would be unbearable.

"Oi dunno as 'is name." He turned to the man who was by now dripping on the floor of Annie's verandah. "Wotcha name, mate?"

"Corbett," he said, "Sam Corbett."

"Get his coat off, Bert," she ordered.

Then turning to the man, "What's wrong with you, Sam Corbett? Have you been drinking?"

Bert answered for the man. "No 'e ain't bin doin' thet, Missus. I told ya, just seen 'im down at the 'orspital. They got some belly trouble dahn there, typhus as I said, and got rid o' all them as could walk. He's one they turfed. Did they throw yer aht, Sam?"

The man nodded and said, "Do you mind if I sit? I don't think my legs will carry me anymore." With that, he plopped down on the floor in the middle of the verandah. He felt as weak as a kitten. He groaned weakly.

"Have you anything catchy, Sam Corbett?" asked Annie, not all that pleased at this invasion.

"I'm getting over inflammation of the lungs, madam. I don't think anyone could catch anything from me now, ma'am." Sam answered. "Had Typhoid first; they didn't want me to get sick again."

"What do you want from me?" She huffed. "Bert, what do you want me to do?"

"I dunno, missus. I jest see'd 'im there, and as I cain't take 'im 'ome wif me, nowhere to shove 'im. Oi jest thought oi would bring 'im in 'ere fer a spell. Yer shed's empty, he could doss down there," Bert said sheepishly. "No way I cud move 'im far, no how."

"Have you anywhere to go?" asked Annie.

"No, I haven't," said the man weakly. "I had intended to find somewhere to doss down, but my search in the rain was rather fruitless. I am sorry to be a nuisance." He spoke in a well-educated voice. He sounded a bit like Master Tim.

"I could sleep here," he said hopefully. At least on the verandah it was dry.

Just then came Rip's sharp bark asking to be let in through the gate.

Annie looked at Bert, "As you are so wet now, Bert, would you please let Rip in."

"Right, Missus. Been on the prowl again, 'as 'e?" Bert chuckled as he dashed out to the gate.

Rip came in, wagging his tail. Smiled up at his mistress and then approached the stranger who was still sitting on the floor. He stood looking at him for a moment and then answered the stranger's click of his fingers. Sam rubbed the dog behind his ears in just the right place, and Rip subsided beside him. Annie was surprised, Rip didn't generally like strangers, but he trusted this one.

"Who are you?" asked Annie. "Where do you come from?"

"I didn't think one asked such questions in this God-forsaken hole, madam, but as you have the right, I'll tell you that I was forcibly working for one Jacob West, a farmer out along the Parramatta Road, until I had served my time. Now they tell me I am free. Free to do what, I do not know. I've got nowhere to go." He slumped more than he already was, now leaning against a sturdy verandah post.

"Free to work, I daresay," said Annie pithily.

He gave a half-laugh, "I daresay, Madam, but as I have been in hospital for many months, for some reason striving to remain alive, I have not had the opportunity to seek work."

"Come orf, it, missus," said Bert. "Don' yer be 'ard on the cove."

"Thank you, Bert," said the man. He was nearly asleep on the floor. They could both hear his stomach rumbling.

"Look 'ere, missus," continued Bert whispering. "Yer know oi kin 'ardly tek 'im home wif me, Missus. Oi dunno wot oi kin do. But, missus, wot abaht lettin' 'im 'ave a doss in yer shed at least 'til the rain stops? Huh, wot abaht it?"

"But I don't know anything about him. Bert, you don't know what you're asking," she whispered back harshly to him.

"Never fear, madam," said Sam as he roused. "Just let me get my breath, and I'll be on my way."

"You can't go out in this, it's pouring," Annie said illogically.

"Well, madam, you can't have it both ways. It is either the rain, here on the verandah, or the shed, whatever that is like. But I must admit, a dry shed sounds like heaven, right now."

"You are far too cheeky for my liking, and don't keep calling me madam," she said indignantly.

"As I don't know what else to call you, I have no choice since my father told me always to be polite, for I was brought up properly. I am sorry that I sound insolent, for that is the last thing I want to be. I'm just so darned tired. I just want to lie down and get warm and sleep. Perhaps this fellow will come to the said shed and help me to warm up a little," he said, hugging Rip to him.

Rip was now sitting with his head on the strange man's lap. He didn't often even do that to her. Reluctantly, she trusted Rip's judgement.

"All right, Bert. You can show him the shed. It is dry there, and there are lots of sacks. Do you think that would do?" She was still looking at Rip.

The man stood up with Bert's help. "Thank you, mad…, sorry, miss, thank you. I will go as soon as I can manage it."

"My name is White. Miss White. Bert, when you have settled Sam in, come back and take him a bowl of soup."

"Thank you, that is kind," Sam said.

"It's roight good soup, too, Sam. Do yer good. Put hairs on yer chest, it will," Bert said.

Bert was soon back and collected the soup. "Here, Bert," said Annie. "Take this blanket to him. Is he all right, do you think?"

"Oi think so, missus. Oi don't think yer'll come to 'arm. But mind yer lock yer door, even if'n the poor cove's so weak, 'e wouldn't 'urt a fly. Ooh, a hot pastie, too? That'll be good fer 'im; they are normally all right." He turned to walk off but said, "Oi've foun' that when a dawg likes a bloke, they's okay. Rip trusts this one."

Annie reluctantly agreed.

She waved to Bert as he returned, calling out, "G'night, missus."

Even though the shed was the length of the block away, she felt the presence of the stranger. She hoped the next day would be fine, and he could take himself off somewhere. There were doss-houses for felons or ex-felons, and that is what he was. "But then, so am I," mused Annie smiling to herself. She could easily be in the same position as him.

There was no sign of him next morning, and Annie did not feel like investigating. She soon was so busy that she forgot him, and after the boy came for the deliveries, Annie had to go to town, so, leaving Rip in charge, Annie locked up the house, something she'd not done before, and walked down the hill. When she returned, she was surprised to see Sam kneeling beside the vegetable garden weeding the carrots.

"What are you doing there?" she demanded

"Weeding carrots, Miss White, I wish to pay my dues," he said, "And then I'll be off. I thank you for your reluctant hospitality."

"I am sorry you put it like this, but I am not used to strangers anymore. I'm ostracised by most people and have no friends here. Being here alone puts me in an awkward position," she explained

"Oh, I quite understand. I can imagine you would think all sorts of things, but I am afraid I haven't the strength." He sounded so tired.

"You wrong me. I didn't think that. But I have lived here alone for nearly three years and ..." Annie finished lamely, shrugging her shoulders.

"It's all right; I'm not always like this. I don't usually take a rise out of people. I daresay it is because I am rather weak on my legs, yet. The food has helped. It's the first good food I've had in over ten years, Miss. I shall gather my things and be on my way," he sounded exhausted. "I had hoped not to have to worry about living."

"Come in on the verandah and have something more to eat. I am about to, and you may as well join me," she said half-heartedly.

"I will gratefully," said Sam. His stomach rumbled hungrily at just the thought of food.

She gave Sam a bowl of very thick soup, two slices of buttered toast and another hot pastie, fresh that morning. "May I say, you are a grand cook? I think it is the best I've ever tasted. Where I've been for the last while, our food would not win any prizes, the opposite. It was borderline basic. If it tasted of anything, then dirt would be the closest I can think of politely."

Annie looked hard at the man, thinking that she was a fool, but felt she couldn't let him go in the state he was in. She said, "Why not stay until you are feeling better? If you are comfortable in the shed, I mean." She was beginning to feel more comfortable with him. He'd had a chance to attack her and had not.

"I do not wish to intrude, and I wish to see what freedom is like, but thank you all the same. But if I were to stay, which I won't, thank you, I would find the shed very comfortable indeed."

"Well, please yourself. It is there if you want it." She was relieved. But she was also sad, for he reminded her of Rip when he came. Perhaps it was because Bert brought them both. The bones of his face stood out clearly; his eyes were sunken, and she'd seen many with this haunted skeletal outline and distended stomach from hunger.

"Thank you. I will be off." He nodded quite curtly. His stance was bent, and she could tell he was still very weak. He left, leaning along the fence as he walked.

Sam went to the shed to collect his few belongings and brought her the blanket and the tin mug he had used for his soup the night before. Again thanking her, he left, closing the gate gently as he did so.

It was lunchtime, and her customers were beginning to appear for their midday pasties and soup by that time.

She was gardening late in the afternoon when she heard the gate click, and as Rip did not bark, she looked up to see Sam enter.

He looked tired and pale. "I am sorry, Miss White. The bad penny has turned up again. I found the doss house, and I am afraid that I could not stomach it. May I eat humble pie and ask if I may come back and resume my tenancy of your shed? I promise you I will not trouble you and will keep out of the way as much as I can." He sounded depressed and resigned to his lot in life. His legs were shaking so much he could barely stand. He was leaning on the side of the cottage.

"Was the doss-house all that bad, Sam?" she asked, having re-thought her attitude all day.

"I don't know why I should still be particular after seven bad years, but I cannot take filth and unwanted livestock that they had down there, Miss White. I always kept my rooms clean and tidy. It was bad enough at West's place, but it was spartan but clean, and at the time, I thought of it as heaven after the ship and the jail. So please, may I stay?" He was leaning against the clothesline pole. He was so weak that he looked ready to collapse again.

Annie hesitated, remembering the prison and ship.

"Please, I'll stay out of your way and will work for my bed and a scrap of food just until I can get about and look for a job. Please?" He looked on the verge of collapse again. She could tell it was no act.

Against her better judgment, Annie said reluctantly, "Very well. I suppose so. You'll have to live on leftovers, for that is all I ever eat."

"Miss White, I am very grateful. I really am. You will not be sorry, I can assure you. I'll keep the garden in order while I'm here. I learned much about that while at His Majesty's pleasure."

So Sam settled in the shed. He made a bed of sorts for himself and seemed content with his life.

At least, it was hard to find out what he thought, and contrary to what Annie expected, she found he said very little and indeed made himself entirely invisible a great deal of the time. As the days went by and he became stronger, she often found him working in the garden for most of the day. Often still on hands and knees.

He saw that the woodpile at the door was always well-stocked, and she discovered that he was even doing little things for her without comment; the gate stopped squeaking, he repaired the clothesline. The grass was kept neat and tidy, and she did enjoy watching him scythe the lawn.

Soon she began to rely on him.

Theirs was a peculiar relationship. She handed out food for him on a tray which he took to his shed, but apart from a few comments made at that time and his thanks for the food, they said very little to each other. She felt she had more conversation with Rip than she did with Sam. She wondered at a man and his evident education, being content to be in such a position. To her, it was no life at all. She rarely asked him to do anything for her. He was just there, a 'nothing', working without pay for a bed on sacks.

One day it got too much for her, and she said tersely, "Haven't you got any ambition, Sam? Don't you want anything better than being my … my, well, slave? What's wrong with you?" she added contemptuously.

He looked at her, straight into her eyes. "What is the use of ambition? It doesn't get you anywhere. What would I do if I had any? In this God-forsaken hole, where would it get me? No, I've done with ambition, except to die." He added the last three words so softly she barely heard them.

She could hear and see the hurt in him. He was a shrunken, stunted man emotionally. He now had sustenance, but it just wasn't enough. The exhaustion he now suffered was even more profound than emotional. He was devoid of emotion, and he'd suffered a spiritual rejection by humanity.

"Are you going to be content to fill your life with weeding my garden and living in a shed?" she threw at him.

"I can't seem to die, so I daresay I might as well be here as anywhere else. I tried the dying, but the people at the hospital wouldn't let me, so I may as well exist here until I finally manage to shuffle off this mortal coil." He fell silent for some time, then asked her with a cutting tone to his voice, "Are you ambitious? Does it get you anywhere? Do you like slaving away each day, dawn to dusk, making things for a whole lot of people who don't care about you? Do you like being a drudge and making a pittance? Where does ambition get you?" he threw back at her.

"You're not much of a man, are you?" she said back just as cuttingly.

"So I've been told all my life," he said bitterly.

Sam spoke so morosely that Annie was shocked. It brought a tear to her eye; she turned quickly from him so he couldn't see. His words had got to her. Never in her life had she been as far down emotionally as that. He was thoroughly crushed. She had been beaten down most of her life, but all she had wanted to do was fight back. The terrible acceptance of this man, of his lot in life, appalled her. She supposed that there were many like him, but she had been so busy living her life that she hadn't bothered to find out. "Don't ask questions" was the rule in this terrible colony, and she was not aiming to ask this poor creature anymore. "I'm sorry," she flung back over her shoulder and went inside.

After this, she spoke to Sam more often. Not that you call their conversation extensive, but at least she made some effort to talk to him.

He appeared to be getting stronger and soon asked her for more jobs, and she thought this was a good sign. With Sam helping her, Annie could get the garden enlarged, and they were soon even able to sell some of the vegetables he grew.

Sam appeared to be a good gardener, and he worked steadily day in, day out. He said little but was now not so morose. He just spoke as though he lived one moment to the next, not expecting anything from life. He certainly was not precisely companionable, but it was actually nice not to be totally alone anymore. He didn't have any interest in life outside the property, rarely leaving it. He asked no questions of her or her life.

She, at one time, asked him what pay she would give him, and he refused to accept anything.

"Bed and board are ample," was his only reply. I have survived on nothing more for a long time.

He was a worry to her, for she felt somewhat burdened by him yet was glad of his presence nearby. Rip certainly adored him.

She wondered what the people thought about her set-up, but as she had no friends in the town, it didn't concern her much. Bert still brought wood, and occasionally she had Willy Knight come and do small jobs, but apart from that, she had little to do with those about her. Both would stop and have a quick chat with Sam. She had noticed Sam's clothing was worn out and wondered how she could get him to replace them. She insisted on giving him money to buy more. He hesitated then accepted, as he could no longer keep what remained of his pants covering him. He had a bag wrapped around his waist to make himself decent. They both headed to Campbell's Store on the docks and returned with a set of warmer serviceable clothes and a set of workwear he put straight on. She also insisted he purchase undergarments and other necessary personal items, including a warm jacket. It was the first time he had left the place in over three months.

One day, soon after this, he suggested it might be a good idea for him to take the extra vegetables down to the market on the small pull cart and sell them.

She was surprised but agreed to this.

Sam came back sometime later with the money. He gave Annie a strict account of what he'd sold and how much. So life went on through summer and autumn and into the colder months, with very little change in their lives.

As the days grew cold, Sam was beginning to look peaky again, and then one morning he started to cough.

"Are you warm enough, Sam?" Annie asked him.

"I am beginning to feel the cold at night, miss," he answered. "I was thinking of trying to get more blankets from Government Stores and also if I could get a brazier for the shed. I don't want to take the risk of a fire in the shed, though," he mused.

"No, I think not," Annie agreed. Then as an afterthought, she added, "If you would care to, you can come in to the fire in the house, if you like."

"Thank you, Miss White. I will try not to be a nuisance." Sometimes his submission annoyed her.

"For goodness sake, Sam, stop thinking like that. I've never met anyone less of a nuisance. I never know you are here half the time. You creep around like a shadow, and you only speak a little more than Rip." She got a smile out of him.

"Well, I did invite myself here, remember. I always feel I am trespassing," Sam said.

"You may have been, but I am sure I don't think so anymore," Annie said brusquely. "I haven't thought of you like that for months. You seem part of the place. I wonder now how I coped by myself." She turned away and said over her shoulder, "If you care to take up my offer, well, it's up to you," and walked into the house.

So when he went up to get his dinner that evening, he found the table set with two places, and she invited him inside. He certainly found it warmer in the kitchen, and when the time came to leave the warmth, he was somewhat reluctant to go to his shed but said nothing but "thank you for the evening" and left. The shed was bitterly cold that night after the warmth of the house, and he shivered most of the night.

The next day Annie could see he was sick and was afraid for his lungs again. "You'd better come into the house, Sam. You can't work in this weather. You'll find yourself in the hospital again. Come and sit in the kitchen and warm up. And you had better sleep on the verandah until you are better. It must be freezing in the shed." He still looked much like a walking skeleton.

"It is not hot," he said succinctly, "I would be grateful."

Sam found the warmth of the kitchen a delight. He showed his thanks by insisting on washing the dishes and tidying up, not letting Annie do anything. She was surprised that he could do so much in a kitchen when as far as she knew, he hadn't been in a kitchen for over nine months, certainly not her kitchen anyway. She thanked him and then asked him to draw up a chair and enjoy the warmth of the stove.

His coughing had eased since coming inside, and so they sat having more conversation than they had ever had. Annie was as reticent about asking him questions about himself as he was of her, but she did ask where, in England, he came from, and when he told her "Sussex," she told him she did too.

The question started exchanges of where they were from and were surprised to find that they had both lived not very far from one another near Billingshurst. They spoke of villages known but did not discuss people. She asked, "Do you miss the life there, Sam?"

"No, Miss White, I do not." He replied with such vehemence that it surprised her. "It was not conducive to my happiness; nothing was."

"Not family?" she asked.

"Certainly not family," he answered with a wry smile.

"Nothing?" she persisted, rather astounded at herself.

"Yes, I daresay there is one thing I miss, and that is reading. At times I would give anything to be able to read, but I have no books, and in any case, I would not be able to read in the shed."

"Would you care to read my books?" Annie asked reluctantly.

"You have some books, Miss White?" Sam eagerly asked as he sat up straight. It was as though a light had turned on behind his beautiful chocolate brown eyes.

"Yes, I have six precious books. On Sunday afternoon, I allow myself time to lie on my old settee here, and I read one of my precious books."

"What have you? May I ask?" His eyes were alight with excitement. Annie told him their titles.

He exclaimed with pleasure, "Dear old Pepys. Please may I borrow him some time, Miss White? I will be very careful of it, I promise. May I look at your copy, please?"

Annie went to her room, brought out the Pepys book, and put it in the man's hands. He took it and held it reverently for a moment, feeling and stroking the smooth leather. He turned it over and ran his fingers over the pages. "What a lovely copy," he remarked. "You must love it." He barely lifted his eyes from the tome.

"Yes, I do," she said. "They were a gift."

They spoke then at length until Annie announced that it was her bedtime. Then in a moment of generosity, she said, "Sam, I imagine it is just as cold on the verandah as it is in the shed, so if you wish, you could settle on the old settee here. It is quite comfortable, and you will be warm."

Sam looked at Annie with some distress showing on his face. "Is that wise, Miss White?" he asked her.

"I can't see why not," said Annie tersely. "I have never asked anyone's opinion about what I do since I came to the colony, and I am not about to now. I have no friends to condone me and have little care for others' interest in me. If I suggest you sleep in here, then I suggest it, no more, no less. And it is no one else's business but ours, but you may please yourself. Turn the lamp out when you have finished with the book." With that, she went to her room.

Through winter, Sam joined her each evening after work had finished, and each evening, he slept on the settee in the kitchen. He recovered quickly this time as his body had not only warmth but healthy food. Now well again, Sam started putting on some weight and started looking, not only well, but could even pass as good looking. He was still drastically underweight, and his bones still protruded, but his eyes were no longer sunken in his head. They enjoyed their readings, their discussions, and their times together over the winter months. Often when reading the Shakespeare plays, they took turns to read the parts. She loved hearing his melodious voice as he read so beautifully. This way, they found the company pleasant. The winter soon passed, and the days drew longer. Sam had been with her for nearly a year. The last three months, he'd slept inside.

Sam had entirely lost his wan look and was very strong now. He found himself waking each day, looking forward to his work with even a smile. There was no further sign of his cough, and he was keen to do as much as he could find to help her. Sam had made a lovely vegetable garden, using up all the land he could utilise. Annie would now sit admiring his lithe physique as he worked shirtless in the garden. He had filled out from the sick scrawny man she first met. His dark hair now glistened with health, and his brown eyes would twinkle and smile when she spoke to him kindly. He was now growing so many vegetables that market day trips were part of their regular routine.

Annie was working six days a week as always. They just went about their daily toil, day after day and month after month.

The days grew longer; they were comfortable reading in the evenings continued until they almost knew the five books by heart. The Bible remained virtually untouched.

Sam still slept on the settee, even in the heat of the occasional hot spring days. It was like he was now guarding her. Rip slept near her door but with his head to the door on guard, not protecting against Sam but protecting him too.

Sam had been with Annie nearly fifteen months. It was one evening in the late spring when Sam was reading John Donne. He felt Annie's eyes burning fiercely upon him. He looked up and caught her eyes, and smiled.

She didn't turn away but kept looking.

He smiled again, wondering what was passing through her mind, but then his smile turned to astonishment at her next words.

"Sam, why don't we marry?" she asked very matter-of-factly.

He looked back at the book, unseeing. He sat there not moving, then he said, "You don't know what you are asking," quite flatly.

"I suppose you think me quite terrible. Being an emancipist and all, I suppose you think me forward," Annie said miserably. Now faced again with abject rejection.

"Oh, no, it's not that," Sam said, "But you don't know what you are asking. I could be an axe murderer for all you know."

"Am I that repulsive to you?" she asked, looking exceptionally sad. Sam noticed her eyes filled with tears at his brusk comment.

"Oh, no! Not that miss! Not that at all, it's just the opposite, Miss White. I think you are both brave and beautiful. Oh, no! Not that at all," he repeated, anxiously attempting to remove any doubt of rejection from her.

"What then?" asked Annie puzzled. "Are you already married?"

He shook his head. "You don't know anything about me," Sam said. "You don't even know why I was sent here. I have nothing to offer you. I don't have a farthing to my name, only what you give me. I am your man, your slave or servant if you like. A kept man. How can you respect me? Someone who has no ambition, nothing to offer at all."

"But I do respect you, Sam Corbett. And for that matter, you don't know anything about me either, so I suppose I am outrageous asking you to share my life without you knowing my past," she said guiltily.

"I don't think I am interested in your past, miss," he said, "I respect you for what you have done here. How you work and what you do. I respect you for all that, but why in heaven's name do you want to ruin it? Aren't you happy the way we are? What do you want? I have enjoyed these months. But I suppose it couldn't last," he said bitterly. "Nothing good ever lasts." He again sounded like the empty, sad man who'd arrived so many months ago.

"Oh, Sam, I don't want to ruin what we have, but I want it to be better. I've been so lonely for so long that I have been so very happy these last months, and I want it to continue, but … I want more, I need more. I wake up shivering when I think of you packing up and leaving. I want you to stay. This way, I hope you would." She sat blushing adorably.

Sam sat, looking down at the book before him, unable to see it but his mind whirling with emotion. "You don't know what you are asking me," he said. "I trust you, Miss White, far more than you'll ever realise."

"I hope you will again," said Annie softly. "I am sorry. I was only thinking of myself. I am so sorry, Sam. Please … we'll try to carry on as before. Please, Sam, I am sorry, you won't let it make any difference, will you?"

Sam didn't answer.

So Annie said, "Sam, I dance to my own tune. I live my life by my own rules, for I have had no one to guide me, and I make the best of what I have, which is not much. I live each day as it comes, and I love what I have, as it's all better than what I had before." She turned and went to leave but stopped and said, "I'll go to bed now, Sam, goodnight."

He nodded goodnight but remained silent. He felt winded, excited and anxious.

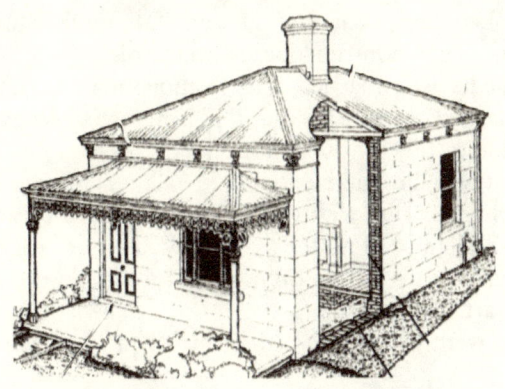

Chapter 3   Discoveries

*A*nnie wondered what she had done, wondered whether her life could go on as it had been. She went to bed and sobbed, "What have I done?" Annie was so angry at herself that she'd now scared him away. She feared being alone again. She wondered about just offering to sleep with him. But he'd never showed any interest in her that way either. Maybe she was just unattractive. She didn't have a mirror, so she didn't know how she looked. She wondered what Sam would say in the morning. Finally, she was sick inside worrying about it, then decided that she had to sleep and made herself think of other things.

Nothing seemed to change in the morning. Sam seemed the same, and they both set about their tasks as usual. Perhaps their conversation was slightly more stilted, but their interactions in the mornings were rarely very talkative.

All day Annie wondered what would happen, but still, they said nothing, but Annie placed the book they had been reading on the table after their evening meal and sat across from him. Rip sat under the table, panting, close to them both.

Sam said, "I have decided that I must tell you my story and take the risk that you will want me to go. I see that it is essential that you should know who you have been housing all these months."

"There is no need, Sam, and it can be no worse than mine. I had intended to tell you my story, too, but there is no need to tell yours. I feel secure about you, and I don't want to intrude." Annie was hopeful that he wasn't going to leave.

"My dear Miss White, marriage is an intrusion. Or at least I have always thought of it that way; that's why I have never attempted it. It certainly didn't benefit my parents," he said. "My mother died when I was three, so I grew up in a non-functioning household."

'At least he isn't married,' Annie thought to herself but said, "I haven't been married either, Sam, but that is perhaps because I have never had the opportunity. I'll tell you my saga later."

"Well, it will be soon enough to talk of marriage after I have shared the story of my life with you." He took a deep breath and started. He was at first hesitant, "I find it hard to draw the story together, as for so many years I have put it all out of my mind that I do not find it easy to find where to start."

"Where were you born? Perhaps that is a start, Sam," said Annie, trying to help.

"I was born to my mother and father in the family home in West Sussex, as I told you, near Billingshurst. There were two of us; Nigel was a few years older than I, and he was the apple of our father's eye. My mother nearly succumbed when I was born and, in fact, never fully recovered, and she finally died when I was three. That was my first big mistake. I took my mother's life away," he added bitterly. "Father blamed me for this." The look of dejection on his face spoke volumes.

"Oh, Sam, that is just ridiculous. You can't be held responsible for your mother's death," she interjected and then fell silent.

"Ah, but I was. In my father's eyes, I was to blame for everything that went wrong. He hated me from that time, if not before." Sam raised his eyes to her. Devoid of tears but full of emotion. "Mind you, even before then, he just ignored me. Other than beltings, he never touched me."

Annie started at that and was about to say something when Sam held his hand up. "No, don't say anything. I told you I would tell my story, and I will. But it must be in my own way. I am not telling it because I am sorry for myself; all that is gone now. And I am not telling you for sympathy, for that is useless, and I wouldn't want it anyhow. I'm telling you because not only must I, but because I trust you."

"Sorry, okay, go on," she said quietly. her hands clasped in her lap.

"I cannot remember having any love at all from anyone in my whole life since the day my mother died. I do remember her cuddles in her bed. She was never well after I was born, but every day we could have a long cuddle, and I'd lie in her arms and just look at her beautiful face, stroking her soft cheek. I was just a nuisance to my father, and he and my brother treated me as such. Remember, I was only three when she died. Therefore, the servants treated me the same. They had nothing to fear from my father, for anything they did to me would be approved by him. I was fed and clothed, and that was it. I was very pleased indeed Father sent me to boarding school at aged six, and there I made some friends, and for the first time in my life, I found that I was normal. I must admit, I had wondered. I loved the lessons and did well, for my benefit, not for my father's. But schooling fascinated me, and I found all my lessons a joy, especially mathematics. Some of those friends went on to college with me, and I grew more and more to depend upon them. I would, more often than not, holiday with them when I was permitted. My father delighted in stopping that when he could too, for he didn't think I should be allowed any enjoyment whatsoever. If he had known I loved school, I am sure he would have taken me away from that too, so I never told him. Later, he allowed me to go to university, mainly because he didn't want me at home, and I was too young to go on the town as my brother was doing."

"Sam, he sounds a beast." Then clasped her hand over her mouth.

"No, he is well thought of in the district and very popular with the County. He does everything one should do in his position, and so does Nigel, lording it over all and sundry. I was just a problem to them, I was not required. However, if I loved school, I wallowed in the delights of learning at Oxford. I studied Pure Mathematics there. I had good friends and loved the work. I never had much money, for Papa kept me on a pittance. So, I could never afford to live a fast life; I had barely enough for my emergency needs. However, indeed I cannot say I hankered after a social life anyway. But there were certain things I did like doing and was unhappy that I forever had to depend on my friends for paying for me everywhere we went, and I would have loved a horse of my own. It made me feel wretched. That I could never reciprocate any invitations, I thought, perhaps, if I went to see my father and ask him to raise my allowance, I could pay my father back when I graduated. I thought then I would start to earn my living in some way. So I borrowed some money from a friend and went home to see Papa and ask him." He ran his fingers through his hair. "I may as well have saved my breath; he refused and indeed blamed me for coming home in mid-term and told me he would cut my allowance for coming home without permission."

He sighed, remembering. "I had nothing in my pockets at all, not a thing, not even a farthing. I wondered how I would get back to college. I racked my brains. Then I thought of Jenkins, the groom, who had been the only one who had ever shown me any kindness. He told me he wouldn't be game, for Anthony knew how things were, and he wouldn't take the risk of losing his job; he'd already been threatened. I understood his situation. So, then I had a bright idea. I would go into the church and see if there was any money in the poor box. I knew that our family had always donated well to the poor; as in, I heard Papa put in coins every Sunday and couldn't see a problem in taking something we gave.

Therefore, that would not be much of a crime. But the Rector came in a found me. I was trying to prise open the lid and couldn't, but Rector caught me in the act and had me arrested. You see, Miss White, he is my father's best friend. Yes, I was arrested and sentenced to seven years in Botany Bay for 'destroying church property and attempted theft', not that I broke anything. My father completely disowned me after that, and he wiped me off the family records; he took great pleasure in rubbing my nose in that titbit of information. The Rector too delighted in appearing in the Assizes to witness against me. He is proud of his closeness to my father. And so, that is how I came here."

"Oh, Sam, what a terrible time you have had," she exclaimed. "I'm not sure if being disowned by a family was better or worse than never having had one." No wonder he looked so sad when he arrived, she thought.

"Well, now you know. Would you wish to marry someone low enough to rob a poor box? Do you know, it didn't hit me until later? Then I wondered how I could have done such a thing." He sounded so bleak.

She absolutely stunned him when she giggled, then laughed, a glorious deep chuckling laugh. "Oh, Sam, well, weren't you poor? But I don't think anyone could blame you; you were one of the poor, weren't you? I certainly don't. What a horrible man! No wonder I don't like church." She touched his hand in sympathy.

He looked speechless and dumbfounded. "You are generous, Miss White, but when you sit and think about it is a pretty rotten thing to do, and I am bitterly ashamed of it." He finally met her eyes and did not see condemnation, but heartfelt sorrow reflected in her eyes. Yet she could see a funny side to it, something he'd never done. She giggled. He did not expect that reaction.

"No, what was rotten is that minister who didn't help you." She could see in her mind's eye the confused, unloved little three-year-old boy who'd lost the only person to give him affection and hugs. Her eyes pooled with unshed tears. "Did none of your friends come to you or your brother or anyone? Surely someone could help." She wiped a tear away from her cheek.

"I did have a friend who came to the gaol once, but I think it so disgusted him that I doubt whether he would have come again if I'd been there. He gave me food, clean clothing, of sorts, it was a coat and scarf, and some much-needed money – it was only a few pounds in coins, but it saved my life. I was very fortunate that I was transported very quickly and so did not have to stay longer in gaol, and if he did come looking for me again, he would have found me gone."

"Oh, Sam," said Annie, thoughtfully. She had thought her lot was terrible, but as she had had no expectations, she didn't worry about people coming to see her. Betsy had come once and brought my blanket and a coat. There were also some coins in the pocket. "I daresay we are alike in that we have no one at all to care for us, Sam."

"Have you no one, Miss White?" he asked.

"No, no one! No, not a living soul; I have got used to being alone and was content until recently. Until you came actually, and I found that I liked company after all. I was quite content to live alone and would busy myself about my own interests, earning enough to stay alive and not expect more." She met his eyes fleetingly.

"Yes, I understand that. I am afraid that I did not care about anything much; I didn't care whether I lived or died. The hereafter can't be worse than this has been if there is such a place. I always trust God, not that I know much about Him, but never in mankind. The God I heard about in school was not the fellow Watmore preached. In fact, I daresay Heaven is a great deal better. I've also learned never to mix up religion and God. I know they are not the same thing. I would have thought that nothing much could be worse than this place." He sounded glum.

"I thought that, too, but have to admit that I like Sydney Town better now than when I first came. Or I suppose I know that I have no alternative, so I don't think about it much. And truly, anything is better than being a felon; at least I am free, we both are Sam."

"It's a peculiar kind of freedom, though. Free to do what though I ask you? And we can never leave, and few will give an ex-convict a fair go," he stated bluntly.

"What do you want, Sam? If you had the choice to do anything else, what would you wish to do?" She looked puzzled.

"Do you know, Miss White, I hadn't given it a thought until you spoke last night. I merely exist, and that is all; I really have no will to live and no purpose. I eat, I sleep, and I repeat. I learned to stop thinking years ago; it was no use. So, I suppose I was rather like a cabbage; I did what was there to do, no more, no less."

"Does my company mean anything to you, then?" Annie asked quietly.

"Yes, it does. I had forgotten how much I loved reading and I have enjoyed your company so very much indeed. So much so that I do not want to spoil that. I could be happy doing just that for a long, long time."

"Nothing else? Do you not wish for ... um, more?" she asked hopefully.

"I don't know. I couldn't sleep last night thinking about it and you and your offer. Of course, I have that lonely ache inside me that I wish I could fill, but I have no idea how to do that. Of course, I have normal physical needs. All I know is that I think I've been happier, and more content here than I have been, ever. I hadn't tried to analyse it until I realised how important being here is to me. I don't mean that you feed me and look after me. I can take that or leave it, but I think I am happy. Does that make sense?"

"I think so." She paused. "So am I, Sam. I have that lonely ache too."

"Do you know, I am rather scared of happiness. I don't think I know what it is. Any satisfaction that I have had, has been transient. I certainly don't know what love is, having never experienced that either. I don't think I'd know it if it hit me. It seems as though you have to give up something to get happiness, and I haven't much to give, have I? You two are all I have; just you, Rip and being here." He bent and patted the dog's ears.

"Yes, I can see that you haven't much to give. You just have yourself, Sam, and that is hard to give away, isn't it? I understand that, but I am not asking you to give that up, Sam. I don't think anyone should give everything up; you must keep your private life to yourself. But I do understand as I feel the same. I have felt like that myself, and believe me, I was surprised at myself when I spoke last night." She looked somewhat shy. "I'm just so lonely, Sam."

"Do you regret speaking, then?" He now looked anxiously at her.

"No, I don't, and even after hearing your story, I will ask again too. But first, you must hear my story. You don't know what I have done. It is far worse than anything you have done. You must have wondered how I got all this; you must have wondered how I got to this colony in the first place. Sam, you must have wondered quite a lot."

Sam said nothing but shrugged. Of course, he'd wondered, but he'd never ask. He just looked at her with quite a glazed look on his face.

His look rather disconcerted Annie. "My turn," she took a deep breath and started her story. She told Sam her story from the beginning. "I was a housemaid in Sir Cecil Broome-Hall's home in London. I began life somewhere, possibly in Kent or Sussex, but I do not know, as I was a foundling. So, I have never known a family. I was placed in an orphanage at a few months old, wrapped in a knitted white blanket and a note that said my name was Anne or Anna, and I was born in July. That was 1773. I was given the name 'White' as that was the colour of the blanket I was wrapped in. The first life I knew was in an orphanage, where I remained until I was twelve years old. Every year in July someone sent me a new white dress. I have no idea who it was. But it was nice to know I wasn't forgotten, I suppose. They always fitted perfectly. The orphanage wasn't unfriendly, but it certainly was not really loving. I was taken into service at the Broome-Hall Manor in Sussex at about twelve. I was even allowed to play with the daughter of the house, who was about thirteen-years-old at the time. I worked hard and gradually advanced in different jobs and later went to work in the family's townhouse in London, where I remained. Lady Broome-Hall did not care for city life, so only Sir Cecil was there most of the time. Their three children had married or moved away and were in various places; one boy joined the army. I was very happy, Sam, and the workload was quite light. The people I worked with were nice; Sir Cecil did not entertain much. Even Lady Broome-Hall was nice to me. He was something in the government, a diplomatic position, I'm not sure, as I never asked." Annie thought back at her lack of interest in what Cec did. She had just accepted him as he was.

"Life just went along smoothly, and nothing seemed to change until I was sixteen and working as a housemaid. You see, I was not good at reading, I'd only done a few lessons at the Sunday School with the other servants, but I always wanted to learn properly but had no opportunity. One morning when I was dusting the Library, I was looking at some big leather-bound volumes trying to make out the meaning of the letters. The funny words interested me. At least I thought they must have been words, but I learned later that they were just the alphabet letters on the volumes of the encyclopaedia, you know, AAA – BAC and BAD – FRC. Things like that."

Sam nodded.

"Just as I was kneeling on a chair trying to work them out, a voice behind me said, "Whatever are you doing, child?" I looked around and stood up fast, for it was the master. He asked me again, and I told him I was trying to read the words. He laughed like mad, and I was upset to think he was laughing at me. He saw my hurt, and then he explained. He took the books down and showed them to me and made me sit beside him to look. I was ever so worried thinking that Mrs Simpkins, the housekeeper, might find me, or Mr Bowles, the butler. The master seemed to understand and asked me if I would like to learn to read, and I told him I would. I look back at it now and wonder about it all, but I was so innocent Sam, and I now know I shouldn't have, but when he asked if I would come to his room at night so that no-one would know he was teaching me, I was quite surprised. He said, 'Don't worry, Annie, I wouldn't let any harm come to you, and I promise I won't touch you. But you see, my dear, I get bored in this house by myself and would consider it a kindness if you would fill in some lonely hours and be my pupil.' I said I would and did. I used to creep down from my attic room after all the others were in bed, and I didn't think anyone knew, or at least not then. He was so kind, and he taught me such a lot. He taught me to speak properly, and we read all sorts of books together. We went along like that for months and months, and, oh, Sam, it's so hard to make you understand. But you know, no one had ever taken notice of me in my whole life. Cec was so kind and gentle, and we were such good friends. After a long while, he said, one night, 'Annie, dear, I am going to ask you to release me from my promise. Can you do that?' I didn't know what he meant until he said, 'Child, I've learned to love you and your wonderful enquiring mind. You have become quite precious to me, and I want to touch you and love you'."

Annie held her head down. Her voice dropped. "Oh, Sam, I couldn't believe it. I just gazed at him and nodded. He lifted me and carried me to the bed and he, well he loved me for the first time. That first time it hurt, but oh, I was just swept away with the glory of it all. I'd never been kissed before, and I'd certainly never been touched that way. He was so gentle, so caring. I never had any sort of affection given to me before, and oh Sam, it was so wonderful." She wiped away a tear with the back of her hand. She dropped her head onto the table and sat quietly sobbing before finally continuing her story. "I loved him so much, and he loved me. Now I look back; he would not have been that old, probably only fifty or so, if that, but I … he was an older man and me but an innocent child. But we were so happy together, and we had so many wonderful hours together. We still read a lot, and he did teach me to read properly. We read absolutely everything, but there were five books in particular we loved. We'd sit up in bed reading after we'd made love. We thought no one knew. We tried to behave just normally during the day. Then one day, after over a year, he told me that he had to go away on a mission to China and would be away for a long while. I was devastated, but he assured me that he would come back as soon as he could, and we'd be together again. He was to go in a matter of weeks. We found time to be together, to make love and read, every day until Cec left. He had been away before, but only for short times, and he often had to go away to his Sussex house. That last time I stayed most of the night in his room. He'd had a big function at the house, and there were lots of men, and they stayed late. I had to wait until they had all gone, and it was nearly midnight before the last one left. I snuck down to his room, and well, it wasn't just once that we were together; we didn't sleep much. Sam, I loved him so very much, but it was more than that; he cherished me." She lifted her eyes to his, tears sliding down her cheeks. "The time flew by as Betsy had me spring clean absolutely everything, including the attics. It was about three weeks after he had gone that the mistress came up to town. The next day the constable came and arrested me. Her father, the Duke, had just arrived and saw it all, horrified. He'd been at Ceccy's meeting. They said I had stolen her ruby heart brooch. To prove it they went to my room and they found it in my drawer. I didn't, Sam. I didn't take anything; I was sentenced and sent here. I'd spent the last three weeks spring cleaning the entire house, even the coal cellar. I'd hardly been into my room but to sleep. I was so tired. Then that happened."

"Oh, Annie, you poor girl," said Sam; he moved closer to her to comfort her in her sadness. "But what happened when Sir Cecil returned?"

"I hoped and hoped that I would hear from him. Betsy, my friend, saw me once and brought a coat and my white blanket. But he didn't come; she said that Cec was still away. I found then that she knew of our relationship. I didn't think he would let me down, and he didn't, Sam. He was away for over a year and knew nothing about my arrest. It's not like he could write to me on his trip, nor I to him. And he couldn't ask his wife. I was still just a servant girl, of course. Lady Broome-Hall's father, a Duke, came and visited her while she was there. He seemed nice, but I felt uncomfortable near him, so I stayed clear away. He was an older man, and he gave me the creeps. Anyway, Master Tim told me Cec was aghast when he got back to find me gone. But I knew nothing of this and hoped and hoped to at least have a letter, but I heard nothing. By then, I was here with Mrs Tremaine to serve my sentence, and now I realise that I was fortunate to be there. It was like she chose me from the crowd. She almost went looking for me. She was so kind. I was so utterly miserable that I couldn't feel happy about anything. Then came the day when I was released from servitude, my time fully up, and Mrs Tremaine told me arrangements had been for me to stay at Mrs Frame's lodging house in Sydney for a few nights. I couldn't understand why but was quite happy to accept the arrangement as I didn't know what would happen. When I got to Mrs Frame's, I had the surprise of my life for Sir Cecil's nephew, Master Timothy, came to see me. We often met in London as he worked with Cec, so he often came to the house. He told me what had happened at home. Cec had been so upset to find me gone and convicted that he had a stroke soon after returning and later was quite paralysed. His daughter had married a Scotsman not long before he left. According to Tim, he apparently refused to talk to his wife, but she came one day, and they were closeted in his office for some time. He would have no one around him but Betsy, my good friend, and Master Tim, in whom he fully confided. He made Master Tim promise to get some money and some things to me when he could and do what he could to see to my future. As this was all done before he died, the family could do nothing. It was mine, untouchable even by his will as Master Tim had already taken them back to his house for safekeeping. All up, it was about £250; some £50 was spent on building and buying this place."

Sam let out a long breath and looked somewhat astounded. He

was by now holding her hand and stroking the back of it.

"So Master Tim got himself into a position where he could come out here as a courier for the Governor. He had worked with Sir Cecil, I think, in the Government. As I said, I had never asked. While he was here, he got busy. He knew when I was to be released, he bought this land and had the house built. He's the one who named it *Rock Cottage*. The cottage was all done without my knowledge. He'd even brought out furniture Cec wanted me to have, and that included some of Cec's things for me. He'd made Master Tim take them home before he died. Master Tim had left some money with Mr Finley to buy this place when the Governor released the land, which I did. But there's more leftover. He brought the cupboard from next to Cec's bed with my favourite books and a letter from him. Cec wrote it just before he died. He even signed it at the end and wrote, 'I love you, my awesome Annie, Cec', in his shaky hand." She looked straight at Sam and challenged him by saying, "He loved me, Sam; he didn't let me down. That letter was the balm to my scarred hurting heart, Sam."

"Oh, Annie," then he realised he had called her Annie and corrected it to, "sorry, Miss White."

Annie smiled, "Annie will do Sam. Well, now you know, Sam. I suppose you would call me a fallen woman, but Cec never made me feel like that. I was apprehensive about the situation, realising that I could fall pregnant until he promised me that he would look after me no matter what happened. He told me that I must hold my head up high. I tried, Sam, I tried so very hard, but sometimes it was impossible."

"Poor Annie," Sam said, "what a story you have to tell." He held her hand warmly now.

"Do you blame me, Sam? What do you think of me now?" she asked anxiously, "Am I so far fallen I disgust you too?"

"Annie," he said, "I think of you as I always have. You are a fine woman and what you have done is your own business, your own life. That has nothing to do with you and me." He paused and waited until she looked up at him. He went on to one knee and said, "Annie White, will you do me the great honour of marrying me?"

With that, Annie's tears flowed. She nodded assent.

He stood up and, drawing her to her feet, took her in his arms and kissed her wet cheeks gently. Then he kissed her properly. For some time, they sat on the settee with her on his lap, her arms wrapped around his neck. She was still in weeping softly but clinging tightly to him. Memories of being loved returned to her. She was savouring being touched affectionately for the first time in ten years. Finally, she pulled herself from his arms. Wordlessly she got up and went and changed for bed.

Sam too prepared to settle for the night. He heard a noise, turning;

she was there in her nightgown silhouetted against the fire. She put out her hand and taking his hand; she led him to her bedroom.

"But Annie, we're not married yet," he said, not believing what she was offering.

She stepped close to him and placed her hands around his neck. "Sam, I dance to my own tune. Everyone thinks I have been sleeping with you anyway. I need to be close to you. I need to be needed, to be wanted."

He did not return to the settee that night. He followed her willingly. He'd not been a man who sowed his seed freely, and he'd been with a woman before, but not for a very long time. He, too, needed to be held and loved.

Their intimate time together that night was a healing solace to them both. Confessions, tears and togetherness were what they both needed. They fell asleep, physically satisfied and relaxed, wrapped in each other's arms; both were emotionally exhausted.

The next day being Sunday, they well and truly overslept. They had relished their physical joining, but their disclosures had depleted them emotionally. He greeted her with a morning kiss when she woke. He'd been watching her sleep and had his head on his hand, looking down at her in awe. His face had now completely lost the haunted look.

She opened her eyes and saw his now very handsome face looking down at her.

He was in awe that she knew all about him and accepted him just for who he was.

She reached up and touched his bristly face, knowing now that he would stay with her. Her loneliness abated. She had now given him the only thing she had the right to offer, just herself, and he'd accepted it. His morning kiss was everything she'd dreamed it to be. She reached for him again, pulling him down to her, and in the early morning light, he watched her face relax with delight as they took their pleasure in each other. She'd never spent the entire night with a man, and she found she enjoyed waking up with him as much as she'd enjoyed the night before. He, too, seemed to like it. He pushed the sheet down a little to enjoy the view before him. She smiled as he did so.

That night Sam went to settle on the settee for the night. Rip was again at his feet. After he had pulled up the blanket, Annie came and stood next to him in the kitchen. She did not realise her nightgown was completely see-through with the firelight behind her. Her glorious long wavy hair reached well beyond her waist, hanging like a waterfall. She was somewhat tearful, not wanting to go to bed alone, and again held out her hand. "Sam, I need you close; I want you close. I need to be held and touched."

He went to her, willingly taking her in his arms and carried her to bed. She clung to him and begged for him to stay with her. "Don't ever leave me, Sam."

Rip followed and lay outside their bedroom in utter contentment. He no longer had to choose where he'd sleep.

Sam never returned to sleep on the settee. Neither had spoken of any emotional connection between them. Neither understood love; both were far too raw for that; Annie had planned a marriage of convenience, theirs would be far from that, but both were content.

In 1802, the marriage of ex-convicts was not always easy as it often took weeks, if not months, to get permission. Yet, in just over a month, Sam was able to tell Annie that he had done all the paperwork. So the Banns were read, and they were allowed to marry. She didn't have a special dress so she made sure the one she had was clean. There was no real church in the colony at the time, as the wooden church that Rev Mr Johnson had built had burned down, and the replacement stone one was not complete yet, so the ceremony took place in Annie's house. They enjoyed their closeness during the nights, and this surprised them both. Their hunger for each other was insatiable, only pausing when she had her menses. Sam still found a way to show his care for her. Sam was affectionate in his kisses but also exceptionally discreet too. His blanket and pillow remained on the settee until they married, as did his clothing, just in case anyone came in. Both gained contentment from the relationship, yet there were still topics that they had not discussed.

They asked Bert Todd, the carrier, and Willy Knight, the carpenter, to be witnesses. These two gentlemen felt they had a real stake in the wedding, for it had been Bert who brought Sam into Annie's life, and Willy had been a constant visitor over the time Sam had been there, and so were delighted to be part of it. Both men presumed it to be a love match. Neither asked. They saw the friendship that had developed between them, and that was enough. They had dressed in their best clothes, and Annie had made a special cake for afternoon tea after the marriage. Rev Marsden said the words, gave a blessing, and the deed was done. Both signed their names in the register. The Minister looked at them in surprise, for few convicts were literate, let alone with such elegant handwriting.

Annie and Sam's life did not alter much after they were married, except that Sam's clothing no longer resided in the kitchen or shed but in her bedroom. They both relished the personal touch they could now give to another person; their loneliness eased. Most mornings started with them taking a prolonged slow waking. They enjoyed a kiss one would provide when passing and the morning hugs they would give each other once dressed.

Occasionally Sam would bend and gently kiss her neck. At first, this would bring tears to her eyes, but lately, she'd turn in his arms and kiss him back. Often they ended up back in bed. They worked just as hard and were increasing their supply of goodies to their customers.

Annie watched Sam closely, for, at times, she wondered whether he was content with their life. She was still quite frightened at what he might say, so she did not ask.

One night, after they had been married for nearly five months, when he was reading some poetry, he burst out with, "Annie, I wish I could find a way to help you more. I wish there were some way where I could ease your workload and help financially. You're working so hard you're making yourself ill."

"Oh, Sam," Annie said, "is that what has been worrying you lately?" She released a deep sigh.

"Yes, it is. I have thought and thought and cannot think of any way for me to do more. I have wondered whether I should start to tutor some child or take a position as a clerk or just anything."

Annie exclaimed. "Sam, I thought you were not happy. I was frightened you may want to leave here and go away." She wept with relief.

He was beside her in an instant. "Go away?" he asked, surprised and taking her in his arms. He lovingly caressed her cheek. "Go away, my dear? Why should I do that? The cottage is my home now, you are my wife, and I wouldn't leave it or you for anything, but I want to do more to assist you. I can't say that this colony offers a great deal for a person with ambition."

"Oh, so you have ambition now, do you?" she asked soggily with a giggle. She didn't know why she was so tearful these days.

"Yes, ambition to do more for you." He dropped a kiss on her lips.

Neither had yet admitted any affection for each other.

After their marriage, both had just let things float. Their marriage was supposed to be one of 'convenience' after all. It was physically very satisfying, and Sam demonstrated that frequently. Their "convenience" would often occur when Anne had finished cooking, and she stood watching his bare-chested body sweating in the garden. He'd see her watching him, and he'd come in and, as he laughingly said, to attend to her needs, or he'd wash up before a meal, which was often then delayed for some time. Rarely was anything asked. During the day, they only had to stand eyeing the other and were met with a raised eyebrow of inquiry and a nod. The other would stop what they were doing and walk to their bedroom. Both were so starved of affection that they craved the physical side of their marriage often. It filled the desolate need that each had for acceptance and intimacy.

"I don't think we'll worry about you doing more, for now, Sam. Just let's be content for a while," Annie said with a smile, snuggling to his chest. "I like the 'more' you are already doing." She smiled contentedly to herself.

So life continued in much the same way for some weeks. Annie was delighted with the change, for she could see that Sam was doing all he could to take any burden from her shoulders, and she was wise enough to let him. She knew that he had woken from the miserable state he had been in for years and now was feeling rather like a fledged bird who was ready to fly. She'd now catch the glint of mischief in his face. He'd make her laugh in some silly way, or he'd chase her, and they'd often end up in their bedroom again. Yet, he still couldn't think of anything he could do to help with their finances without leaving her to cope alone with all they did on the place.

One morning after they had been married some six months, Annie came into breakfast looking very pale and wan, having been sick again. Tears were streaming down her face, and she was a picture of abject misery.

Sam went to her and reached to take her in his arms. "Why, whatever is the matter, Annie joy?" Sam asked anxiously. She threw herself into his arms and sobbed into his chest. "What is it? Are you ill?"

"Oh, Sam, whatever will I do? What will happen to us?" she muttered incoherently into his shoulder.

"Come, lass, tell me what it is?" He sat and pulled her onto his lap

She pulled back in his arms, "Sam, I think I'm going to have a child. What will I do? What will we do? We didn't think of it, did we? How can I do my work if I am having a child?" She sobbed even harder.

He drew her to him, and she hugged him tightly as she now sat tightly nestled in his arms. Hers were wrapped around him as she sobbed into his neck.

Sam chuckled, placing many little kisses on her cheeks and forehead. He was still laughing delightedly as he said, "Didn't you think it was possible, Annie? Our, um, activities have been, well, um well frequent and satisfying, haven't they?"

She nodded.

He continued. "I know we haven't talked about it, but I daresay it was an inevitable result of marriage, you know. I'm surprised this had not occurred earlier. I'm particularly pleased it didn't before we married, though."

"But I didn't before, Sam, not with Cec, nor with us. So, I thought I just couldn't have a child." She sounded distraught. "And Sam, I'm nearly thirty." She set to sobbing again

"So am I, by the way, my dear. Well, it just shows that it was never your problem." The smile he had on his face comforted her.

"Don't you mind, Sam? You aren't upset?" She drew back and searched his face.

"I will only be upset if you are, my lass. Actually, I rather like the idea, don't you?" He was now grinning from ear to ear. He now nibbled at her neck then kissed her nose then continued to distract her.

"I suppose I could be," she said after a long passionate kiss. "But how are we going to manage? How will I be able to do all the cooking when I am, well, when I'm huge?"

"My beautiful lass, you'll have to teach me to cook, won't you? You'll see. We'll manage very well." He kissed her again and cuddled her tenderly. He finally felt her relax against him.

"Sam, I'm scared, really, really scared," she admitted, hiding her head in his now soggy neck.

"We'll learn together, my dear. We'll ask and learn and be ready." She sat being comforted for some time.

He sat just holding her, unable to believe in his good fortune. He gave a long-contented sigh.

Sitting nestled in his arms just felt right. Annie didn't wish to move, ever.

Later that week, they went together to the midwife, Mrs Pitts, to talk to her. Annie needed to be sure she was expecting and wanted to ask some questions. Having never known her mother and never really being told the facts of life, she knew very little. Sam, having grown up in a dysfunctional family, knew even less.

Sam came with her to support her. He was still somewhat overwhelmed with the change in his circumstances. He had not occurred to him either. They had never even mentioned children. Now he realised he needed to learn all he could.

By the time Annie was large with child, Sam could cook the goods that she had always done for her customers and do the necessary gardening. Sam admittedly had to cut down on the weeding and buy more vegetables than usual but could manage their tasks. Annie felt the last two months badly. Her feet were very swollen. She still managed to make the pastry, but from there, Sam did the rest, although, he'd tried making pastry too, but he was no chef. Annie felt quite ill, but that only lasted the first few months. Later she'd started sorting a place for the baby. She emptied the bottom drawer of their dresser and set it up as a crib. They still had little, but they needed little. She looked forward to when she would be back at work and taking over some of the tasks again.

They had spoken a great deal about the coming child while lying cocooned in bed at night. It was still rather a wonder to them both.

Annie had been alone all her life, with no blood family, now with the coming of this babe, she had not just one person who cared about her, but there would be a second one too. Two confused, hurt, lonely people who were still learning about living with one another, and now the thought of a third totally helpless soul in their midst was a bit daunting. They lay in bed each night discussing some portion of their future. Little by little, Annie grasped the horror of his childhood, and her own in an orphanage in comparison was quite happy. She knew there was still much he was not telling her. She told him about the appearance of a swing in a tree beside a creek at the orphanage. It was her delight. At least she'd had companionship. Even when she went to Broome-Hall, the staff had made her welcome.

Still, neither had opened up to their feelings for the other as they didn't quite understand the emotions themselves.

As parents-to-be, they pondered over the gender of the child and the name they should give him or her.

Sam would rest his hand on her mobile stomach as the child moved. He was in awe of her. He'd sit watching her sleep, he'd watch the wave of emotions flash across her face, and he'd wait for the inevitable sigh that nearly always came at the end. The closer and larger she became; the more caring and attentive Sam was of her. The feelings she stirred in his frozen heart were overwhelming.

Late one evening, they lay in bed and discussed names for the child. The girl's name was easy according to Sam, for his own mother's name was Anne, and so he was adamant that the child's name should be Anne also, after both the child's mother and his mother, but it would need a second name as well, and he suggested Grace, which Annie loved.

Looking up into his face, Annie said, "Then, in that case, a boy should be Sam." He objected. He said that he didn't like his name much, for his mother told him that his father had chosen it, and he always felt it belonged to a weakling. He wanted to give his son a name that was after someone he could look up to. The choice of a name took quite a lot of discussion, and in the end, they came up with Daniel, for Sam told Annie that Daniel had always been one of his favourite Bible heroes, and it was a name that suited him, man, boy and baby.

Annie was surprised that he'd mentioned the Bible. She asked about it and if it meant anything to him. His answers shook her.

"Annie, I believe in a God who is loving and forgiving, but one with rules that we must obey. I believe all that about Jesus being his son too and that only by believing in Him can you be saved. I believe it, but I am not quite sure what to do with that knowledge. Only I'm beginning to understand that connection between the two, the Father and Son bit. But Annie, what I don't understand is how people can corrupt Jesus' beautiful teaching from the Bible and turn themselves into almost earthly demons." He spoke with intensity. "Rev Watmore is the perfect example of a Pharisee, in my understanding. He's a religious zealot, not a loving Christian. Oh, Annie, I have learned that there is a vast difference between the two. My sweet, I see more love and acceptance in your loving arms than in the scores of sermons I had to sit through in his bigoted church."

"I didn't get to church much, and when I did, it was to learn to read and write. I never actually found out what it was all about," she said sleepily on his shoulder.

Sam went on to talk to her about what was written in the Bible. "Annie, we have one, so why don't we do some reading from it for a while?"

She nodded sleepily against his naked chest. Soon her rhythmic breathing told him she was asleep. He, however, had a myriad of new thoughts running through his mind.

They wondered what would happen if the child decided to come while Sam was doing all the cooking. They now knew it would be some hours before it arrived once the pains started. He laughed, for he didn't think he would be able to 'think straight' if that was the case.

Daniel, however, was an accommodating baby, and he was born on a Sunday afternoon in November at their quietest time. The delivery was not very bad when one considers that Annie was now thirty and having her first child.

Mrs Pitt, the midwife, was a pleasant person and quite enthusiastic about any birth. "'Tis the miracle of life every time, lassie," she said when she first met Annie. She had given Annie a great deal of comfort and suggested that they call her anytime they wanted, for she was a great one for bringing up babies, as she informed them. She willingly answered any questions they asked. She was giving them just enough details for them to understand without being overwhelmed by what was ahead of them. Over the months, she'd taught them more and more.

Sam was satisfied with her, for she seemed much cleaner than the usual run of midwives he heard about elsewhere. She'd certainly been helpful to them.

Mrs Pitt knew they were both perfect innocents about bringing up a baby. She assured them she would help. She told this to Sam while cocking one eyebrow to him and saying, "Yer don' know much 'baht littluns does yer, Sam?"

He was happy to admit to it. "We know nothing, Mrs Pitt, absolutely nothing." Sam confided to her somewhat nervously. "We know we must feed and change it, but not even how often. Neither of us has ever even held an infant."

When the time came, Mrs Pitt and Sam were the only two with Annie. Sam was horrified that Mrs Pitt insisted he stay and assist. She made Annie walk around the room between contractions and lean into Sam's chest as each hit. For such a big strong man, her pain forbearance made him feel weak. The crushing pressure of her fingers on his own was excruciating. For the delivery, she was vastly uncomfortable lying on the bed. Nothing was progressing, so Mrs Pitt said, "All right, plan B."

They both looked at her, confused. Annie was in agony.

"It's taking too long. We'll deliver the child as the local women do. It's easier on the mama too, but not so on the midwife. It does my back in each time, but it's quicker. They deliver squatting. Sam, does ya have a stump or a stool of sorts?"

Sam found her something suitable, and they prepared for the birth. Rip took up his place outside their door.

Annie had nearly panicked when Sam had left her. She had not heard their conversation. "Sammy, where are you?"

He returned in a short while with a stump in his hands. He placed it down and put a small cushion on top.

Mrs Pitt made him rewash his hands with soap on his return. "I'm a person who likes things clean. That means hands too." She sent him to soap up his hands in case she needed him.

For the delivery, Mrs Pitt placed Sam sitting on the end of their bed and had him wrap his arms around Annie.

Annie then rested her arms on his legs. Her nightgown was pulled up around her waist and thus braced; Annie was able to bear down with ease. She could lean against him and relax between contractions. He took her full weight.

Sam was whispering encouragement to her and as she was just pushing the child out. He said, "Come on, Annie, my joy, my love. You can do this," and he kissed her neck. "I'm here, my sweetheart. I'll not leave you." Or "You can do this, my beloved."

Annie had heard but did not acknowledge the comments until much later. With each contraction, he said something loving and encouraging.

Their son arrived with a healthy scream. They now had this strange little wiggling, squalling scrap of humanity to look after and very little knowledge of how to do it. Mrs Pitt showed them the basics. How to change a napkin, wash the child, even how to give it a relaxing rub.

When she showed them how to change him, she said, "Watch out for his shower." Sam had no idea what she meant until the first time he had to change his son in the middle of the night. Sam got a face full as soon as Danny's napkin was undone. Aghast and revolted, he gagged. He was far more careful after that, holding the napkin over him each time he changed him. By the next day, he chuckled when Danny repeated the vile attack.

Mrs Pitt also showed Annie how to feed him without him getting too much air. Then how to burp him, but thankfully Daniel seemed to have his mind on only two things, feeding and napkin changes, and so life took on a semblance of normality again within weeks of his birth.

Annie was weak and exhausted for the first days, barely moving from the bed. Sam did most of the care for their son. Sam kept his cooking to a minimum, with the soups only. Annie only moved to use the chamber pot and return to sleep. Mrs Pitt came each day and checked her. On the third day, Annie felt better; Sam allowed her to get up but not dressed.

Sam was concerned as he did not want her seen by any of their customers. He wrapped Annie in a blanket and sat her out of view from the front window in the sitting room. She was able to watch him work, and therefore she relaxed. She woke when he picked her up and carried her to bed. "Rest, my sweet girl," he said as he gently lay her down. He knew Danny would be awake soon. She needed to gather her strength.

He'd got into the habit of, when he could, sitting next to her when she fed Danny. She was so weak and he needed to hold her up, but then because he loved to do it. He'd sit with his arm around her, his cheek resting on her head.

Sam would catch the beautiful look on Annie's face when he'd walk in as she was feeding their son. She was so at peace, and the look of love and adoration on her face made his heart jump. He'd watch the infant caress his mother's breast as he drank. Sam would catch his breath and feel a lump in his throat. He was so surprised that he did not understand his own emotions.

Annie would look at Sam the same way sometimes, often after she had just fed their child. She too would catch her breath at just how much Sam now meant to her.

Sam insisted on Annie doing light duties for several weeks. Coddling her until she announced that she would tear her hair out if he didn't allow her to get back to cooking again. Their bedroom activities, however, took two months to resume. Sam was not going to instigate it; that once again had to come from her. She had just laid a baby. When it did finally happen, he walked into their room when she was crying on her bed. He took her in his arms to comfort her. They forgot about cooking until Danny awoke.

When she attempted to explain that she was no longer attractive to him, he proved her very wrong. Annie had been worried; Sam's words haunted her, from during the birth, but he'd not followed them up with any more, nor had he been as affectionate. Her response to him reassured him about her physical need for him.

Chapter 4   Helping Her

Sam found time was hanging on his hands and once again had that lost look on his face occasionally. He seemed very unsure of himself again. Sam knew himself to be insecure and was still afraid of hurting her.

One day he said, "Anne," since Danny's birth, he had taken to shortening her name, "Do you think I could attempt to build a room onto the house for Danny? We are getting rather cramped in our room, and it will be hot in the kitchen for him in the summer. What do you think?"

"Well, it is a good idea, Sam, but do you know how to do it?" she asked, not knowing his skills in this area.

"I could try, I suppose. But I don't wish to waste your money, and I have none of my own." He was concerned.

She shot him a look that could have carried daggers; she looked somewhat exasperated but merely said, "I think *we* have enough money to ask Willy Knight to do it. Perhaps he would let you help." She looked at his face and saw it brightened.

"Should *we* do it, though? I don't like to suggest we use your nest egg. That's why I suggested that I try."

Anne brightened when she replied he would use the money. "Let's go down to see Mr Finley and see what he thinks. Now we own this place completely; I am sure he would think that any improvement would be a good thing."

"But I still think of that money as being yours, Anne."

"For goodness' sake, Sam, we're married. We have a child together. Everything I have is yours too, as it's the law. Cec wanted me happy, and I am Sam. What have you been doing all this time? We work together. Earn our money together. You never take anything for yourself unless it is absolutely essential. Don't you think you've earned it? And, there's still over £180 left."

Her question made him think, but he still felt unworthy of her. Sam shrugged his shoulders; he said, "You know that I have never earned any money and never wanted to, but now I have a family, I wish I could find some way of bringing in some cash."

"Please, Sam, please don't say that." She proceeded to assure him of her total reliance on him. "We work on this business together, Sam. We earn together. As you say, we are a family." She blushed and looked at him shyly.

"I know, but … oh, I don't know." It was her special money, but Danny was her son too. "All right, let's go and see Mr Finley."

That afternoon after they cleaned up, they took Danny and, of course, Rip, who still never let them out of his sight, and visited their financial adviser. He was happy with the suggestion that they add to their house. Mr Finley admired the 'wee bairn' and thought the laddie would grow to be a "strong tower of strength to them".

Sam hoped so and quietly thought that he hoped young Danny had inherited all the good things from his family and not the bad ones.

They had no baby carriage, horse, nor other means of transport, so as they had arrived, with Danny in his arms, he tucked Annie's arm through his, and they walked back from town, Rip again hard on their heels.

After their visit, they decided on their way home to go and find Willy Knight and consult him about the proposed extensions. Not knowing where he was working at the time, they went to his house where they found Mrs Knight surrounded by what appeared to be hordes of children. They left a message and returned home.

"Home Annie, doesn't that sound nice?" He bent and kissed her lovingly, releasing a sigh of contentment. "I've never really had a place I felt at home. Somewhere I was happy."

He missed the wave of sadness that crossed her face.

That evening Willy arrived to talk about the building and was surprised that Sam had made drawings of what they wanted. Willy didn't seem to be able to make out what the drawings meant. He said, "I jus' build a building, yer see, Sam." Then explained the way he went about it all.

Sam was intrigued, for he was not conversant with the ways of builders. In his ignorance, he expected that they always began with a sketch plan of what was wanted. He wondered how one went about building a large construction if anyone built as Willy did.

Sam looked forward to seeing how it all happened.

Willy and his mate soon arrived to start the job.

Sam was able to watch from afar while he did his work; during the afternoon, he was able to see more of what the men did. Willy did his measurements with a piece of light rope knotted at the precise places that Willy wanted and then squared by the same method.

Sam didn't wish to interfere but couldn't help thinking that building from a plan would be a much safer way to build. However, as Willy could neither read nor write, Sam could see that his plan would have drawbacks.

All the timber came roughly hewn so that Willy and his mate worked it to the desired shape, size and thickness with an adze that was as sharp as a razor.

Sam admired the skill of the men and how they used this instrument. They could achieve such smoothness and evenness that was unbelievable. They worked quickly, and it was not long before the room was taking shape.

Little Danny would have a room of his own before his first birthday, and his father had learned a great deal about the primitive but very stable building methods in the colony.

Sam took over the final touches himself. He painted the room inside with whitewash and cut out and fixed shelves to the walls where Annie could place all Danny's clothes.

These two lonely people had had to change their thinking and way of life so much since the advent of their son, yet he was both a constant delight and source of frustration to them. At times they wished for their previous peaceful existence, especially after a troubled night when they still had to crawl out of bed at their usual time, dawn. And at other times, he'd wake giggling, and he delighted them.

His first smile almost overwhelmed them, for neither knew much about babies and certainly nothing about the expected development pattern.

Mrs Pitt was often consulted, for she was a tower of strength and a fount of information. She assured them that her brood had been healthy children. What she told Annie seemed to work with Danny, and he seemed to avoid most of the small baby problems.

It was not long before he crawled, followed by walking and soon running with Rip, his great companion.

They had been worried, at first when he was a baby, that Rip would resent the newcomer, but thankfully, he was not a jealous dog and delighted in the small Danny.

Because of the new addition to their house, Sam had made the acquaintance of one Josh Comfrey. Josh was employed to build some substantial buildings in the colony. He had been a well-known builder in England and was convicted for some misdemeanour. Several of the leading citizens were beginning to use him to build their houses.

Sam spoke to him about how Willy Knight had built the new room and asked if that was usual. He found Josh had vast knowledge in this area, and he was well versed in the proper use of plans and told Sam so. Sam had been very interested in constructing houses since Willy's small effort and found himself spending some time sketching plans for mythical homes. He showed them one day to Josh. Some of the designs he had just made up, but others he drew from the memory of his visits to friends' places in England.

Josh noted their precision and correctness. He asked, "Where did you learn to draw like this, Sam?" for Sam had not only drawn to scale all that was needed for a building but had worked out the specifications as well. Josh, of course, could see a significant number of flaws, especially on the specifications, for Sam had drawn the wrong sized timber for many of the items, but basically, they were good. "Would you do plans for me, Sam, if I showed you how to do it properly?" he asked.

"Josh, I couldn't. I've just been amusing myself. I know little about it." Sam was now worried that he'd been over-keen in his ability.

"Yes, I know that, but you've got the right idea and can draw well. You're pretty good at calculations, too, which I am not. Where did you learn all this?" Josh enquired while still inspecting the pictures he was holding.

"I suppose I learned something at Oxford, Josh. I did Mathematics there, and I daresay that helped." Sam admitted carefully.

"You went to Oxford? Then I daresay it did, Sam. Will you help me? I will pay well," Josh inquired hopefully. This was just what he needed.

"You mean you would pay me?" asked the astonished Sam. His insecurity still sat deep within him.

"Yes, of course, Sam. I don't think you'd need a lot of teaching. I can do basic ones, but you add little bits that the customer wants and make them look good. They always want to know what it will look like when it's finished. I'm not that good. Can I come to your house and tell you what I want? You see, I just do a floor plan, but you draw what you think the place would look like."

"Could I do that, Josh? Would you really pay me for what I did?" asked Sam eagerly. Sam joyously thought of helping with their income, and this could be a marvellous help. "I suppose it wouldn't pay much," he thought, "but I'll give it a try."

When he arrived home and told Annie, he was so excited that he grabbed her, swung her around, and kissed her passionately.

She was giggling at his joy but welcomed his excitement.

Later that day, Josh came to the house, armed with large rolled-up sheets of blank paper and examples of his previous work. Sam could see that Josh's drawings did not have the polish his did, but he could see that Josh knew what he was doing.

Under Josh's tutoring, Sam learned to draw the desired architectural plans. He worked hard on this new project and soon contributed some designs and drawings that pleased his new master. At first, Sam worked on plans that Josh had already used. Josh made him work out quantities of materials required, then, he would correct his mistakes. Josh said, "My pupil has progressed very well" to Sam one day, and he was soon able to help with new projects.

Annie was pleased that he had found something to contribute to the family's income, but she missed the reading at night, for Sam was usually working on his plans.

One night Sam didn't pull out his paperwork; he said, "Anne, I think I have mastered my homework, so let's have some reading tonight, shall we? You've no idea how I've missed it."

After their poetry reading, they would often go to bed and cuddle. Lately, Sam had been so tired he'd fallen straight to sleep. Tonight she said, "I'm so glad you have, Sam. I thought you were so involved with Josh's work that you wanted to give up our poetry and Shakespeare." She was feeling a little forgotten and was surprised just how much it hurt.

He picked up the book of John Donne poetry and flipped over to a specific poem. "Tonight, my dear Annie joy, we're going to read this one, *Elegy XIX: To His Mistress Going to Bed.*"

"But Sam, that one we usually skip. It's well, um, way more than suggestive," she said, blushing.

"I know, and it's just what I feel like," he chuckled at her shocked face "but tonight we're going to read it, and then we'll… well, you know what we'll do. Because my Anne tonight is different."

She looked puzzled but sat listening.

Sam started reading, and she sat gazing at him, her chin resting in her hands as she adored his face, and watching his mobile mouth form the beautiful words. With a smile on her face and a tear filling her eye, she listened and loved. Annie had finally admitted to herself she was in love with her husband.

The realisation had hit her hard and now she could not tear her eyes from his handsome face.

"Come, Madam, come, all rest my powers defy,
Until I labour, I in labour lie.
The foe oft-times having the foe in sight,
Is tir'd with standing though he never fight.

Off with that girdle, like Heaven's Zone glistering,
But a far fairer world encompassing.
Unpin that spangled breastplate which you wear,
That th'eyes of busy fools may be stopped there."

Sam read the passionate words. He lifted his eyes, catching her blush. He dropped his eyes and kept reading, a smile spreading across his lips as the words roused his desire for her.

"Unlace yourself, for that harmonious chime,
Tells me from you that now it is bedtime?
Off with that happy busk, which I envy,
That still can be, and still can stand so nigh.
Your gown going off, such beauteous state reveals,
As when from flowery meads th'hill's shadow steals.

Off with that wiry Coronet and shew
The hairy Diadem which on you doth grow:
Now off with those shoes, and then safely tread
In this love's hallow'd temple, this soft bed
Ill spirits walk in white, we easily know,
By this these Angels from an evil sprite,
Those set our hairs, but these our flesh upright.

Licence my roving hands, and let them go,
Before, behind, between, above, below. ... "

Sam groaned with desire. "I cannot read more, my love, I need you."

He gently closed the book and placed it on the table. He looked towards her, sighing, "Oh, Annie joy, my dearest love."

He bent and gently kissed her lips. Her eyes were shining with happiness. "I, too, have missed our reading, but, as to not wanting to be with you, no my dearest love, I have hated not being with you, but I had to concentrate on this new work, for I am well paid to do it. I will at long last be useful to you. I have been so happy to think that I have found something to help us financially that I have worked on it hard. I hope that I'll be able to do so well at it that it will ease your burden."

Annie's gaze had not left his.

He now stood her up and put his arms around her. "Do you know, my dearest Annie joy, my heart; just how much I love you, I'm no longer afraid to say the words, and I just want you to know how much you have done for me."

She was lost for words.

He kissed her lovingly and long, his eyes drooping with passion, "You have given me such a wonderful life. You made me live again, and I am so grateful for you and to you."

"Oh, Sam," Annie said. "I love you so much too. I didn't know what happiness was until I met you and then we had Danny. And I don't want that to change anything. I think I first realised when I cried myself to sleep each night, and I feared you leaving. I thought I was happy as we were, but when I realised that I love you, it almost hurts, but yet it's, oh, it's so much better. I heard what you said to me while Danny was born, but you never repeated anything later. I thought they were just words and that you had not meant them. Then you didn't touch me for so long."

"I was frightened that I had spoken too soon, Anne. So I said nothing more." Sam bent and kissed her very passionately. "I meant them, though. Every one of them, but I wasn't sure you had heard."

"I had, and it gave me the strength I needed." She pulled his head down to hers again. "I had hope, Sam, it was something to cling to, but I still didn't know what love was, and therefore I did not realise that is what I was feeling. Now I know that I love you too."

"Well, I am happy that now you know, Annie joy, for you are my world; you gave me a reason to live again. You cared, even from that first day when I was so sick. You accepted me. And that I can now earn some money, yet still be able to help you. As you know, I have wanted to do something that would ease your burden. Do you know, my darling girl, that every time I draw a plan of a house, I draw it for you, I think of what you would like and I long to be able to build one like that and put you in it?" He held her tightly to him. "One day, I will be able to do that, Annie joy. One day I'll build it for you, your dream home. I'll make sure there's even somewhere we can dance. It will have firm foundations and be built of stone, just like you've always dreamed about."

With Danny asleep, Sam lifted her and carried her to their bedroom.

He said, "I love you so very, very much, and now I need to make good on my promise and finish that poem our own way." He gently laid her down, and kissed her in such a way she was left with no doubt at all.

She was unable to reply as Sam satisfactorily silenced her. She was, however, already undoing the buttons of his shirt. She now knew the dance of love was yet to come.

Chapter 5   *Plans and Drawings*

Sam pushed open the gate, and Anne looked up to see him stand back and let Mr Comfrey enter. Danny came hard on their heels. Sam turned to fasten the gate as the others turned towards the house.

Anne came to the door to greet them, saying, "Welcome, Mr Comfrey. Have you brought my men home early, or is there something I can do for you?"

Josh pushed his hat to the back of his head, "A cup of tea would be grand, Mrs Corbett." He laughed at the worried look on her face. "Nothing to worry about, I assure you. Don't look so worried, my dear. Yes, to answer your first question, I have brought your men home early because I wanted to talk some new plans over with Sam and thought I might as well bring young Dan home, too. I think he deserves it, don't you, Dan?"

Danny was a sturdy seventeen-year-old who always seemed to have a grin on his face. Life was a joke to Dan; he thought there was always something to smile about. Life at *The Rock* revolved around the son and heir of the place. He laughed at Josh's remarks and said, "Don't worry, Mam, I haven't been sacked yet, but I imagine it won't be too long before I am."

Sam looked indulgently at his son, who, he knew, had become a great favourite with the builder, and nothing in the world would persuade him to release the lad from working for him. Danny seemed to have found the place in Josh's heart that a son of his own would have been, but Josh, who was blessed with only daughters, vied with Danny's parents for ownership of the lad. But popularity with the adults did not turn Dan's head, for he was an easy-going young man who took such things in his stride.

Danny had entered the house first, giving his mother a big hug and a kiss that showed his admiration. He turned and pulled the large kettle onto the centre hob of the stove. He opened the firebox and peered in, satisfied that there was enough fuel, then said, "He mightn't sack me, Mam, but he is such a hard taskmaster that I am seriously thinking of leaving his services and starting up in opposition to him. This town could do with more builders." He put his hand to his forehead and feigned pain, then chuckled.

With this, Josh roared with laughter. "You impudent young scallywag," he said. "You make me shudder at the thought of it."

The men chatted as Anne put a cloth on the table and set various cakes, biscuits and some honey down. She put large cups out and made tea while listening to their talk. She filled the cups when the tea was drawn and sat down quietly, not wishing to disturb the flow of the conversation. All liked their tea, black and sweet.

In the intervening years, Anne and Sam had started greying, but since discovering their love some sixteen years before, they were no longer bitter about their lives and the advent of Danny. The absolute joy of watching him grow up gave their lives a new purpose, meaning, and a most satisfactory depth. Both were somewhat surprised that no more children followed Dan. They were sad she'd never fallen pregnant again, but such was their delight in their son, they were content.

Sam had achieved his ambition some years before of being able to get Anne away from the eternal grind of cooking and slaving over the hot stove. At forty-seven, she felt that she'd had a glorious life of leisure now and was spoiled as she had never experienced in her life. She adored her two men, Sam so tall, confident and assertive, not to be recognised as the cowered man who tilled the garden crawling on hands and knees due to his weakness, some eighteen years ago, and Danny who seemed to go through life as though it was nothing but a joke.

Sam had become very proficient in his drawing of plans. He usually worked for Josh Comfrey, but on occasions, other builders employed him. He was always proud of the finished product. The owners always asked to get one of his views to see how their purchases would appear. The various builders always tried to make the final building as close to his drawings as possible, knowing what the owners wanted.

Josh had employed Danny since he was fourteen and he was getting to be quite a proficient carpenter and builder. He loved his work and was often able to suggest improvements to the plans that Sam was currently working on. It often became a round table conference when a new project was mooted, and ideas pooled.

There was a new building in the offing, and Josh wanted to discuss possibilities with this team. "It is the biggest job I've had, Sam, and I don't want to make a mess of it," he was saying.

"May I ask what it is, Mr Comfrey?" asked Anne.

"Why, yes, of course," Josh said. "It is a store and offices down on Darling Harbour, Anne. Quite a large one and different to my usual houses. It is to be brick, and we have to do a lot of work on the foundations and work out what sort of soil there is down there, so we have to make it firm and solid. There is lots to think about."

"And can Sam do it, Mr Comfrey?" she asked anxiously.

"I am sure he can, can't you, Sam?"

"I am going to have a good try, Annie, love. I've been talking to the engineer and the architect. I am sure I can plan it; I hope you haven't made a mistake, Josh, by asking me," said Sam.

"I have confidence in you, Sam, and I am sure you won't let me down. If you wish, you can take your plans to Thorburn to look over and see what he thinks. His work is overwhelming him; he will be glad he hasn't got to do all the basic work."

"Are you sure? I don't want to upset the architect."

"You won't," said Josh. "I've already told him you are doing the preliminaries, and he is delighted. I showed him some of your work, and he was very interested. Don't be surprised if he starts using you for some of his stuff. Can I have some more tea, please, Anne?"

Anne had been so engrossed with what he said she forgot to be a good hostess and apologised. "Do you think Sam can do it, Mr Comfrey?"

Sam laughed and said, "Are you worried that it might fall, dear? Oh, ye of little faith! If Mr Smithson says it is all right, it will be, so don't worry."

Anne was once more content to sit and listen while they discussed the details. But soon, the conversation took another turn.

As Josh looked out the window, he said, "Sam, I often wondered why you don't get rid of that big fat rock sitting in your front yard."

Annie gasped. She'd used that giant rock to put her signs on for her home bakery.

"Get rid of it," asked the startled Sam, looking at his wife. "Get rid of it? But how?"

"Well," said his boss, "It occurs to me that someday it will have to be moved because it's a dashed nuisance where it is, and someday an excellent road will have to be put out there for there are lots of houses going up down towards the harbour. One day the town will be so thick around here that it will have to be moved."

"Are you particularly wedded to it, Annie?" Josh asked her

"No, I just am used to it being there," she replied.

"But how, Mr Comfrey?" Danny asked.

"You are a pair of duffers, aren't you? What's the use of being in the building trade if you don't know how to get rid of a rock?"

"I suppose I am so used to it being there too that I never thought of it," said Sam. "Would someone use it, do you think?"

"Why not use it yourself, man? Slice it up and use it to build yourself a new house. You must have outgrown this cottage years ago."

Sam sat stunned. He had never thought to use the rock as a source of building material. "But it would cost a lot, Josh, and I don't think I could afford it."

"There's a lot you and Danny could do, and that would make it easier for you," Josh suggested.

"But we don't know how to cut up stones, Mr Comfrey. We aren't masons," said Danny.

"I know you aren't, lad, but you could employ someone like old Bill Sanders. It wouldn't cost you much, as a matter of fact, Sam, that's a good idea. Old Bill is sick and unable to keep up with the young building team, grumbling a bit. I know his daughter wants him to slow down, and this might be just the answer for him."

"Would it cost much, Mr Comfrey?" asked Danny.

"No, son, he doesn't want to give up working but knows he can't stay with me for long, and I think he'd be happy to come. I reckon if you offered him a few shillings a week and let him take his time, he'd do it. It would take about a year for him to do the job and shape the finished stone; compared to buying bricks or similar; it's worth it as that cost is offset by not buying building materials. He's a good tradesman."

"He is that," said Sam. "It will take a deal of thinking, Josh. I'll sit and do the Math properly, but that should be less than £8 in wages. I've always wanted to give Annie a better house. I have it all planned but didn't think to use what we have on the place. Fancy, my dear, what this place would look like without the rock. I would miss it, but I daresay Josh is right; someday, it would have to come down anyway. Thanks for the thought, Josh."

Later that night, Anne saw that Sam was deep in thought and as they got into bed, he told her what he had been pondering. "Annie love, I think Josh's idea of cutting up the rock could be good. Think about it. I know that old Bill Sanders is nearing the end of his working life, for I've talked to him about it. He doesn't want to just sit at home and do nothing. I daresay his daughter fusses a lot, and Bill can't stand it all the time. So, I think he might like to take on something he could take his time over. What do you think?"

"I must admit it startled me, Sam, when Mr Comfrey mentioned it, and I thought of what the place would look like without the rock." Then Annie added wistfully, "I've nestled behind that rock for over twenty years now, Sam and I think I would feel rather vulnerable without its protection." She chuckled as he drew her into his loving arms. "Sam, seventeen years ago, I would have been insecure without it there, but now my dearest love, you are my rock." She bent and kissed him as she leaned over and blew out the lamp.

He took her in his arms again and cradled her to him. "I understand, dear, and yet think of what it would be like to have a new house. It is what I have always wanted for you."

"I am very happy in this cottage, though, Sam. I have so many wonderful memories here. I don't wish to change anything. But, my dear, if you wish it, I will go along with whatever you say. As long as we are together." She was willing to do whatever Sam felt was best for his family. Their love for each other had deepened dramatically over the years. Their marriage started as a marriage of convenience but had grown into a deeply loving one. Sam always sought her input in all decisions, but she was happy to leave the final ones to him more often than not. They fell asleep as they had done many times before, cradled lovingly in each other's arms.

Sam lay listening to her rhythmic breathing. He decided to follow Josh's suggestion and at least sound out old Bill.

Soon after this that Anne saw an old man come through the gate early one morning. He knocked at the door, and she was not surprised when he told her that he was Bill Sanders, who'd come to look at the rock. He was a stocky, grey-haired man with bowed legs as though he'd spent years on a horse. He walked as though it hurt, and Anne didn't wonder that he could no longer keep up with a team and do what the young men would call a fair share of the work. Anne could hear him chipping away at the stone, and then he came back to her to tell her that the stone looked all right and appeared to be a good colour. He showed her some of the pieces, and she was surprised to see the markings on them that were not apparent from the outside of the nearly black rock.

"Can you make a house out of it, Mr Sanders?" Anne asked.

"Yus, missus, it's real good stone that, and she'll make up real good. Kin I git on wif it, or should I arks Mr Corbett?" he asked anxiously.

"Well, I daresay you could get on with it if Mr Corbett sent you up to look at it. Are you feeling well enough to do it, Mr Sanders? It won't be too much for you?"

"No, missus, Mr Corbett says I kin takes me time, and thet ud suit me good. It's me laigs, yer know. They ain't what they use ter be. But I'd like ter do it, I would."

"Well, make yourself comfortable and have lots of rest breaks, and I will call you for tea soon," said Anne.

"There's no call fer yer ter do thet, missus. I ain't used ter gettin' spoiled."

"Well," replied Anne. "You must take your time and have rests often, but I will still call you for tea, or I can bring some out for you."

Anne watched him work over the next weeks and thought to herself that the team's men must have had little to grumble about, for the old chap never seemed to stop. It was hard to get him to take time off for more than just short breaks. She tried hard to ease him down as often as she could. She found him an interesting man. He had come to the colony a free man, which was unusual. He explained that he had come when his wife died. His daughter had come when her husband had been transported. She had set up a lodging house while waiting for his freedom. He was supposed to have been assigned to her when he got his pass and off the chain gangs. Sadly, the man had died during his initial imprisonment. So, Bill lived with her. Knowing that there were few lodging houses in the town, Anne asked if his daughter could be Mrs Frame; she was quite amazed to find that she was. He was happy there with his daughter, but she was one for keeping everything spotlessly clean. "Too fussy my Beccy is," he said with a smile.

"I stayed with her when I was freed, Bill," Annie explained. "I felt safe and secure, in an unsafe world that I now found myself living in."

Bill smiled. Like most parents, he loved hearing nice things about his daughter.

Sam and Danny were pleasantly surprised to see how quickly the stacks of formed stones grew. The stones were dressed and ready for construction in some heaps, and others were of rough pieces that came right off the big rock. Bill was working from two places. On days when Bill felt well, he cut stone on the far side of the yard. This meant he had to man-handle the cut pieces further. He couldn't leave the slabs out there in case anyone fell over them, although Sam and Danny were quite prepared to carry them into the yard when they came home. But most days, he worked in the yard where the rock jutted in through the fence. Then one day, Sam arrived in Comfrey's dray. Onboard, it had a wheeled trolley that made the handling of the larger bits much more manageable.

The sandstone itself was beautiful. It had lovely swirling patterns of deep ochre throughout the pale fawn rock. Bill was an expert at cutting the pieces so that the most was made of natural patterns. Some days when his stiffness was at its worst, he would sit down beside the rough stones and spend the time dressing each stone to prepare them for the construction of the house. He had worked at the easily accessible parts of the rock at first and tried to work it so that he could step up to get to the higher pieces, but he knew it would be difficult. But, to his surprise, one of Josh Comfrey's wagons appeared one day and unloaded a lot of scaffold poles. Charlie, one of his old teammates, was driving. He called out to Bill, "This what yer want, mate? The boss thought yer might need 'em. 'E's sending a couple o' blokes to set 'em up. They'll be 'ere in a minute." With this, Charlie drove off chuckling.

Bill was so surprised he went into Anne to tell her what wus happening. "It's a bit of all right, missus. I wondered 'ow I wus gunna do it 'cos tis gettin' a bit 'ard."

"Will you be able to get up on the scaffold, Mr Sanders?" Anne asked anxiously. "I don't want you to fall," she added.

"Na, missus. I won't fall. I bin up scaffolding all me life. 'Sides, it ain't real high, and the blokes kin put it up, so I kin get up easy. You'll see," he assured her. "An' missus, please, I'm jus' Bill."

He was quite correct; the men put up the scaffold to have easy access to each tier. He would work until the timber needed moving and then wait until Comfrey's men came to shift it.

Anne was beginning to see what it would be like without the rock. It worried her at first, and then she decided to concentrate on her new house and not be concerned about it. She was now resigned to have to leave her little secure cottage. When Sam wasn't around, she'd tear up. This place had meant so much to her over the past years. She'd be sad to leave.

One day Bill announced to Sam when he came home, that it was about time they prepared the foundations for the house and a cellar. There was much discussion about the cellar, for they had to find a place that was not solid rock. A place where they could dig deep enough to form a large hole. Sam felt that it was vital that they put a cellar in if possible so Annie could keep food cool. She thought it peculiar that most houses had cellars in England and perhaps didn't need it as much as they did in Sydney. But until recently, there hadn't been very many houses that would be big enough to have such a luxury, except the rich people, of course, and there were comparatively few of those.

It set Anne thinking of how the town had grown and how its appearance was changing. When she and Sam came to the colony in 1794, many people still lived in tents; they turned into the rough wattle and daub huts. These huts were made of local wattle branches placed as uprights jammed into the earth – other branches woven through these as a framework and the whole covered inside and out with clay mud. The roofs were thatched with whatever was available, often the local tea tree. These huts were predominantly of one room, but some achieved greater things. The floor was of hard-packed dirt. They often had a lean-to fireplace and chimney held up by a single freestanding pole. If the chimney caught fire, which often happened, you simply removed the pole holding up the rickety chimneys and it collapsed in a heap but didn't burn down the house.

By the time Anne had attained her freedom, there were brick houses in the town, made of bricks from the Needhams brick pit and kilns at Brickfield Hill and tiles for roofs. So the township began to look somewhat different. Thinking back to then, she sighed to think that her life would have been very different without Sir Cecil. Sam and she may not have met, and both may have even died.

She watched when the first stone buildings were built of sandstone, quarried from various nearby parts of the colony. Governor Macquarie came in 1810, and he was keen to see better buildings in the settlement. So, buildings boomed in both quality and quantity. Sam benefited from all the new work. They still retained the formal appearance of those in England with narrow eaves and bare fronts. Still, the colonists rapidly found the benefit of placing a verandah on their houses, and the shading of wider eaves was an asset, especially on the north and western sides. So gradually the appearance of the buildings changed somewhat from England.

Sam was somewhat traditional in his taste, and so the house planned for Anne was with narrow eaves and bare front. The cellar proved to be no problem, for they could dig quite quickly, and Danny found he delighted in spending the summer evening hours before sunset digging in the soft soil and setting the space for the planned cellar. At one end, Sam hit rock, and Bill suggested that as it was sloping down towards the floor, they could utilise the rock by cutting steps into it and so save them making a staircase. He was concerned that they might have a seepage by doing that, but he hoped he could overcome that.

Slowly Anne could see the formation of her new house appearing. Under Bill's direction, Sam and Dan worked hard at it every bit of time they could manage, but they could see it could take years to finish at the rate they were going, especially as Bill was finding the work very hard. Anne found that by the time Bill got up the hill from the town each morning, he had to rest for some time before he could begin work. It was often mid-morning before they heard any chipping. He was gone by late afternoon so he could find his way home in the daylight.

She asked Sam about this, and they suggested to the old man that he may care to sleep on the comfortable couch on the verandah from Monday to Friday and go home for wet days and weekends. Bill jumped at the chance. He thought much of these kind people who had befriended him and given him a job of work to do that suited him. His new conditions allowed him to work longer hours and with better rests in between work sessions. On his bad days in summer, he even had a comfortable place to rest through the heat of the day. He could sit, shaping the rough stones on the verandah through the crucifying heat of the days, then get back to work as the evening fell. Bill was full of stories, and they enjoyed their evenings listening to his talk. The house went ahead very quickly now. One by one, the new stones were laid. Each stone he shaped for its unique position in the house.

Just one year later, just after Easter in 1820, the house was declared finished. Anne had taken great delight in making blue gingham curtains for her new windows. She entered into the decoration of it. All the time the house was being built, she had been hooking rugs, and so by the time she could move in, all her soft furnishings were complete, and now they could shift the furniture. When she saw her old furniture in the new spacious rooms, she was a bit horrified for they looked so small and shabby, but Annie was determined to say nothing and set to polishing and refurbishing all she could. There would be time enough to think about new furniture. The only items she would not touch was the bedside cupboard Mister Tim had given her years before and the bookcase Sam had made her. She had been happy with these pieces for so long that even though they looked somewhat foreign in this new place, they were old friends, and she wasn't one for discarding what was valuable.

The first furniture in the colony for the common folk had to be knocked together with few tools and local timbers. Only the officers and the free settlers could bring any furniture in ships in the early days, but later better-quality items were available at a price. Also, those who could set about making better furniture and some fine pieces were made as time went on. The new craftsmen utilised local timbers like the red cedar, swamp mahogany, and even she-oak. Gum and wattle, too, came up well when French polished. But Anne did not have outstanding items, just the ones from Cec and a bookshelf Sam had made for her.

Sam made quite a few pieces himself, and she would not have changed them for anything and would not hear of him criticising them. He had made them for her, and that was enough. So, their beds and tables mainly were the rough, heavy ones that she'd had for years. Dan didn't notice that they looked out of place, but he did think that the rooms looked large after the cosy rooms in the cottage.

"We need more things to fill the rooms, don't we, Mam?" he asked.

"Oh, I don't know that we do, Danny," Annie answered casually. "It is going to be very easy to clean the rooms, and that will make a difference to my housework."

"Do you like the place, Mam?" Danny asked with rather a worried frown.

"Oh, Danny, how can you ask? It is a marvellous house. I didn't think I would ever have one so fine," she said. "Aren't you pleased with your work?"

"Yes, I am pleased with it, but it sort of looks different to what I expected with all our stuff now in place," Danny said after a long thought.

Annie ruffled his hair. "We are so used to being crowded that we will find the extra space rather odd for a while."

"Well, even so, it isn't a big house, Mam. You should see Mr Fields house that Mr Comfrey is building. Its rooms are at least twice as big as these, and it has so many rooms that I can't even remember how many there are, probably twelve or fourteen of them, I would think."

"Far too many for me, son, there are only three of us; what would we do with all those rooms? What would I do with a house that big? Besides, you would have to have many servants to keep it clean, and I would hate that."

"This won't be too much for you to look after, will it, Mam? We don't want you to work too hard. Pa wouldn't like you to get too tired," Danny asked, quite concerned.

"Your father spoils me, silly. Anyone would think I was fragile. Anyway, now you have brought the last of the furniture in, go and get your father and Mr Sanders and tell them tea is ready."

"Have you got the fire going in the new stove already? You shouldn't have done that. I would have done it."

"Go away with you, lad; it was my utter delight. I was very keen to get to it. I just wish it was hot enough for me to put a batch of scones in, but we'll make do with biscuits."

When Sam came in, he gave Anne a letter. "Charlie Grimshaw brought it up for you, love," he said. "It looks as though it is your Master Tim writing."

Anne turned it over and looked at the sender's address. "It is, too, Sam. We've not heard from him in years." She carefully opened the folded letter and read. "He is coming out. He is coming on some Government business and hopes to see us. He should be here in a few weeks; he is on the *Mary Jane*. We must watch for her. I daresay she will be a fast schooner. Do you know it, Sam?"

"No, I don't, but I imagine the Government would book their officials on a fast boat, not like the ones that brought us, dear."

Anne read the letter to him. "Isn't that good? And we'll be in our new house. He will be surprised to see it."

"He will be surprised to see Sydney, too, love. The town is considerably larger since he was here last. It was in… '97, wasn't it? He hasn't even met Danny."

"Yes, in '97! What a lot has happened since then. Oh, here's Bill, come in, where's Danny?"

"He is comin', missus. Jes' a gettin' somethin'," Bill hobbled to her.

"Well, sit down and have tea while it's hot, Bill," Annie said. Even though the house was complete, there was more rock to be shaped and then on-sold to offset costs. Bill only had about sixty chunks of rock to go.

The *Mary Jane* proved to be a swift ship for Tim Styles appeared one afternoon not two weeks later. Sam was working in his new office that he'd turned into a well-lit drawing-room, which had been Danny's room in the old cottage. Sam heard a vehicle stop at the gate and then a knock on the cottage door. He knew who it would be when he saw the very well-dressed gentleman on the step.

"Come in, sir; I daresay you must be Mr Styles." Sam welcomed him warmly. "I am very pleased to meet you."

"And I daresay you must be Sam Corbett," Tim said with a puzzled frown. "But I know you, don't I?" he asked.

"Do you, Mr Styles? I don't remember meeting you. But you must come over to the house. Anne will be most eager to see you again. She has been quite excited at the prospect of your coming."

"I see you have a new home. Outgrown the old one, eh Corbett? I see the big rock has gone too."

"Not outgrown it, for we have been very happy indeed in the cottage, thanks to you, sir, but as the rock had to go, we decided to turn it into a house. A good idea, don't you think?"

"Yes, I noticed the, err, void and wondered. I was quite bewildered at first, thinking I was in the wrong place. Many things have changed in Sydney, and I expected that; I just did expect the rock to be in place." Tim looked puzzled.

Sam laughed, "The immovable rock that proved to be moveable. Do come across to the house. She named her bakery business after it, you know. So now there is no bakery, there is no rock."

Sam led the way and called to Anne as they entered the house.

"Oh, Master Tim! Oh, Mister Styles, it is so good to see you. Please come in." Anne led the way to the front room with its new furniture of comfortable chairs and a sofa. "Please sit down, and I shall run and get tea."

"No, Annie, please sit down and let me look at you." He looked for some time and then said, "You're a fine woman, Annie, you always were, and I see you have a fine man, who I am sure I have met you somewhere but cannot remember where. It will come to me. But tell me both of you, what you are doing and how you are progressing? And a boy, too, Danny, isn't it or perhaps more than one?"

"No, Mr Styles, just the one boy, and we're so pleased to have him. He's seventeen," said Sam. "I hope you will call on us again and meet him. He is at work at the moment."

Sam looked at the man and felt that he had to be one of those solid Government officials who took life very seriously and had, over the centuries, given Britain its great name of decency and truth. Sam liked what he saw, even though he presumed Tim would be relatively narrow-minded in his way and wondered what Tim would think of the colony, for nothing could be more different from the life he would know in England. He was content to sit and listen to his Anne and their visitor sharing something of their lives over the past years.

He heard Anne say, "So you are now Master of Broome-Hall Manor? Does this mean that you are Sir Timothy?" she asked.

"Yes, I am. Sir Cecil's two sons died, one of stupidity and one in the war, and as I was the next heir, I inherited, and so my family and I live there. The boys had died when I was here last time, but you didn't need to hear all that then. You were coping with enough. My wife and I have changed things quite a lot there. I think we have made it a happier place now."

"Have you a large family, Sir Timothy?"

"Sophie and I have a nice bundle, as I call them. Six children, three of each; Robert is sixteen, and the baby is little Georgina, who is six."

"A lovely family, but what happened to Master Albert and Master Henry?" Anne asked.

"Well, Albert was rather a wild one and ended up breaking his neck in a pointless horse race. He left a widow and a small girl. Henry was in the army, and he was killed at Waterloo, so it was all left for me to sort out. It was rather a mess, for Albert lived what he called 'the good life', but it is fine now. Albert's wife has gone back to live with her family, and I hear she is about to marry again, and Henry was not married; he was even wilder than his brother."

"And Lady Broome-Hall? Is she still alive, Sir Timothy?"

"Yes, she's a heartbroken lady but very much alive. She is in a Grace and Favour house in the village, and I must say I cannot imagine her ever leaving this life; she has a tenacious grip on it. The Dower House burnt down some years ago."

"She must be very old, Sir Timothy?"

"Yes, nearly seventy, I believe, but no one knows for certain."

"I must get tea. I shall not be long," Anne said.

"You seem very content, both of you, Corbett," Tim said to Sam.

"Yes, sir, we are. We have been very happy and pray that it will continue for many years." Sam's eyes followed Anne as she left the room

"No thoughts of going back home?" Tim asked.

"None whatsoever! This is my home. England does not have happy memories for me."

"You seem to be prosperous enough; what do you do?" Tim asked, intrigued.

"It isn't what you may call prosperous, but we manage." Sam told of his work drawing plans for the building trade that and he and Danny worked together where possible. "I'm not quite an architect as I draw the houses from others plans. I present the owners with a finished look at the buildings they have ordered. The builders try then to make the finished building as similar as possible."

"I imagine it is far from what you were doing at home, Sam?"

"Yes, far from it, but I am grateful for what Oxford taught me; my Mathematics has been most useful and has given me an occupation that delights me as well as it means I can supply my family's needs."

"Oxford, eh? I thought something like that was in your background."

"Oh, yes, I have all the right background except for one thing, and that is that I came to this colony as a felon. Whether I deserved it or not is another matter. England and my father's peers were not much interested in the truth of it. None could believe he allowed me no money."

"You sound bitter, man." Tim was worried.

"Bitter? Is that not the greatest happiness a man could have? No, sir, I am far from being bitter." Sam swallowed. "I admit I used to be. Not a bit of it now; this place has given me a wonderful wife, a son. Very bitter and resigned to my fate when Anne took me in. She let me sleep in her shed, Sir Tim."

His eyebrows went up, but Tim said nothing. After tea, Tim said, "I must leave now, but may I ask myself for a meal so I can meet the rest of the family?"

"Yes, please," Sam and Anne chorused. Then Sam added, "Will you have much time, sir? How long will you be here?"

"I have been in the colony for two days and have much to do with reports to write, but I will usually be free in the evenings, so if I may, I would like to come... well, let's see... today is Tuesday. What about Thursday evening? Would that be all right? I have to be at a Government House tomorrow evening."

So that was agreed upon, and he left.

As Sam was working the following day, he was surprised to hear Tim quietly call from the cottage's door and come in.

"I had to come, Sam, for I realised where I had seen you. I know who you are. You played rugby for Oxford, didn't you? I was sitting at dinner last night when it suddenly came to mind, and without thinking, I said *Garney* out loud. That's right, isn't it? But you were also at Christ's Hospital in Horsham some years below me."

Sam simply said, "Yes." He looked despondent.

Tim continued. "I came because I didn't know whether Anne knows and thought I shouldn't mention it before her."

"That's all right; she knows most of the story, just not the title bit. I told her long ago." Sam sighed in great sadness. He really did not have to face this situation.

"Good!" Tim quizzed him. "Where did the Corbett come from?"

"It was my mother's name. My father was only too pleased for me to use it instead of ruining his, as he told me." Sam ran his fingers through his hair.

"Surely you couldn't have done anything so bad that he couldn't get you out of trouble?" Tim was astounded at what Sam had just said.

"No, I wouldn't have thought so. But father was only too pleased to be rid of me. He didn't lift a finger to help. You see, he had Nigel, and I never did matter." Sam's voice was devoid of emotion.

"That is another thing, Sam. I was sitting with John Burnside at dinner, and when I came out with your name, he asked, 'Do you know the Garney's?' So, I replied 'yes'. I said something about the name just coming to me, and he went on to tell me that your brother Nigel is dead. I'm sorry to tell you like this."

"Nigel? Gone? Heavens, my father, will be devastated. When did it happen? Do you know?"

"Yes, apparently, it must have been about five years ago. Nigel died of some fever, I take it. I am away from home a great deal, and it must have been while I was absent. I am sorry."

"Please don't be sorry. I must admit I had no real love for my brother, but no hate either. As we grew older, we grew apart. He dared not anger Father. I am sorry that he is gone, for that puts me in a bad position. I suppose I am now the heir. My father could not break the Entail without my consent unless he's disinherited me, and that would come hard with him knowing that I am the future Earl of Meldon."

"So, you are Lord Samuel, Viscount … what?"

"Clarestow, I daresay, but not for long, I assure you, I will get out of it as soon as I can," Sam said with some anger in his voice.

"But won't you use your titles, Sam? It would get you places here,"

Tim asked, quite concerned.

"No way in the world, Sir Tim! I am Sam Corbett, and that is the way I am staying. I have no desire to be an Earl or anything else in that line. Do you know, sir, how my father is?"

"Yes, I do, as a matter of fact, but drop the sir bit please, Sam. As you outrank me," Tim requested.

Sam nodded but remained silent.

"Sam, Meldon Hall is not too far from my own estate. We join borders on one side, and I happened to see him recently. Just a matter of a few months ago, and he was hale and hearty then."

"Thank God for that." Sam gave a single resigned nod. "It will give me time to think this out. I do know of your place, sir."

"Yes, I daresay young Dan comes into this. Does he know? Or Annie, for that matter?" Tim asked.

"No, not about that, and I wish I could keep it from them. So, both yes and no! Anne knows all of my story except the title. Dan knows only of my conviction, not even my real name. I have some thinking to do." Sam ran his fingers through his hair again. "When Anne and I married, we did so under the name of Corbett Garney. Our marriage is legal, but I explained what my father was like, so we agreed never to use that name. Dan was born as both and duly registered legally, just in case. Something at the back of my mind made me conform to all the things I hated. However, he does not know." Sam groaned with almost agony.

"I will be very interested to hear the outcome. Someday you will have to tell Danny, and he will have to make up his mind about returning to England or whether he wants to pass it all over to the next in line. Who is it, by the way?"

"My cousin is Charles Garney. Do you know him?"

Tim acknowledged that he did.

"He would be much more suited to succeed than either Dan or me. I hope the boy decides to refuse it all." Sam groaned again. "Oh, dear God, what a mess! Maybe my father has told them I am dead or even disinherited me. He always threatened he would. Then I wouldn't have to think about it at all. After all, to all intents and purposes, I am, to him, anyway. His very last words to me were of his intention to disinherit me fully. I thought he had; he may have. I have absolutely no idea, so mind you, he may have done so already. Just because Nigel is dead does not mean I am next in line; maybe Charles is."

"That is hardly fair to Daniel. He should at least have the opportunity to try it out, but it is up to you after all. But remember, Sam, the call could come at any time."

"Tim, what happens if I am already disinherited? Then he'll be angry that he'll think he should get something and won't." Sam was getting so stressed over this. "Tim, the timing is just all wrong. He's currently courting, and if she finds out, well, it could and probably would taint her answer. She's a builder's daughter, and, I can't see her as a Viscountess." He stood and ran his fingers anxiously through his hair. "Yes, I, however, will go and tell Anne; she will help me know what I should do when the time comes." Sam was very concerned; Anne may not like it at all. He'd told her everything else. "Tim, if Dan had a son, things might be different, but he doesn't, but he may have …"

"I will leave you then and see you tomorrow evening." Tim took his departure.

"Tim, thanks so much for coming to me privately. There is one question I will ask you. Tim, if you live so close and we do get the title, would there be any chance that you would oversee the Estate? I know Charlie won't want it, and with the three of us, we could break the 'Entail'. I may even use the place for some charitable thing. Father would absolutely hate that so that it would please me greatly."

Tim looked aghast but nodded and croaked, "Err, yes. If that is your wish, but let's not cross that bridge just yet."

~

Soon after Tim's departure, they all grieved over the loss of Rip, the faithful companion who had been Annie's shadow for twenty years. He'd been unwell for weeks, and all knew his death was just a matter of time. Anne went to call him for dinner, and she didn't return.

Sam found her sitting on the verandah next to her beloved companion. Her hand was on his still, cold body. She was not crying but sitting stunned, staring straight ahead. The look of loss and grief was apparent on her face. She was swallowing her tears, trying hard not to cry.

Sam went to her and sat with her, his arm gently around her. His gentle act was the straw that broke her.

She turned to him and wept, deep hacking sobs for the loss of her canine shadow.

Rip had gone.

He had come to her as a skinny unloved stray pup soon after her release. He had not been fully grown and had doubled in size.

They had all talked about his passing; it was inevitable. Rip had rarely moved from the verandah these days; he'd wee, drink, eat and sleep. He'd not been well enough for a walk for months. Now he was gone. Peacefully and with no pain, but the loss of a friend was hard.

Danny heard her sobs and came to see what was wrong.

Sam watched Dan's face as the realisation of the loss of his best mate hit home.

"Oh, no!" He sank down next to them and patted his little mate for the last time. Dan fell silent, but he, too, was swallowing tears of his grief. Yes, Rip's passing was expected, but the sadness and grief were still almost unbearable.

Sam suggested that they bury Rip where the big rock had been. Exactly where Sam had found refuge.

In silence, Danny went and retrieved a shovel from the shed. Ann went and found a piece of cloth to wrap him in, and Sam retrieved a lamp. Together the three dug a grave for their little shadow. Sam gently placed him in the rich soil, and they all took turns in covering him. They didn't know if they should say a prayer, but Sam remembered a passage from Zechariah about even the bells of the horses are dedicated to the Lord.

So together in the dim lamplight, they listened as Sam read some verses from the Bible. Genesis 1 v 25 was the first one *"And God made the beast of the earth after his kind, and cattle after their kind, and every thing that creepeth upon the earth after his kind: and God saw that it was good."*

Zechariah 14 v 21 *"Yea, every pot in Jerusalem and in Judah shall be holiness unto the Lord of hosts: and all they that sacrifice shall come and take of them, and seethe therein: and in that day there shall be no more the Canaanite in the house of the Lord of hosts."*

"I'm sorry, love, but I don't know of any other Bible passages that mention God's care for animals, but I remember one particular verse about God's love for us. It's from the New Testament. It talks about God's love for us, and I figure that He cares as much for His creatures as he does for us. John 3 v 15 -18"

"That whosoever believeth in him should not perish, but have eternal life. For God so loved the world, that he gave his only begotten Son, that whosoever believeth in him should not perish, but have everlasting life. For God sent not his Son into the world to condemn the world; but that the world through him might be saved. He that believeth on him is not condemned: but he that believeth not is condemned already, because he hath not believed in the name of the only begotten Son of God."

"I figured that God does care for us all, even if we don't care for Him. This is the God I learned about at school. The loving and forgiving one, I try to remember the words I learned at school about Jesus, but Watmore's words overshadow them sometimes. He certainly doesn't live up to Jesus' words. Anne, the only other thing I can think of is there is also the Ecclesiastes chapter 3 passage" He took a deep breath before he read, *"To every thing there is a season, and a time to every purpose under the heaven: A time to be born, and a time to die; a time to plant, and a time to pluck up that which is planted; A time to kill, and a time to heal; a time to break down, and a time to build up; A time to weep, and a time to laugh; a time to mourn, and a time to dance. A time to cast away stones, and a time to gather stones together; a time to embrace, and a time to refrain from embracing; A time to get, and a time to lose; a time to keep, and a time to cast away; A time to rend, and a time to sew; a time to keep silence, and a time to speak; A time to love, and a time to hate; a time of war, and a time of peace."*

The three stood looking at the mound of fresh earth in their front yard. Sam gathered them both into his arms. The three stood hugging, mourning Rip's passing together.

Sam and Anne spoke in whispers as they lay in each other arms that night.

"Anne, I figure that if God can care for all the animals, including horses and dogs, surely He had our lives all mapped out for us too."

They had to trust that whatever happened, God was still in control of their lives.

Chapter 6   The Waiting Game

*F*or a long, while each time Sam heard the gate open and saw a stranger enter, his heart turned over, but as the months, then years, then a decade passed, he was able to put the thought of accession to the English estates aside. He presumed his father had disinherited him.

Sam's friend, Major Tom Turner, kept in regular contact. From the time Dan was about eighteen, Tom brought a young friend with him on his visits, another Major named Ned Grace. He was from Kent but knew the area around West Sussex. Neither ever questioned Sam, and they were always welcome, as Tom brightened Sam's life. Ned, although over twenty years younger than Sam, became a good friend with Danny.

Danny and Ned often sat outside on the verandah, talking while the two older men chatted of Kent and West Sussex. As Danny had not been there, Ned described what it was like. Anne occasionally stayed when she brought them tea but typically left them to themselves.

Sam and Annie were content to keep Major Tom updated with the family's happenings. Tom was really the only other friend he'd made; Sam guessed that if he was the one who'd been asked by his father, his reports would be favourable. However, Sam was surprised that Tom was as interested in Anne and Danny as well. Ned seemed interested in Sam's early days. He tried to dig out his story as a convict and then release. For some reason, Sam did not wish to discuss it with a stranger yet ended up telling him more of his hardships than he'd planned.

Sam had now disclosed his life to Anne, and they both decided to say nothing to Daniel, for Sam felt sure that his father would count him as dead, so it would be useless to involve Dan in something that may never happen. They did give in a little by telling him a little of Sam's background and education but not a great deal and certainly nothing about the title.

Dan seemed to understand that speaking of it distressed his father and so did not press the point. He also didn't ask either Tom or Ned. Dan did, however, presume that Sam came from a highborn family. Such things seemed so far away he didn't think much about it. Dan's life altered little. He married his beautiful builder's daughter, Vanessa, and his family grew with the advent of beautiful daughters.

Their lives had changed in the ten years since Tim Styles' visit. Sam and Anne were once again living back in the cottage. It was much improved as they had rebuilt it and added a new enclosed verandah out the back. They re-shingled the roof as it had perished.

Dan was now married to Vanessa Comfrey, and they had three children. The oldest was born only seven months after their marriage. They needed the space of the larger house. Dan was in partnership with his father-in-law's building business and making a very successful job of it. He and his family lived in the stone house, and Sam and Anne happily had moved back into the wholly refurbished cottage when Vanessa had the first child. They installed a new enclosed stove as Annie had worn out the old one, and bought a new mattress and even a proper wardrobe for their room. They took the special cupboard and Cec's bookshelf; however, much of the other furniture was now too old. The old table still was there, as was the settee Sam had slept on, but they were still functional. Anne still insisted on keeping these few items, and some Sam had made for her over the years.

At fifty-seven, they adored being grandparents. Anne and Sam delighted in his little family; they dearly loved Vanessa. She was the youngest of the three Comfrey girls. The children were Jo-Anne, Lucy-Anne and Mary-Anne. The two oldest were usually called Jo-Jo and Lucy, but the little two-year-old usually got her full name.

Sam still hoped that his father had spread the word that he, Sam, was dead and so would have named his cousin Charles as heir.

Tom was a closed book and would not say if he knew at all.
However, the day that Sam had dreaded for so long finally did eventuate.

One sunny afternoon, Anne looked up from her sewing on the front verandah as the gate opened, and she gasped as she saw two London-dressed men enter the front gate. She abandoned her sewing, casting it on the ground in haste and hurried in to get Sam from his desk and just said, "Come quickly."

He met them at the door. They asked if this was the Corbett residence and were they addressing Mr and Mrs Corbett. On receiving the affirmative answer, the older of the two men said, "May I introduce myself, Sir, I am Simon Pennecuick, and this is Justin Robb. I am a junior partner of Pennecuick, Robb, and Pennecuick, Lawyers in Horsham in Sussex and London. May I enter? I would like to speak to you."

Anne looked at Sam and saw that he had turned so pale that she thought he might pass out. He seemed to have hold of himself and stood aside, motioning the men to the sitting room.

Sam said, "I presume, Mr Pennecuick, that my father is dead?"

"If you could show me papers, sir, to verify your identity, I will explain." Mr Pennecuick saw Sam's reaction. "I know you were convicted under your mother's name and that you are unlikely to have paperwork other than that, but it will suffice."

Sam nodded to Anne; she went to their bedroom and soon returned with their Conditional Pardons, Marriage Certificate and other papers. She gave them to Sam, who in turn passed them to Pennecuick. He studied them carefully and then asked several questions about who Sam was, his father, where he had lived in England and how he had spent his life, both in England and in the colony. When he came to their Marriage Certificate, Pennecuick's eyebrows raised, and he looked up at Sam but said nothing.

Sam was impatient and started to say something, then changed his mind, sighing deeply and sat back in his chair waiting until the man had finished his perusal of the papers. He tried to fill in the time by watching the second man, who neither spoke nor moved. Then Sam could not stand the tension any longer; he then asked, "Mr Pennecuick, I take it that my father is dead. Is that so?"

"The Fifth Earl of Meldon passed away on 5 March of this last year, 1829, and as I am satisfied that you are his heir, I now tell you, My Lord, that you are Lord Meldon, the Sixth Earl Meldon, as your brother, Lord Nigel Philip Garney, then Viscount Clarestow, died some fifteen years ago. May I congratulate you, My Lord, and wish you well," Pennecuick added pompously.

"Thank you, Mr Pennecuick, I accept your last remark as well-intended, but I cannot see anything for congratulations. How soon can I renounce the whole thing?" Sam still lay back in his chair, twiddling his thumbs. His heart was in his mouth, but he gave the impression of not a care in the world.

"My Lord!" said Pennecuick, aghast and nearly choking, "My Lord, you must not! You cannot! There is a large Estate waiting at home for you and much to be done. Also, My Lord, there is the new Viscount Clarestow to consider, Lord Daniel Garney, if I am correct, I must see him as well."

"I do know how big the Estate is, sir, I grew up there." He paused before adding, "Yes, my son, but I must ask you to put off seeing him for a while, for this will come as a surprise, and I must prepare him," Sam said somewhat briskly.

"Do you mean, sir, that he knows nothing of his position?" the solicitor asked, stunned.

"Of course not; I have never told him as I always hoped he never would know. You see, I always hoped that my father considered me dead, and his very last words to me were that he fully intended to disinherit me and would do all he could to let the estates pass on to my cousin Charles should the need arise." Sam's temper was beginning to unsettle. "I so wished he had done this." He jumped up and paced around the room.

"But, My Lord, that would have been illegal. He could not, at least not, unless you were insane. He knew you were not so, as your father had someone in this colony reporting to him of your welfare, and he was very up-to-date in his information."

Sam swung around, stunned. "Did he, by jove? The old devil. I guessed but never really believed it. Do you know who it was by any chance? I heard of Nigel's death from Timothy Styles; he is a dear friend of my wife's. I hoped I never would succeed. I had hoped Charles was looking forward to being the next Earl. How did he take the news that I am still alive?"

"It was not he, My Lord, who told the Earl. I believe it was a Major at Hyde Park Barracks. He was some local lad from your home area," the lawyer admitted reluctantly.

"Ahh, that would be Major Tom Turner. Yes, that would be right. I knew Tom was in contact occasionally with him, but he too was a closed book. I knew father had someone over here; Sir Timothy Styles, now Broome-Hall, didn't know who it was. I had hoped and guessed it was Tom." Sam was relieved as he liked the Major, so he knew any reports back from him would be in a good light.

"My Lord, Sir Cecil Broome-Hall's household and the Garney's did not, um, communicate willingly. The Estates march on one boundary, and there was some animosity between Sir Cecil and His Lordship, I believe." Mr Pennecuick had gasped when he heard Timothy's name. "It was only last year your father told Sir Charles Garney that you were still alive and would succeed as soon as he, Lord Meldon, died. So, Sir Charles has never been under the misapprehension that he would be the heir. I might add that he is delighted that he is not heir, for he is most happy on his own Estate and does not wish to leave Oakland Park. I carry a letter to you from him, which I will leave with you. He is overjoyed at hearing you are alive; he repeatedly asked the Earl for information, but his lordship would never answer. Sir Charles knows nothing of your life or why you came here." Mr Pennecuick looked uncomfortable. This entire situation was totally unexpected. He had presumed that the new Earl would jump at the position.

"I suppose you do, Mr Pennecuick?" Sam said with a resigned tone to his voice.

"Yes, My Lord, we do, but of course, that is totally confidential." Mr Pennecuick looked sad.

"Oh, I don't mind anyone knowing. It's a pity that society also doesn't realise I was forced to it because my father halved my only meagre source of income of £5 a month. Everyone here knows of my theft. Half the colony came as felons, you know. As was my dear wife."

"Ah, yes, your father had investigations made of Countess Meldon as well, My Lord." Turning to Anne, he said, "My Lady, I am sorry, but the late Earl found that you had been sent out here under erroneous accusations and that knowledge made him happy. He made steps to allow your return should you wish to. I also have this paperwork. Your status is now Free Settler, not even an Emancipist. He had your conviction completely quashed. Please do not ask me for details. For I'm not in a position to answer them." He handed her a sheet of paper. "Suffice to say, He took great pleasure in submitting the paperwork where Lady Broome-Hall renounced the theft as trumped up. We believe she was so upset when he contacted her. This would have been over ten or fifteen years ago when Lord Nigel died. Sir Timothy was already Baron by then."

Anne gasped. She took it, but this made Anne swell with anger and indignation. She was about to speak, but Sam cut in, catching her hand and squeezed it.

"What a devious old character he was, my love. If it gave him some pleasure, I am glad. He didn't find much pleasure in anything except Nigel, and as we have been so happy, we cannot deny him some, even if it is at our expense." Sam spoke softly in a very calm voice. Anne was stunned at his words but stayed silent.

Sam continued to hold her hand, gently caressing it. He carefully removed the sheet from her hand and laid it aside.

Mr Pennecuick looked at the gracious lady sitting close to Sam. He felt so sorry that he'd not been allowed to tell her of the overturning of her conviction years before when it had been finalised. He felt so uncomfortable. "I assure you, My Lady, that the investigations were carried out in the strictest secrecy. Great care was made to ensure that. He had Lady Broome-Hall admit to the Magistrate that it was mere jealousy." There was far more to it than that, but it sufficed. That may well come out in time. Then turning back to Sam, he said, "My Lord, I have a letter from the Earl, and I hope you will read it and give him a good hearing whether you feel he deserved it or not. I am sure you wouldn't mind if I say he was a difficult old gentleman. I don't know if he was sorry for what he did to you. He wrote it some eight weeks before he passed."

Sam opened his mouth to speak, and he was cut off as he'd just done to Anne.

Mr Pennecuick held his hand up, "Yes, I know all about it. I think deep down he was sorry for the life he made you lead."

"I doubt it, sir, but I will read the letter, what I do with the information… well, I just don't know. I will never know why he resented me so much, but I must admit I never thought to hate him. Even as a small boy, please remember I was three years old, I never knew a different life. He never showed he cared for me at all, so I never missed what I never had. I did miss my mother and loved her dearly, but she was gone from my life early. I was, however, sorry for him, which was very peculiar in the light of it all. If it were not for my wife, I would not be alive today. She saved more than just my life. She made me the man I am today." Sam squeezed her hand gently again.

"Perhaps, My Lord, I should leave you now and come back sometime when you have digested all the papers I have brought with me." The man paused and looked Sam in the eye. "I have copies, so destroying them will change nothing. May I make the suggestion that we might return tomorrow at a suitable time? Would that suit you, My Lord?"

"I daresay it would if Lady Meldon agrees. Three would suit." Sam grinned at Anne, who was startled to hear him address her that way.

"Then, My Lord, Lady Meldon, if we may be excused, we shall see you tomorrow." They bowed themselves out.

They watched until they were out of sight.

Anne sat looking bewildered. All she could say was, "Sam?"

Sam smiled at her. "I suppose we did expect it, Anne, but there's no denying that it is a bit of a shock now that it's come."

"I nearly fainted, Sam, when you addressed me as Lady Meldon. I'm not really, am I? I thought you wouldn't accept it. You said you wouldn't." She had a touch of fear in her voice. "Please say you won't."

"Come on now, be honest, Annie-girl, don't you fancy yourself as the Countess of Meldon Hall?" Sam laughed at her. He bent over her and kissed her.

"No, I do not, Sam Corbett. It is the last thing I want. Me, who was proud to be a mere housemaid again. No, Sam, I do not want it." Annie was indignant.

He was grinning at her. "All right, my dear. But you know I would give you the world if it would make you happy, and you are the one to make a choice."

"Have you changed your mind, Sam? Do you want it after all?" she asked, concerned.

Sam walked over to her; he pulled her up from the chair, and put his arms around her and said, "My darling girl, no, I don't want it, but I know what I am giving up, and you do not. I want you to think hard about it and all that it means before I sign all those darned papers and give the lot to Dan. Then it will be up to Dan and Vanessa to pass it on again. What a pest it all is; I did hope it would not come to this. If we'd had a daughter instead… But the good Lord saw fit to give us a son."

"Whatever will Dan and Vanessa say? I wonder how they will take it. Oh, Sam, I am afraid of that. They may do all the wrong things, and we may lose them. I suppose it could all go to Vanessa's head and be silly." Anne looked very worried.

"I must admit it is one reason why I haven't told Dan recently. I have on occasion thought I might, but I really am not sure of their reaction."

Anne knew she should try to sound encouraging. "I suppose we should have more faith in them. When should we tell them?"

"I'd better read these letters first and then tell him as soon as he returns home." Sam sounded resigned to the inevitable.

"I'll make a cup of tea. I think we need it." She left him holding the bundle of paperwork.

Sam took the papers that the lawyer had given him and sorted out the letters from his father and his cousin. He sat with them on his lap for some time, then picked them up, one in the left hand and one in the right, not knowing which he should open first.

He sighed deeply, and taking his knife out, he broke the seal from his father's and read. On the front of the letter was his name written in a shaky hand. He had never liked his writing.

Sam Corbett Garney,

Anne returned to find him sitting with the open page in front of him and a sheer look of misery on his face. He was halfway through it. He looked up at her, his face so white and bewildered, and she knelt beside him and put her arms around him. His face showed distress and was grey.

"Sam, my darling, I do wish it hadn't happened. We've been so happy, haven't we?" She loved this man so much. She hated to see him so hurt. To have to now deal face to face with his ghosts. "Your face looks like how I felt when I thought you were going to leave me. I offered myself to you and was rejected. But Sam, then the next night came, and we've not been apart for a night over the past twenty-seven years. You are my life. You are my love. What are we going to do? Will everything be ruined?"

He held her close to him, and his voice muffled in her hair; he said, "Not if I can help it, my darling girl. Not if I can help it at all. Come on, where's that tea, although I feel I will need overproof rum after this, a full bottle of it?"

She poured out the potent brew and gave him a mug.

He read on, finally coming to an end, he said, "You'd better read it, Anne. It will hurt, but you must. To know the truth of what I have said if nothing else." In it, his father has summed up all Sam had told Anne over the decades.

Anne took the letter and looked at the writing, which was strong and vigorous, not written by an ailing man. It was dated six months previously.

It simply started with just his name and no endearment.

Meldon Hall
West Sussex
5 January 1829

Rock Cottage
Sydney

Samuel,

You will not have heard that Nigel has died, and you are now the heir. I cannot think that you will take pleasure in this, for you never really fitted Meldon Hall and all it pertained. Yet, even you and the life you have led these past years must realise that you have a duty to take up where I must leave it and return to your inheritance. If you had been a girl, Charlie would now be the Earl. However, Charlie does not want it either-he told me he'd break the Entail given half a chance.

I have employed someone to watch over your life in the Antipodes and report to me, so I know about your activities. Reluctantly, I must admit you have made something of your life even though it really was not fitted for a Garney, but thankfully you have not called yourself that. I believe you are married to someone, who is a good woman who has served her term. I hear she has been a good worker and has kept herself apart from the rabble. On investigation, I found her blameless, and I have had her conviction thoroughly quashed, which, I admit, gave me pleasure to arrange. I hope she will make a wonderful Countess of Meldon. I'm glad you have a son to carry on the Garney line, and maybe my grandson will make a better success of life than you have when you bring him to Meldon Hall for some polish. I hear he, too, married and had three children.

Life has dealt me a bitter blow in losing Nigel, for he was the only son I wanted. I think your mother would have understood you better than I ever did. I admit, I never gave you a chance, but I had my reasons. It may have been better if you had been female. Your mother lost the will to live when you were born, and I never did come to terms with that. Had she lived, things may have been different, who knows? She at least cared for you.

I hope in this last request you will not let me down. I have never asked much of you in your life, and I hope you may see your duty to the title. Bring your wife and let her live in some comfort. Bring my Grandson and my Grandchildren give them their rightful heritage. I so wished I'd had a chance to meet them.

Philip Garney,
Fifth Earl of Meldon

Anne's hands were shaking by the time she finished the letter. "Sam, I can't believe it. If I had not read this myself, I would never have believed it. What a sad, miserable, horrible man he could not even address you as 'Dear Samuel'. He obviously could see nothing in life but himself and his ego. Oh, my dearest love, what Sammy, that little boy, must have gone through. I feel it so much. You never did tell me how bad it was. But this …" she waved the letter, "This is both disgusting and blatant hate. Pure vitriol! There is no mention of you as his son, but he refers to Danny as his grandson and even the great-grandchildren. He's almost even approving of me. Why did he hate you so?"

Anne looked up at Sam and could see the deep hurt scoured on his face. After all these years, the rejection was still etched deeply within his being. It was a total and utter rejection. This absolute spurning still cut deep. She did what she could to ease the pain.   "Sam, this is a disgusting letter for anyone to write, a deliberately hurting, vile letter that the lawyer should have burned rather than let anyone, especially for you, read it. It is beyond understanding. I will give him the benefit of the doubt and say I hope he did not know what it contained." Anne had been through much in her life, but to come face to face with such shocking hatred of the small defenceless boy, poor little Sammy, he had lived with virtual banishment. It was more than she could understand. She wept for that small boy.

They sat in silence for some time, cradled in each other's arms. Then Anne sat up when she thought of Dan's reaction. "Sam, you have no need to worry now about what Dan will say. I mean, if you show him that, he will understand why you never wanted him to be tarnished with it."

"Should I show it to him, Anne? Should I dare show him what my father thinks of me? The absolute hate, the malice. I couldn't, lass. I have some pride." His eyes bore deep into hers.

"Yes, Sam, you must. He will feel as I do and we must share this situation with him, for he must know the full story. What does your cousin say? I hope there are no more unpleasant surprises today." Anne wiped away an angry tear, thinking of the puzzlement of that little boy. Daniel was the image of his father, tall, dark and very handsome with adorable warm brown laughing eyes. Anne saw that three-year-old child as Danny was at that age. "Sam, even I never realised it was so bad. Dan must be made to understand. Was he the same with others?"

He had Charlie's letter still in his hand, as yet unread.

"Yes, and no, Charlie and his family and I always got on well. He was another my father didn't like, so sadly, we saw little of one another except at school, but I can't think that Charlie would feel favourably to me unless it is because I stand between him and an Earldom. However, I'm truly sure he never even wanted that either."

"Well, read it and see," she encouraged him.

"I will. I will read it to you, for I see already that it is somewhat different." Sam read the letter from his cousin aloud.

Oakwood Park
Billingshurst
West Sussex
20 April 1829

Rock Cottage
Sydney

My Dear Sam,
I had no idea where you had hidden all these years and did not know that you were even still alive until your father came to me after Nigel's death. Even then, he told me little, except that you were in the

colony. *I have no idea why you went out to that God-forsaken hole of a place, as I presume it is. Nor do I understand why you have not written. However, it is good to know you are all right, and you have a wife and family. Now that your father is dead, I hope you will soon return. You will have been told by now that I am the executor of your father's will, with old Pennecuick, Simon's father, and so will try to sort things out before you come.*

Oh, I do offer my condolences on his passing, but at the same time, I have a feeling you do not need them. I feel that it will almost be a relief.

It will be good to have you as a neighbour at Meldon Hall. You must put some life into the place, for it has been dead for a significant number of years. The people there are hurting greatly and need care. I am longing to hear all your adventures, for I am sure you have had some. I believe you now have bushrangers in the colony; I hope they are not too troublesome.

Do write and tell me about your family, all I know is that you have one. Your father was as close as an oyster. I do not hesitate to say that you will find life more congenial at Meldon Hall now but do let me get rid of all those retainers that remain that made your life so hard. Believe it or not, some still are there. You need a new agent, and I suggest that you get whomever you hire to employ entirely new staff and pay off the rest.

You will not know that I married Alice Chambers and now have six children who keep me poor, but I must say, happy.

My regards to you and yours,
Charlie

Sam smiled, relieved, as he put the letter down. "A somewhat different tone, eh, lass?"

"Will you, or we, have to go back, Sam? To fix things up, I mean. Oh, Sam, what are we to do?" she exclaimed, quite startled.

"Not if I can get Mr Pennecuick to do it for me. Now, what about getting Dan in here? I heard him come home a while back." Sam thought for a bit. "Love, when Tim was here a year ago, I asked him if he'd oversee it for me, just in case. I had an idea of something that I know my father would have absolutely hated. If I can't break the Entail, then this is what I may do."

"The children are playing outside; I will send Jo-Jo for him." She left him to get the child.

Six-year-old Jo-Jo ran into her father and said, "Daddy, Granny and Gramps want you. You know there was a man there and another one, and do you know they called Gramps Lord? Why would they call him God? That's not right, is it?"

"Little girls should not listen at doors. They never hear what they should hear. I'll go and see what Pa wants." He bent and kissed his wife. "Now, girls, you are to stay here." He walked out.

"Jo-Jo tells me you want me, Pa," said Dan as he reached the door of the cottage. He looked at his parents sitting where they had been since the lawyers came. They looked as though they had had a shock, for they hardly looked up as he said, "What's this about a man calling you God, Pa?"

His parents looked startled.

"It's all right," Danny laughed, "Jo-Jo told me that a man visited you and called you God."

"Sit down, son," said Sam, "we have something to tell you. Something perhaps I should have told you a long while ago but hoped it would never come. I had a visit from my father's lawyers today to tell me that he was dead."

"From what I gathered, Pa, you would not be too upset about that," Danny sat relaxed.

"Not about that, son, but what Jo was telling you was correct, but she didn't mean God. She meant Lord."

Danny laughed. "Do you mean to tell me that you are some long lost Lord or other? What do you mean?"

The inflection in Sam's voice had told Danny that this was no laughing matter, that something was going on here that he would not like.

"Well, you see, Dan, my father was Lord Meldon, the Fifth Earl of Meldon, and as my elder brother Nigel died some time ago, I am now the Sixth Earl of Meldon, your mother is the Countess, and you are Viscount Clarestow, and therefore I am Lord Garney, and you are Lord Clarestow."

Sitting bolt upright, Danny exclaimed, "What? And you never told me all this, you never thought to tell me? Pa, how could you just throw this at me without warning? I am not hearing right, am I?" Danny was angry, outraged.

"I'm sorry, son, I somehow imagined that my father would tell all who needed to know that I was dead and that I wouldn't have to think about it. Remember, I was sent here as a convict. He told me he'd disinherited me, and I thought this was so. I have used my mother's maiden name of Corbett as my own, thinking I was no longer entitled to use my own. Anyway, I was the younger son. It never occurred to me that Nigel would die without male issue and leave me as heir."

"But didn't you think I had a right to know? Surely, I should have known. This affects me, you know. It even affects Vanessa too," Danny said cuttingly.

Dan got up and was walking around the room with his hands clenched tightly. Anne had never seen him so angry. She shuddered at the thought of him speaking to Sam like this.

"Now calm down, son. I know it is a shock, but I will try to explain," said Sam.

"Explain, Pa? You have a lot of explaining to do. Did you know your brother was dead? Something tells me you did." However, Dan came and sat down again.

"Yes, I did. Sir Timothy told me when he was out here that time. Son, in England, once you have been disinherited, you cannot undo it. I was not to know Father never proceeded with this. He told me he would. I took him at his word, and he'd never changed his mind before."

"But that was years ago. You could have at least told me then." They had never seen their son so worked up, but then he'd never been told he was a Viscount before either.

"I could have Daniel, but I thought it was best. To what point? So that I could rub it in your face that you weren't to gain anything because of me? That my actions had removed us from succession? From money, wealth and a title? For that is what I had thought until today." Sam put up his hand to stop another fusillade from Dan. "No, Daniel, you will listen to me. When Sir Timothy told me, you were just courting Vanessa. You were seventeen."

"Don't say anything against Vanessa, Pa."

"Of course, I won't, you silly fellow. I love her. Daniel, you will sit and listen to me. I don't often lay down the law, but this time you *will* listen. When I grew up, I knew nothing but hate, and it wasn't until I went to school that I found friendship. Being a Lord's son didn't mean anything to me; I was just Sam at home, a child everyone thought ought to be put out in the rubbish. An unwanted weakling, unworthy of even a hug. When I got to school as The Honourable Samuel Garney, I made friends, and I liked it. I had lots of friends, and it went to my head. I had many boys who hung on to me just because I was a Lord's son, but not for me, not for 'Sam', but I didn't know that until I heard some of them speaking one day and found that they weren't friends at all. It was a rude shock. Wherever I went, I found I had that trouble, even at Oxford, where I expected that they would be more mature in their friendships. But I was wrong. It got so that I couldn't tell who friends were and who weren't. It was not until I was in prison that I found I had only one true friend, and he was a reluctant one. His name was Daniel," Sam said softly. His eyes flew to

Anne. He'd never told her that.

Dan replied, "Yes, fine, I see all that, but what has that got to do with Ness. She's not like that."

"I know she isn't, son, but did you know that at the time? You remember that she was very hesitant about choosing between you and young McFarlane. If she had known you were heir to an Earldom, you would always wonder whether she chose you for that or for yourself. She chose you for just being *you*, and we all love her dearly, you know that."

"Yes, all right, Pa. I am sorry, I see what you mean. But you've had lots of time to tell me since. Why didn't you?" Dan was hurt, but his anger was ebbing.

"Son, being a Lord does not make one happier. It also comes with much responsibility. All I can say is it is a bad, bad nuisance. You will find that out soon enough; trust me in this. Unfortunately, now you will find out just how shallow people are, and I wanted you and Vanessa to be mature enough to cope with it. You are now twenty-seven and can cope with it, but I hate to think what it will do to your little ones. We don't want them spoilt, and yet that will be virtually unavoidable. They will be courted and married for *who* they are and not for themselves. In that way, my conviction may benefit them, for only someone who loves them for themselves will overlook that. Can you imagine how we shall be inundated with callers, even here, if and when this gets out? And Danny, my conviction will stop us from being presented at court, and you will probably be ostracised at home. This colony is a hotbed of gossip at the best of times; that titbit of information will be like a sabre cut to your heart."

"To be practical, Pa, what does it mean?" He was beginning to see the reasons behind his father's silence.

"Dan, I didn't even tell your mother about the title until Mister Timothy came out a few years ago and told me about Nigel. She married me for being me. She wanted to marry me before she even knew why I was sent out." His eyes fell softly on her. "She is my world, Danny. She is all I need. You have that with Ness."

Anne reached out and took her husband's hand.

Sam explained to Dan about Mr Pennecuick and his offsider being here to talk about legalities, and they would return the next day. Dan would be able to ask all the questions he wanted to, then. "But I daresay something will have to be done about the Estate. I will tell you here and now, Dan, that I want to renounce the title and all that goes with it as soon as it can be done. This means it will fall to you. I hope I will not have to go to England to do it; I hope that Mr Pennecuick senior has had enough sense to send out the papers in case needed. He said something about duplicate paperwork." Sam took a breath. "That is presuming it can be done at all. I'm not sure what the law is anymore. The last time I heard, it could be rescinded if three heirs renounce the Entail. If we can do that, we can sell the entailed buildings that come with the title. Lock, stock, and barrel."

"But where does that leave me, Pa?" Dan was beginning to be fearful.

"It will make you the Seventh Earl of Meldon, son, and then it is up to you to decide what to do," Sam said matter of factly.

"If I renounce it, then what happens?" Dan was stunned.

"Then, as you only have daughters, unless Vanessa produces a son, it will go to my cousin Charles Garney, who has an estate nearby, and he doesn't want it either, according to Pennecuick. He's the 3rd heir and is in favour of cancelling the Entail. But I must say that Charlie is more suited to it than I am. You can read his letter; it's something no one wants to touch. I reserve my opinion about it to you, son. I don't want to influence you one way or the other. But I am afraid there will be no way out of the title unless they have changed the law, but that you must at least go to England and see what you are inheriting before you either decide to stay or give it up." Anne went and made tea for them all. She was clanging pots in the kitchen and unable to hear what they were saying.

"What properties are there, and is there any money, Pa?" Daniel was beginning to realise that no matter what his decision, his life was to change radically.

"Meldon Hall, which is a huge pile that various ancestors have added to. Think of a huge English Castle, then double it and add a wing or two, and you're about there. It could host five hundred in the ballroom alone and still have room for a full orchestra. I suppose it could be a pleasant place providing the people in it are happy. I wasn't. The Estate lands are large and divided into several farms, as far as I recall. Each of those paying rent. Remember, I had nothing to do with it and am therefore very hazy. There are so many rooms I certainly have not seen them all. Some I was not even allowed to enter. I will say right now that I will not touch anything of my father's money, but if my mother left me anything, I would take that. Again, I must ask them. I wonder if she did, though, for as Mr Pennecuick junior seems to have known about me, he surely would have seen to it that I would have received it. So, I won't bank on it. But I do imagine that there is a large amount of money involved. There is a hunting lodge, and I think few smaller houses scattered in various Counties. I'm not actually sure what there is."

Anne arrived back with a tea tray. Both men acknowledged her with a nod.

"I won't bank on anything either, Pa. In any case, it all seems like a fairy tale to me. I really haven't absorbed it yet. But I must go and tell Ness, Pa. I daresay she will be excited." As Dan said this, he frowned but looked at his mother and smiled. "May I go and get her, Pa? But I think I will tell her myself if you don't mind."

"No, go ahead, lad," Sam said. "And Daniel, I truly am sorry I have been so hoping that father had disinherited me."

"Sam," said Anne, "Before Danny goes, he must read the letters."

Sam shook his head, "No, love, he wouldn't understand."

"Yes, Sam, he will. It's the only way he'll understand fully," she said.

"Letters, Pa? Who are they from?" Dan asked.

"One is from the Earl, and the other, from my cousin, Charles Garney. Dan, I cannot say I really want you to read them but go ahead if you feel you must. Admittedly it will give you some understanding of my attitude." Sam passed the two letters to Dan, who sat and read with intensity. Dan looked up and saw his father's face.

Sam sat back and watched his son's face as he took and devoured the letters. He folded his arms and waited for an explosion of ire that he knew would follow. After a few moments, he stood and went to the window ... waiting.

Dan found it hard to find the words, then he choked over it as he cried, "Oh, Pa. How could he? How could any decent man or father hate a little boy as much as he did? I understand, Pa, now I understand." He stood up and grabbed at his father, and a colossal aching sob shattered him.

Anne watched her two men as their tears mingled, then she joined them.

Dan then held his father away and looked straight at him. "Pa, I don't think I want anything from him either."

"Danny, sadly, you must go and see for yourself. It is a very huge thing, and you must be able to get it all in its right perspective. You might be able to do something with the place..." Sam looked at his son; he had a mischievous smile on his face. "Danny, you might like to do something he'd hate, like turning it into an orphanage. He'd turn in his grave to see that happen to it. I could not see Meldon Hall without thinking of all that happened to me, but you have not had those experiences and may fall in love with the place, and maybe it is the right place for you. It is yours by birth. I don't know, but it is for you to decide. Either way, you have my blessing. In any case, this has all got to be talked through; we have days and days of talking yet. Now, be off and go and tell Vanessa. Together we can break the Entail, as it takes three of us who have attained our majority.

Charlie will be the third, and he too will want that weight off his back."

Dan looked puzzled. "Break the Entail?"

"I'll explain about Entails later. It's different to the title. Go and talk to Ness," Sam said.

Anne made more tea while they waited for them to return. She kept her eyes on the house, waiting.

It seemed a long while before she saw Dan escort Vanessa over towards the cottage.

"Isn't it exciting, Mama Corbett?" said Vanessa as she greeted Anne. "Oh, or do I say Lady Meldon?"

Anne could see that Vanessa was silly with excitement. She was a peasant girl, who never seemed to really grow up, but she was a good wife and mother, and Danny adored her, as they all did. This news would be enough to throw anybody off-kilter, and Anne knew that Vanessa could be tiresomely giddy at times. Yet she did love her because she loved Danny. Anne thought it was one reason Sam had kept the news to himself, hoping that it would never eventuate. Anne really didn't know if either of them were fitted for such a life as Meldon Hall would demand, especially Vanessa. Anne could only picture a place like Broome-Hall. One had to be brought up to that sort of thing. She had lived that life as a servant and could not imagine going back. She sighed as they sat down. She'd worked in a place like that and was overwhelmed to think that at the moment, they owned one similar. She'd not heard Sam's description of the house.

Sam answered Vanessa's questions patiently, which mainly were what she and the girls would be called. She was excited to know that they were all titled Ladies.

"Ness, your title is Viscountess Clarestow and the girls, and are all Lady ... their first names." He waited while she rolled this over her tongue. "You would be officially introduced as The Right Honourable, The Viscountess Clarestow, but you are Lady Clarestow. Your signature is now Vanessa Clarestow." Soon the young couple settled down and asked questions about the whole situation.

Sam told Dan that Mr Pennecuick would have all the paperwork to save him from going to England. He said to Dan and Vanessa that they prepare themselves for a trip to England. All the formalities could be done over there after seeing the house. "If you decide to renounce the title and estates, Dan, you can do that easier there than here and then come home knowing that it was all decided, and you can be Dan Corbett again. I will sign nothing until you have given me your final word. If all three of us are in agreement, then we can do it. So you must be sure if this is what you want. Charlie and I are happy to sign. It would revert to his line after you're gone anyway."

"What is our name, Pa?" asked Dan. "Aren't I really Corbett at all?"

"Yes, son, you are. Your mother and I were married as Mr and Mrs Corbett Garney, and you were Baptised and registered the same. So really, all we've done is cut off usage of the Garney, but it's on all the paperwork, yes, even on your marriage certificate, for I added it when I submitted the application. I was pleased to drop it, Danny, and I think it was the only thing I did my father approved of me ever doing."

"We wait then to see Pennecuick tomorrow, Pa?" Dan asked.

"Yes, that is all we can do." Sam was a little more relaxed.

The next day the lawyer arrived mid-afternoon with his silent shadow in tow. Dan and Vanessa sat listening to the explanations of the serious-faced man. Sam and Annie became more and more depressed as the discussion continued.

Mr Pennecuick explained that the law stated that although three could break the Entail of the property, this did not cancel the primogeniture, or in Sam's case, the right of succession, as Nigel had died. So, he couldn't pass Dan his title no matter how much he wished to. Mr Pennecuick did say that Sam did not have to use it. There were moves afoot in Parliament to modify the rules; however, they had not passed, and he was not sure they would before the Estate was fully settled. The inheritance was absolute. Sam was the Earl for the moment, and Danny was the Viscount. Whether they used the titles was a different matter. To say they were shattered was an understatement.

Sam felt positively ill. Both, however, decided to just let the titles die. However, if they couldn't get rid of the building, they could use it how they wished.

Chapter 7   Sorting the Mess

*S*am was surprised to receive another letter from Charles Garney

the following week. It was written some ten months after the first one.

Oakhurst Park
West Sussex
18th December 1829

Rock Cottage
Sydney

My dear Sam,

I have to write to you with some bad news, I am afraid. Word of your past has been released, and the county is buzzing with it. This is how it came about.

Alice and I were dining with the Richardsons, and after the ladies left us, someone asked about you and did I know whether you were alive or not. I told them that you were and were happily settled in New South Wales and that I hoped you would soon return to take up your inheritance.

I daresay you remember the Reverend Mr Watmore of St Mary's? You must, of course, a man I never did take kindly to. Well, when I greeted him, he chuckled and asked whether we really did want a criminal to return to the county. I objected most strongly, and he laughed sneeringly again. Then he said, "Did you not know that your cousin went to the colony at His Majesty's pleasure? I am surprised you didn't know, but I knew Lord Meldon did everything he could to quieten the story. Now I see how well he succeeded."

With this, he absolutely gloated at my barely disguised surprise. But again, I objected and demanded proof. I should have kept quiet, but I was most distressed. He laughed again. "Oh, I have proof enough, Garney. I was instrumental in sending him there. He tried to steal my poor box; you know."

The horrible fellow thought it was amusing, but most of the others were very quiet about it. Knowing how short of funds your father kept you, I fully understand your reasoning.

I remember your father standing in the aisle at church and loudly dropping lots of coins for people to hear. As an altar boy, Sam, I had to help the Vicar empty that same poor box one day. I expected it to be full of gold. Alas, it was full of pennies with three sovereigns, and those I know my own papa put in. So all those coins your father dropped in were not worth one single sovereign. Well, that is by the by, the next day, I went to old Pennecuick and demanded the entire story with nothing left out, and he told me all but was adamant that you did not actually steal it, but Watmore only found you with it in your hands. I am appalled, Sam, not at you, but the episode was taken to such lengths. The old fool Watmore was always a tool of your father's, or vice versa. Either way, your father would have been able to quash it without any trouble. Worse things have been covered up with influence. The volume of peers' by-blows in the area is being hushed up, as their parents, of course, donate liberally to his slush fund. I do not think the church sees much of that as A; it would be hard for him to explain where the money came from, and B; he's always saying there is no money in the coffers. He willingly Baptises all those illegitimate children with their parents watching on, and then once he had the Nobility and Toffs signatures and the child's names inscribed in his books, he has them in his pocket.

All I can say is that, pardon me, but I dislike your father and this man now even more than I did when he was alive. Oh, but what reception you will get from the county, I hate to think, Sam. I really am appalled at the thought of what you may go through and wonder whether I can help in any way to make it easier for you. You must be assured that I will do all in my power to help all I can, and so, too, will Alice.

I am very fond of you, Sammo, and look forward to making the acquaintance of you and yours.

Regards,
Charlie.

Anne had taken Sam the letter and sat with him as he read it. She knew he had a meeting later that week with his lawyer. When Sam received this screed, he was not quite sure if he was angry or happy. This letter contained much that would make the decisions easier to make.

Sam replied to Charlie's letter the day he received it.

Rock Cottage
Sydney
12 May 1830

Oakwood Park
Billingshurst, West Sussex

Dear Charlie,

I was so pleased to receive both your letters. I read your first after reading one from my father, which deserves nothing but to be burned. I will, however, keep it as evidence of hate. To remind me why I don't wish to come back. I am sorry that you had to write the second, for I feel you must have been much upset at the news and how you heard it. I shall send a note of disapproval to old Pennecuick that he did not warn you in private of the reason for my coming to the colony, but please do not be any further distressed. I would have told you a long while ago but was made to promise that I would not. Father had told me he'd legally disinherited me, and I thought he had; I have only recently found that he could not do so. Here I am known as Sam Corbett. It was my mother's name.

I found life here in the colony a delight since I attained my freedom, for soon after the latter, I met and married my beloved Anne, who taught me what happiness was when I did not know the meaning of the word. For I had never known love Charlie, but you know that. I should say that I attempted my crime because my father would not increase my allowance. Instead, he halved it to £2 10 0 from the £5 a month I was getting. I had not a farthing to my name. He also would not let me come home. I had nowhere to go. Yes, the money in that box would probably have been put there by him, quite loudly, in the middle of the church service on Sunday as that's what he did each week, as we know. I did not realise it was so little. Enough of him!

We have a son, Daniel James Corbett Garney (we have never used the name Garney), he is married to Vanessa, and they have three adorable little girls aged six, four and two. So you see that as Dan has no son, and I doubt if he will, as Vanessa was very ill at Mary-Anne's birth, you are the 2nd in line after Danny now.

Mr WC Wentworth, to name one. Do not worry about my being a felon; a significant number of people here have that against their names, and many are very decent people who came in much the circumstances that I did.

Here we are known as emancipists, and many have achieved great success. I have gratitude, I think, not for what Watmore did, but that it landed me here on these shores. My years of service were not too good, but I am much suited to this life and am more than content. Not to mention a delightful climate. I have no intention of returning to England. I am sorry to disappoint you, but I see no reason to do so as I am not in the least interested in 'my inheritance', as young Pennecuick calls it. He is much upset about that, but I cannot help it. I will not and do not want to go to Meldon Hall. What has it done for me except to teach me what unhappiness is? I'd like to see it rot or burn to the ground.

However, in my place, I will be sending Dan and his family. All were born free and not labelled as a convict nor as an emancipist either. I was hoping to have all the legalities of renouncing to Dan fixed up here to inherit instead of me, but I've been told this is not possible. I cannot say he likes the idea at all. I had never told Dan of the situation. As I said before, I believed my father had disinherited me. At first, Dan was furious, then excited, but on mature thought (and after reading my father's letter), he is now quite reluctant. I might add that I never did tell Dan much of my background, other than as a convict. So, it was all a great surprise to him. It is now quite amusing, really, to see how he wavers from elation at being a peer to the horror of taking it over his comfortable life. His wife is the same. She is a builder's daughter but is a delight.

We hoped we could keep the news from this unusual small town, but it was a forlorn hope, and already the parasites are flocking around. A freeloader accosted them at the markets last week. Dan is seeing this horror for himself and is disgusted. Before this, we were accepted as just the norm. It is instead a pest, but I daresay it will be a nine-day wonder, and it will all cool down when Dan and Vanessa set off for Meldon Hall.

I cannot tell when Dan will leave, but Charlie, may I hope you will care for them? They have no earthly idea of what they will find, and I have not prepared them for Meldon Hall. They are alternately looking forward to it with excitement and dread. It will be a rude shock to them as I have told them little about the house itself. I thought it best not to. To make matters worse, Dan has only had a simple education at the charity School and what both his mother and I could teach him. His Mathematics is good as I majored in that at Oxford.

Charlie, I believe with the three of us, we could also break the Entail, as it needs three heirs of age to do this. If we three cannot break the Entail, I would consider making the house over to the London Orphan Asylum and making it the best Orphanage in the world. If we do not, then I have had a very naughty thought. Father absolutely hated waifs and orphans. I have no idea why, but he did.

With that in mind, I send you thanks and great regards,
Sam.

Sam posted his letter and settled back into his colonial life. He was sad he could not renounce his title, but that did not mean he had to use it. He'd asked Pennecuick to look into it. The Entail was, however, different. Danny felt the same, but he needed to go and see the sprawling place for himself. Sam knew what he'd left behind and was renouncing; Danny didn't.

Anne refused to even contemplate going.

Sam smiled to himself, wishing he could be there when Dan and Vanessa first saw the sprawling edifice. It really was an awe-inspiring sight. Sam remembered being banned from entering numerous ground floor rooms. However, he did not mind as his favourite room was a small sunny library he'd discovered at the back of the old wing. It had more books in it than he could ever read. Most were extremely old. He was about seven when he first wandered into the old wing. It was spring cleaned annually but otherwise unused. It was dusty and distant from everyone else in residence. Sam had great pleasure reading some of the many old tomes he discovered there. Most were leather-bound and gilt-edged. Some even printed on velum. When he touched these, he had always made sure his hands were clean. He had learned at school that body oils can hurt manuscripts. It was a room that had been his childhood sanctuary. His father never looked for him, and on wet days he'd curl up under a rug, and as long as he appeared for meals, no one ever sought him out. It was about his only happy memory of home.

~

Eight weeks later, Dan, Vanessa, and the girls left for England at the end of July. It would take at least four months for the ship to arrive. Sam had asked Dan to send word on arrival.

Claridge's Hotel
London
18th November 1830

Dear Mam and Pa,

Just a note to tell you that we have arrived in England after a long, long voyage. I daresay the ship was comfortable, but I was very seasick and never seemed to get my sea legs. Vanessa stood up to it very well, but I am glad you insisted on getting a nursery maid who was a good sailor, Mam.

It made such a difference. All the way, I could not help thinking of what your voyages out must have been, my very dear ones. You go up much further in my estimation, and I respect you even more than I already did. We travelled in style, but you? My heart truly breaks when I think of it. Your cousin Charlie and his wife Alice met us, and we are now at Claridge's Hotel in London. They have been marvellous to us and seem to be determined that they will protect us all they can. I almost expect Charlie to carry a sword to keep us clear of enemies. We are staying here as I think he is worried about the reception we will get from our neighbours at Meldon House, here in town and has gone to a great deal of trouble, I think, to see that our first visitors will be welcoming ones. I have not yet seen Sir Tim but expect he will come for a visit once we're settled.

We are all going to Meldon Hall tomorrow. As you know, it takes nearly all day to travel the forty miles or so. I am pretty apprehensive about it now. Until tomorrow...

Two days later
...I will say little about our surroundings until I become more used to them. Overwhelming is the word that instantly comes to mind. But I do say it is somewhat different to home, isn't it? As I walk through the place, I will keep in mind how horrible grandfather was and how I'd love to turn it into an Orphans' Asylum.

This is still supposed to be Autumn here, and it is frigid; we wonder what Winter will be like when it arrives? Is it always cold here?
Love,
Dan, Vanessa, and the girls.

Sam and Annie were relieved they had arrived safely. It was mid-March when they received another letter. The second was from Charlie and contained both good and back news.

Oakwood Park
Billingshurst
West Sussex
1 December 1830

Rock Cottage

Sydney

Dear Sam,

Dan and Vanessa and the three little ones are ensconced in Meldon Hall. Dan mentioned yesterday that they almost needed an inside carriage to get from one end to the other. I know that I have never been into all the rooms, even now it's empty. I bet you haven't either. I vaguely remember you saying you were actually banned from some in the main section. I shake my head at that.

Anyway, after two weeks in London, we travelled in separate coaches, but just before Meldon, Alice and I joined them, for I wanted to see the looks on their faces when they first caught sight of their new home. I am pleased I did, for I wouldn't have missed it for anything. Vanessa literally ogled at it. I must say it is impressive, but as you say, it was an unhappy place until now. Dan and his Vanessa are such innocent children; I fancy they are somewhat overawed by it, especially having servants. I gather this is not something you have over there.

I must tell you that I rid the place of nearly all the old retainers and replaced them with people of my own choosing. Old Pennecuick was upset about some of them, but I insisted. I showed him your letter, and it gave him no option but to acquiesce to my instructions. I would not have anyone near the place who was here when you were, bar that groom of yours, he is the only one who spoke about you with kindness, Anthony something or other, Jenkins, I think. He's old-ish but seems to know his stuff. So, I kept him on. I have actually made him in charge of the stables. He told me that's better than being made Master of the Horse at the Royal Palace.

The new agent, Graham Long, is the son of my own agent, Maxwell, and a really steady young man. He is well trained and has been working under Chambers' agent for several years, so I feel happy about him. Do you remember the Chambers? David was at school with us. They are near neighbours; I married their daughter Alice. What would Dan and Vanessa have thought of old Burge, Thompson and Simmons? (I shiver.) These new people are friendly servants. I am pleased I rid the place of the others. Simmons is a nasty man. He had two sons remember? One was as bad as he. He went to Sydney as a soldier. I heard he was killed recently by a falling tree.

Anyway, they have had some pleasant, welcoming visitors and so are settling happily. They are doing well, and you may be proud of them. Incidentally, I see you in that boy of yours, and I note that you *have both brought him up well. He is all that an Earl should be, Sam. You can be proud of him. Especially considering he knew nothing of the Title. I cannot hear enough about your life out there, Sam. I never tire of Danny telling me; I am becoming really fond of him. His joy of life is so adorable. Alice tells me she feels the same for Vanessa, and she, of course, adores all the little girls. Your life there sounds so exotic, yet straightforward. The weather certainly sounds better.*

I send my regards to you both. I have on good authority that you are both truly wonderful parents. I am sorry I will not have the opportunity to meet you again, Sam, and get to know Anne, who Dan and Vanessa both tell me is the best mother in the world.

Your friend and cousin,
Charlie

Sam smiled as he could imagine much of what Charlie wrote about. He was pleased Anthony had been kept on. He realised he must be getting on for seventy at least. He'd been to only one he felt he could ask for money on that final visit. He was pleased he didn't get the sack.

~

The following mail, Sam received more paperwork from the solicitors, and he tried to get his head around it. Charlie had as yet not said much about the state of the building, but it must all be in hand as Danny had sent no word. Sometimes the eight-month plus turnaround in letters was a major frustration.

He replied to Charlie's letter and got on with life.

His skills for the architectural drawings had picked up to such an extent he was busy dawn to dusk. Not much work was coming his way from Josh Comfrey, and this puzzled him. He made a note to go and visit him to make sure all was well.

Sadly, Sam forgot.

~

The following letter arrived in April.

Oakwood Park
Billingshurst
West Sussex
3 January 1831

Rock Cottage
Sydney
Dear Sam and Anne,
I just have to write about an incident that happened this day.

Your young people have been received very well, but I must admit they have not attempted to entertain a great deal, and that has been wise. Society is decidedly picky when it comes to who is acceptable. Dan and Vanessa have, however, had some unpleasant experiences about which I will now speak. Today your Dan showed his true breeding, and I am proud of him.

We were all at an official reception this afternoon, and most of the County was there. It was at Malvern Hall; you know the Duke of Malvern's place. I presume you've met him. When the Duchess was alive, she was stuffy, but the Old Duke is a nice fellow. He's interested in you and what you've been doing out there. For some reason, the Duke is always asking if I'd heard from you. He felt very sorry for you when you were here. I gather he knows your story somewhat. It seems he had a soft spot for your history. Anyway, this particular day he was wonderful, Sam. He has gone way beyond his neighbourly duty for Dan and Vanessa. He decided to throw his house open for a Garden Party for Danny and Vanessa as soon as the weather warmed up. All boded well, and the day dawned bright and sunny if somewhat cold. Well, it was apparently the first time old Watmore met them, and that's when sparks began to fly. Let me tell you what happened...

You remember Watmore's favourite saying is, when he meets someone who is doing something he is not pleased about, he asks, "Are you prepared to meet thy Maker?" I'll wager he said it to you more than once. Well, he still says it, and often while in church, naming and shaming some poor wretch. The Duke of Malvern brought the Reverend up to introduce him to Dan and Vanessa, but he stayed at Dan's side. After the introductions, Watmore extended his hand with a sneer. Dan looked him up and down, put his hands behind his back and, drawing himself up to his full height, almost spat the words out. This is what Dan said, in quite a loud voice, so many heard him.

"Mr Watmore, are you pleased with yourself? Are you prepared to meet your Maker? I would think about that if I were you. You, a minister of God, refused to help a starving lad in his time of need. You turned your back on him so proudly and then rubbed his desperate plight in his face. You, a minister of Religion, personally convicted a starving lad whom you Baptised and regularly saw at worship and were employed to aide and guide. I say minister of Religion because this is not the Christian Faith my loving parents taught me about. It's certainly not Jesus' love and compassion. Mr Watmore, I would be so afeared to

meet my Maker with this as my resumé, I would be falling on my knees repenting daily."

With that, Dan nodded politely to the Duke of Malvern, who stood beside him. Taking Vanessa's arm, he turned away and said, "Come, my dear, the area is suddenly very stuffy," and led her away. The Duke spoke one word to Reverend Watmore then cut him. He turned his back on him after just saying, "Go!" Sam, the Duke, was livid, almost seething at Watmore. If he had not been so old, I think the Duke would have struck the man. The looks he gave the man – Oh, dear, I would be fearful of being in Watmore's shoes. Have you heard the term "Shooting daggers with his eyes?" For that is what the Duke did. He was enraged, absolutely seething. All he said to the man was, "Go," but in such a way that even Watmore did not argue. More amazingly – Watmore went.

Oh, Sammo... It was a great moment; I can tell you. Watmore almost had a fit, for he has been quite pleased with himself about all this. Lord Malvern smiled quietly at Danny, even putting a hand gently on his shoulder and left Watmore walking away alone as Dan, Vanessa, and the Duke walked back to the crowd. They were then joined by his son Johnathan (known by us as Nathan), the Marquess Roxborough.

Others, too, turned then their backs on Watmore, finally realising the full story of your conviction. I was so pleased with Malvern, I would not have believed it of a Duke. I think the episode will have stopped Watmore's game now. The truth is filtering throughout Society already, and Dan finds more and more doors opening for him. Although I feel sure your young people will not remain for long. Dan has asked me many interesting questions. He gives no information, but I can see he thinks very deeply. He has grown in emotional stature, Sam. This has all been quite an experience for him, and I thank you for sending him to us. I only wish he could or would stay and let some of my young blades learn a little of his sense, but I feel his heart is many miles away with you both.

I must tell you that I think Vanessa is not standing up to the strain, though. She seems to be fading a little, if not outright unwell. This will definitely be one thing that Dan will take into consideration.

Yours very affectionately,
Charlie.

As usual, Sam sat down to answer this letter immediately.

Although work for Comfrey's Building was falling off as Josh was ill, business was slow at best. However, Sam's work for other builders kept him occupied, and they were paying him more if they wanted his drawing quicker. So although orders were slowing, funds in the bank were building. He picked up his pen, trimmed the nib and started writing a reply to Charlie.

> *Rock Cottage*
> *Sydney*
> *24 April 1831*

Oakwood Park
Billingshurst
West Sussex
Dear Charlie,

I have received your letter of the 3 January and am both pleased and perturbed. Dan began writing a great deal, which has fallen off lately, and I wonder what is happening. There does not seem to be a deal of happiness at Meldon Hall, and I worry about our young people. I truly appreciate all you are doing to help Dan and Vanessa and wonder what they would have done without you and Alice. The Duke seems like kindness itself. I sadly never met him, but give him my thanks.

The thought of your assistance makes me realise how I miss not seeing you and meeting all your progeny. They must all be a fine family. I thank God that you were there to help Dan and shall be eternally grateful for it. But I cannot help worrying about Dan and wonder whether he is in some trouble. Needless to say, Anne and I miss them desperately. Our life seems to be empty without the family rushing in and out of our cottage. We, too, are worried about Vanessa. She is never strong, and I cannot think the life there would suit her, for she is a perfect mother and would miss not having the children about her and having to confine them to their own quarters in the nursery wing, as is usual in Meldon's type of situation. I realise that that was one good thing about the size of the place, for me, anyway, for I didn't have to see my father very often.

I am hoping you will write again soon and also that Dan wi…

Sam paused in his writing and looked out the window at the carriage pulling up at the cottage.

He called out, "Annie, Anne, love, come quickly!" Putting down his pen, he walked quickly to the front door.

Anne rushed from the bedroom, thinking something horrible had happened to him and found Sam trying to hug two of his small granddaughters at the same time. While looking out the doorway, she could see Dan and a very ill Vanessa and the girls alighting from a carriage. "Dan, Vanessa, my dears," she raced to her side as she did not look well.

With that, they all met in a group embrace outside the cottage. They all spoke at once, and none could really sort out what the other was saying until Sam called a halt.

"Come on in, and let's sort this out inside," Sam said.

He said for the coachmen to take the luggage around to the house at the rear.

"Yes, I'll go and make tea," said Anne.

Dan and Sam went with the coachman, and the girls and Vanessa followed Annie.

When, five minutes later, Annie handed Danny a potent brew of dark black sweet tea, he exclaimed, "Darling Mam, now I know I am home. You've no idea how we have missed your mugs of strong tea," said Dan, giving her a big one-armed hug. "Breathe the air, Ness, eucalyptus. We are home, love. Mam, they call the insipid tiny china cups of amber fluid 'tea'. You need another one or four after it just to quench your thirst."

"Why didn't you give us warning, Dan? We've been a bit concerned that you didn't write much," Sam said while still hugging his granddaughters.

"Sorry about that, Pa, but you know, it was so hard to write about what was going on that I just didn't. Anyway, I thought it was best to come and tell you." Dan shivered. "It's certainly not as conducive to one's comfort as here. Funny that mere money doesn't make you happy, does it?"

"So, you are going back, lad?" asked Sam anxiously.

"No, Pa, never again! You see before you Mr and Mrs Daniel Corbett and the three Missies Corbetts. At least we will be when all the paperwork is finalised. I know you were waiting for us to decide what we're going to do. We've resigned ourselves to our fate in this penal colony and love the idea of it."

Anne came bustling in with a tray, "Did I hear right, Dan. You're going to renounce the title too?"

"Yes, Mam, as much as I can. I can't do anything legally, of course, I'll tell you about that in a bit, but we don't have to use it. The Entail is another matter. We can break that as Charlie's family don't want it either. I don't think it will be too hard to sell. It's impressive enough for an up-and-coming peer to lust over it. It is all over, well we're hoping it will be anyway, and we will start living again."

Anne beamed at him and said, "Take your time, son, we want to hear all about it but, tea and scones first."

Vanessa had not said anything since she arrived, and Anne could see that she was pale and listless, so she asked, "Where are the children now, Vanessa? They were here a minute ago."

"Yes, Mama Anne, but I told Nanny to take them to their bedrooms and settle them in. They will be all right. Nanny is a treasure. She is going to light the fire and make them all a drink."

"That's kind of her, though she'll find the fire already set. We go over and light it occasionally," said Anne.

"I sent a message to Josh on the way, Mam, and asked him to come and dine. I hope that is all right. Do you think we could manage?" asked Dan.

Anne grinned. "Just as well I have that roast on, Sam. We must have known something. I felt that I needed to cook a big one for some reason. It's a big joint. I only have to add extra vegetables." Anne said, smiling lovingly at her husband. "Vanessa, I have to tell you that your father is not well, though. Sam's done as much as he could to assist, but Vanessa, your Pa has been very sick, and he's not been working."

Vanessa looked shocked and teared up. Anne looked at her and thought that her reaction was not like her.

At first, they just sat over tea, happily looking at each other and feeling content to be in each other's presence. Dan started looking embarrassed, then came to the stories of hurts and harshness, non-acceptance and rudeness, but for Charles and his family's kindness and love and respect, Sir Tim and the Duke of Malvern, Nathan and their friends, Danny, would have returned earlier. Dan told about their joys and sadness, heartbreak and love for a country they felt was impossible to live in.

Sam noticed that Dan left out the confrontation with Watmore; he'd let him know he had heard about that already. "I am sad that I sent you, Dan, for I wouldn't have deliberately hurt you for anything." Sam grieved for his son and the feeling of rejection that he'd experienced.

"We had to go, Pa, and we are so glad we went. It was such an adventure, and we do feel we are very privileged to have had the experience, weren't we, Ness? You should have warned us about the Hall, though." Dan grinned when he saw his father give a gentle shake of his head.

"Yes, Dan is right; it was all fascinating, but I am glad we do not have to live there. It is so cold and at times so unfriendly." Vanessa shivered at her recollections.

"Apart from that, we are glad we saw what you had to put up with all your young lives, both of you. Sir Tim took us to Broome-Hall Manor so we could see what it was like. He was wonderful. It is the only way we could ever really understand, Mam. But we couldn't stay; neither of us wanted it. We love our life here so much that there is no comparison. I suppose everyone wishes for riches and a life such as there, but we found it really shallow and, oh, I don't know…. I suppose it would be all right if you had been born to it, but it just didn't appeal to us."

"What is Charlie's family like, Dan?" asked Sam

"They're great. Pa, there you have an example. The two eldest boys are Henry and Samuel Thomas, who is called Tom. They are what you would term *wild*. They hang around the other young peers and drink themselves stupid. They are only twenty-two and twenty-one, then the girls Frances and Caroline. How old are they, Ness?"

"They are nineteen and seventeen, Danny." Vanessa didn't sound as bright and chirpy as she always had.

Anne was somewhat worried.

"Then two youngest ones are Richard and Alice May; Richard is away at school, so we saw little of him, and Alice May has a governess or some such. Henry is a nice chap but so involved with a social life that he is forever off to some social thing somewhere. I hope that he will settle down because Charlie will set him up at Meldon Hall to get it sorted, and as he is hoping to be getting married sometime soon, so he should be all right. Tom is an out and outer who, I think, worries Charlie a lot. He doesn't seem interested in a home and just wants to be a man about town. He went through his allowance twice in the time we were there. His allowance per month is more than we both make in a year, Pa. I know Charlie doesn't like the set he moves in and wishes he could interest him in something good. I told him that what he should do is send him out here, and I'd teach him how to work, but Charlie wouldn't countenance that. Charlie replied, 'Garney's don't work'." Dan laughed. "I said, 'This one does'. Even Charlie can get a bit stuffy at times, Pa. Actual hard work is foreign for them, something which menials do. He was not impressed with what we said about our life here, so we didn't try to make them understand; we just kept quiet."

"It is different, isn't it?" said Anne, taking all this in. "For years, I hated it here. I supposed because I was forced to live here, but for many reasons, I realised that you live life the way you make it. Here in the colony, you can make your own life. You don't live on what someone else made and the social expectations; even as freed convicts to some degree, we get that say in what we do. Here, we can do what you wish, and if you work at it, you can make something of yourself. In England, if you're born poor, you seem to stay that way. If you're born rich, you have to live a certain type of life. Do you know over there you can never marry out of your class?"

"Yes, but, Mam, I was horrified. It isn't always what the rich people say, either. We found that the servants were just as intolerant if not more so." Dan said. "Over there, I would not have been allowed to marry Vanessa. So we didn't elaborate, we just said her father was building his portfolio." He chuckled.

"Don't I know it? I used to be one of the lower classes, remember?" said Anne. "They are often bigger snobs than their masters. Even taking the same precedence as their masters."

"That we discovered too," Danny said.

"Poor Nanny had a bad time," said Vanessa, "We had to tell her not to say that she had been a felon, for Charlie and Alice were aghast at our bringing her with us, that we had to tell her to keep it from all the servants. Even then, it leaked out somehow, and they made her life absolutely miserable. We would have sent her home in any case if we hadn't come. She doesn't ever want to go back again to England. We sent her off to see her mother, but it was not a success. Her mother was both pleased and happy to see her, but her sister-in-law and other relatives shunned her completely. It is sad when you think that her infringement was a minor one. She picked up a lace handkerchief, and thinking it was her own, she pocketed it. One stingy lace handkerchief. Sadly, it being lace, its value came to over 1/-. I think she will now marry here and settle down. She was not content here before. She has a beau."

Vanessa asked to be excused, and as she stood, she nearly fainted. Dan and Sam escorted her to the house. By the time she arrived, she was so unsteady on her feet Danny carried her directly into their bedroom and laid her on the bed.

Anne noticed she was no longer as thin as when she left. She had been underweight since her illness after the birth of Mary-Anne. Her new weight sat well on her minute figure.

Danny took some time in emerging. When he did, he was ghost white.

Vanessa had not wanted to tell Danny until they were home, but she was expecting again. He should have guessed as she'd put on so much weight, but she told him she'd just been eating far too much good food that she had just piled on a tummy. It's why she was feeling so ill. She worked out she was about six months gone and should be due late June or possibly early July.

Dan had taken her in his arms as she finally admitted her condition to him. He felt as though he'd been kicked. She was very compact as her condition did not show greatly. The style of the gowns also helped her hide her state. Danny was as anxious as a mother hen, and Vanessa was just plain scared. Her last confinement had been difficult enough. The doctor had suggested she try not to fall conceive again. The usual joy of a child was totally absent with this news.

The look on Danny's face when he finally emerged from their room shocked his parents.

Sam didn't have time to write to Charlie for a week or so, and when he did, the contents of his letter were very unplanned. Vanessa was expecting again. She was far from well, and Dan and Sam decided to do nothing re the signing any paperwork until the child was born. If it was a boy, things would possibly change.

Finally, Sam wrote again to Charlie. He'd not posted his last letter.

> *Rock Cottage*
> *Sydney*
> *1 May 1831*

Oakwood Park
Billingshurst
West Sussex
Dear Charlie,

This is not a letter I ever wanted to write. I had another half-written when Dan and Ness arrived home. Charlie, things have changed. Vanessa is expecting a child. It's why she was so ill over there. She is due in June or early July. I now cannot make a move until I know if they have a son or not. This totally changes everything, so I'm not going to sign the Entail cessation paperwork. I've had it sitting on my desk for months now, and each time I pick it up, I feel it's almost burning me.

Anne and I have even prayed about what to do and feel we should wait for the moment. Even Danny said this. Charlie, what I'm going to write now will throw the spanner truly into the works.

I may not sign the Entail cancellation at all. It all depends on the gender of this child. If it's a boy, the point will be moot anyway as he will be the second heir instead of you, and therefore won't be allowed to sign for twenty-one years.

Sam.

Dan found that picking up the threads of his old life was not as easy as he had thought. Josh had not come for dinner the night they arrived, and when Dan saw Josh later that week, he was surprised at how the ill man looked.

Josh had been so ill that his business was suffering. He had looked for a replacement when Dan had gone to England, and this had not been a success as the man, Perkins, had made merry with his money when he was ill, and the business was so run down that Josh had not been able to get it on its feet again. He hoped that Dan would again come into the business and get it going again.

While Dan was away and Josh was trying to get other builders to work for him, other companies had come to the colony and taken a great deal of the work away from Josh. His best workmen had left to go to the opposition, and he been left with scruffy workmen. He now had no apprentices and had no one competent to teach any boys the trade. So, all in all, Dan found that he had come home to find that he had to start right from the beginning again and support not only his own family but help to keep Josh too.

Sam had wondered about the business, but Josh had been tight-lipped about it and therefore kept Sam in the dark. But as Sam had been working on his own for all the new builders too, he had felt he had no right to question Josh.

Sam soon found that Josh's company was bankrupt. He had fallen behind on some of the buildings he worked on. When Josh became ill, he had the contracts taken from him. He now had nothing left. He moved in with Dan and Vanessa. Very soon, they realised that Josh was almost beyond work now.

Dan and Sam started from scratch by planning and building small cottages again, something they had not had to do for years. With Sam's planning skills, they built some attractive connected cottages from brick and slowly the business began to grow again.

They had now used up all their capital and money was tight. Funds took some time to come in. They had to live on the small rents they could get for their cottages, and they found it was tough going.

Sam's drawings now had to support three generations of his family.

"It's all a bit different to life at Meldon Hall, son," Sam had said one day. "I haven't signed the paperwork, you know, son."

"Yes, Pa, I almost wish I'd never heard of the place. Things were going so well before we went away, and now, oh Pa, we are far from getting out of the woods. I'm sorry I was so angry. I can now fully understand your reasons," Danny said.

"I haven't asked, but I gather you did not accept money from the estate, Dan?" Sam asked quietly.

"No, I didn't. Charlie wanted me to take some. He couldn't understand that we could live on what he called a pittance, but I thought a clean cut from it all would be best. In any case, I was quite sure I could come back to my old job." Dan fell silent for some time.

Sam waited, giving him time to process his thoughts.

"Going back is never the same, Pa, is it? Even coming back here," Dan said somewhat mournfully.

"No, it's not. One can never seem to go back, and things stay the same. That is one of the many reasons that I would not return to England," Sam said thoughtfully.

Dan looked straight at his father.

"Dan, something is eating at you, more than just money, isn't it?" his father asked him, quite concerned.

Danny nodded, "Pa, I am anxious about Ness." He wiped his hands across his eyes, angry that he'd teared up. "Dear God, I wish we hadn't left this place. Having said that, she may still have fallen with this child if we'd stayed here. She was ill enough after Mary-Anne was born. My base desires overruled sanity. Oh, Father, what have I done to her?" Their gazes locked and held.

Sam could see tears appear, and Dan's lips were quivering. "I am sorry, son. We have noticed that she has not settled. No one is ever too old for a fatherly hug. Come here, son."

Danny was so in need of one, and Sam embraced his son. Danny walked into his father's loving arms. He wrapped his arms around his father's waist and hugged him back. "I'm so sorry, Pa. Sorry I doubted you; sorry I lusted over material possessions; just so damned sorry for everything." Dan relished the firm embracing hug. It had been some years since he felt too grown-up for a parental hug. "I'm sorry, I also thought I was too old for hugs, Pa." He laughed while still in Sam's loving arms.

"I'm always here for you, Danny, my boy." Sam kissed the top of his head. It wasn't often he could even do that anymore as Dan stood eye to eye with him, alike in so many ways.

Finally, Danny pulled away. He wiped his cheeks with the base of his thumbs. "When we heard about all this, she was so excited. I was myself and, as you know, I was irate too. When you showed me that horrible letter from your father, things seemed to make sense, though. Father, I'm sorry. As I said, I'm so sorry for how he treated you, sorry for my behaviour and well, just sad things turned out as they did. But since the news, we have been in either a state of excitement or being dashed down." He paused, thinking of how he'd phrase the subsequent comments.

Sam again stood waiting.

"Pa, I presume you heard about the incident with Rev Watmore? I bet Charlie couldn't keep that to himself. It seems no one else had been prepared to stand up to him. From then until we left some weeks later, people stopped going to St Mary's. Doors actually started opening to us, but their welcoming was shallow, to say the best. We could tell they were reluctant, to say the least." "Y e s ,   s o n ,

Charlie told me." Sam smiled to himself. "I wonder if Watmore is as content now as he was before."

"Pa, up and down, that's the story of our life now. Ness wanted what Meldon Hall offered and liked being a Viscountess, then hated all that pertained. She loved the people who were friendly but hated all the undercurrents. She was very homesick but wanted to stay to see it through. Then we came home to find her father sick and old, their business ruined. Yet, she hates being without the wonderful comfort and ease she had at Meldon and now is down to cooking our own meals. She hated the girls being in the nursery, but now she hates having to do everything for them that we've had to give Nanny up. It's all just too much cost, and I don't know how to help her. The pregnancy in itself is so not helping. She wonders if we are denying the girls a chance to make good marriages but then hates the thought of having them live far away from us. She is just so unhappy, Pa. What am I going to do?" Danny pleaded.

"Son, why don't you take some of the money and live comfortably here? That's always an option, something to seriously think about, then you could get a nice house and you could have the best of both worlds." Sam said, hopefully sounding confident. "Just because I won't take his filthy money doesn't mean you can't. And there's plenty of it."

"Pa, I might have too," Danny said mournfully. "It goes against the grain, though, doesn't it?"

"Dan, just try to be as patient with her as you can, son. Love her, hug her and encourage her. And tell her that you're considering the money too. You're stuck with the title. Time is a great healer, and your mother and I will do all we can to help. I know it is easy to say that, but you just have to stick with it until we all settle down. She will get better, I am sure. The pregnancy is not helping her settle. We will do all we can, Danny. I'll write to Charlie."

Meanwhile, the week Sam posted his letter to Charlie in England, Charlie's son Henry moved into Meldon Hall in West Sussex. He had officially been sent to clean out some of the previous Earls paperwork, however, he'd been partying instead.

Henry had, in fact, been cleaning up one of the rooms after he'd held a huge and rowdy party and thought that he'd just sit at the old desk and have a rest. He pulled open one drawer and started sorting it, then another, all eight drawers he sorted. Most of the paperwork was rubbish, and he binned it. It was still better than cleaning up the party mess. It took hours but was worth every moment of his time. As he pulled open the last and bottom drawer, he heard the scraping of paper as he tugged it out. He got down onto his hands and knees and retrieved a handful of crumpled paper from under the drawer. He glanced at the writing, read the first few lines and gasped. He called for his horse and rode home with the crumpled sheets in his coat pocket.

On receiving the sheets, Charlie sat and immediately wrote to Sam and the lawyers. The news was life-changing for them.

Sadly, it was not soon enough.

At the end of May, Vanessa went into early labour and died two days later. She got to hold her son briefly, then lapsed into unconsciousness. It was a month or more before the child was due. The baby, however, lived. He weighed just over two pounds but was alive.

Daniel had a son.

Everything now had changed.

Chapter 8   Unforeseen Events

It was not easy to get back to normal after Vanessa's death.

The little girls were sad, Danny was in shock, Anne was trying to cope with being a mother to four crying children and not managing. Sam did what he could, but nothing could bring her back. He still had to work.

Danny shunned assistance and took the blame for her death on himself. If Sam put a hand on his shoulder, Danny would shrug it off and walk away.

After some weeks, Sam saw him smashing into a pile of wood, splitting the logs. He was putting so much anger into the swings Sam wondered at the wisdom of approaching him, yet he walked out and stood watching. Out of danger but close enough to not be missed by Danny.

Sam could see his tear-stained face as he swung the big axe.

Finally, Dan stopped and fell to his knees, sobbing.

Sam walked and joined him on the ground. Dan was beyond discussion, so Sam sat just hugged him. After some time, Sam gently pointed out that the children needed him. He had to pull himself together, or his mother, too, would crumble.

Dan turned to his father and just said, "So?"

Stunned, Sam lost it. "Damn it, Danny, do you think you're the only one hurting? It's not your fault that Ness died, just like it wasn't my fault my mother died. When Josh collapsed and died, that's not your fault either. Your mother will be next if you don't help her. Only this time, it may well be your fault! Because I can tell you now that she is exhausted. She's trying to do all this herself; it will be our fault if she dies." Sam, however, didn't leave. He sat with his loving arm still around Danny.

Sam stood and pulled him into his arms. He hugged Danny until he stopped sobbing. A hug had broken through where every-thing else had failed. Sam's loving, caring response was healing for Dan. "Dan, do not look at the future, just get through that hour, then that day or that week. Just deal with one day at a time."

Danny looked at his father aghast. He could not risk losing his beloved mother too. After a few minutes, Danny nodded.

In those first days after her death, Danny had walked and walked, denying that it had occurred. Then the shock set in; Dan wouldn't get out of bed for two days. On the day of her death, Josh, Vanessa's father, had collapsed, and he died two days after he heard the news. The two were buried next to each other. Dan cried for two weeks. He'd been angry and sad, but it was the guilt that hit him hardest. He couldn't bring himself to even look at his tiny son.

Sam had not known how to help him. Sam had tried the gentle approach that hadn't worked, so the tough love was the final thing he could try. Sam had only lifted his voice to Dan once before, and that was the day he told him about the title. But now Anne was at risk, and he'd not let anything happen to her. He held his son at arm's length. He looked him directly in his eyes. "Son, your mother is not well. Look at her lips, they are blue, and it's not from the cold. She's not coping. I don't want to lose her too." He saw the look on Danny's face, but he didn't wait for an answer but walked back inside to help her prepare dinner for everyone.

Anne saw Sam coming. She had seen the confrontation and thought to herself. "That certainly wasn't normal, but what is normal?" Anne was numb with tiredness. "Will anything get back to what it was before? No, nothing could be ever again," she mused. She was so tired she was ready to weep.

Sam walked to her and brushed her cheek with a gentle kiss. He went into the kitchen and started preparing the vegetables for dinner. His mind went back to the first years together. When she had fallen pregnant with Danny, she'd taught Sam how to cook. This was now one way he could assist her. He couldn't do it all, but he could get everything prepared for her, then he would take over the care of their grandson.

Anne rocked her tiny grandson. Looking down at the fragile child, she wondered what his future would be. For the first few months he was kept in a darkened room, or had his eyes covered when outdoors. He was dark-haired and brown-eyed like his father and grandfather. Anne was intrigued that all three men in her life had this trait. Danny and Eddie had both had brown eyes when born. Mrs Pitt was intrigued as she said most of the babe's she delivered had blue eyes. Anne stroked his downy cheek. He was so like his father. The memories of Danny's birth flooded back to her. Edmund was so tiny but seemed to be healthy despite his early and terrible birth in May. She hoped he would not grow up with the stigma of his mother's death, as did Sam. "While I am alive, little one, you will have no feelings of that kind." She gently placed him over her shoulder and burped him.

Little Edmund Daniel James Corbett Garney had a wet nurse, Agatha Wells, called Aggie, who lived not far from Rock Cottage. Anne insisted on Aggie coming to the house every three hours and feeding him at their home every day to have as much family life as Anne could give him. Every three hours during the day, Anne welcomed the wet nurse for the baby's feed, then she'd go home again. Aggie took the babe home after the last feed at night and returned him after the first early morning feed. Annie did everything else for the child. This worked well for everyone. She didn't want a woman of Aggie Wells' stamp living with Dan and the girls, nor did she want Eddie to be wholly brought up with the Wells children who were a dirty, unkempt, untrained lot. So the best they could manage was to let Edmund stay with the woman at night and spend the day at the Corbett's after he'd had his first feed. Also, Anne wanted to make sure that Aggie washed as often as she could be persuaded. Aggie's own baby was now ten months old and weaned.

Anne was exhausted.

The last few weeks had been burdensome, and she felt she was far too old to be bringing up a young family with four small children. She had started too late herself and now to be caring for a baby again. It was hard. Jo-Jo, Lucy, and Mary-Anne were good girls; they helped where they could.

Seven-year-old Jo-Jo seemed to be more concerned about Anne than the welfare of the tiny brother who demanded so much attention. "Gammy, you have to lie down and sleep too," Jo-Jo said anxiously.

Anne gave her a big hug and thanked her.

The weeks passed. Danny was coping, making it one day at a time gave him the ability to make it through each day.

Sam was still working far too much, but Danny seemed to be emerging from his dissociative fugue state of grief. Sam's talk seemed to have worked. The family was barely holding together.

Life must go on.

The men were now doing better with their business. Dan now spoke to his parents regularly. He was learning to cope, but the guilt still ate at him.

They completed a row of semi-detached cottages and some had pre sold, others were rented. Money was once more not such a worry, but Sam was getting too old for hard building work, and he felt his workload was exhausting and often looked tired. Danny wasn't much better.

Anne felt that even though he missed Vanessa very much, he must feel some relief knowing that she was now out of harm's way and could not be hurt anymore. She was drowsy, she'd been deep in thought when she heard a voice calling her.

"Where be ye, ma'am? Is yer in the cottage?" Aggie called for her.

Anne roused herself, surprised that she had fallen asleep. She was glad that her little bundle was safe in her arms and that she hadn't let him fall. "Yes, Aggie, I'm here on the verandah. Come in. The baby is still asleep. He cried whenever he was put down. Do you want to feed him now?"

"Yus, missus, it's time. I'll take 'im in, missus."

"He is still sound asleep, though."

"I'll take him an' I think ye should go an 'ave some proper sleep, too, missus. Yeah, I come'd a bit early as I thinked you didn't look too good yesterd'y. Yer'll be better if yah take a nap. Ye look thet tired. G'arn, put yer feet up while ye kin. I'll take a bit more time wif 'im so yer's can nap."

"I think I might, Aggie. I do feel tired nowadays." Anne was so tired she could hardly make it to her bedroom.

Sam was, in fact, very apprehensive about Anne. She did not have the energy she used to have. She had two high coloured spots on her cheeks that made Sam think she had a heart complaint. He quietly was concerned that she may have something wrong. He knew that so many depended on her that she knew she had to rest as much as she could and keep going. He watched over her intently. He was also aware that she was worried. She had too much to do.

Sydney was still growing at a great rate. There were now nearly twenty-five thousand people in the town, and there were many improvements for the residents over the latter years. There was now a water supply of sorts. Soon it was expected that water could be piped to some of the houses. Thankfully, years ago, Sir Tim had installed both a tank and a well for her. This was such a blessing; it had been one thing they'd never had to worry about. It was vastly different from getting water from the Tank Stream as most had to do in the early days.

Sam had always been able to keep the tank at the cottage clean and filled from the well, which made things easy for Anne.

The streets in the town were looked after better now, and so vehicles found it easier to negotiate them. In the last years, the houses were of much higher quality, and Sam and Dan could now get contracts for some very decent-sized places. The various building businesses were booming in the colony, and there were some very prosperous businessmen.

Sam and Dan tried to keep their family away from much of the rabble and life in Sydney. Anne, of course, never wanted to be part of it much. So, they all shunned the social life, preferring to just spend time with the family. Tom Turner still visited, as did his friend Ned Grace. Both were very nice men and pleasant to talk to. They filled them in on the happenings of the town.

One day Ned visited alone, he confided to both Sam and Danny some of his own noble history and was supportive of whatever decision they were to make. This instigated many deep discussions between the three men.

One could still see chain gangs of convicts, and convicts were still being flogged. In fact, the colony still had its harsh side, and Sam wanted to protect his family from that side of the town life. The girls were very carefully guarded and not permitted to wander alone. They had few friends, for they never wished for a social life. Vanessa's sisters all had families, so the Corbett children could visit their cousins a great deal and mix with other young children.

Charlie's letter, written in May, reached its destination in July. Sam had torn open the missive from Charlie, wondering what catastrophe had befallen them now. He was sitting at the kitchen table with Anne. He had no idea why but felt that something important would be in this letter. He sat clutching the screed in his hand, absolutely stunned.

Anne made tea for them both and brought the large mug of sweet black tea for Sam. She saw him now sitting with a letter in one hand and a £100 note twisted in the other hand; he was staring out the window. The look on his face was both astonished and dumbfounded. He was sheet white.

She'd seen that before, but this time his expression was different. This time, he had a smile on his face.

She had heard him exclaim, "Nooo!" as he was reading. He turned to her and said while looking at the letter, but with a tremendous smile on his face, "Oh, mother, I love you so very much."

"Sam, what's wrong?" She fell to her knees at his feet.

His eyes were twinkling with delight as he sat back at the table. "Um, nothing I suppose, love. Here, you had better read this." He handed her the letter from Charlie that he'd just read. "I think this will solve our problems with Danny, love."

Anne took the letter and, sinking to the floor, read it aloud, stopping at the first mention of money.

> *Oakwood Park*
> *Billingshurst*
> *West Sussex*
> *5 May 1831*

Rock Cottage
Sydney

Dear Sam

I made a decision in the absence of information from you. I had moved Henry into the Hall for what amounts to a security measure. He did this the week Danny left. I knew whatever happened, it would take a year before the next action, and I thought I'd rather the place not be left vacant, so I told Henry he could stay until further notice.

I write to let you know that Henry has finally cleared out the desk in the main office. In it was a copy of your mother's Will. He brought it to me immediately, and I took it directly to Pennecuick and Co.

Sammo, she left you £25,000. Totally clear of the Estate funds. Your father never intended you to know about this, but as it was jammed at the back of his drawer, he had obviously lost it or hidden it. Apparently, Pennecuick Senior knew about it, but could not act without the paperwork, so he had not told his son. Either way, you said you would take money only if it came from your mother. Nigel was mentioned in her Will, too; however, she left him £1. Yes, just one measly pound, and he was her firstborn son. If he were not mentioned, then I suppose he could contest the will.

I have since shown Pennecuick and Co, and it is entirely legal. As I said, Snr knew it existed, as he drafted it himself, and the money is safe. It seems your father's behaviour to you was seen by her before she died. Your father had no say in how she left her money that was settled on her after their marriage with the strict stipulation that it was to be for her alone and she could leave it to whomever she wished. Sam, it was not part of her dowry. This came to her, possibly from her father when he died, and it was tied up so legally that your father could not touch it. The lawyer had invested it before her death. As that was some fifty years ago, over £40,000 at least is coming your way. The £100 is merely an advance in case you needed it.

As I said, Henry had moved into Meldon Hall after Danny departed, and I was content with this. However, he is not running it as I had hoped, so I moved him back out. His marriage plans have fallen through, and he's drinking heavily now. It will sit vacant until I hear from you. I may send Henry to you to straighten out. He needs a good shake. Maybe some time and hard work in the colony would help.

Sam, you have not yet completed the Entail cancellation, and I'm not sure if you are aware that there are movements afoot to vary the Entail laws, which may affect things. If you do not do this soon, the rules could change, and the Entail may not be allowed to be changed.

I will write more once the money had been transferred, but I have included some pin money to tide you over.

Charlie.

Sam had murmured, "Mother left me £25,000," he read.

"Oh, Sam!" She put her cheek on his knee. "Well, this solves one problem." She turned to Sam and grinned. "Dan can hire some staff now and even move to a better house if he wishes." She giggled.

He reached down and lifted her onto his lap. "You're not wrong there, my dearest love, and this is money I will take. For it was given in love." He pulled her close and kissed her passionately.

Anne wrapped her arms around his neck, returning his affection with delight.

Eventually, Sam released her.

She said with a giggle, "Sam, with £25,000, you'll never need to work again."

She looked at her fifty-three-year-old husband; he was still so handsome that sometimes he took her breath away. His temples now showed some grey, but this made him look more distinguished. She gently brushed her hand over his bristly cheek.

"Keep reading," he said,

She dropped her head and read the rest of the letter. "£40,000, cor Sam!" She, too, had a smile on her face and then giggled. "Your father wouldn't like this, would he?" Her eyes were now dancing with joy, and she then threw back her head and laughed. The magical tinkling sound he had so missed, now echoed around the room.

He joined her jubilation and reached for her hand, kissed it and together they laughed.

Sam finally said, "Annie, my love, my father would blooming-well hate it, and therefore, I love it so very, very much."

The relief of no financial worries relieved Anne, and the concerns she was unintentionally carrying, finally released.

"We're going shopping!" Sam grinned, "Right now."

Sam hired some help in the house with the £100 that Charlie included in his last letter. He paid off all the outstanding bills and bought some treats for Anne, Danny and the girls. Then, he bought himself a new silk top hat.

Knowing that neither ever had to work again, Sam gave up his work and stayed home with Anne. Dan completed the projects underway but did not take on any more contracts.

~

The next afternoon the three of them sat drinking tea and realised something. All three knew now they had no option. They had to go back. They owed it to Edmund.

On Tom Turner's last visit, he mentioned that he would retire as he was approaching fifty and was looking for accommodation. When Sam asked when and the answer was October, Sam's eyes lit up. Tom Turner would move in as caretaker.

Ned could come and stay when he wished. Sam knew that he had a friend he saw at Government House. This gave him a Sydney base.

Rock Cottage
Sydney
29 July 1831

Oakwood Park
Billingshurst
West Sussex

Dear Charlie,

This is another blooming letter I never wanted to write. I should have written when the child was born in May, but we were unsure he would live.

Vanessa died having Danny's son. He is named Edmund Daniel James Corbett Garney. He was born at least a month early but now seems to be thriving. He's now two months old. This totally changes everything, and I'm not going to sign the Entail cessation paperwork as it's now pointless. Eddie is, of course, underage. Neither Danny nor I ever intended to come back and live there, but while he was away, their business here has failed, and his father-in-law, his boss, became ill and died soon after Vanessa's death. Her mother died years ago, and her sisters have both recently moved to Parramatta. So, our ties here are now somewhat tenuous.

Charlie, your news of my mother's money also changes things somewhat. This enables us to now alter our way of thinking. News of our titles has seeped into the community here, and things are far more complicated than I anticipated.

Charlie, I'm going to throw another spanner in the works. I have written to Annie's friend, Sir Timothy Broome-Hall. I believe you know him. I had spoken to him over ten years ago about the future use of Meldon Hall when he told me of Nigel's death.

*(*Breathe Sam …*)*

Sam lifted his eyes and looked out the window at the small rock on the front lawn. It was a marker for Rip's grave. He thought back to that first night; Rip came to his side and licked him, then curled up at his feet. It was this simple act that persuaded Anne to let him stay. She trusted Rip.

He sighed and kept writing. The following sentence was one he never wanted to write. He'd already delayed too long. He dipped his pen in ink again and kept writing.

Charlie, I am keeping Meldon Hall for Edmund. It's not fair for him as a tiny child to have his future heritage thrown away, and he has no say in it. However, it will not continue as the way it has ever been before. It will not be run as a regular Estate. I plan to use it in such a way that it would make both my father and Nigel turn in their graves. (The idea of this pleases me greatly.)

Tim is in contact with many orphans who are by-blows of the aristocracy through his work. Danny and I are keen to now use the Great North Wing as a home for these children. The Hall will be fully staffed by those you have chosen and other top-quality staff. I wager many of those will not be prepared to stay, but Tim knows of some who will come. Some are of similar situations themselves. The Music room or equivalent will be turned into a classroom with some of the best teachers to educate these poor children. These children will be brought up to enter society if they wish or work in a Trade or Businesses. Even work in the Government in such a way that will make the Nobility there cringe. I will expend the money from the Estate on giving these unwanted children all the love I never received myself. I could so easily have been one myself if my father had been given a chance to rid himself of me. Sometimes I actually wonder about my own parentage. That would explain much.

Consequently, we will consider coming back for a period, if not even permanently. Charlie – how did this happen? Danny and the girls will come too. He is young enough to remarry, for he is but twenty-nine. If we all come together, then we will at least have each other for support.

I will write more about this later. We now have enough funds for cabin fares for us all, but this will not be for some months as young Edmund is too young to travel, but he is a happy babe. We will come when he is weaned.

I cannot believe that I am going to do this, Charlie … I am going to need help. I do hope you are still willing to assist.

Sam,

The blooming Sixth Earl of Meldon, after all

Sam didn't want to post this missive but knew that for his grandson, who only that day smiled at him, this was his duty. Sam also poked out his tongue, and Eddie mimicked him. This set everyone laughing. Sam's heart melted. No, he could no more steal this lad's heritage than give him away.

The day before their mid-October departure, Danny took the girls and visited Vanessa's grave and the girls placed flowers on her parents' graves as well. Tears formed but did not fall. Dan knew that his future now rested in England.

Thankfully Ned had been a tremendous support and gave him encouragement. A lump formed in his throat as he walked away; he'd turned to look back and said his final goodbyes and the girls ran ahead. The path that lay ahead of him, he must now walk without Ness.

The family had packed up, rented their house and cottage to Sam's friend, Tom Turner, and are all booked on the *Hooghly*. They stayed their last night in the house, and early the following day, a wagon arrived and loaded up the luggage and bits of furniture they intended to take with them. Annie had bought some fabric and intended to teach the girls to sew to help pass the time. Before they boarded, Anne and Sam stood and wept over Rip's grave. He'd been such a faithful friend for so long. It was hard to think he'd been gone for nearly twenty years. He was buried where the big rock had once stood. Exactly on the spot that Sam had collapsed. His grave was now marked with a new tree and the smaller rock Sam had placed on it soon after he was buried, and they asked Bert to tend the tree so that it wouldn't die in a drought. They all still hoped that one day they would return. One day! They would not close that door. The two bits of furniture they took with them was Anne's bedside cupboard with the secret compartment and Sam's bookshelf he'd made for her. She absolutely refused to leave them behind. She insisted on a few other bits of sentimental value.

Much to their surprise, they found they would be travelling with Governor Darling and his family. As they were settling in, Sam twice bumped into a lady going into their cabin. The second time she stopped and spoke to him. After introducing herself as Amelia Westaweller, she simply said, "Sam, you need to trust the Darling's". He remembered visiting her father's Manor house with his brother Nigel. He stood and watched her disappearing and then went and reported the strange conversation to Anne.

There was much cheering as the ship pulled away from the dock. Sam discovered later that this was from the pleasure of the Governor's departure rather than from friends saying goodbye. So Sam escorted his family to the other side, away froth rabble.

Tom and Ned had come to see them off. He thought the Darlings did not appear until the town was out of sight, but he found them cloistered on the far side of the ship too. The lady he'd bumped into was standing waving to the Darlings with a group of others. Ned stood close to her. Sam looked at the Governor and decided to take her words to heart. He'd see what opportunity arose. When it did, they were met with kindness. Sam and Anne reciprocated.

Sam had sent word to both Tim and Charlie on the *Renown* a month before they sailed, to expect them. To say Sam was afraid to return was a vast understatement. It was a horrifying thought to them all to find that they were to be on board with Governor Darling and his family.

The Darlings, however, were initially equally horrified, knowing who they were travelling with. The convict Earl was on board. Their first meeting was uncertain, to say the least. Sam greeted them with hesitation and anxiety, for they knew themselves to be convicts even though now titled. Sam's fear would not be needed, and their greeting was such that it quelled Sam's last worry. When Mrs Darling saw Annie trying to cope with a baby and three young girls alone, she immediately reached out to assist. Sam had booked their passage under the name of Corbett, but the truth was already known by the Darlings, and when Mrs Darling explained this, Annie burst into tears. When the younger woman, Mrs Darling, offered Annie help, her offer was met with tears and a nod. "I only had one child myself, and that was so long ago. Little Eddie's mother died in childbirth, and Mrs Darling, I am thrown. I don't want to leave. I have no desire to be a Countess. I just want to stay me."

"We will help each other, dear, as I'm expecting another one. It will be born before we arrive, so I shall need your help as much as you need mine," Eliza said, looking at her new friend.

Anne replied with, "Oh! Of course."

"I had a Nanny in Sydney, but she was unable to return with us as she had not fully served her time. There was something fishy about her case, and I promised to look into it on my return." Eliza rubbed her stomach. "Settle down, little one," she said to the unborn baby. Mrs Darling continued, "Amelia West was her name. The children adored her. She told me her story, and oh, Anne, the treatment she suffered was horrific. She was raped by her owner and now has a child."

Anne related the story to Sam, and he put the pieces of Amelia's life together. He realised that Amelia Westaweller was the same lady. He knew her father to be titled too.

Governor Darling was still officially Governor. When he

discovered that Sam had been a convict and was only on a Conditional Pardon, he penned a letter of permission to return to England due to extenuating circumstances. Thus, Sam was given an Absolute Pardon. Governor Darling made a comment to Sam that took over a year for him to understand its meaning. "They may take my position from me for my actions, but in this, I can at least set one more action right."

~

With over three months ahead of them on board the *Hooghly*, the two women broke through the protocol barriers of society. Ralph discovered that Sam was only a year younger than he. Soon the two families were friends. Nearly four months in a confined space with children shattered any protocol. Mrs Darling said, "Call me Eliza, dear," and she decided to teach Anne much of what she would need to know, like protocol and precedence, when she arrived. "Anne, you take precedence over even me. Do not be ashamed of who you are and what you were. Stand tall, and do not be hesitant. Bluff, my dear. I do it all the time. The more powerful the person, the more scared I am. I have mastered the art well." She chuckled. She then did her magic wave and passed her hand over her face transforming it into her official persona. Eliza then giggled, and Anne realised what she meant. The Darlings were travelling with four children, but she was expecting another, and it would be born before they arrived in London. They already had two sons and two daughters. Eliza and their older daughter, twelve-year-old Cornelia, took to caring and entertaining Danny's three little girls along with her children while Anne cared for the baby.

Sam and Danny also talked over much with Governor Darling. When the Governor heard Sam's full story, the fatherly compassion overtook him, and he reached out to Sam with great friendship. When he heard of what Sam intended to do with his inheritance, he was unsure if he was horrified or delighted. The Governor knew of the house to which they were returning and its great stature in England.

Sam's worry was cast aside by the Governor. After less than a week on board, Sam and he were friends. A few weeks later he decided to show Governor Darling, or Ralph as he was told to call him, the letter his father had written to him. Sam took the opportunity of a gap in the conversation one day, "Ralph, as we were settling into our cabins, I met a lady on board who gave me a word of advice. She said that her name was Amelia Westawaller. She said I could trust you; she reinforced that. As I do trust you, I will show you this." Sam handed Ralph the letter from his father.

Ralph sat and read the short screed. He looked up at Sam; his face was red in anger and with tear-filled eyes. "How can any father write that rubbish? I fathered ten children, Sam, we have lost three, and my heart was crushed each time. The pain doesn't go, but you learn to cope, one day at a time. So for a father to have such blatant disregard for a small child, let alone his only surviving son... Oh, Sam, my heart bleeds for you."

From then on, the barriers between them were entirely removed, and Ralph understood Sam's motivation for his unorthodox actions with a poor box. Dan sat listening to the two older men. The three men entered into much planning, Anne and Eliza joining them in many of their discussions.

Sam and Anne also discussed in their cabin the incredible coincidence that they were travelling with them. Things could not have actually worked out better.

Eliza's time came to give birth. She delivered a healthy girl they named Charlotte. After a few more weeks on board, they celebrated Christmas.

In a private conversation afterwards, Ralph admitted to Sam he must himself face an inquiry on his return. He asked Sam if he would keep him in his prayers, and when Sam looked shocked, Ralph realised that Sam did not understand what this was. "Did your father really teach you nothing about anything? Do you not know about even the basics of faith?" Ralph asked, stunned.

Sam shook his head. "I remember bits, sir, from school, but no, I was not taught by father. Please remember that it was a clergyman who gave evidence against me. I've had no reason to love the church." Sam looked apologetically to Ralph. "Anne and I read the words of Jesus in the Bible. I do not see that this is lived out in the church. Rev Marsden is much the same calibre of a person as Rev Watmore and not conducive to showing emancipists much love. We try to live as we think Jesus would like, but we don't really understand it all."

"Oh, dear, Sam, you can do no better than reading about Jesus directly from the Bible. Still, Eliza and I can explain the difference between the religion of these fanatical zealots and the true faith in Jesus. They are vast distances apart from each other. Some are not even Christians in my reasoning."

Over the remaining weeks on board, the discussions of the five adults covered many topics. By the time they arrived in London, the three Corbett Garney's were well on the way to understanding the vast difference between God's love and forgiveness and the religion taught by some. Danny had grasped the difference already but also had not known how to put it into action. He knew what Watmore taught was not the love his parents taught.

Eliza's eyes would rest on Anne and soften with compassion. The experience of these two people horrified her.

Anne asked Sam if it were all right if they invited them to stay, and Sam was delighted to say, "Yes, absolutely, Anne. It will be your home too. Ask whomever you wish."

"But Sam, is there enough room?" she asked quietly.

Sam's eyes caught Danny's. He was grinning from ear to ear and answered, "I think we'll manage to fit them in somewhere, love," Sam smirked. "Invite whom you wish, sweetheart. Whenever you wish."

The last month onboard, Eliza took Anne aside privately and said, "My dear, I know I am a little younger than you, but I have moved in society, and you have not. Would it offend you if I showed you some grooming and deportment hints? I could not do this before due to my condition."

Anne face lit with joy. "You would do this for me, Eliza? I am so worried I do not know what to do and would love it. I have been wracking my brain to remember all I saw, but I was never taught."

~

They spent an hour a day practising curtsying and walking with a train. Eliza also showed Anne how to dress her hair. Also, what gowns were worn at which times of the day. Sam had always insisted on table manners even when they were alone in the cottage. After they married, he set the table for every meal, as though it were a banquet table. He had taught Danny and the girls as they grew. After Anne could do all her lessons perfectly, Eliza said, "You're ready, my dear, to be presented."

"Oh, no, Eliza, that will never happen. We do not return to join the rabble at court; we are returning to stir them up." She smiled with a naughty little grin. "Do you really expect that I would even be acknowledged? I was a housemaid and then a convict. Even though my conviction was quashed, I am a nothing, Eliza, and I expect nothing."

"Anne, are you sure?" Eliza said. "I would be proud to present you."

"I am honoured, Eliza, but I am resigned to my lack of breeding. I do not even know who my parents are. I am a foundling. Like Sam, I knew no affection in my youth. Hence our desire to assist others in the situation we found ourselves in."

"The offer remains, if you so wish, my dear."

Anne hugged her and said another thanks. "In ten years or so, we may ask you to present Jo-Jo if you're willing."

The first week of February, the *Hooghly* docked in London. The two families, being first-class passengers, were unloaded before the rabble in either the intermediate or steerage classes were allowed to disembark. Charlie and Tim were there to meet Sam and Anne, and they were greeted with great joy.

Anne greeted Tim with a warm welcome before he did something he'd wanted to do since her release many years before. He hugged her again. Charlie did likewise to both Sam and Danny.

The cabin maids escorted the three little girls off the ship, and nine-month-old Edmund was carried by a fourth.

Sam introduced the Darlings as friends and then said their farewells. They would meet again at Meldon Hall when the Darlings could come and stay. They made their farewells.

The Darlings were met by government carriages and whisked away.

Charles and Tim had decided that they would all stay at Broome House in London, and Anne was delighted. It held special memories for her, and she wished to show the place to Sam. She had no secrets from him, and she also wanted to show Sam her tiny attic room.

Tim, too, knew her story and thought it would be good for her to lay some ghosts. He planned to let them wander where she wished. "Annie, your time there was very happy; none of the same staff is still there, not even Betsy. Although I thought you may wish to see her sometime. She lives in the country."

Anne's eyes were heavy with tears, so she just nodded. Betsy had been the only friend she'd ever had.

Sam looked at his wife sadly. He slid his arm along her shoulders and drew her close. What a sad thing to have to claim. He had no desire to see Clarestow House just yet. He'd have to face that torture later.

Anne took the sleeping baby from the   ship's maid, and the group walked to the first carriage.

Charlie said he'd meet up with them in West Sussex and would bring along all their luggage. He had a few things to do in London and would try to see them before they departed, but not to worry if they didn't meet again in London. He'd be staying with them at Meldon Hall, so he would have much time to catch up later. He was just glad to see Sam home.

The time in London passed quickly.

They spent a week sorting out the legalities of the Earldom. Sam also produced the letter from Governor Darling allowing his return to England, as did Anne.

Tim escorted the three of them to various outfitters, and they each purchased an entire wardrobe of clothing for each member of the family that suited the English climate. Anne also insisted on many serviceable gowns rather than ball gowns. Sam persuaded her to buy two, but she had no intention of wearing them. Each was so beautiful she could not resist them. The look on Sam's face when she had shown him was all she could desire. She decided to wear them for him and for him alone. Something she could dance in when alone. They each also bought various heavy capes for warmth and new clothing for all the children.

He had laughed when she said to him the night of their engagement, "Sam, I dance to my own tune. I live my life by my own rules, and I make the best of what I have. I live each day as it comes, and I love what I have." He'd reminded her of that often over the years. He'd taught her how to dance in their tiny sitting room, but he promised that they would dance in the Music room at the Hall. He knew what it was like. He could see her in his mind's eyes where they would twirl and whirl and swish to the beautiful music in their minds. Sam looked at her face. The stress of the past year had been erased, and she was as calm and as beautiful as ever. Even the blue tinge from her lips was gone. He knew too well the stress from financial worries. The months at sea had worked its magic.

~

It came time to leave London and head for the new life ahead of them. Anne was nervous, the little girls excited to be returning to the house with the toy room, and Dan and Sam were just stressed. Charlie had completed his business and met them again in Broome House. He had decided to travel with the family and Tim on the trip to Meldon Hall. Neither were accompanied by their wives.

As they drove through the countryside, Sam pointed out various places from his childhood. They passed Christ's Hospital School near Horsham after the lunch stop, and Sam told her of the happy days spent there. Even though it was only half a day from his home, he lived-in as a boarder from the age of six.

"But Sam, they look like reverends, baby reverends," Anne giggled and exclaimed when she saw the uniforms. She bent forward to watch the students for as long as she could. Danny couldn't tear his eyes off the strange uniforms.

Sam, Charlie, and Tim all chuckled.

Tim replied with a laugh. "Yes, they look like that, only we were so proud of them. In winter, they are warm as they are woollen."

Charlie added, "And they are actually quite comfortable too."

"Did you all go there?" she asked, surprised.

The three older men nodded and grinned.

"Charlie and I really got to know each other there. Father didn't realise he'd been sent there too, and we kept quiet about it. Father hated him too." Sam said, grinning at his cousin. "He was a year behind me, but they were fun days, weren't they, Charlie?"

"Sir Tim? You too?" Danny asked Tim.

"Yes, lad, but some years earlier, they were a few years behind me, but I knew of them both when I was a senior. They were still in junior school. I'm now sixty-five, Sam, you'd be fifty-nine, and Charlie, you're a year younger?" Tim said.

The two younger men nodded to his enquiry.

"Anne, my love, they were the only really happy years of my life. I was too young to realise that my home life was not normal and not old enough to be really concerned about much more in life than enjoying school. For years they were all I had to hold on to." Sam lay back on the comfortable leather squab seats as the countryside whizzed past. She took his hand and gave it a squeeze.

The three youngest children sat on the laps of Sam, Anne and Dan, and Jo-Jo sat between Dan and Tim, opposite her grandparents. The baby was resting on Sam's shoulder. All four children were asleep.

As the coach swept around a long sweeping bend, Sam leaned over to Anne. An enormous stone building came into sight. "Anne, we're here." Sam had not warned her about its vast size. Although he had said, it was larger than Government House in Sydney.

What she saw was at least twice as big as she expected. Soon she realised that this was only part of the facade. The lawns and gardens were immaculately kept. Then she caught sight of the rest of the building previously hidden by the trees. It was more than twenty times the size of Government House. The driveway was smooth and even. The whiteness of the building sprawling out over the vast lawn looked like something from a storybook.

"Oh, Sam," she could not tear her eyes away from the horror of what she saw. "Damn it, Sam. How the blooming hell are we to live there?"

Sam chuckled. Only Anne would put it like that. To her, the fantastic palace-like building was a total inconvenience. To her, their tiny three-roomed cottage was a palace. "Um, my dearest love, that phrase is something that is probably left unsaid over here. Mrs Darling would blush bright red, and my sweet, not very Countess-like." The grin on his face belied the correcting words. He totally agreed with her.

Charlie and Tim were trying hard not to laugh. Neither succeeded in keeping a straight face. Their crinkled, twinkling eyes gave them away.

"You mean I can't say, h*ell* or d*amn*?" Annie chuckled. "And I suppose *blooming,* either, I bet? I'll try to remember." She grinned wickedly. "Unless I'm provoked. If Rev Watmore is anywhere near me, I promise nothing."

"Fair enough, Anne, but Danny has already given him a good job, I believe." Sam looked at his son and winked. "Thanks for that, by the way, Danny."

"It was my absolute pleasure, Father." Dan grinned in reply.

All watched Anne's face as she realised the immense size of the incredible palace-like building when it finally came into full view. The facade went on and on. Their carriage clattered over the rough arched stone bridge, which heralded the waking of all the little girls. They then drove past the twin stone guard towers, past the Dower House set back from the main road, then she saw a folly and temple-like structure in the distance. The overwhelming size of the building grew and grew as they moved closer.

Sam looked at his wife's gentle face. Tears were sliding slowly down her cheeks.

"Sam, I can't do this. You should have warned me. This is nothing like Broome-Hall Manor. You did say it was bigger, but this … this is, … damn it, Sam, this is a palace. Even bigger than a palace. Dan, now I realise why you said, 'Oh, some rich peer would buy it'. Sam, it's terrifying." Her eyes widened more as they drew closer. She then turned on Dan, "You could have at least warned me, son."

Dan grinned in reply. "Now you understand why Ness had issues, Mam."

Chapter 9   A New Start

*T*he girls squealed with joy, remembering their visit from only a year before. For them, it was a fairy palace. Sam forgot it was their heritage too. He had a flash of guilt. Their squeals awoke the sleeping Edmund, who proceeded to screw up his face in an unpleasant way. The carriage windows were hastily dropped, and fresh, cold, sweet-smelling air entered the travelling carriage as they pulled up under the portico. The Corinthian pillars of the portico were over thirty-five feet of gracious white marble edifice. There was a sweeping semi-circular ramp up to the front door encircling a partially sunken garden. This allowed carriages to drive to the front door fully undercover. It was only then that Anne realised the immense size of the building. The carriages were minute compared to the monumental entranceway. The two front doors alone were over twenty feet high, and each one was over six feet wide. As the carriage drew up, both doors were flung open. The red carpet was already out and waiting for them to alight. Staff were lined up inside to welcome them. Sam knew that it usually took some two hundred employees to run the Estate. There were but twelve in the Hall. Some six gardeners were also waiting along the side of the driveway as they'd driven through. They had stopped work and stood to attention. He'd nodded to them as they passed. Sam chuckled at the speed with which the family exited the conveyance. This was undoubtedly the quickest way to empty the carriage, as his grandson urgently needed his napkin changed. Thankfully it had not leaked onto his lap.

Charlie and Tim had found two maids who wanted to work with children, and they were hired on the spot by Charlie. They introduced themselves as Abigail and Mary. They took charge of the four small children. Mary said, "Miss Jo-Jo, would you like to go to the nursery?"

Seven-year-old Jo-Jo was thrilled. She remembered the amazing toy room. "Can I see if I can find my way, please, miss?" She led her youngest sister up the grand staircase towards the fabulous children's playroom.

Abigail said, "I'm called Abby, Miss Jo-Jo; I'll take your brother and Miss Lucy-Anne." Abby also took the smelly baby and his change bag from Anne.

The children thus dealt with, the men stood in the foyer watching Anne survey her new home. She was all eyes. Looking all around her as she stood in the impressive foyer. Even the ceiling was extraordinary. The moulded plaster was painted in white, and the decoration picked out in gold. Everything around her was beyond her wildest imagination. "Sam, this is really ours?" she asked her grinning husband.

He had an absurdly silly grin on his face. "Yes, love, all ours. Should we paint it royal purple? How many orphans do you think we can fit?" With both eyebrows raised, he had a child-like innocent look on his face and smirked at her reaction.

She gently punched his arm. "And I suggested maybe thirty. Sam, this would fit three thousand of them and still have rooms spare." She fell silent; after a while, she said, "And I asked if we had room for the Darlings. I puzzled over your reply."

"Now you know why I laughed." Sam looked at Danny and smiled, his grinning face one of absolute innocence.

"Is this the biggest house in England?" Anne asked in earnest.

Charlie said, "Um, no, not quite. Stowe House in Buckinghamshire is bigger, but it's of a similar design, although their entrance looks similar from a distance, at ours, you can drive up to the front door undercover. At theirs, you must walk up the steps. So you get wet on arrival. Windsor Castle is some, one-thousand rooms, and others are bigger."

Sam explained, "You must admit, love, I did say that it leaves Government House in Sydney for dead. I'm guessing ten of those at least might possibly be the size of the front facade, but this goes out the back too. And then there's the Great North Wing. You can't see that from the front; it's as big again. A few others may challenge it for size, but it would be getting close to the top of the list. Some of the royal palaces, like Blenheim Castle, may give it a run for their money, but well, I think they'd like to buy this if they could. The estate at Stowe House has more open land around the house, and they had wider wings with big curved wings in the rear. Chatsworth and Harewood are reasonably sized, but we have bigger stables than most of them. Then our Folly is far superior as it has a fully completed temple with guest accommodation. Wentworth Woodhouse would be the biggest, and we're not too far behind that one, it's in Yorkshire. It has some three-hundred rooms; we're over two-hundred though; so we're not likely to see it. We're about the same size as Gracemere Castle in Kent, but it's a real Castle with crenellated walls and all. That's Danny's friend, Ned Grace's family seat. Oh, forget I said that, shh! The entire ground floor of our Great North Wing is a Ballroom, easily fitting some five hundred couples. It has underfloor heating with orangery attached to its conservatory at the end. It has its own palm garden section in it. Father even had some pineapples growing in there at one stage."

Charlie looked at Sam, then Anne, and smiled. "My house, Oakland Park, is much more manageable, and of course, you know Broome-Hall Manor. Hence my reluctance to take on this mausoleum. Both of those only have about a hundred rooms at the most."

"Eighty-seven at the Manor," Anne nodded, still stunned. Her tears had obscured her gaze, so she brushed them aside angrily.

Standing silently behind them were the new butler and housekeeper that Charlie had chosen. Charlie beckoned them forward and introduced them. They were introduced to Victor Jamison, their new butler and Dorothea Murchison, the housekeeper, and eight of the other new maids and footmen.

Anne, having been a housemaid herself, caught herself bobbing a curtsy, then chuckled. "This is going to take some getting used to, Sam," she said softly. She was clinging tightly to his hand rather than to his arm as she should have done.

Charlie raised an eyebrow to Victor as if asking an un-uttered question. Victor nodded. No words were spoken. Tim and Dan stood to the side, watching and waiting for the new owners to be ready to move out of the foyer. Charlie again addressed Sam. "Sam, Anne, Victor says I can let you know something of both their backgrounds. Shall I just say both are especially suited to their new positions due to their own births. Abby and Mary, other staff are similar, but not with titled parents, and the rest are sympathetic. Only two have left, and that was because of health reasons rather than disagreements with your plans. Neither could cope with many children. Given the murmurs of excitement circulating the community, I think it will mean you will have a stream of staff searching for positions. I am stunned at the number of similar stories I am hearing. I had no idea this was such a big problem, Sam; I see how vital this work will be." Charlie explained. "Graham Long and Victor can work through the applications if you're happy."

Sam nodded and agreed to Charlie's suggestion. "As long as we have the funds to pay them an excellent wage, no skimping on that, Charlie." Anne stood listening but stayed mute.

Mrs Murchison stepped forward and said, "My Lord, M'Lady, please excuse me if I'm speaking out of turn, but personally, I'm thrilled to be known for who I am and not be ashamed to admit it. My father was an Earl, and we're thrilled to be able to help the little innocent mites who find themselves in situations similar to ours. We were all born innocent and have had to live with the consequences of our parents' actions." She bobbed a curtsy then stepped back.

Victor Jamison was heard to say, "Hear, hear, Thea."

Sam caught a look of adoration on his face for her. "So, you're all on board with our project? You're not ashamed to work with us?" Sam asked

"Sir, you will have our undying appreciation if we can help others in the situation we found ourselves in. Some of us grew up with knowledge of our parents. Some parents even acknowledged us in private, but there it ended. Abandoned as soon as we gained our majority. So, sir, we're all in this to the end." Victor also smiled then stepped back. He then grinned. "Sir, my father was an Earl too. At least he had me trained as a butler."

"Fabulous, then we have much work to do, don't we?" Sam said.

Victor agreed, grinning. "Too right," he murmured under his breath.

"So, are we in the Master suite?" Sam smiled at him. Sam finally took a step towards the immense sweeping staircase in the overwhelming foyer. The first flight of stairs led to a landing where they split and swept around both sides of huge the circular entrance.

Charlie replied for Victor, smiling broadly; he said, "Yes and no, Sam. I refurbished your father's bedroom, but not as a bedroom. I turned your father's bedroom into an internal privy, exactly where his bed used to be." He let this sink in and met Sam's wicked grin with his own, and Sam made no comment but chuckled.

Charlie continued, "So you're now in the new master suite. It wasn't finished when Henry was here last year, so no one has ever slept in there. I thought you'd appreciate that joke. Sam, I have left your mother's room untouched," he said as he led them up the grand circular staircase.

They kept walking towards the master suite. Anne saw portraits on the walls as they passed, but none looked at all like Sam or Danny as she expected they would. She laughingly thought she could see herself in them more than Sam. She could see no resemblance to Sam in any one of them. Most, if not all, of them, seem to be light-brown haired with blue eyes like hers. None had Sam's chocolate eyes and colouring. She wondered if maybe Sam's mother, Lady Anne, was dark? Hopefully, he'd show Annie her portrait if there was one.

They walked on for what seemed an age. Finally, the group reached a solid white door with gilt highlights. Charlie threw open the portal and inside was the most beautiful room. Its simplicity was in stark contrast to the over ornate palace-like building they had just inherited. The walls were pale blue, and the furnishing offering shades of plain blue velvets, luxurious yet simple. The furnishings were neither ornate nor gilt. Bare solid timber. "Oh, Charlie, it's perfect," said Sam.

"Charlie, I can breathe in here. This will become my sanctuary," said Anne. "The only two changes will be my own bedside table and Sam's and Cec's bookshelves. The rest is perfect."

She walked to the window; the vista before her made her gasp. Stretched out before her were the most exquisite gardens she'd ever seen. They extended as far as the eye could see. Anne stood stunned. Suddenly an idea occurred to her. "Charlie, you said, 'Father's room' and 'Mother's room'. Are we expected to sleep apart?" She didn't wait for him to reply but turned to Sam. "I'm sorry, Sam, that is not going to happen. If we have to, I'll go home." Anne stomped her foot. "If I have to sleep apart, trust me, I'll leave."

Sam chuckled. "No love, we are very unfashionable, we will share a room, and we shall use the rest as we wish, including the other bedroom, maybe as a special 'sleep over' room for the grandchildren."

Charlie smirked and again caught Sam's eyes with a wink.

Sam mouthed 'jealous' to his cousin, then grinned again.

Charlie nodded, then grinned back. If he loved Sam as a young lad, he was fast learning that the bond had deepened. He adored his older cousin back then, and now he knew that had not changed.

Anne nodded and took a deep breath. "Okay, I can do this if I can escape into here, Sam." She went to look out the window again. "I'll do it for Eddie and the girls."

Danny had followed them into the room. "Oh, this is delightful. I think I'll strip my room too. This I could live with," he exclaimed.

"Ahh, Danny! I did not think you'd wish to be in the same suite, after … well, you know, so I prepared one for you if you'd like to follow me. It's just down the corridor." Charlie led Danny about five doors down and across the hall. He threw open the door, and Dan was greeted with the room of his dreams. Decorated in dark green velvet and white, with lots of unpainted light timber. The furnishings were as plain as his parents' rooms. Not a fribble nor furbelow insight. "Oh, I love it, Charlie. I won't need to change a thing," Dan said with glee.

"Tim's nineteen-year-old daughter Georgina chose this colour scheme. It seems she too has simple tastes. She may have hoped to be placed in here if she were invited to stay at any time."

Dan smiled to himself when he thought back to his parent's cottage in Sydney. This suite was more extensive than their entire cottage. The suite contained more than just a bed. The enormous four post bed was curtained with steps to climb up to the feather mattress. Next to it was a full dressing room, a sitting room, a bathing room, and an internal privy. Oh, the luxury. Dan's mind flashed back to Vanessa, remembering how she loved the commodes in their last room here. She would have adored this. He had a wave of sadness pass his face. Dan turned and looked at Tim, who had just entered. He'd followed them into the room behind Dan.

"Well, it's an hour hard horse ride from our place. Some of the rooms were so tattered they needed immediate repair. So we did it our way. Charlie and I felt your folks wanted things quite plain, so that's what we did. I know what your Sydney cottage was like, as I had it built for your mother. Dan, I also saw the house you built for her. So I knew you'd like things as simple as we could make them. Dan, your father's room is, however, untouched from his childhood. Your grandfather would not even let the cleaners in it as he left it to rot. We did get rid of the dust, but that's all."

Dan nodded thanks; he'd tell his father later. Dan wanted to see it himself. He fully expected it to be as stark as his father had described to him. The ghastly room he had been placed in last time was now gone. No more frills and peony roses painted on the walls. Memories of Vanessa would not haunt him in this new room. Here was a fresh start. He loved her still but knew she was gone. One day at a time, that's what Pa said, just one day at a time. Let tomorrow wait until tomorrow. He, too, released a breath and knew that he'd have lots of support.

The family settled in well. Tim and Charlie's wives and families came for dinner that night, arriving only two hours after them.

Sam took Anne up to the nursery and showed how well looked after the children were. Once she saw the vast expanse of the playroom, she gasped. From the door, she could barely see the other end of the room. The three little girls were riding on toy horses. There were dolls houses and a line of the most exquisite china dolls that Anne had ever seen. They were obviously very old but looked almost new.

She had never had a toy herself, and even Dan had only had a blanket as she had, but never a toy. It was this realisation that finally made her sink on a chair, and she wept.

Sam was beside her in an instant, drawing her into his arms. "Anne joy, my love, if you can't cope, we'll go home."

Her wet eyes met his. "No, Sam, it's not that, this is their heritage; we nearly stole it from Edmund and the girls. We nearly gave it away, and can you imagine what he would have done when he grew up? I now understand Danny's initial anger." She lay her head on his shoulder and gazed around the room. "Sam, how are we going to stop them all from becoming spoiled?"

"Easily, my beloved, we're going to love them and teach them its importance. And we have a staff of people who will do the same. All of us will be on first name terms; yes, even the staff, and everyone will be loved and treated as equals. Just as God made us. Each of these unwanted children will be given a huge and luxurious loving home. Anne, you told me you dance to your own tune, well that's what we'll do here. We shall run our estate to our own tune."

Annie nodded, then gave a wicked smile. "No one is going to stop us dancing to our own tune here, are they, Sam?" She chuckled. "They have to find us first. Have you been into every room?"

He shook his head and bent to kiss her. "No, my Annie joy, my beloved, I have not been in into every one. I was banned from many of them in this main section, but I loved the old section. I did discover some special rooms. One, in particular, I wish to show you. It's got books in it, special books. Not even Watmore could find me there. For now, I am the Sixth Earl of Meldon, and my Countess will not let anyone mess with me."

She gave a wet chuckle, and as he pulled her up, she said, "You'd better believe that I won't. Come and show me what your favourite toys were, for I bet they are still here."

Sam led her to an army of painted toy lead-soldiers and a farm set. She was intrigued at the numerous feet of the soldiers poking up through the sand trays. He looked embarrassed. "Father was a soldier," he shrugged. "I, um, buried him, often." Sam grinned innocently at her.

Anne laughed. Amazed that some fifty years later, they had not been moved. The last hands to touch them were his.

~

Then came the first Sunday after their return. Sam, Anne, Danny, and the children attended the church with Tim and Charlie's entire families. Charlie stayed close as he knew that a fight would ensue. He hoped that Sam would not actually punch the man. Sam led Anne to the family pew and ushered Dan in first with the girls.

Anne had the baby in her arms.

The elderly Rev Watmore saw the new Earl lead his family and then usher his wife and son with the four small children into the family pew. He grinned gleefully, snickering to himself.

Charlie's family sat behind, and Tim's behind them. There was no way either of them was going to miss this confrontation. Each sat through the ceremony with their arms folded.

At the end of the service, Sam waited for Rev Watmore to exit the building. None of the family knew what to expect. All knew something would definitely be said. Anne knew that after such a vitriolic sermon, Sam would not let this man stay. He now held the living for the parish, and it would not be staying with this hypocrite. When the old man finally came out of the building, he looked more shrivelled and sourer than he had when he'd entered. He knew the living of the parish and his position as the incumbent was at the pleasure of the Earl. He realised his vitriolic sermon this day may not have been the wisest. This was one Earl who was not pleased with him, and Watmore now knew it.

Sam stood in front of the shrunken, bitter old man. He took a step towards him and drew himself to his full height of six foot two inches. He looked down at his nemesis, only this time it was not him standing in fear. Very quietly, Sam said, "You have a week to pack your things and move. I do not care where you go, but go, you will. Your sermons have not changed, Watmore. You are caustic and hateful, preaching heresy and dissidence, and I will not allow this." Sam took a small step forward. "My people will learn to love the God I know." Sam, who towered over him, took another step towards the cringing man, who had to step backwards. Sam continued softly, but so others could still hear. "My people will learn the Bible as Jesus taught it, untainted by hate." He took a third step towards the man, who had stepped backwards again. "My people will learn the difference between religion and the true loving faith of Jesus. What you teach is not Christianity. I will not have that irreverence spoken in my church." Sam's voice was still quiet, but Anne and Danny could hear the seething anger behind his words. Finally, Watmore had met his match.

Sam went to walk away but turned back after only one step. He raised his voice a little. Many could now hear him. "Oh, and Watmore, I will not give you the title of Reverend, for they are Godly people; you are like the Pharisees that Jesus himself condemned. I am not judging you, for you have shown just where you stand by your own words and actions. Change before you meet your maker. When I was a small boy and being persecuted, you turned your back on me; when I was a young man and was hungry, you reported, then prosecuted me rather than help me. You had a chance to redeem yourself last year, and yet you mocked and scorned my son and his wife. You are a person I do not want living anywhere near my family. If I were you, I'd seriously sit and read the Bible you now ridicule because soon Watmore, you *will* meet your maker." With that, without waiting for any reply from the old man, Sam turned, took Anne's hand and walked away.

He turned to Tim and said, "Tim, get the Sacristan to lock up the church valuables now, please. Make sure that man leaves with nothing at all but his clothing. Return the balance of his money to the poorest in the town, as it is ill-gotten. Use the food in his house to feed the hungry." Sam said as a parting shot, "Put his remaining possessions out on the street for the needy to take. Only leave what is required for the next incumbent. I want all traces of him gone."

Charlie and his wife Alice were standing to one side and heard the entire conversation. Tim and Sophie stood with Anne and Danny. Tim put his hand on Anne's and Dan's shoulders, giving Anne's a little squeeze to show support.

"Willingly, Sam," Tim said.

Rev Watmore was gone three days later. As instructed, only his clothing had been packed. The Verger oversaw his cases being packed, and he was seen with two suitcases, waiting for the mail coach heading north. No one asked where he was heading; no one showed any interest at all. Some stood and clapped as he passed. His departure signified a change in direction for the area. Now they were ready for a fresh start.

The following Sunday, Charlie took a service of Morning Prayer. For the sermon, Sam spoke of what his plans for the village were now going to be. He set out his goals for the change in the Hall and asked if he had the support of the people. "Come to me and talk to me. Do not be afraid to approach my Agent too, but if you have issues, see me. If you have any needs, see me. I am the same boy who was convicted of theft, trying to get the money from that very poor-box padlocked at the back of the church. There is nothing you can say to me that I won't understand. I may have lived in a big house, but I had no money, no love, and no one who cared. Trust me and work with me, and we can change this town."

The congregation erupted in various murmuring conversations. The organist forgot to play the following hymn. Soon one old man stood. "M'Lord, we all agree we can't go on as we were. We've let a lot of things slide, but we were too afeared to say anything. We're all with you, M'Lord, fully." He started clapping and was joined by everyone else, who then stood as they did so.

~

By the end of the month, the first small child had arrived, her name was Sally. Her father was a Duke, and her mother a noble lady. No names were given, although her history was recorded in a new sizeable leather-bound register, so she could one day be told her parentage. She had been taken in by some of the staff on the mother's Estate. When she turned five, they were told to find somewhere else for the child to live. At this age, she fitted in well with Danny's three small girls in the nursery.

Over the following months, other children were brought to the Hall. Most were under eight. All were loved and cared for. A new minister was brought in directly from college; he was young and enthusiastic and charismatic.

Sam had interviewed some eleven others, and none had the *joie de vivre* or the joy of life that he required, nor the basic loving beliefs he wanted to be taught. Sam wanted someone who would teach the Bible as Jesus lived. In Hugh Williams, he found such a leader. The man was twenty-eight and had a smile that brightened the room. When Sam found that he also was the illegitimate son of a peer, he knew he'd found the right man.

Hugh had never expected to even get a parish, especially if his history was discovered. To be given one directly from college was beyond his wildest dreams, and such a parish. His father had sponsored his training, then virtually said, "You are on your own." Hugh was stunned that Sam had somehow weaselled the private information out of him. Hugh smiled to himself.

"Reverend, there is a condition attached to your employment. You must teach the Bible as Jesus wanted us to learn. He, too, disliked the Pharisees and their dogmatic teachings. Loving all, letting Him and Him only judge all people for their sins. Sins can be listed, but no judgements are made unless it's self-judgment. That is for God only to do justly. I need this church to be a loving and accepting church. Can you do that? Will you work with us?" Sam watched how these words were received. "Hugh, I do not mean you are not to challenge us, for you are. But I need the truth to be taught, just God's pure truth. Can you do that?"

Hugh met Sam's eyes; he met them honestly. "Sir, if you meant half the things you say, then we shall work well together, but I fear of none but our Lord. I can't believe you actually want me, knowing my own history." Hugh settled into the large empty Rectory.

Hugh fitted into the family and was, sort of, adopted by those at the big house. A place was set for him every meal but breakfast. He didn't always turn up, but he knew he'd be welcomed if he came.

Sam, Charlie, and Tim had cleaned out the Rectory after Watmore left, finding much in there that was obviously not belonging to the previous occupant. Some named items were returned to their owners. The entire village decided to assist in the refurbishment of the Rectory. So Hugh had moved into a freshly redecorated building. The past had been erased, and he had a fresh start. "Hugh, you are perfect for our new plans," And he was.

Sam sat through Hugh's first sermon grinning widely. Alice had taken Eddie for the sermon, and Sam sat holding Anne's hand with their fingers interwoven.

As they had entered the church that morning, each person was handed a small slip of paper. It was folded, and they were told not to open it until they were asked to.

Hugh spoke on evangelising. He asked everyone if they knew what that was. He watched as most of the congregation shake their heads. "Evangelising is telling people about God and the good news of Christ. It's how to share your faith."

He then asked everyone to open the slips of paper. There were two shortlists on each one. He explained, "This was how to talk to others about God and Jesus. How to talk about the most important decision in your life you will ever need to make. I want you to memorise them." Hugh continued, "If you follow these five simple guides, they will help you remember how to talk to anyone about God and Jesus."

1. GOD   2. MAN   3. GOD   4. What if you do?   5. What if you don't?

"See? That's not that hard, is it?" Hugh explained that if they followed these simple steps, anyone could share their faith. Even if you are blind or can't read. He instructed everyone to keep this instruction in the pockets of their coats. Then he went on to expand his words.

*1. God Created the world; how? – Well, it doesn't matter; we are not called to understand **how** He did it, only believe that He **did** do it. He made it perfect.*

2. Mankind sinned and stepped out of God's will. So evil entered our world.

3. God makes a pathway back to Him through Jesus, who died to take our sins, and therefore we are forgiven, thus restoring the balance.

4. We either believe it, and accept His forgiveness.

5. We reject it and believe there is nothing else and that living is pointless, condemned forever to nothingness.

"Seriously, it's that simple," said Hugh. He fleshed it out a little, but those five things stuck in Sam's head. Sam was thrilled. This was just what he wanted. Someone who truly believed. Hugh spoke in such a way that everyone from the small children upwards could understand.

~

Six months on, twelve new children were living at Meldon Hall as well as Danny's four.

Within the year, changes were beginning to be made to some of the larger rooms. A school was started in the upper rooms of the North wing as Sam had always wanted. The music room was deemed too small, so they used one of the large sitting rooms in the old wing. The children were well fed and loved.

Anne discovered that many had never had a loving hug. Now they had many. The newly employed staff showered the small mites with more love and attention than they could believe. Some were initially unsure of the physical touch, but they responded when they saw the other children cherished and hugged. They blossomed. It worked both ways, and the staff, too, were loved back. Most had never had a brand-new set of clothing, now they had many. None could read, and one by one, they began to flourish. Victor and Thea were often seen hugging a crying child.

Both knew the loneliness of their positions and the desperate need for such affection. One significant change Sam instigated was that he encouraged staff to be allowed to marry. He said to his thirty-two-year-old butler, "Victor, any staff members who wished to marry can stay on working." Sam would be happy with that. Also, that staff children would be welcomed to the clan.

Victor was so stunned he stood silently. Servants didn't marry. It just wasn't done. "Do you mean that if I wanted to marry, I could? Really, Mr Sam?"

"Yes, that's what I mean, so for goodness' sake, go and ask Thea, will you? You look at each other as I look at Anne." Sam grinned at his stunned face. "You can also then become house-parents if you'd care to."

Victor nodded. "You know?" Victor asked, amazed.

Sam nodded, "I've been in your shoes, Victor. We're not that different. What right have I to control your happiness? I hope she says yes. If she has qualms, send her to Anne."

Victor mumbled thanks and waited until Sam left before he went and hunted for Thea. Their relationship had already progressed beyond walking out. Now he could propose.

The next time Sam saw him, Victor nodded to him, followed by a grin. "Thanks, Mr Sam, she said yes."

"Good! Work out new rooms with Graham. Hugh will do the honours, I presume. Take the afternoon off, and both go and see him as soon as you're ready. Victor – we're happy to stand as witnesses if you'd like." Victor was so overwhelmed, so much so he could only nod thanks. The lump in his throat precluded further conversation.

A month later, Sam and Anne were witnesses at their wedding, Hugh presided in a private ceremony. Sam was surprised to hear Thea had never actually been married but took the title of Missus when she grew old enough to work as a housekeeper.

Graham had arranged an entire apartment for them. They were staggered when Graham had said to them when showing their new married quarters, "Mr Sam said you may not need to move then if you have children yourselves." He grinned at Victor and offered his congratulations.

One person who regularly visited, almost daily, was Sir Tim. Robbie, his eldest son, often came; and his youngest daughter Georgina accompanied him on most visits. She was now twenty and a delightful down to earth young lady. Danny began to look forward to her visits and realised that he was now in a position to broach the subject of any possible interest she may have in him. It was some eighteen months since Vanessa died. He thought that before he spoke to her, he should ask her father. So on their next visit, Danny looked for an opportunity. It came just after lunch. "Sir Timothy, I was wanting to talk to you if I may. It's about Georgina." Danny was anxious.

"I was wondering if this were the reason for this conversation," Tim said, grinning. "I'm jumping the gun, but if you're wondering if she's interested, then you're in luck; at least if her talking about you non-stop all the way home after each visit means she is, then yes."

Tim's grin was encouraging to Dan. "Yes, sir, it is. I was wondering… that is… um, I wondered if I have your permission to court her? Is that what's done here?" Danny was as anxious as he had been over ten years ago, when at seventeen when he'd asked if Vanessa's father would allow him to walk out with her. It had been some years before he was allowed more.

"Oh, Danny, I could not be happier. You are just the sort of no-nonsense lad she needs. You not only have my permission but my blessing too. She's in the new schoolroom setting up for classes tomorrow. Go find her, lad." Tim was delighted. He knew Georgie was obsessed with the young fellow. He watched the spring in Danny's step as he hastily left the room. There was eleven years between them. Dan had been a widower for over a year and had not intended to remarry, but Georgie was different, and he was thrilled that she also loved his four children, and they adored her. Smiling to himself, he went to find her.

Once Danny left to find Georgie, Tim went looking for Sam to tell him. Victor pointed to the direction and said, "The main library, sir,"

Tim found him sitting in the East wing library and staring at the immense walls of books. He barely acknowledged his presence for some time then said, "Six books, Tim. We had but six blooming books. We had the Bible, three Shakespeare's, John Donne and Diary of Samuel Pepys. That's it! Tim, cast your eyes over all these. Where do I start? I was never allowed in this room when I lived here. I didn't know. I had no idea there were this many books in the world, Tim."

Tim sat next to his younger friend, seeing the worry on his face. As he got to know him better, he saw more of the hurt that was so deep within his soul. He saw that hurt surface soon after he moved back into the house. Rather than talk to Sam about this or even acknowledge an issue, he changed the subject. He had his own hypothesis about some things. Instead, Tim said, "Sam, I just had an interesting conversation with Danny. He's going to ask Georgie for her hand. He has my permission, but I thought I'd better warn you."

This comment certainly succeeded to scare Sam's melancholy away. "What? Oh, Tim, that is absolutely fabulous." He sat upright and looked intently at his friend. His face suddenly alight with joy. "Isn't it?"

Tim nodded, saying, "Yes, fabulous." Grinning at Sam, he added, "I said I'd meet them here; knowing you were somewhere around, I thought they could find us here."

"Tim, there was a while after Vanessa died that I feared for him. He still blames himself for her death. He said it was caused by his carnal lusts. It took months before he realised that it was just the way of life. But, oh, he took her passing hard. Her father, Josh, collapsed after she died, then he died too. Josh was also Danny's boss. Tim, it was such a terrible time. Anne was not coping, and she was failing. Eventually, I had to almost yell at Danny to pull himself together, or his mother would most probably die too. So yes, I'm over the moon," Sam said. He was still looking at the walls of books around him.

"Is Annie around?" Tim asked.

Sam shook his head, "Victor just led me here. This was the section of the house I'd been banned from, by my father. I've asked him to let Anne know where I am and to meet me here as soon as she came in from her walk." Sam shook his head as if to shake off the thoughts. "Tim, I had found a tiny library of ancient books in the old wing when I lived here, some two hundred ancient tomes. I must go there again with her and show her, but Tim, this …" He waved his hands at all the books, "… This is awe-inspiring. All these books, Tim, this is real wealth. Why would he lock me out of this?"

Tim sat in silence for a minute before they heard light footsteps approaching. Anne opened the door saying, "Victor said to meet you in a library and that there are books in … Oh, Sam!" She froze, looking at the thousands and thousands of books on the wall before her. "Sam …" She brushed happy tears from her eyes.

He came and stood beside her and let her look at the walls of leather-bound volumes. "They are ours, love. In all the years I lived here, I was never allowed to enter this room. I've been too busy until today, and I walked in and nearly collapsed. Anne, my love, this truly is wealth."

Tim sat watching the faces of these two dear people. He'd learned so much about life through them. He'd learned about compassion, love, forgiveness; he had re-found his faith because of them too. The simple child-like faith, he knew to be true to Jesus' teaching. He knew that these two were more at home in their tiny cottage than in the fantastic heritage they were now standing in. Their wealth was in family, faith and the passion for both books and dancing of course. As he watched their reaction, he knew that it was time for the next revelation. Georgie's conversation with him on their return visit from their last trip had explained much. Now to see if it were true. Charlie had to be told, as he had to arrange the next meeting, and it would take some arranging.

Chapter 10   Explanations

$\mathscr{T}$he engagement party for the Viscount Clarestow and Miss Georgina Broome-Hall was a Gala event. All the aristocracy of the area were invited; most accepted the invitation. However, all the children of the house and the staff were also invited and came along too. Sam and Annie had also included all the local parishioners and Rev Hugh Williams. They attended *en masse*.

Charlie arrived with Alice and his children, Henry, Tom, Franny, Caro, Rick, and Alice May. They knew Meldon Hall well as they all often visited when Henry lived here for those few months.

Tim and Sophie arrived with all six children. Robert, the heir, was unmarried and pining for a mystery love from some years before; Timothy Cecil, known as TC; Sophia, Adam, Victoria, and their youngest child, Georgie, who was glowing. Still so excited that Danny had actually noticed her. Even more delighted that he returned her affection. Soon this would be her house.

Danny was astounded that he'd fallen in love again. He'd felt guilty that he was betraying Ness for some time, but he and Georgie talked of her, and he realised that this new love was not a betrayal but a new beginning. He was pleased Georgie had met her on his previous visit.

Charlie sought out Tim and to say their special guest had arrived. Charlie had just seen the crested carriage pulling under the portico and went to greet it.

Tim took Sam into the Library. He almost had to drag him into the room, as Sam felt he should greet the newest visitor. There they waited.

Tim had said to him, "Sam, I have an urgent matter to discuss with you, sorry, but it can't wait."

"What's this about Tim? I need to return to prepare for my guests," Sam said.

"No, you don't; you need to be here, and you're now going to get some answers to some questions. Charlie and I discovered this by sheer chance, but well, it was Georgie who first guessed. We've waited until we could introduce you without, well, finding a strange reason for this guest to be here."

They turned when they heard the door open.

Charlie entered first; he was followed by a tall elderly man with greying hair clutching a whale tooth-topped walking stick. He looked intensely familiar, yet Sam knew they'd not met.

Their eyes met and locked.

Neither moved; they barely even breathed. This man looked more like Sam than any portrait hanging on the walls. Sam walked to the man who'd just entered. Yet his eyes moved to Charlie, then back again.

"Who...? What...? Who are you, sir?" Sam whispered, almost unable to voice the words. He saw an older version of himself.

"I, Sam am a weak man who was too afraid to acknowledge something I had done sixty years ago, when I was twenty, and have regretted it every day of my life, until today. For it's taken me until my eightieth birthday to meet my oldest son."

Sam gasped but let him finish.

"Anne Corbett Garney, your mother, was the love of my life. I am James, Duke of Malvern, from Malvern Hall across your eastern border and, Sam, I am your father. Anne, your mother, was my lover. I ... um, we got caught out by Garney, and I could never see her again. I tried for over three and a half years, and then she was gone. I never even got to see you up close until you were sent to school. I used to watch you from a distance when you played sport at school. I saw every single game, Sam, you played. I could never even acknowledge you, but I loved you from afar. Anne died when you were three; only then did I marry. Until then, I hoped something would happen to Philip and that we could marry." He paused, gathering his thoughts. "Samuel, you are my son, and I never knew how badly you were treated until it was far too late. I'm so sorry, so very, very sorry. I have loved you from afar for all these years. I have done what I could without making the situation worse for you."

Sam opened his mouth to speak, but the Duke put his hand up to silence him.

"When you were imprisoned, I had you shipped out quickly as I saw the conditions you were in at the gaol. I made sure you were not in a chain gang when you went to New South Wales. When your time was over, and I tried to find you, but you'd gone. I had people hunting for you for some eighteen months. My sources couldn't find you anywhere. We knew your paperwork had been processed, but you'd vanished. When we did track you down after another year, you'd married Annie, and she was expecting Danny. So, I kept watching you, unable to assist you in any way. I was so tempted to write to you. I started many times, each one ended up in the fire. It's not the thing you can exactly put down in a letter, so I left well alone." The Duke had sunk into an armchair. "When Danny arrived over here last year, I knew the truth would finally win out, for he is the image of my own son Johnathan, or Nathan as I call him. At the garden party, Nathan's wife, Phoebe, picked it in an instant, as he was the image of me when I was young. I knew Nathan would realise as soon as we were together. You are not unlike me yourself, son. But there is more to the story."

Sam was totally speechless.

That's why his father hated him because he wasn't his.

Sam went from stunned, to amazed, to chuckling, in a matter of minutes. His face suddenly broke into a wide grin. He sank back onto the floor on his *derriere* and chuckled, then gave a deep belly laugh. "Sir, this is the best thing that you ever could have told me. I am thrilled. Absolutely blooming-well thrilled. Your story has explained my entire life." Sam looked to Tim, and grinned, "Get Anne, Tim. Now please."

Relief washed over the Duke's face, and he finally smiled and released a deep sigh.

Tim hastened to leave the room and find Annie.

She, however, had seen Sam's hasty departure and was waiting outside.

Tim ushered her into the room quickly and shut the door again.

She saw her husband in his evening attire, sitting on the floor at the feet of an old man and laughing. She could only see the back of the old man's head. She walked towards Sam.

When he saw her, he reached out for her hand. "Anne, my beloved, come and meet my father. My real father and therefore your father-in-law," Sam said excitedly. He was grinning so widely his teeth sparked in the candle lights.

"What? Huh? How?" Anne walked to the side of her husband. She finally saw the face of the elderly man in front of him. She gasped. "But you're dead," she exclaimed.

"No, my Anne joy, this is the Duke of Malvern, but he and my mother ... well, I think you can work out that bit. I think this has answered all our questions, and I am at peace. This explains absolutely everything." Sam's face was relaxed.

She looked from one face to the other. She gasped in awe. "Ohhh," then she, too, chuckled.

A few comments were made before the Duke said, "Dear ones, there is more to this saga, and indirectly it involves Charlie and Tim. Please sit, everyone, as this bit will be a shock to you all. So please let us make ourselves comfortable."

In the library, the five now made themselves comfortable. "Annie, my dear, come sit with your father-in-law, for I need you close. Sam, don't look so concerned; she is *not* mine." He took a deep breath. "The reason my Anne and I were able to have a liaison is that the Earl was himself involved deeply with another local lady. They were not so discreet, and I saw them meet at the Folly quite often. As you know, it's visible from the roadway into the estate as well as other vantage points. You would have passed it as you entered. I knew this left the way clear for me, and I arranged to meet my Anne elsewhere. Well, you do not need more details about that; suffice it to say your mother fell pregnant with you, Sam, and at that same time, the Earl's lady also fell pregnant. Her husband had removed to London some months before this occurred. They covered it well for some five months, then she 'went on holiday'. However, Anne, having been caught in the same situation, could not hide it for long. Her husband must have realised her condition and one day he followed her. We were caught, um, *in flagrante delicto*, in the act, if you will. You can, of course, imagine the scene; it was not pleasant. He barely allowed us time to dress, he dragged her home crying. Both ladies were by this time some five months pregnant or more. The Earl's child was born not far from here, in the Dower House, and later placed in the orphanage nearby when the baby was some months old."

"The lady named her child…" he looked at Annie, "Annabella, partially as a derivative of her own name. The child's father cared for her greatly, almost idolising the little girl. He even visited her often while she was little, donating funds for her care and upkeep. He seemed to adore the little girl, visiting frequently. When aged twelve, the child was placed in a good house where she could be watched over and provided for. However, we gather it was almost too much for the child's mother, having her so very close. Although, I hear she, too, adored the child, even encouraging her to play with her own older daughter. After some three years, something must have occurred, and the child was transferred to their London home; I don't really know why, but suddenly she was gone from the area. This happened when she was fifteen, and for two years or so, everything just jogged along. Her mother visited often; then, during one visit, she must have been informed of something that horrified her. Her husband had been sneaking the girl into his room at nights." The Duke patted her hand, for he could see she understood the implications of his words.

Anne's eyes left his face and flew to Sam's. Tears welling in her own, for this, was her own story. She brushed them away, eager to hear more.

Sam knew this part of her story too.

The Duke paused until she gathered herself.

Letting a sob escape, Anne finally managed to say, "Please continue, sir," she finally said. Swallowing, she clung to the Duke's hands tightly.

"Yes, Anne, you, my own daughter-in-law, are the Earl's child. So, in reality, Danny is in his rightful place after all. Charlie, Tim, I know this to be true as I have followed her life until she too disappeared. When I found out who Sam had married, I was utterly delighted." He relaxed back into his seat. "The saga is now complete. Sam, my dear boy, your re-purposing of this place is apt, is it not?" He looked from his son's face to the faces of the three others in the room.

All were stunned at the latest revelation.

"Well, I never!" Charlie exclaimed.

Tim had a look of empathy on his face as he said, "Annie girl, I swear Sir Cecil never knew. He would have told me, I'm sure." Tim said. "He would never have touched you if he had, I'm sure of that."

Anne caught Tim's compassionate look and smiled at him reassuringly.

Sam went to his wife, taking her in his arms as she sat next to his father. "My beloved Anne, I am so sorry. For you to be his daughter, though ..." He was still stunned at what had been revealed. "For us to both meet and marry on the other side of the world. Anne, it's no wonder he moved heaven and earth to have your conviction overturned, and it's no wonder he had sway over your mother so she would do it for him. For I gather that the lady was Lady Broome-Hall?"

The Duke nodded.

The enormity of the Duke's revelation hit her, and she turned to Sam and sobbed into his shoulder for a short while, but in moments it turned into wet giggles. She lifted her face to his, and he saw her eyes twinkling with joy. "Sam, I'm a Broome-Hall and a Garney; I know who I am. I have what I have always wanted to have for the last fifty years, a name. But regardless of all that, and by far the most important, I am your wife." Regardless of who was watching, she kissed her husband. With Sam now holding her close, she turned to the Duke. "I'm speaking for Sam, but sir, we want to get to know you better, much better. And we won't take no for an answer. But there is one thing I must do first. Tim, Lady Broome-Hall is still alive?"

Tim nodded, "Yes, she is well, although she seems frail."

"Then I am well overdue for a visit, don't you think? For I'm not asking permission, but I would like you near me." She gave Sam a wet grin. "I need answers, and I'm determined to get them before it's too late."

"As if I would let you go alone," Sam said.

The Duke said, "She knows about you, Sam, so that is no secret to her. You can be open with her about that. What a complex situation? However, I am glad you have both taken the news in this way. I suggest that I stay the night; I shall plead age and beg a bed for the night. But for now, we have the engagement of my grandson. Let us join them. Tomorrow they can be told the entire story. Tim, Charlie, it's up to you two how far you want this known. Sam, for us, I'm proud to be your father, but you are an Earl and me, well, I'm a Duke, so in public, I should be 'Sir' or 'Lord James', in private I'd love to be 'Father' if I could ask." The questioning, pleading look in his eyes delighted Sam.

"On one condition, Father. I would dearly love a loving hug, for I have never had one from any father." Sam stood in front of the elderly gentleman and drew him to his feet and then into his arms.

It was only then Sam wept. Great hacking sobs of the past sixty years escaped from him. Releasing the hate for the man who brought him up, to now accept the man who had loved him always. Tears of acceptance and of love.

The Duke wept quiet tears of joy.

Anne herself was sitting astounded at the revelations she'd just heard about. She felt a tear or two trickle down her cheeks as she watched her husband's first loving paternal embrace. She was the daughter of the Earl. She now knew who her parents were. She also now knew she was of equal birth to Sam. She smiled, precisely equal, and their plans for the house would be perfect. They yet had to tell Danny. Her eyes flew to Tim. How would he feel knowing his daughter was to marry the son of two illegitimate children? Both were also, in essence, convicts.

"Annie, I can see what's just occurred to you. I know your face well enough to read your thoughts," Tim said gently.

Sam pulled from his father's arms. "Cripes, Danny! We have to tell him before the announcement." He wiped his face.

The Duke sat down again, somewhat overwhelmed himself.

"No, we don't; we'll tell him tomorrow," Tim said. "Georgie already knows. Well, your side of it anyway, Sam. For it was she who put one and one together and encouraged us to arrange tonight's meeting, even to writing the wrong time on the Duke's invitation. She guessed when she first met Danny as he was standing near Nathan last year. She doesn't care, and neither do I. You both deserve everything that's come your way, and neither Charlie nor I am in any way jealous."

Charlie sat next to Tim shaking his head. "I have enough to do at home; there's no way I'd want this millstone around my neck. What's more, it is still in his family, and I think it's why he wanted you back, Sam. If you'd married anyone else, I think he may have disinherited you as he said." Charlie was grinning from ear to ear. "His blood grandson will inherit after all."

Charlie thought about how Henry treated the place during the few months he lived here, party after party. He said to Sam, "I'm thrilled for you both, actually. I had no idea about Annie's story, though. The sly old devil he was. Apparently, what was good for the goose was not good for the gander."

Sam came to Annie and took her hand. "Well, my dear, our bloodlines are good, but the family trees may take some explaining. Our grandchildren, though, might not need to know all the details." He bent and kissed her, then offering her his arm; they stood waiting for the others.

The Duke sat bouncing his walking stick between his knees; he was smiling from ear to ear. "Now we've been here too long. I think we'd better go and announce my grandson's engagement." He stood, then with his hand rested lovingly on Sam's shoulder, the Duke said to his oldest son. "Sam, just one more thing, I love you. I always have, be assured of that." Then, without further ado, he turned to lead them all back to the arriving guests.

Sam left the room grinning. For the first time in his life, he felt as though a weight of rejection had been lifted from his shoulders. He swallowed the lump in his throat and followed his father from the room with Anne now on his arm. "His father," he couldn't believe it. He just grinned.

Sam and Anne took their places at the door and welcomed all the guests as they arrived. Charlie and Tim hovered, making sure they were coping.

Victor announced everyone as they arrived.

The evening passed in a blur for Annie and Sam. The revelations had unsettled them both. They knew how Danny had taken the news of the Earldom was how was he going to accept the information of what he'd learn on the morrow. But for tonight, he was happy. The little girls played with their new friends, and the room was filled with colour and laughter. Tim and Sophie made the announcement of the engagement. Standing close to them when it was made were Sam and Annie.

The Duke came and stood next to Sam, and though a few recognised a resemblance and raised a few eyebrows, no one said anything. They smiled and nodded, understanding dawning on some of their faces. Most there knew Sam's story and also of his rejection by the Earl.

Annie looked up at handsome husband, "Dance with me, my wonderful Sam, for now, I am not ashamed of my lowly beginnings. I told you I always danced to my own tune; I just never realised that it was a dance made for two. We were meant to be together."

The Duke heard her comment and smiled.

Sam swept her into his arms, and they danced around the stunningly decorated Grand Ballroom of the Great North Wing. The thirty-piece orchestra played dance tunes, one after the other. Sam did not let her go.

Anne was wearing one of her two magnificent ball gowns. It was a sapphire blue gown and had a pure white lace overskirt draped over the skirt dropping at the back to a train. The vivid blue made her eyes shine brighter than they normally did. Happiness shone from both their faces as they only had eyes for each other.

Danny noted their happiness and smiled, a feeling he knew well.

The following day, after a late breakfast, Sam ushered Dan into his office.

The Duke was already waiting for them. He was clutching his walking stick firmly.

Annie was due to enter in a few minutes with Georgie and Tim. Sam knew this would shock Dan and needed to break it alone, except for his father.

The Duke sat unobtrusively in the corner.

Dan glanced at him on entry, but other than a swift nod, concentrated on his father.

"Sit down, Daniel," Sam said seriously, pointing to the leather-covered settee near the Duke.

Dan sat silently; he wasn't often called by his full name, especially by his father.

"Dan, last night, certain revelations were made that, although won't change things legally, affect us all." Sam was getting tongue-tied. "Um, well …"

"Want me to take over, son?" the Duke asked.

Sam nodded.

Dan noted the last word and drew a quick breath.

"I'll not beat around the bush lad, in simple words, Daniel, I am your grandfather, not the previous Earl," the Duke said bluntly.

Dan opened his mouth to speak, and the Duke put his hand up to silence him. The Duke smiled at Danny. "Before you utter a single word, listen to the story. However, before I tell it, son, get the others ... and bring Georgie too." Sam opened the door and beckoned in the waiting family members.

Georgie came in first and sat beside Danny, clutching his hand tightly.

He went to say something, but she hushed him. A micro frown crossed his face. He hated situations like this.

The Duke told Dan what he'd told his parents last night. Adding only that he was surprised that it had taken so long for someone to catch on. "Dan, you are the image of my other son, Nathan. One day you'll both get to meet all your cousins and know that all I say is true. Nathan has known for more than a year. Since I heard Dan was coming here last year, actually. His wife guessed as soon as she met you, Dan. It's just as well I told him the morning of that garden party at our place, just before it started." He turned his attention back to Dan. "When we met last year, I thought you'd guess yourself."

"No, sir, I had no idea at all," Dan replied.

"Oh, lad, when you dressed down Watmore, I could not have been more pleased; I was proud of you. I so wished to acknowledge you right then and there, in front of everyone and hug you in front of all watching, but I could not. I had already made provisions in my will and knew Nathan had to know why. I had also written a letter to him explaining the situation. I gave it to him that night. Samuel, my dear boy, you are my eldest son, and I have always been proud of you. Nathan is some five years younger, and Gracie is two years younger again. Their mother, Adelaide, died over ten years ago. I told her soon after we married. So, she always knew about you. It's why I could get away to watch you play sport. She even came with me sometimes. We were tempted to introduce ourselves, but you may have guessed. While the Earl was alive my hands were tied."

Daniel sat mute. Way beyond anger, hurt, wonderment, or any other emotion, just dumbfounded.

Tim added, "Georgie was the one who put all the pieces together, Danny. However, it had to come from the Duke; we could only guess. Last night we invited him early, hoping he'd spill the beans. He did, but far more than we ever knew," Tim said.

Dan put his arm around Georgie and drew her to him. "You knew and said nothing?"

"No, Danny, I guessed, but it's not exactly the thing you can say to your fiancé, is it? Oh, 'and did you know your father is the illegitimate son of the Duke of Malvern?' I wasn't even sure it was true, but Danny, you look like Nathan, far too much." She snuggled to him. "It changes nothing for me."

Dan looked at the faces of both his parents. "There's more, isn't there? I know you both too well. However, this explains so much, doesn't it, Father. That letter, the Earl never calling you 'Dear' or 'Son'. Just vicious demands. Yes, this explains much."

"Yes, son, you're right; there's more," Sam said. "Father, will you continue, please? I do so love the sound of that," he said, grinning.

"Yes, son, so do I." The Duke's walking stick was held gently, and he bounced it occasionally as he spoke. "Okay, so to continue ..." The Duke retold his story, "Your grandmother had been totally ignored since the conception of Nigel, the Earl's son. The Earl had done his duty, and there, his attention finished. As you may gather, it was not a love match, but an arranged one. They disliked each other on sight, but that is by the way. She provided him with the required heir. Then he left her completely alone. I married Adelaide for much the same reason."

The Duke filled Dan in on more of his story, adding, "I knew I had a son, Anthony told me that, but I could not see him." The Duke saw a frown of puzzlement cross his face. "He's your father's groom Dan. He was my eyes and ears. Oh, I want you to know I loved her so much." The Duke wiped his eyes and smiled wanly. His stick now stilled but held gently. He then told Danny and Georgie about Anne's history, adding, "Philip made sure his daughter was well cared for, and he supplied her with warm clothing and even built her a swing, according to Anthony. I know of this as he had to drive him over to the orphanage to deliver them each year. More he felt he could not do. All this I only know from Anthony. When she was twelve, she was placed into service at Broome-Hall Manor."

Daniel gasped, knowing his mother's story.

"Yes, Daniel, the Earl's daughter is your mother. The story is muddied, and you may know more from her, but the next contact the Earl had with his daughter was when he was both horrified and delighted to find that Sam and Annie had married. He was able to get her mother to quash the conviction somehow, and ..." He paused, watching Dan's face.

"Your mother is Lady Broome-Hall? But she was the one who accused you of theft," Dan said, aghast.

The Duke answered. "Yes, she is your mother's mother. Earl Philip somehow got her to admit that she'd trumped up the charges and have Annie's conviction overturned. This is the section that still puzzles me, for up until then, she adored you, Annie. Well, the Earl moved on your situation as soon as he could. No child of his was going to be known as a convict. This would all have been about the time Nigel died. We think Earl Philip must have had no idea what had happened to her as he made no attempt to assist her for ages, then suddenly, they seemed to have acted. We all thought she must have travelled with Sir Cecil and then died. However, when Nigel died, Philip knew he must acknowledge Sam as heir. He did that only after he knew whom your father married and that he had a son." The Duke fell silent.

No one spoke. All were digesting the information just heard.

Georgie took Dan's hand and brought it to her lips. "Danny, we're going to have the most loving orphanage in all of England. All the children here will be loved and cuddled and everything your own parents were unable to have. We can do this, Danny. Please let me help," she pleaded.

It was too much for Dan. He turned to her and gathered her into his arms. "It's too much to grasp," he whispered. That was all he managed to say for some time. There were no tears, just stunned confusion that he was not who he thought he was, yet he was still the bloodline heir.

Sam and Annie knew how he felt. They were both still in shock. They were both loved children, born to the wrong parents. For them to be led to take in abandoned illegitimate children of the nobility and bring them up as they should have been was now a project they were proud of. They smiled knowingly at each other. Anne snuggled close to Sam. Sam then catching Tim's then Charlie's eye, he smiled.

Danny finally spoke. "Sir, when we met before, you stood by and supported me even then. I liked you from the first. Now I don't just like you – I love you. I've never said that to another man other than my own father. To say I'm stunned is a vast understatement, but it now all makes complete sense. Father that letter." He shuddered. "And Sir Tim, I think that Sir Cecil was told who she was by Lady Broome-Hall. I think that's why he could not …" he left that sentence unfinished. "Cor, Mama, she's still alive." He'd swung around to his mother.

"Yes, son, she is, and we're going to visit her soon. The Duke, Pa, Charlie and Tim are coming with us. Georgie, I'll need you to stay and look after things here. Can you do that for me?" Annie looked at her future daughter-in-law.

"Willingly, Cousin Anne," she grinned. "I can't wait to hear what she has to say for herself." Georgie snuggled closer to Dan. "She certainly has some explaining to do."

"Ooh yes, that makes us cousins of sorts, I suppose, doesn't it?" Anne herself gasped.

"Not exactly Annie, as I'm Sir Cecil's nephew, related through him, not Lady Marianna Broome-Hall," Tim said. "So, I think we'll drop the cousin poppet," he said to his daughter.

"Annie, my dear, there is one more thing you should know. You were Baptised here when you were a week old. The Chapel at the Hall has your Baptism record, as I snuck a look at it this morning when I went for my morning prayers. You were Baptised as Annabella Phillipa Joy Garney White and were not Baptised alone as on the same day two-week-old Samuel James Corbett Garney was Baptised with you. You were born only a week apart and both on this estate."

"What? My name is Annabella Phillipa Joy?" she said, "I have a real name and a birthdate?"

"Yes, your father chose it. He apparently insisted on the 'Joy' being added, Jenkins said. Sadly, I have to tell you that Watmore Baptised you both, so he knew their secrets all these years. The Annabella or 'beautiful Anne' was a mix of Marianna; remember I said it was a derivative of her name? Philip was the Earl's name. Remember I said Jenkins was the only one who knew about us, Sam. And remember I said I never saw your mother again. It's true, but we did, however, write, and Anthony Jenkins delivered the letters. She told me where she kept the letters; if you look in her large travelling jewellery case, there is apparently a secret compartment at the back with my letters in it. I doubt the Earl found it, but that's where she told me she kept them as they never travelled, and she therefore never used it for jewellery. By the way, Jenkins, Anthony is his name, carried our letters as often as we could write them. Then they stopped. He brought me the news she'd died. She'd not been able to leave her room since you were born. I don't know what she actually died from. But I know she was too weak to stand in the end. I knew a lot about you then, about you both actually. Anthony often added some tidbits of his own when delivering them. I wanted my letters back after she died. But I had no way to access the place. I nearly came last year when Henry was here, but it's a bit hard to explain why an elderly Duke would be walking around your house, especially in the private lady's room. So, I stayed away. Please say I don't have to anymore?" Lord James was misty-eyed.

"Never, sir, I'd love you to move in. However, that might take some explaining in itself. I shall, however, make up a suite for you so you can stay when you wish. So, you can get to know your grandson and great-grandchildren." Sam took a surprised gasp. "It's just occurred to me. My middle name is James."

The Duke nodded. "Yes, after me, and Samuel, because God heard us."

"Daniel is also named James, and so is little Edmund. When I think of the name meanings, James is 'supplanter', and Edmund is 'Richly protected'. Daniel means 'God is my judge'. My friend who visited me in gaol was named Daniel, and he told me. All are so fitting." Sam smiled at his father.

"More than you know. Sam, I am James Samuel. Your mother knew, as did the Earl. I laughed, though, when I heard what you named your son. Do you not know that Nigel is a French version of Daniel? The Irish version is Neil."

All looked at him, stunned.

Sam shook his head, trying to understand the twisted history. "Nigel snuck me money when he could. Father found out and was livid. So, I told him to stop it. However, he still did when he had spare cash. I never had a problem with him. I suppose I did love him; I was sad when I heard he died. I don't think he ever knew our history."

Dan took Georgie's hand and drew her to the window. "With all these revelations, I cannot think. I just need to hold you, my dear. But before I do, are you sure you will marry into this motley lot?"

"I could imagine nothing better, my dearest love. Remember Danny, it was I who first saw a possible connection. Knowing the hatred, I wondered if there were not more to the story and knew this would explain all." She reached up and pulled his head down to hers and gave him a brief kiss, watched by her father, his parents, grandfather, and Charles. "I am content, my dear. You will have to think of a much better excuse than that to extract yourself from marrying me. Like already having a living wife."

"No, she's dead. But, I will tell you more about Vanessa as with four children I must and will speak of her to our children. I'm glad you got to meet her." He bent and kissed her. "Georgie, Ness was the daughter of a convict builder, a simple girl with no guile. No hidden peers in that line, at least."

Georgie nodded and snuggled into his arms.

The Duke leaned back in his chair. "I think the next years will be an absolute delight to this old man. Sam, I want you to meet my Nathan. He's itching to meet his older brother; he's always wanted one, you know. He can guide you in anything these two can't." The Duke reached out his hand to his son. "I can't abide skeletons. Now they are all out in the open; I can breathe again. Nathan's son will have to be told, but from there, it gets too distant. Sam, did you get the money I gave her? I told her to say it was her father and not part of a marriage settlement. Therefore, the Earl would not be able to touch it. I could do it no other way."

"I did, sir, but only after Henry moved in here last year. Mama's will was hidden in his desk, and Henry found it stuffed at the back of a drawer. I have it, though, father; it's the only money I would touch. The estate money we will spend on the Orphans and the estate, but we will not touch a penny of it, not even now. For all personal expenses, we use your money." He looked at Anne as he spoke.

She agreed. "We shall make over much of it to Danny as it is now yours by right. We have enough. The estate costs can come from it, but personally, neither of us will touch any of it."

"Sir, Mr Pennecuick invested it for me on her death, and the return was over £40,000. So, we have ample. When I think my wage last year was £12." Sam chuckled. "More than sufficient, thank you, Father."

"We'll see what the future brings, Sam. Now is there any chance of tea? With all this talking, I'm parched. Then I think we should all retire to the Chapel to show you what I found in the Baptism register. After we give it a glance, I would not mind if we followed that with a little prayer of thanks. What do you all think?" Lord James grinned; he bounced his walking stick like it had a spring on it. He had a beatific smile on his face.

Sam rose and tugged on the bell-pull.

Victor brought in the tea tray then left. They sat discussing the next visit.

"I need to see her, don't I?" Anne said, showing some anxiety.

The five men all nodded.

"Tim, is she up to it? I have no wish for her to drop dead at my feet." Anne asked with concern in her voice.

"She's hale and hearty. Trust me. I was dealing with complaints from her staff only last week. She now only has a footman of sorts, a rough-looking chap, and a maid. Everyone else has now left." Tim chuckled, thinking of how that meeting would go.

"Fine – then can we all go this afternoon? I want you all with me. I'm not doing this alone, and we're all here." She was holding Sam's hand very tightly.

Tea drunk, they all stood and walked to the Chapel. Anne had not yet been able to find her way there by herself, so she had only seen it once on her grand tour of the house soon after their arrival. They had been so busy every day since then that she'd not thought of it. Sam had asked if Anne wished Hugh do a service at the Hall instead of going down to the village church, but Anne said she'd rather go to the church. She loved the fellowship afterwards and relished the villagers and being able to chat with them.

There was a candle burning in a sconce on the wall as they walked in. From this, Sam lit the rest of the candles until the room was alight and welcoming. Anne stood looking at the warm glow of the stone chapel, the sunlight shining through the stained-glass windows.

The Duke walked to the side of the Chapel and picked up a large ledger. He flicked it open and ran his finger down the page. "Sam, come and see for yourself."

Sam read, "Samuel James Corbett Garney born 12 July 1773; Baptised 26 July 1773." His parents' names were both there. He read the following entry: "Annabella Phillipa Joy Garney White born 19 July 1773; Baptised 26 July 1773."

"White? Father, what's that for on Anne's?" Sam asked.

"Marianna's maiden name was White, so as they weren't married, it was added too as that was her legal surname," his father replied.

Sam and Anne looked at each other and laughed.

"What have I missed?" The Duke said.

"The orphanage called her 'Anne White', and that's what we married as. I was wondering if our marriage was actually legal, but now I know it is. Thank goodness." Sam reached out for Anne.

She walked to him and wrapped her arm around his waist. "Sam, can you believe that it's over sixty years since we were together in here? I didn't even know my birthdate, you know. I just knew it was July 1773. The only thing I have is a hand-knitted white blanket that I was found wrapped in. It's why they gave me the name White, that and the white dresses that arrived yearly. There was no paperwork except a note that read, 'Her name is Anna, born July 1773'. To be back here together is truly amazing." She was emotional but was not weeping.

They all stood in front of the altar, and hand in hand, the Duke led them in a prayer of thanks. After he finished, the others filed out, leaving Anne and Sam standing in the Chapel alone. Both were still stunned by what had been revealed to them the day before.

"Anne, I find it so hard to catch my breath. Is this really happening? I think when we have spoken to your mother, I may be able to swallow the whole. With what we've learned already, there may yet be more to tell." Sam laid his cheek on her sweet-smelling hair.

"Sam, to know who my parents are… well, I still can't get my head around that I actually know who I am. To know that I have known my mother most of my life is even more incredible. When I think back, yes, I feel there is more to her story. For up until then, I swear she liked me. Surely she could not have wanted me in prison though, not if she felt anything for me and apparently she did. I have to know, Sam. I'm still so angry with her. Seethingly angry!"

"I dare say we will find out soon enough, Annie Joy, my beloved," Sam said as he turned her around and led her to the Chapel door. He released her then started snuffing the candles near them. Sam snuffed the remainder of the candles, leaving just the one in the sconce near the door. He bowed his head and gave a final prayer of thanks, and then he turned to leave.

The group gathered in the foyer at two that afternoon, Anne wrapped in an old hand-knitted white wrap.

The Duke greeted them all with, "Ready? It will be interesting to see what this day brings." He took Anne's hand and kissed it lovingly. "Lady Anne, may I escort you to the carriage, please, my dear?" He tucked her hand into the crook of his arm. "Come, my dear." They led the group outside to the porticoed entry. The Earl's crested carriage awaited them.

The Duke greeted the elderly groom at the carriage door. "Thank you, Anthony. It's so nice to see you again. Things will be finally put to rights today."

"Always happy to be of service, Your Grace. The bones are getting on a bit, but I'm pleased that all has turned out well. If the destination is anything to go by, I would not miss this trip for the world, Sir." The seventy-five-year-old retainer stood grinning at Sam. He said nothing more but shrugged and gave him a bit smile.

"Yes, today, all is revealed." The Duke smiled at the man who'd held his secret for so long.

Sam grabbed both his hands. "Thank you, Anthony, for always watching out for me. Now I understand so much more and what was at stake."

Anthony nodded and smiled again. "And I will continue to do so, sir. It's always been my honour."

Danny seated himself silently. Anne and the five gentlemen settled themselves down for the short trip. She was sitting between her husband and father-in-law.

"I'm so frightened, Sam," she whispered. "What happens if it all goes wrong?"

"Then we're no worse off than yesterday, are we? Annie love, we have nothing to lose," Sam said comfortingly.

"Let me go in first, please," Tim said. "Sir, if you would lead the rest in, with Annie, you last. Danny, I know this is going to be difficult but say nothing. You must let her tell you herself. There's a lot more going on here than any of us understand. Some things just don't make sense, and we all need answers."

Dan nodded.

Charlie sat silent, wondering what else they would find out.

Sam felt Annie cling tightly to his arm. She was shaking.

Chapter 11   Long Awaited Visit

The carriage drew up at a quaint, two-story, thatched-roof cottage and a footman of sorts came to the door. He was a scruffily dressed individual. This place was a vast come-down from Broome-Hall Manor. Tim alighted first and said, "Give me five minutes, and then come in. She probably won't be happy, but we won't allow her to say no. No matter what happens, you'll see your mother today, Annie. The Duke and Charlie are to come in first, then Danny, Sam, and Annie, you three last." He walked through the gate, and they watched him walk inside without knocking. They heard him call, "Hello, Aunt Marianna, you have visitors."

The group waited the prescribed five minutes and then followed him inside in the order he'd requested.

Lady Marianna Broome-Hall sat on a settee, beside the fire, under a beautifully hand-knitted old white blanket. She looked sad, gaunt, and shrunken.

Tim stood beckoning them into the sitting room. He introduced them as they entered. "I'd like to introduce you to some people I think you need to talk to, His Grace the Duke of Malvern; Sir Charles Garney; Daniel, Viscount Clarestow; his father, Samuel, Sixth Earl Meldon; and The Countess of Meldon, Annabella Phillipa Joy, whom I believe you may know."

Lady Broome-Hall caught her breath. Then burst out, "Ohh, oh. My darling Anna, my Bella, oh my Joy, I'm so sorry; it was the only way I could protect you." She then clasped her hands over her mouth, aghast at what she'd revealed.

Surprised and shocked at the outburst, Anne stood her ground. She was still seething in anger at what this woman had done to her. Anne wished her eyes would fire daggers at the woman. There was yet way too much she did not understand to forgive anything yet. "Protect me from what, madam? I never harmed you." She huffed in anger, emphasising the last word. With shock, she recognised the brooch the old woman wore and now touched.

"Anne, be gentle," Sam said softly, "Let her speak." He took her hand and ushered her to a chair.

"Fine, but it had better be good," Annie said gruffly. She plopped herself down in the nearest chair and folded her arms angrily.

"Can I ask you all to please take a seat? You're all too tall, and it hurts my neck. Anna, please come sit next to me. No, no, do not argue. You can growl at me later if you wish." The old lady patted the seat next to her.

The men didn't move.

Anne had opened her mouth to say something. She wanted to say no but moved next to the old lady and sat on the settee as far from her as she could. As she sat, she let out a humph of anger, then she folded her arms again. She felt like a petulant teenager rather than a mature woman of over sixty. Anne found she was as in awe of the old lady now as she had been when working for her. Until the day of the accusation, the lady had always been quite kind to her.

The old lady stated quite abruptly, "Tim has explained why you are all here and what you know. However, there is something you do not know; that is why I did what I did. Duke, Sam, boys, sit, please. You lad, I'll speak to you in a bit," she said to Danny as her face softened.

Annie gazed at her in surprise.

She looked at Anne and studied her face intensely. "For forty-three years, Anna, I have prayed for you daily. From the day they took you from me. I won't ask forgiveness, and you will understand why after I have finished speaking. I would do it all again, mayhap somewhat differently, but yes, I would do it again."

Anne and Danny both gasped.

Sam looked puzzled. He knew enough about life to know that whatever occurred must have been dire.

The Duke sat silently with his whale tooth walking stick sitting upright between his knees, both hands clenched tightly on its top; his knuckles were white. His face was unemotional, but Sam knew he was anxious.

Anne saw gleams of love in the old woman's face as she looked at Danny.

There was a gentle knock at the door. The maid brought in a tea tray. Anne looked at her and gasped. "Betsy? Is that really you? What are you doing here?"

"Yes, Annie, it's me, and I'm sorry," she said. "But it was for your own safety, Annie. Truly!"

Anne looked at Sam, puzzled.

Lady Broome-Hall said, "Betsy dear, please pour and take a seat yourself as you're part of this, and it's time for the truth to come out in full."

Betsy nodded, "Yes, ma'am."

They all sat in absolute silence while Betsy poured and handed around the delicate china cups.

There were minute shortbread fans placed on each saucer. The loudly ticking clock and the chink of the cups were the only noises heard in the room for some minutes.

Anne felt like she'd choke on the biscuit if she bit into it.

Finally, Betsy took a cup herself and sat near the window; she was slightly out of the conversation circle.

Odd looks were passing from one to another.

"Right, I know why you all think you are here, but you could not be more wrong. Anna, firstly, I knew what was going on with Ceccy soon after it started. I was not jealous; I was almost pleased for you both. I also knew it started with him teaching you to read, yes, and everything else. Although I was upset that it happened, I understood for both of you. Our marriage was, let's just say, lonely. I figured that you know all that part of the story, or you would not be here, Duke."

Annie looked at the old lady with a stunned look on her face.

Lady Marianna took a sip of her tea. "I want you all to listen and no one to interrupt until I'm finished. Anna, the week before Ceccy left for his long trip, there was a big meeting at the house, wasn't there? Betsy told me of a group of about twenty men who met there, and they had a heated discussion over some political situation. Amongst them was my father, as well as the Earl of Summerville and many others. You were serving them along with Betsy and probably too busy to notice who was there."

Anne nodded. "Yes, but …"

"I said no talking; all will be made clear."

Annie's mouth snapped shut.

Lady Mari looked at her daughter lovingly. "I need to fill you in with all the sordid details, or it will not make sense to you."

Lady Marianna took a deep breath and then continued. "However, I have to go back much further, to when I was thirteen, the week I, um, shall I just say when I became a woman, my father visited my room that same night and enjoyed stealing my innocence and taking great pleasure inflicting much pain on me. The more I struggled, the more he hurt me.

So, I learnt not to struggle. That continued for a week, every month for over four years, for he had learnt I could not get with child at that time of the month. Betsy's mother, Sarah, was my personal maid; the rest of each month, he used her most nights to slake his lusts. She was only sixteen. When I married, Sarah was already pregnant with his child, we didn't tell him. I took Sarah with me when I left, knowing that I needed to get her out of my home too. Ceccy knew all about that. When Betsy was born, she was allowed to stay with her mother, at the Broome-Hall Manor. After I married Ceccy, our three children came in quick succession, barely a year between them, but it kept Father away from me. Ceccy started spending more and more time in London for work, that's when I met Philip and Anne. Anne and I became friends. We were both unhappy in our marriages. Ceccy had moved to London by then, and I was alone and lonely. I really had no intention of starting a relationship, but it sort of just happened. You came along when Betsy was about five."

No one dared even murmur.

She paused for a long breath. She waved her hand in a rolling motion as though to progress through the story. "If you had been born a week earlier, when Sam was born, we three talked about you being brought up as twins, but that didn't happen. I was angry that Philip cut James's any access to Anne, but he would not listen to me. Anna, your father insisted on placing you in an orphanage when you were some months old. I'd been in the Dower house some six months by the time he took you away for me. Anne was very ill after your birth, Sam, and she never recovered. She kept you with her for six months, not letting you out of her sight. It was when Philip took Anna away that he demanded Sammy be sent to the nursery. She wept but understood. He was jealous. She had her love child, and he couldn't. He had said something to her that if both children had been boys, he was going to swap them so he could bring up his own son."

Lord James nearly choked when he heard that.

Lady Marianna met his eyes and knew his sorrow. "That, of course, didn't occur. So, Anna, you were sent away. My heart tore that day. We each visited you often. Each year I made you a new white dress, and I'd sit watched you playing on the swing Philip made for you. Darling Anna, I visited as often as I could. I so wished to hug you and tell you I loved you, but I was bound by society's rules. Philip also watched you and saw you sneak away when you were little and sit under the tree by the creek. He'd make arrangements for you not to be sent to work as other children were. So, he built you a swing there. No other child ever used it. Then, when you were twelve, you came to us to live." Lady Marianna looked so lovingly at Annie that she was stunned.

"You asked for me to come to you?" Anne discovered that she was wanted.

Lady Marianna nodded. "I wanted you close to me." Her voice was so low that she almost sounded embarrassed. "Betsy was seventeen by then, and I encouraged her to be friends with you, and so you became. Mind you, she needed little encouragement. She has always known the full story. She loved you on sight."

Annie looked over to Betsy, who nodded at her.

"Three years later, when you were only fifteen, Ceccy took you both to London as my father was coming for a visit, and we wished to keep you both well away from his reach. Sarah and I knew he had a penchant for young girls, so you and Betsy moved with Ceccy to London. I couldn't risk you even being seen by my father, knowing his reputation. I saw that the inevitable would happen with you and Ceccy, but at least you were not related. With your background, I knew your life would be, well, difficult anyway. I was sad, but I knew he loved you by then, and that alone made it bearable. We were totally living apart by then. I visited London often, but it was to see you, my darling girl."

She took another sip of her now cold tea, gathering her thoughts and emotions. "So let me return to London. Years had passed. That last night Ceccy was there, he had a big political meeting at his house. Unbeknownst to you, my dear, the cream of London's politics was there, plus a few others. That included my father, Julian, Duke of Cheatham; and numerous others, including the Duke of Summerville. He was from Warwickshire, which is where our main family seat was. Ceccy had a hunting lodge nearby, and that's how I knew him. He'd come and hunt with Father. Anyway, Summerville had apparently much the same penchant for the young girls as my father. I heard that he forced his daughter Margaret, or Peg as I knew her, to marry an old friend of his so they could both, um, enjoy her."

The look on Danny's face was one of absolute disgust. To hear all that was being revealed and realise that this was his own great grandfather. He was appalled.

Lady Marianna saw his reaction and whispered, "Sorry, Danny, but you have to hear it all to understand."

He nodded an acknowledgment, knowing she was right.

She continued with the saga. "I had become friends with Peg on those hunts too. The story I later heard is that her husband took to her somewhat violently one night soon after they married, and she pushed him away from her. He fell, hit his head, and he died. Then she was tried for murder and was sent to gaol and then transported. It was so sad as she was so nice. Her younger sister told me when I asked after Peg. So, I was not alone in my suffering."

All but Betsy gasped. Anne's eyes were now locked to her mother's face. She felt the blood drain from her own.

"It was this though, that gave me the idea of how to keep you safe from him, my darling girl." She drew a deep breath again and ploughed on. "My father noticed you, Anna, and it was far more than just scant interest. He spoke to Ceccy about you, asking about your history. Darling Ceccy didn't guess why, although he should have known better. He waxed lyrical about you, my sweet girl. Betsy overheard and realised what would follow. Remember, Ceccy thought you were just a maid. He knew of no other relationship between us at that stage. After he had his stroke, I told him. I had to, Anna and he didn't like what he heard."

Tim caught her glance at him. "That's why he would not let you near him?"

She nodded. "Cec blamed me and for good reason. Darling man, he was horrified at the reality, I suppose that made you his stepdaughter. Betsy had reason to know the entire story. It is as much her story to tell as mine. For, in reality, she is, of course, my half-sister, and it's why she is here with me. She came when Cec died and stayed as Sarah had died. Father took great pleasure in using her too when he found out who she was. I did not know. He was a sadist and also enjoyed inflicting punishment while doing the abuse. He particularly liked the girls young and innocent."

Anne swung around and looked at Betsy aghast.

Betsy met her eyes with a nod. "He took to my Ma, if you get my meaning, Annie, when she reached her womanhood. She were just a girl. He was violent and abusive with us servants. Few of us girls escaped his notice. According to Mama, he employed young girls and then sacked them when they fell pregnant with his children. Mama would have been let go if Lady Mari had not taken her when she left. A few months after Lady Mari married, my Ma had me at Broome-Hall Manor. Mr Ceccy knew who I was. Ma'am had told him everything and why Mama was being brought in her condition. I'm not really sure if he believed her though, or he may not have been quite so keen to talk about you. Annie, I have reason to know this is true. Just before you came to live with us, it was my turn. I was only seventeen and innocent as a lamb too. I fell pregnant with his child but thankfully lost it early." Betsy was watching Anne digest the information.

"You're my aunt?" Anne asked, absolutely astounded at what she'd just heard.

Betsy shrugged and nodded. "I suppose I am, but I'm still your friend, I hope."

Anne felt light-headed and nodded. She could not stop the tears that now freely flowed down her cheeks. She shook her head in disbelief. This is not what she'd expected to hear. She felt ill.

Lady Marianna continued, "Anyway, back to the story."

"There's more?" Annie muttered.

Lady Marianna nodded, "Yes, more. The next day Ceccy left for his Asian trip. Father arrived and asked the butler for you. Thankfully you'd gone shopping and were not at home for some hours as Betsy had given you a half-day off. So the next day, he came back again. This time, Betsy had you cleaning out the attic rooms, remember? I arrived as soon as I could. I'd had to see Philip before I came, and it took time as he'd been away somewhere. I couldn't very well march in and say what was happening to our daughter, could I? It took me nearly three weeks to get to London. Betsy was at her wit's end by the time I arrived. You'd cleaned absolutely everything. She even got you doing the coal cellar that last day, do you remember?"

Annie nodded.

Lady Mari smiled. "While you did that, Father was sitting upstairs waiting for you. He was lusting after you and was furious at your absence. When you didn't appear, Father announced to Betsy that he was coming to stay the next day. I arrived just after he left. Anna, I couldn't protect you any longer. I had to send you away, and it broke my heart, but I would not let him near you; I know what he was like. I fully expected that one day he'd kill some girl, but I never heard if he did. Anything in a skirt was fair game; trust me, I know. He seemed to take even more pleasure if he was related to the girls. Some of the other staff at home had daughters whom he abused too. Knowing who you are would have made little difference, so telling him would have only made the chase sweeter. The only way was to get you well out of his reach. That meant sending you to the colony as a convict as Peg had been."

Annie gasped again. No wonder the lady cared for her.

"Anna, dear, I'm so sorry, but I made sure you were safe with Mrs Tremaine. She is the sister of a friend of mine. I wrote to her often about you and she to me. I paid her well to employ you. Then Timmy got everything else sorted. He had no idea of my secret, but I ensured you had access to the money Ceccy wanted you to have. I knew Tim had been told by Ceccy to buy you a house and see you looked after that, but I couldn't very well give you money without them asking why. Sorry, Timmy, but I needed Betsy to listen to your conversations so I could have things ready for you. So, I brought a wad of cash and accidentally left it with Ceccy on one of my visits. I had not told him at this stage. Annie, over half of it came from your father and a half from me. I made sure that the land Timmy got you was heavily subsidised. Philip paid £20 for it here, and you paid the rest. It wasn't much, some £12 or £15, I believe, and you were safe."

She saw Annie nod but she stayed silent.

"If we left you much more, questions would have been asked, and we were still trying to avoid that. Being a convict, Father could not bring you back. Philip sorted the rescinding of the charges as soon as Father died. I had already signed a withdrawal of the accusation, just in case anything happened to me. As soon as my father died, we submitted the paperwork the next day, actually, even before he was buried. I think overall you were better off there than here. Sadly, Nigel died soon after; Philip was shattered. Your grandfather was an absolute creep, Anna. I married Ceccy to get away from him; Ceccy knew from my bruises and welts on my back that my father had abused me severely for the weeks before we married. We even waited for a month before we consummated our marriage to ensure I was not carrying Father's child. He had had fun with me the week before our wedding, not caring if I fell pregnant then; as a child could then be explained away. He took all his debauched anger out on me in full that last week."

Lord James wiped his cheek. This explained so much.

Lady Marianna drew her breath like a dry sob when remembering her evil father. "Ceccy and I had the three children and then went our separate ways. But he was gentle and even affectionate, but we did not love each other. It's the deal we struck when we married. He needed an heir, a spare and an extra if I wished, so I had Amelia Elizabeth. I admit I was not maternal with them, as they were not conceived in love, and I was sad when both the boys died, but when Timmy inherited, I was actually delighted, as I had always liked him. The boys had got themselves mixed up with the fast set, and it destroyed their own lives. Henry had a wife and daughter, Mildred, and she went home the day after he died. I've not seen either her or their daughter since. Now I think of it, I wonder if Father had at her too? Anyway, thankfully, Amelia took my advice and moved far away. I encouraged her to marry her Scottish Baron. Ceccy did see that her grandfather was never allowed near her. I insisted she marry early and for love. She met a Scottish Baron at her Presentation Ball and married him soon after. His name is John Macdonald. They have two sons, Fergus and Hamish, and John calls her Elspeth."

She sighed. "Although I've not seen her for years, she was safe in Scotland and was away from your grandfather. Thankfully she writes often, so do her boys." She chuckled, "Amelia is blonde and John a redhead, so I bet the boys are both redheads, but I have not met either of them. She does not know about you; at least, I don't think she does. She will remember you, though, from when you were young. I will tell her if I may?"

Annie nodded; she had tears welling in her eyes; she had forgotten about Amelia Elizabeth. She had a half-sister. They'd been allowed to play with her occasionally when she came from the orphanage. Amelia was a year older than her. She nodded again. "I'd love her to know. I'd love to meet her again one day too. I adored her when I was first at the Hall. She married soon after I moved to London." She turned to Sam, "Can we visit her?"

He nodded.

Lady Marianna was sitting straighter, and the stress that had been visible on her face on their entry was easing. "Good, now where was I? I told Betsy to put this in your drawer." She touched the ruby heart brooch on her chest. "Philip gave it to me when you were born. I wear it every day. I got it back after the court case and pinned it over my heart, and one day I shall wear it out as I continually am touching it. It will be yours when I'm gone, Anna. To use this as my weapon was a double-edged sword, but it had meaning. I knew you'd get to see it, recognise it, and even hopefully hold it. Anna, I saw you in gaol from a distance when Betsy visited and then again when you walked onto the ship. I was completely hooded and collapsed into Philips's arms as you disappeared from view. I never thought to see you again. I supplied a coat for you in gaol, and Betsy brought you the white blanket I had made you. The one you now wear. It matches this one. Betsy had found it in your room. I didn't know you had been allowed to keep it at the orphanage. Betsy was allowed to bring them to you; we had put some coins in the pockets just to ease things for you. I'm glad they got to you, but you were now out of your grandfather's reach. Oh, Anna, I'm so sorry."

Annie could hardly breathe.

Lady Marianna wiped away a tear with a sob. She sniffed in a very unladylike way and wiped her eyes with the backs of her hands. "Years passed, Mrs Tremaine wrote so I knew what you were doing. Then the seven years were up for you both, but some months apart. Ceccy had died some years before. He was so angry with me he wouldn't talk to me. He said I should have told him about you, and he would have kept you safe, even from himself. It was more disgust at himself, as he felt I should have told him you were my daughter. After he died, I knew Tim was out there for some months working for the Government, and Mrs Tremaine told me what he was doing for you. I sent her some money while you were with her, and she told me she gave you some when you left. Sam too, was due for release, but Philip told me they soon lost track of him. He had someone watching over him while there."

Sam's eyes lit up. "Yes, that was Major Tom Turner. He is a friend of mine, and he's renting our house. I recognised his accent as coming close to home. I was surprised he wanted to be friendly with me, as I was a convict at the time. I found out from Tim there was someone and worked out it would probably be Tom. Then the lawyers confirmed who it was, I laughed. Tom's a good bloke, and I was happy for him to watch over us," Sam said. "It was the first time I had a twinkling of the possibility of care of any sort."

"Good, I'm glad you know about Tom; he's, yes, a nice lad." She had another sip of her tea as she met the Duke's eyes. "Now to continue. We had lost you, Sam, as I gather you had too, Duke?"

The Duke nodded. He bounced his stick occasionally; his knuckles were no longer clenched on its top. "I, too, had someone watching over you, lad."

Sam smiled and wondered if it were Ned as he'd appeared out of virtually nowhere.

"Philip knew you'd been assigned to West's farm. Tom couldn't get much detail but knew you were not in a chain-gang and were still alive. Nigel then died, and Philip was shattered that you would have to inherit after all. He told me of his threat to you, but it was just that and said in anger. I told him how hypocritical he was."

Sam met and held his father's eyes. "On release, I fell ill from sleeping rough. I had nothing but the rags on my back. I slept in the bush for a long, long time and drank from puddles and creeks. I fell ill with inflamed lungs. I could barely breathe. I was in the hospital for a very long time too. I actually have no idea how long. Ma'am, on release, I just wished to die," Sam said, tearing his gaze from his father to his wife. "Anne will tell you the state I was in. It wasn't pleasant."

Their eyes met, and both could see the vision of his skeletal body. Anne teared up again at the memory of his condition. Remembering how reluctant she was to take him in.

Lady Mari continued, "I knew Anna was safe and well. When I found out Anna had taken you in, Sam, you were about to be married. Tom wrote that he'd lost you for nearly eighteen months, and you stayed well-hidden after she took you in. Well, actually I could not have been more pleased, as I knew your history too. We had both prayed you would both be kept safe and alive. Phil and I were ecstatic when we discovered who you were married to, as we were worried she would end up in an abusive relationship. Even Phil acknowledged that you would care for her, Sam. When Tom told us of the pregnancy, I was delighted. Phil, too, as it meant his own real grandson would get the title after all. He was still ready to disinherit you until you married Anna. He was somewhat obsessive over the bloodline, you know." She glanced at Charlie, who'd raised his eyebrows in horror. "I admit you both kept your heads down while there. It was hard to find out much about either of you."

Lady Marianna saw Charlie had blanched. "Leave it alone, Charlie; it was just that he had no love for your father. No skeletons, so don't worry," Lady Marianna said.

Relief swept over him. "I would have broken the Entail, you know." Charlie grinned, much relieved. He explained to Annie, "My papa married the lady the Earl liked when he was tricked into marrying Miss White."

She chuckled. "I think that's ultimately what changed Phil's mind about naming you as heir. He had no love for you either."

"It was mutual," Charlie added with a grin. "Papa hated him too. Mama certainly would have refused him. She only had eyes for Papa."

Sam took a deep breath and began his story. "After I was thrown out of the hospital, I had nowhere to go. There were cases of typhus from the lice there, and they didn't want me to get that. I collapsed in her front yard under an enormous rock, willing myself to die. I had seriously had enough of living. I tried everything to be dead. Each morning I woke, I groaned. After Anne took me in, I lived in her shed and slept on sacks. I weeded her garden for some months. I barely had enough strength to stand, so I weeded crawling. I was so ill and I was malnourished after the years at West's. Anne nursed a reluctant me back to health. Initially, she was equally unenthusiastic. I was skeletal and literally starving. West's rations were scant at best. You know she makes the best thick soups and pasties in the world," Sam added with such a look of adoration on his face Lady Marianna drew her breath. "I must have looked like a walking skeleton when I arrived. No wonder she was afraid of me, but she let me stay. One day, I realised I didn't want to die anymore, and I looked forward to each morning. To her cheery hello, and I wished to help her any way I could." He met his father's eyes and saw sorrow in them. "One hot night in the shed, I opened the door and noticed there was no moon; I could see a myriad of stars. It was like a fairyland. I'd done the same two weeks before, but there had been a full moon, and not many stars were visible. Stars don't shine without darkness. It suddenly occurred to me that you see the bright lights more clearly when things are at their worst. So when I saw the stars that night, I felt like I'd been trampled by a galloping horse; my emotions got the better of me. I was so overwhelmed with feelings I had no understanding about. I was noticing her, wanting to help her, but I had no idea why. However, I had something to now live for... Her!" Sam again met Anne's eyes from across the room; they shone with returned love. "I realised I had fallen in love with her, without understanding what love was." Sam and Annie's adoration was written on their faces when their eyes rested on each other.

The old lady was now sitting up straight, and the lines gone from her face. She didn't look so drained anymore. A smile transformed her face. "Danny, I have followed your life too. You had all found your feet, and life looked up for you all over there. You all seemed content. However, I wasn't quite sure about my grandson marrying a builder's daughter, but I believe she was lovely."

Danny nodded. "She was, ma'am."

Lady Broome-Hall continued, "Well, Tom still wrote about once every six months with a report. I heard about each of the three girls' births and heard about the trip over here. Then once here, I heard about your visit to your grandfather's house." She nodded to the Duke. "Not that you knew who he was, Sam. Then I heard of Watmore and his behaviour to Danny. Cantankerous old busy body. I was so thrilled you put him in his place, lad. I would have loved to have seen that." Her eyes twinkled. "I heard that you finally had a son but sadly that Vanessa died after he was born. I'm so sorry about her passing, Danny. I then understood the reasons you were all coming back." She paused, finally looking at Tim. "Having said that, congratulations on your engagement too. Georgie is a good girl, and I feel you will get along well. Funny that Timmy will be your father-in-law. Unlike most girls her age, she has sense. Your Robbie does too; he's like you, Timmy. Found his mystery girl yet?"

Tim shook his head but didn't want to get side-tracked. "Georgie is the one who put all the pieces together."

She nodded and continued. "Danny, you will do well together." She smiled, "Strange, eh, Duke, to think we now share a grandson and great-grandchildren." She relaxed back into her chair. The years had shed from her stature. Her smile rewound the years, and she was now at peace.

The Duke nodded, then turned his attention to Sam. "As I said, after your release, Sam, I too had a soldier writing to me. It was Major Ned Grace who lived in Parramatta. I met him some months before he went when he was only a lad of about nineteen, and we struck up an odd friendship. When he enlisted, I believe I was the only one he told what name he would be known by. He is the second son of The Duke of Gracemere over in Kent. He should have enlisted under Edward Lockley but didn't want the family knowing where he is, so he's hiding under the name of Edward Grace, but is known as Ned."

The Duke saw Sam nod, but then realised he'd let the cat out of the bag over that information. "Ooh, I probably shouldn't have said that, but well, please, make sure you keep it quiet. But this is part of the whole story. I happened to overhear the break-up of his engagement. I initially commiserated with him, then I heard who it was. Knowing Elouise

Wickham, I sympathised with Ned, when in reality, I should have congratulated him on his escape. Right place, right time, for me. I was sad that the shrew got her claws into his older brother David though. Anyway, I sponsored Ned when he enlisted and bought his commission as Major, that's by the by, Ned went to Parramatta as a Major and kept an eye on you for me, Sam. From a distance, though, and yes, I told him why, then Tom introduced him to Dan. It seemed a time for confidences. Ned only went out in 1820, I asked him to look out for you, but he kept his ears open for what you two were up to. Nice chap, a true gentleman."

Ned had come visiting with Tom often over the last years. Ned and Danny were only four years apart in age, and they got along well. "So is he related to Charles Lockley then?" Sam asked, intrigued.

The Duke shrugged. "I don't know him, but possibly. I don't know Ned or the family well."

Sam thinking how similar Ned and Charles were in looks; they probably were related and kept it quiet. He smiled to himself. The group sat silently for a few minutes, each digesting the story they had heard so far.

Lady Marianna reached for Anne's hand. "So, my Anna, that's why I sent you away. Otherwise, I would have left you with Ceccy. It's an odd situation, but I knew he would be gentle with you. Anna, you were to Ceccy what I was to Phil, the absolute love of our lives. I wish he could have taken you on his trip, but then you wouldn't have met Sam. I think, in the long run, you've been even happier with Sam," she said.

Anne nodded with tear-filled eyes. "I felt loved by Cec, I felt cherished, but I love Sam in a totally different way." She turned to Sam, and her face lit up. "We complete each other, and now I think I know why. Even now, if I think of my life without him, I can't breathe."

Sam moved across the room and sat close to Anne. As there wasn't room on the settee, he sat on the arm of the small couch and drew her to him.

Anne melted into his lap, her arms wrapped around his waist and her head on his knee. Her shoulders were shaking in released grief. Her life was so different from what she'd thought. She'd gone from feeling so angry, ready to explode and seethingly livid before she entered the room, to the absolute disgust. She was shocked that her grandfather was a filthy, dirty old man who used even his own daughter and granddaughter to satisfy his base desires, and then sorrow for her mother and Betsy. If only she'd known, but that would have involved confessions that could not have occurred back then either. Now she was sad, absolutely gut-wrenchingly, sad. Sad for all the missed chances to be loved, sad for herself but overwhelmingly sad for her mother and father.

"Anna, Philip and I loved you the only way we knew how in the situation we were in, and that was to send you away from us. It broke my heart, Philip's too, but I could not let you see my adoration for you. While you worked in the rooms at the Manor, I watched you, so wishing you I could tell you who you were. You were my love child, not a duty child; you were the child from my heart." She touched her brooch. "I see you still have the blanket I made you. I cried many tears over that. I would not let you go until it was finished, so I took my time in making it. Did you ever find the hearts knitted into the edging? Or your initials?"

Annie shook her head. Looking at the old white blanket, she wore around her shoulders as a shawl. She drew it off and looked intently at the designs. Sam kept his hand on her shoulder.

Her mother lifted the edge of the shawl and pointed out the design of hearts around the edging. Annie had never looked that hard at it and had never noticed them. Then Lady Marianna showed her the tiny initials embroidered into each corner in the middle of the garden of grub roses 'APJGW'. All were sewn in white thread and looking like grass of the flowers. She then pointed to the blanket on her own lap. It was identical, only larger. Both were aged, and much loved. She showed Anne the same initials on her own blanket but with PG and MW on either side of them. She met her mother's eyes and was soon in her arms, sobbing their sadness away. Her entire life, she'd spent thinking she was a nothing. Now she had a father and mother who'd always loved her and had sent her away to save her. Betsy had confirmed all the story was true.

Eventually, she found her voice, "How could he, Mother? May I call you that in private? How could he be such a dirty rotten old man? It's filthy and disgusting." She gagged as she spoke. "It will take time to digest everything that's happened in the past two days. However, I'm still amazed I have a name, let alone a family, even an aunt." She turned to Betsy, giving her a wet wan smile.

"Yes, in private, I'd be delighted, Anna." She patted Annie's hand. "Right. Now the air is clear. How you feel about me will be up and down, but I do ask that you do consider the entire story before condemning me." She looked up at Sam. "You copped it worst, lad, and I'm sorry for that, Sammy. It's what your mother called you, you know, and it's how I have always thought of you. Sam, your mother Anne and I were friends; I told you that's how I met Philip. I felt somewhat cruel betraying her, but she was relieved when she found out. It took Phil's dictatorial attention from her. He didn't like her, but she was his. He was a hypocrite when it came to affairs, and I told him so. Hence you two were Baptised together. He swallowed his pride enough for that, but then that ragbag Watmore intervened. Phil had no love for your mother at all. Nigel was all he wanted, and once he had him, he ignored her completely. If he spoke to her at all, it was very rudely. Duke, you were good for Lady Anne. I'm glad she had some happiness in her short life. I did like her, but I felt so sorry for her too. Philip had been forced to marry her by her own father. When she was not even seventeen, he manoeuvred them into a compromising situation, and even though nothing had happened, they had to marry. Anne had only met Philip once before they married; they were engaged for nearly a year. She was eighteen when Nigel was born. Nigel was born nine months after they married. Her father wanted the Earl for her, and she, of course, had no choice at all. So, when Philip and I met, it seemed inevitable that we'd end up together. But Sammy, I'm sorry you had such a horrible experience. Watmore is responsible for much of that, and I was pleased when you removed him last year. However, if Phil had given you a half-decent allowance ... Well, that's past history, and I'm not discussing that part of it anymore. Watmore played on Phil's guilt. The Earl often paid for that, trust me. Duke, I'm sorry Phil cut you out of the lad's life, but hopefully, our last years will be different. Anna, that depends on you."

Annie drew a deep breath. Stunned at the many revelations just made, even more so to find Betsy was her aunt and Lady Marianna was her mother. However, having had a day now to digest that fact, she asked. "Are you happy in this cottage ... Mother?" Her voice broke on the last word. "We have lots of room at our place. I think we could possibly find a room or three hundred if you and Betsy would like to move in? We could get to know each other properly. Although, I must warn you what we are doing there." She smiled at Danny and Sam, "Now we know our true stories, we shall continue with our plans for these peer orphans. For now, I feel it is even more apt." Her eyes caught Danny's eyes. She'd already felt Sam squeeze both her shoulder and the hand he still held.

Danny nodded and gave her a grin, any animosity now gone from him. He'd seen that his parents had known nothing of the situation unfolding before them all.

"I'd be delighted, my dear Annabella," kissing her daughter's cheek. She turned to the Duke, "See Duke, our olden years will be golden years." She shooed Annie and Sam away and beckoned Danny to sit next to her.

After he was beckoned, Dan went and sat next to his grandmother, telling her of his four children. She chuckled when she heard that the youngest girl was named Mary-Anne.

Sam and Anne walked to Betsy and were deep in conversation with her as Dan spoke to his grandmother for the first time. Anne drew her friend into her arms, both in tears, all now forgiven.

Charlie and Tim excused themselves and walked outside to get some air. They, too, had much to discuss. Both were in shock at what they had heard.

The Duke sat watching his new family with a beatific smile on his face, bouncing his whale tooth walking stick on the floor between his legs. His eyes were twinkling with joy. His eyes met Lady Broome-Hall and held them, each smiling to the other.

Chapter 12   The Darling People

*T*he short trip back to Meldon Hall was accomplished almost in silence. Anne was still in shock. The men on either side of her holding her hands and stroking the backs of them. The three men opposite, the Duke, Tim, and Charlie, sat quietly. None of them knew what to say, so they said nothing. Anne and Sam had much to think about and ponder over, and they needed to be alone. Danny, too, was trying to absorb the revelations that had occurred over the last two days. On arrival at the Hall, Georgie met them in the foyer, and when she saw the stunned look on Danny's face, she took his hand and drew him into the gardens so they could talk in private. He would tell her of the day's revelations.

Charlie ushered the Duke into the sitting room and asked for tea. Tim followed them.

Sam drew Anne aside as they too needed to be alone. To talk, to hold each other, and to digest their past. Everything they had known about their lives was cast aside. Neither had been abandoned as they thought, and both had been loved and wanted by their parents. It is just that their parents were not who they believed them to be.

Once alone, Sam drew her to him and into his arms.

He cupped her face in his hands and looked deeply into her beautiful blue eyes. "There is so much I should say, but this is all that is needed to be said. With all the revelations made this week, I still love you. No, I love you even more. You are still my world, my entire life, and however this will finish, I will be here beside you. I need you, and I want you. I always have." He gently brushed his fingers across her soft and downy cheek and then bent to kiss her lightly on her lips.

She began to cry again. The same deep hacking sobs that Sam had done the day before on his father's shoulder.

He held her close and comforted her. Together they would work out what their next steps were to be. After some minutes, he drew her to the large leather armchair and sat down, pulling her into his lap.

There they sat for some time, just gaining strength from each others closeness. Her arms wrapped around his neck and his around her waist. The tumult of the revelations would be long-lasting. "I do want to get to know her, Sam," she finally said after nearly an hour of silence. "I meant the invitation, Sam."

He knew that she needed to process all that the afternoon had revealed. He had lain awake thinking of his own discoveries most of last night, the joy to discover that he still had a chance to know his father. She now needed to do the same. "Whatever you need, we will do, my beloved Anne Joy. Isn't it funny that I have always called you that, only without the capital 'J'? To think that our lives were woven together for so long and that we had no idea of any of it? So intricately linked and loved from afar. Maybe it's why we were drawn to each other in the beginning, for my love, we are the other half of each other."

She nodded against his neck. She just needed to keep him close, to touch him, to be hugged by him. She'd felt this way the first night they were together. How long she sat, she did not know or care.

Sam held her, loving her. They both looked up when there was a knock at the door.

Charlie stuck in his head and said, "Are you both okay?" He looked concerned.

Sam looked at Anne, and she answered, "Yes, Charlie, I think we are. We just have a lot to digest."

"Good, because we have to leave, Sam; Alice sent a note she needs me at home. I'll be at your beck and call, as will Tim. Don't hesitate, but Sam, we're leaving your father in the sitting room. I'm still stunned by that revelation, let alone the rest. It was the brown eyes, you know that made her wonder." He shrugged. "If you're both up to it, I'd suggest you spend a bit of time with him, as he too is in a bit of shock. He hadn't seen that coming."

Anne moved from Sam's lap and went to farewell the departing men. As she went to leave the room, she turned to Sam and said, "I want no secrets. With mother probably moving in with us, all the staff will know soon enough. Many have already guessed your relationship to the Duke, for you look too much like him. I'm not going to hide anymore, Sam. I'm going to hold my head high and do as I've always done, I dance to my own tune. If society doesn't like it, well, that's their problem. So, let's go and say goodbye to our family. Funny Charlie is my cousin, not yours."

The two men were seen off by the three smiling faces of Annie,

Sam and his father. As they drove out of sight, Sam turned to go indoors. The butler had not seen the two men standing so close together before and blinked at what he saw.

Sam looked at the Duke, who nodded. "Victor, I'd like to introduce you to my real father, the Duke. Hiding it is quite useless unless we never see each other, for we are too much alike. Nathan too! It's a long story, but I want you to gather the senior staff and meet us in the sitting room in half an hour. We will reveal who we are, for trust me, you will all need to know."

Victor had been stunned enough when Sam suggested that he propose to Thea and they have special quarters arranged. Victor nodded; for the Earl to call him by his first name was unusual enough for a butler, however for all the senior staff to be treated as equals was astounding. He was honoured that they even volunteered to be witnesses at their marriage. Victor would do anything for this man.

So, thirty minutes later, the senior staff filed into the sunny sitting room. Some of the revelations of the past two days were revealed.

Graham Long smiled; his guesses were correct.

Sam said, "You all need to know as the Duke of Malvern and Lady Broome-Hall will be regular visitors from now on. Lady Broome-Hall and Miss Betsy White, Lady Anne's, aunt, will actually be making their home with us. I expect that you will all respect our privacy and not discuss this outside the Hall. The junior staff do not need to know more than necessary. Some may guess, but it need not be either confirmed or discussed at length. You all know what we are doing here; we did not know our own histories when we embarked on this adventure. We call you by your Christian names as to us you are friends who work with us, rather than employed staff who work for us. I intend to give these children a loving, stable home, and we need you to assist us. As you now know our birth backgrounds, we are equal to you. Our backgrounds just reinforce to us the need for this to be done."

Anne watched them each nod and smile. Anne turned to the housekeeper. "Thea can you prepare a suite for Mother and make it one of the best ones? Make sure that Betsy is comfortable too and close to her. I want full guest treatment for her. For without Betsy, my own life would have had a tragic ending. Be kind to her, for she has given up much to protect me all of my life."

Thea smiled. "Then I'll prepare the Queen's suite for her Ladyship, ma'am, and the Princess suite for Miss Betsy."

Anne nodded. She'd not yet seen all the suites but realised that there would be some very fancy rooms available.

"And I'd like a room or suite to be made available for His Grace too." Sam turned to his father. "For I hope you will stay regularly."

The Duke grinned. "Too right, I intend to stay often. We have much to catch up on."

Thus sorted, the staff were dismissed.

~

Things went on as before the engagement party for nearly a week, only now there was much more laughter.

The Duke stayed two more days before Nathan arrived. Anne left Sam alone with his father often.

It was Wednesday when Nathan arrived to collect his father, and Sam finally met his younger half-brother.

Sam was unsure of his reception, but Nathan walked up to him with his hand outstretched, shook it and then drew Sam into a bear hug. When they broke apart, they stood looking at each other. Nathan broke into a broad grin. "Sam, I can't believe it, but I know it's true. We look too similar."

The three men went into the den and sat ensconced for over an hour before Sam sent for Danny.

The meeting was all that Sam hoped it would be. They knew that outside these walls, whispers would be made. Inside them, they could be just one family and a happy one at that.

Nathan loved the idea of an older brother and asked his permission to make time to discover more of each other's past. Sam was overwhelmed and still battling with the idea of a family who not only loved him but wanted to be with him too. Nathan also asked if he could bring his son JD next time. James Douglas was the same age as Danny and recently married.

It suddenly occurred to Danny that he had both an aunt and uncle nearby and another aunt in Scotland. And he now had cousins and even grandparents. He could hardly wipe the smile from his face. It had always been just him. Nathan and the Duke finally departed, and the house fell quiet for the afternoon.

As the day was fine, Sam took Anne for a walk in the garden. He'd wished to show Anne a surprise he'd had made for her.

Sam had made her a swing and hung it in a tree. After the revelations by Lady Marianna, he understood its importance to her. There was little he felt he could give her, as neither were interested in the worldly luxuries and usual trapping of society. However, a swing would be perfect.

Anne saw it before Sam said anything. "You did this for me?" she exclaimed excitedly. "It's just like the one I found as a child. The one Father made for me."

Sam grinned. She was like a schoolgirl again. "Yes, love, for us to play with. Hop on, and I'll push you." She did, and her squeals of joy were adorable. In her sixties, she still had the pleasure of life as a child.

Their son Dan had inherited this from her. Sam wished he could see this side of her more often.

She would make Sam laugh often, tricking him, teasing him, and generally having great fun. He, in return, was constantly thinking of ways to make her smile so he could hear her joyous laugh.

Sam's grin was plastered on his face when they walked back home arm in arm. He'd stop and pull her into his arms, kissing her and then making her giggle.

They talked of their time in Sydney. Of the night she first asked Sam to marry her. Of the revelations they had made to each other the next night, of their first night together in unadulterated lust. They drank in each other's neediness.

They stopped before they came within view of the house. Sam took her in his arms and teased her by giving many little kisses before she pulled him close and drew his head down to hers. Her love for this man was breath-taking.

When he finally raised his head from her luscious red lips, she said, "It seems all so long ago now. I still blush at that first night, Sam. It's hard to believe we've lived over half our lives together but that we were woven and tied together before we met over there."

As they topped the rise, they saw a carriage parked in the portico. Annie said, "Oh, do you think it's Mother and Betsy? I said I'd send a carriage for her, but I haven't heard from her yet. She said she'd let me know she was coming."

"No love, look, there are two luggage coaches too. Let's hurry; we must have guests. I wonder who it could be?" Sam and Anne upped their pace.

Victor greeted them with the information they required. "Sir Ralph and Lady Darling have arrived, sir. I have shown them into the formal sitting room. They said that you offered an open invitation to them."

"We did, Victor, indeed. Get Thea to prepare a suite of rooms for them and their children, as I hope they will stay awhile. They are good friends," Sam said.

Victor broke into a grin. "Good sir, then they shall get the best of everything. May I ask, sir, do they know the way things stand?"

"Not yet, Victor, but they soon will, so no shadows remember. With Mother coming soon, nothing will be able to be hidden," Anne said. "We won't tell everyone, but the Darling's need to know."

Victor nodded. After he showed them in to their visitors, he bustled away to prepare for their stay.

Eliza Darling stood looking out at the magnificent gardens. "Oh, Anne, these are delightful," she said to Anne just before she greeted her with a hug.

"Sir, welcome to Meldon Hall," Sam greeted Ralph. "I believe the 'Sir' is now official? Should have happened long ago in my books."

Ralph said thanks, and the four sat and enjoyed their reunion.

"Please tell us you can stay for a while. I'd love to let you know what's been happening. For trust me, much has," Anne both asked and explained.

"I'll answer that, Ralph. We'd be delighted. We need to breathe in some genuine friendship after the shallowness of London," Eliza said before her husband had a chance to even open his mouth. "We won't be getting another placement of any kind for all sorts of reasons, and so we must find somewhere to live. We're looking down near Brighton, but Ralph has not yet found anywhere. Would you mind us here for a short stay while we look around? It's less than half a day from here, and Ralph can *reconnoitre* at leisure. If you have any suggestions, let us know."

"It will be so wonderful to have true friends close by." Anne took Eliza's hands. "You are welcome to stay for the entire season if you wish, or longer. We might just be able to squeeze you in somewhere." Eliza laughed with Anne. "Remember when I asked Sam if there was a spare room? I had no idea what we were coming to. Eliza, there are hundreds of rooms here, hundreds and hundreds. I think you could stay, and we wouldn't even know."

Eliza caught her husband's eye, and with a look, he nodded. Sam and Anne caught both actions. "We've been hearing all sorts of exciting and interesting titbits of news about what you're planning to do here. Is it all true? You're going ahead with your plan then?"

Sam caught a raised eyebrow from Ralph to his wife. "Ralph, if I can't ask these dear friends directly, then they aren't good friends." She turned back to Anne. "Now, this sounds exciting; tell us all about it."

They sat discussing the peer orphans for some time. With some already incorporated into the household, they were willing to outline some of their plans. "Eliza, we have the peer orphans, but also a couple of war widows and a few injured soldiers, and they are all working hard. All are given the best chance we can and then supplied with references. Hopefully, they will be offered places in various houses around the country. We're beginning to have trouble sourcing people to train." Sam explained.

While there was a break in the conversation, Anne looked at Sam for approval to let them know the recent happenings.

He nodded assent.

She started, "Eliza, Ralph, as you will be staying, I must tell you that we're expecting another person, two actually. I must tell you about her and, well, explain that we have both had recent revelations made to us, and if you're in residence, you will find out soon enough, so we'd rather tell you ourselves. Firstly, we're both not who we thought we were." Anne paused but, catching Sam's eye, said simply, "Sam...."

Sam picked up the story and told them all. "Having heard our sordid story, you may wish to rethink the friendship," Sam said once all was revealed. "However, I will give you the salient details."

"No, why should we? It does not change who you are to us. You are friends who are good and true and honest. This conversation proves this to us. This makes our friendship even more valuable to us both." Ralph spoke for all his family. He had yet to tell them of the happenings in London. However, he knew that any revelation would not change their opinion of him.

Sam had broken the news to them of their previously unknown parentage. The recent revelations were still raw, but as time passed and they had time to digest the disclosures, it made more sense. When they re-read the Earl's letter to Sam, even that made sense.

Eliza spoke to Annie about the past year for them and the incidents that occurred. "Anne, we have been living with Mother in Cheltenham, and she is an active philanthropist. When I heard what you were doing here or planning to, she said she knew of some children in need and wondered if you would give them room. I only have to let her know, and she will either bring them or send them." Eliza looked to both Sam and Anne.

"Of course, we are ready for many of the poor dears. Now we know our stories, we are even more determined to show these abandoned children some love. If they have any histories or knowledge of their parentage, that would be even better. As one day, it would be nice for them to know who they are."

"Excellent," said Ralph. "Err, Anne dear, one of the things she has come across is a group working with rescued women off the street. They were once upright women who had fallen on hard times, and when their soldier husbands died, mostly in the Napoleonic wars, or in whatever other war action they saw or even sailors lost at sea, their only recourse was to turn to the streets to feed themselves and their children." Ralph wondered at their reaction, but there was none but compassion. So he continued. "My mother-in-law, Ann Dumaresq, Eliza's mother, has employed some and has trained them for various household roles, but we need more households to employ them. Some have children, all need assistance. I was wondering if you need more staff to assist with the children?"

"Yes, we do. We're having trouble finding staff after finding out who they will be looking after. This could work very well for us all." Sam was thrilled. "Anne Joy, this is wonderful and will solve our problem." Sam was grinning. "This works as a double win, sir."

"Darn it, Sam, drop the 'sir' will you. Okay, I'm knighted, but you're still an Earl; you still outrank me." Ralph chuckled.

The housekeeper knocked and entered with Victor. He placed a hand on the small of her back in a slightly possessive action. "Sir, I've come to let you know the children have all gone for a walk and have taken your young ones with them," Victor said

Thea finished, "We hoped this was all right, but you did say they were staying. Also, that your rooms are ready." Thea curtseyed.

Victor added, "Mr Sam, I have sent the carriages to the cottage, for our other visitors will be here tonight."

"Thank you, Thea and Victor." Sam looked at Anne, grinning joyfully. He was looking forward to Anne being able to really get to know her mother. "Yes, the new visitors will become permanent residents, and the Darlings will be staying for some months. So, can you add some desks for the children in the classroom too? They can join our boisterous group."

"Certainly, Mr Sam," Victor gave a bow.

The four stood and followed the housekeeper to the door.

Eliza chuckled. "I love the informality of your household ,Anne. I love what you have achieved here in the past eighteen months," she said as she walked with Anne to their rooms.

"Eliza, the senior staff know everything about our backgrounds. We decided they should know all as Sam is a young version of the Duke. As to informality, we are equal by birth; why should we lord it over them? Both Thea and Victor are children of Earls. They all still feel we should be far more formal, but I threatened them that if they called me M'Lady, I'd pack up and go back to Sydney. I'm Mrs Anne, and Sam is Mr Sam most of the time, and we can cope with that. They only married recently, so our butler and housekeeper get along exceptionally well. It helps with the harmony of the household. They are like houseparents for the orphans. We really are one big happy family here, Eliza." As they walked, they kept talking. "Eliza, why don't you ask your mother to come here too? She can help the new ladies and girls settle in."

"Oh, Anne, would you mind? I so hated leaving her all alone. That would be delightful, and she and your mother could keep each other company too."

She left the Darlings to settle into their rooms. On the way back, Thea escorted Anne to view the other rooms she'd prepared.

Anne had checked the enormous Royal suite allocated to her mother. It was bigger than the cottage she'd been living in. Anne smiled to herself.

Two hours later, the other carriage drew up to the porticoed front door. Two older ladies alighted and stood looking at the foyer around them. Sam and Anne greeted them warmly; he escorted Lady Broome-Hall upstairs to her new rooms.

Anne greeted Betsy with a huge hug and followed them. "I'm thrilled to have you here with me, Betsy. Even more so, to know that for all those years, you looked after me. I told Sam that in all my life, you and you alone were my only friend." As they walked upstairs, Anne said, "So you are here now as my aunt, my friend and a guest, who just happens to be helping my mother. From now on, you will be introduced as her companion. Just so you know."

Betsy gasped. "But, Annie! No, you can't! I do not deserve to be elevated to such a huge status. If you knew the grief I went through, knowing there was no other way to help. I so wish I could have told you everything, but I had been sworn to secrecy. Annie, Sir Cecil knew before he died, and I told him about your grandfather's visits after leaving on his trip; of course, he knew my relationship to him. However, that the Duke had abused me too, he did not know. He was so sad but understood. You were out of his reach over there, and you were safe. It was that knowledge that made him decide to confront your grandfather. Annie, it was when he challenged your grandfather that Sir Cec had his stroke. He got so angry, and he collapsed when he confronted the old man." Betsy filled in a bit more of the circumstances of this incident. Anne stood listening, saddened but understanding. Betsy was about to say more and started, "M'lady …"

"Betsy, you, my dear, are a Duke's daughter; I, a mere Earl's daughter. Both of us are illegitimate; in this house, we are equals, the same as Sam. Understand?" Annie stood looking at her only friend.

Betsy nodded, realising that her life from now would be very different. Anne grabbed her arm and showed her aunt-friend to her new rooms. Before they entered, Betsy grabbed her arm again and continued her story. "Annie, if you'd gone voluntarily, he would have brought you back, you know. He'd worked out who you were. You were too like M'lady for him not to realise. We thought of trying everything. It was the only way to save you." Betsy could not leave the story untold.

"Betsy, it's okay. Now I know, I understand. My time was served with a lovely lady who was kind to me, then Tim took over. It was tough for a few months until business picked up, but I still had the nest egg I could fall back on. I had a better life there than I would have here. And Betsy, there I met Sam." She sighed. "Everything I went through was worth it just for that."

Thea walked just in front of them, and opened the door for Lady Broome-Hall and Sam.

Anne said, "I hope you like it, Mother. Sam tells me this was the Queen's room. As we have no intention of inviting Royalty here, you're the next best thing. By the way, Betsy is no longer your maid but your companion. She will be included as such in everything from now on. She is my friend and stood by me all those years. This is one way I can thank her. In this house, we are all equals. She can still assist you, but you can help train some of our new staff arriving soon. Our other visitors can explain it after dinner. Oh, the Duke also has rooms here, and he's in the King's suite just down the hallway."

Thea left the three ladies alone, and returned downstairs. Sam followed her out.

"Mother, as I explained to Betsy, she's a Duke's daughter and I'm only an Earl's child. In this house, she outranks me." Anne chuckled. "Mother, Thea and Victor are in the same situation too."

"Thank you, Anna, I should have done that for her years ago, but, it never occurred to me. From today we are all making a new start. I have a request though; we've been talking about what you should call me in public. I think that, 'Lady Mari' would do nicely; what do you think? It's what Betsy calls me anyway."

Anne kissed her mother and nodded. "Come and look at Betsy's suite. She's next door." The three ladies did not go out into the corridor but walked through three interconnecting rooms to another suite. This one was decorated in the palest greens with pink peony roses tastefully trailing down the walls and painted as a trailing design around the cornices. The three central rooms were joined by a sitting room, and each had a dressing room and a bathing room with its own commode chair.

Betsy gasped. "This is more beautiful than the master bedroom at Broome-Hall, Annie. I don't deserve it."

"You do, and much more. It's about time you lived who you should be. I shall also be introducing you as my aunt. Elizabeth White is a common enough name not to raise any eyebrows."

Betsy was weeping in awe of the delightful room. "I really don't deserve this, Annie. I'm just me."

"It's precisely why you do deserve it, Betsy," Lady Mari said. "Accept it in the spirit in which it is given, my dear."

Betsy nodded, unable to talk.

Sam sent a note to his father with a dinner invitation.

The Duke arrived in time for the evening meal welcoming Sam with a hug. "I still can't believe you want me in your life son."

"No, Father, you're not quite right there. I demand you in my life," Sam said. "You have some parenting to make up that I missed." He had a twinkle in his eye. It was reciprocated. Anne saw what Sam would look like in twenty years or so. Dinner that evening was a joyous event, and before they sat down, Sam spoke to the Duke. "Anne and her mother have been in discussion. We think she shall be known as 'Lady Mari'. We can be less formal in private, but in this house, I want the informality that everyone else enjoys. Betsy is her new companion and is to be Miss White."

"Good then I shall be 'Lord James'," his father said.

Sam had introduced him by his full title and then said he was to be known as Lord James.

The Duke sat happily, bouncing his walking stick again. Sam noticed that he did this when he was relaxed and happy, and he was doing this more and more often. It seemed that the faster he bounced it, the happier he was.

Within a fortnight, Lady Ann Dumaresq arrived and settled in, as did the eight new maids and four of their children. More were to follow, arranged by some of her friends in London.

Sam asked her and her philanthropic friends to send any they found, as all would be retrained. Many were war widows who had fallen on hard times. They were thrilled to be given positions and trained for their new roles. Anne and Eliza interviewed them and worked out where each would be best utilised. Lady Mari and Betsy each got new maids, and it was decided that they would be taught how to become 'ladies maids'. Both were daughters of soldiers who had died. Neither had wished to go on the streets but thought they had no other options. Erica and Caroline were only sixteen and seventeen. When offered an alternate life, both jumped at the chance. Others had some education, and they were assigned to assist in the classroom and became junior teachers in time. Another sixteen-year-old, Miriam Lock, one of the London girls, had an excellent education and had fallen on hard times when her soldier father was killed and her mother died soon afterwards. She was nearly fifteen when that disaster had befallen her. She had been taken in by a kindly lady for a year; sadly, she too had recently died. Miriam had been rescued by Lady Ann as they were about to leave. So, she came too.

Two weeks after Lady Ann's arrival, Dan and Georgie were married by Rev Hugh Williams. It was only a month after their engagement party in June. Banns had been read, and as Georgie didn't want a big fuss, only the family attended. That, of course, meant all the

Broome-Halls, the Garneys and the Duke's family too. Anthony Jenkins
and Betsy sat close together at the back.

Miriam asked if she could help out with Sunday school as she
adored children. Hugh was thrilled, if somewhat distracted.

In October, Danny announced that Georgie was expecting and
that their child was due around Easter time.

Their parents and grandparents were delighted.

Lady Ann Dumaresq and Lady Mari were often seen together
surrounded by numerous small children and usually a team of mongrel
dogs and puppies. By this stage, some fourteen orphaned children lived at
the Hall, plus the four of Danny's and four staff children. The need for
more staff grew. Lady Ann put out feelers, and more war widows soon
arrived.

Anthony Jenkins came and saw Sam one afternoon in his Office.
"Mr Sam, I was wondering if I could have a moment of your time."

Sam turned to the elderly stable master. "Anthony, for you
anytime! I can never thank you enough, but I am all ears. For you never
ask for anything."

"Well, Mr Sam, it's come to my notice that with the growing staff,
the gardens and stables have been left somewhat devoid of extra hands.
Stan has met some injured returned soldiers who require employment.
Some are maimed, and some severely scarred. All have usable skills. Do
you think we could possibly find a place for them?"

"Fine by me. Anthony, Charlie said that we'd need more, but it was
the least of my worries with everything else occurring lately. How many
can you get? Finances are not an issue; it's staff accommodation that will
limit the quantity. Bring as many as we have rooms for. We can always
convert more rooms if needed. And see if any others have teaching skills.
We need a few educated ones as well. I want to start a school for adult
classes too. I want to have somewhere staff can learn to read and write
and even teach others less fortunate to be trained for various positions. Do
you think any would suit those roles?" Sam grinned at Anthony's surprised
look. "Just one thing... who the heck is Stan? I don't recall any Stan's on
the payroll."

Anthony chuckled, "He's the Darling's groom, come footman, Mr
Sam."

They discussed the various positions Anthony thought they could
work in, and Sam gave him the go-ahead to find whom he wished.
"Anthony, see Graham Long and work out how many we can fit. Do you
think they will come?"

"I can but ask, Mr Sam, and thank you, sir." Anthony hobbled off
and went into the Estate office to discuss the required staff with Graham

Long.

They worked out twenty new positions for men that could easily be used, and many would not need skills. Those who didn't know anything, they would train.

The Darling's groom, Stan Davies, was a fount of knowledge of where to find these sorts of men, and it was he who had put the idea into Anthony's head. Stan was a returned soldier himself and had been kept on retainer when his fighting days were over. He'd been thrilled when he was told to appear for service as security for Sir Ralph while the court case was on. When it was over, he'd stayed on, now employed by the Darlings.

Stan went to London with Graham and Anthony; together, they selected twenty of the least likely men to be employed anywhere. They went with strict instructions from Sam, though. They must be sober, God-fearing and otherwise clean-living men. Sam would have no seedy drunkards on the estate, or they would be promptly dismissed without reference if they stepped out of line. Anthony could have hired four times as many. He assured them that once they had trained this group, he'd return for more. With skills and a reference, these men could work anywhere. Some begged to come and learn unpaid, and three of the most desperate, Anthony and Stan brought back with them.

Graham said they'd have to sleep in the same room as they had no more room in the men's quarters. Most of those had been made over for the new women with family.

All three were so ill they could barely stand, mostly from lack of food. With good food, the three recovered and threw themselves into any job asked of them. When they could move about, their first job was to clean the men's staff quarters. If they could manage that and get well, they would then go on to a training programme. That's all they needed, hope.

By the time a month had passed, the gardens were trimmed as far as the eye could see. The soldiers were old hands at keeping their swords clean and sharp, so a scythe was easy for them. Hedging took some more skill, but they were all quick learners. The knack of using hedge clippers took time, but they were outdoors, and the weather had been fabulous. As the work was slow and done by hand, they could all take their time. An amputee with a stump leg could work as fast as a man with one eye lost from a sabre wound. The hedges were trimmed back by others, and some learned how to cut bushes into topiary shapes. Each had skills that were utilised and encouraged. Some dug over the kitchen gardens and even planted a children's garden. The children were encouraged to come with the teachers and learn how things grew. Some may one day need to know how to do this.

After some months, the estate manager, Graham, let the

Employment Agencies know that they had staff training at the Hall and not to hesitate to ask for specific requirements. All staff sent would be accompanied by references. The central Domestic Bureau in London was now frequently in contact with Graham for staff of all sorts. This allowed new ones to be brought in and trained. Each of the senior team loved their new roles as teachers, and soon new faces were the norm at Meldon Hall. They still had more than they could place, and many needed more training

Chapter 13   The Dance Goes On

Sam and Anne insisted that laughter or whistling be encouraged by all who wished, so the staff frequently heard it; someone was often whistling as the cleaning was done. Sam explained that this would not be allowed in other great houses, but it was desired here. Bullying would be punished by instant dismissal, with no reference, as would abuse of any kind, and all female staff's treatment and respectful treatment of all the female staff was demanded.

Failure to obey and they were to be put out on the street that day with only the outstanding pay owing. All were warned; however, the issue never arose.

The Hall was a joyful and fun-loving place.

Some six months after Victor and Thea married, Thea quietly admitted to Anne, "Mrs Anne, I'm expecting a child and will need to train another to take over my position." Then she proceeded to burst into tears.

Anne could see she was upset and fully understood; she too had fallen pregnant when she was thirty. She called for tea, and they sat down for a chat. The upshot was that Thea did not really wish to leave but said that she would not be able to stay on. Anne giggled. "Why, Thea? Do you wish to leave?"

Thea looked shocked. "Oh, no, Mrs Anne, but, well, I'll have a child to look after."

Again, Anne chuckled. "Oh, my dear Thea, we are not an ordinary house. We'll work around it. It's not like you actually do the cleaning yourself. I had to work up until Danny was born and then from a month afterwards. If you feel you can and want to stay, then we'd love to have you stay on."

Thea gaped at her, "But, ma'am, I'll be huge."

"Then hold the rails carefully as you walk the stairs. In this house, a baby is not enough reason to leave us." Anne smiled at her. "So, will you stay? Victor can help, and the baby can be in the nursery with Danny's brood. You can still be available while feeding . Goodness knows how many others we could have by then."

Thea gave a wet smile and nodded. "Oh, Mrs Anne, I'd love to stay. Really I can use all the staff and nursery too?"

"Yes, absolutely!" Anne said. "Now, let's go and tell Sam and Victor."

About a week later, Lady Mari beckoned Anne to her one day during morning tea. She'd been sitting looking out the window in the sitting room. "Anna dear, I'm bored, and although I love seeing all the children around me, I was wondering if I could teach some of the little girls to sew or something? Or even play the piano. Lady Ann and I wanted to run these things past you first. The girls will also need some, how do I say this delicately... moral lessons. The earlier you start, the less likely they will get into trouble. They must be taught it's fine to say *no* should they be caught in an indelicate situation. They also have to know that they can tell other adults. I know this from experience, as you will understand. Sadly, this is rife in many so-called noble houses these days. Hence the need for what you are doing. If I'd been wiser, I would have had Sarah and Betsy sleeping in my dressing room while father stayed with us. It just never occurred to me he'd go after Betsy then too. Anne, I want to protect every little girl I can and this is one way I can do it."

She and Lady Ann started teaching in the music room by firstly letting the little girls listen to music. "Come settle yourselves down; we are going to teach you some 'music appreciation', dears. If you learn to love the music, soon you may wish to make it yourselves." Lady Ann was a skilled harpist, and Lady Mari, a brilliant pianist. Sam had purchased a new grand piano for Lady Mari, and the harp that sat in the music room was tuned for Lady Ann. Together they sat playing the most moving melodies. The children were sometimes brought to tears while listening.

Anne often stood at the door just out of sight and swayed to their melodies. One day Sam sought her out as she stood listening. He walked up behind her and slid his hands lovingly around her waist, turning her gently to him; he motioned her to be quiet. She slipped her arms around his neck and drew him close. He whispered, "Dance with me, this is our tune," as he drew her further out into the corridor, and they danced, enjoying having some actual music to swing to. More really moving to the music than actually doing any particular dance. Her head was on his shoulder, and they would often stop and kiss. She smiled as they moved to the music together.

She gasped when Sam whispered, "Let's try the new German Waltz?" They'd seen it done but never tried it themselves. Her mother was currently playing the piece in 3/4 time, and Sam pulled her close to him. Their bodies were tightly pressed together, and he swung Anne down the wide corridor as they listened to the music. "Do you remember the night I told you I loved you? We'd been married for just over a year, and I'd just read the John Donne poem, well, some of it, and I couldn't hold it in anymore. Anne, my joy and my delight, I've never regretted a single day spent with you. You are my heart, and you still make my heart dance with joy. You gave me the will to live."

They had stopped moving but stood locked together. He lowered his head and gave her a peck of a kiss, then kissed her again but for longer, then as she stepped to him, pushing her body hard against his, the kiss deepened as he crushed her to him.

Neither heard the music stop, nor the door open.

Lady Mari and Lady Ann stood watching them. The look of joy was ecstatically written on Lady Mari's face.

Anne thought she heard something and opened her eyes to see they were being watched. She had just been kissed silly in front of her mother, and she didn't care a whit. She met her mother's eyes with a smile and a giggle.

At sixty-two, the two lovers smiled at the watching octogenarians and, with a chuckle, they left them grinning in the doorway as they walked to their room.

~

It took over six months for Ralph Darling to find a suitable house in Brighton and months more to make it fit to live in. When they finally moved down and sadly took Lady Ann Dumaresq with them. Lady Mari missed her greatly and would often sit alone in the sunroom.

A regular visitor to the house was Lord James, he'd also often stay over. Occasionally they would end up in the music room and at the piano.

Betsy was often buzzing around or sitting with them chatting. They had all become friends and, having known most of the same people most of their lives, often sat talking about them.

The week the Darlings left, Sam and Anne sought their parents out. They had rarely had a chance to just be the four of them alone since their revelations.

There were still gaps in the knowledge of each other. Questions still needed to be asked and answered, but in private. This day they finally found themselves together, just the four of them sitting in the orangery, just off the conservatory, enjoying just being together. Betsy was often with them; however, she was busying herself, teaching the new women some of their needed skills. She felt useful and loved her new position in life; Anne had asked her if she could keep her eyes on them for some time.

Sam and Anne were discussing all sorts of things from each of their pasts. Lord James then quietly said, "You know, you have heard our sides of the story, but you have both only had snatches of yours, son." Sam had previously revealed that Anne had proposed to him but few details of how it occurred. The look on both their parent's faces were a surprise and a delight. Sam sat with his arm carelessly draped around Anne's shoulder. She was nestled against him. She held his hand that he placed around her neck, and she clasped that in her own and held it against her cheek.

"Tell me, dear ones. I want to know it all. I have missed so much I need to know," Lady Mari said.

"She inherited a lot from you, Lady Mari. You know she proposed to me? To say I was stunned was a vast understatement. I'd been living in her shed, then on her settee for some months through winter. I was too ill to leave her property; hence no one could find me. One night we'd been reading one of her books, and she floored me and blurted it out. We weren't in love, as neither of us knew what that was, but we liked each other, even trusted each other, and we'd become friends. We each didn't even know why each other had been convicted, yet she wanted to marry me. As I said, we weren't in love, that came later, after Danny actually, but we liked each other's company; we'd become friends, and that was a start. The nobility marriages are arranged with much less base. Neither of us had any friends."

Sam paused. He rested his cheek on the top of her head. "Father, I'd collapsed next to an enormous rock in her front yard. It partially protected me from the tremendous thunderstorm overhead at the time. My strength was totally gone. Bert, the man who delivered her wood, found me and asked Anne if I could sleep in her shed. I realise now what I must have looked like, a walking skeleton, but I'd been in hospital for many weeks trying hard to die. I'm so glad now I failed. I didn't mention I'd been found by some aboriginal people. I didn't tell you all, as I thought Tim and Charlie would have been horrified. I have not even told Anne the full details of that missing year and a half. I had walked from West's farm and was trying to reach a town. I didn't make it. I passed out from hunger. I'd not eaten for three days, and the only water was puddles and brackish creek water."

Annie gasped. He had never revealed as much to her.

He whispered something to her before continuing. "Since I've been here, I have learned from the library that I had typhoid and then probably double pneumonia on top of it. I found some pink berries that tasted like apples, but I wasn't sure how many I could eat before they made me ill. Anyway, I had passed out when they, the aboriginal people, came across me. I have no idea how they moved me, but I woke up in a stick humpy near a fire. They fed me more pink berries and other fruit and food. They gave me a fish they cooked. I was too weak to feed myself; I could barely keep my eyes open. They sat me up and poked tiny bits into my mouth. It was the first fresh food I'd had for years. Oh, it was like the food served at the Royal Palace to me. A beautiful doe-eyed girl with a huge smile and dimples pushed it into my mouth. She would only let me eat little bits at a time. I could have devoured an entire school of fish. I was so ravenous, but somehow, they knew I shouldn't overeat at once. Every few minutes, they fed me a bit more. They were right. After half an hour, my stomach rebelled, and I got violently ill. She patiently started all over again. They brought me some water in a wooden thing, and I drank delicious, cool, clean water. Then they fed me more."

Annie snuggled closer.

He drew her closer. His head shook sad, slowly in remembrance of the episode. "Day by day, I revived. They laughed when I tried to start a fire. They taught me to pick and grind wild grains, how to catch fish and many other skills. I watched while they danced, they called it a *corroboree*. You could see the animals they mimicked, the stories they told in dance. Oh, it was brilliant. The most fun I had was when I was taken to watch them catching ducks. There was a pond near the camp, and I noticed that sometimes they would arrive with some ducks. They had no guns and carried no spears, so I had no idea how they caught them. Then one evening, they motioned for me to follow and be very quiet. All our communication was by hand signs. I learned a few words, but their language is complicated. Anyway, I was pushed onto a rock and motioned to sit still and stay silent. I did. I was intrigued." His voice lightened. "We sat deathly still for nearly an hour. Two of the men were waist-deep in water in the creek. At dusk, I saw a flock of ducks fly overhead then swoop down and settle on the creek; as soon as they arrived overhead, the two in the water sank to neck deep, and stayed still. The ducks settled, and although at the far end of the pond, they were not worried about us being so close. I peered into the gloom and saw one, then two, then more disappear, and a hole appeared in the middle of the ducks. They just kept disappearing underwater. I gasped in awe at the skills of the hunters. Soon the two men appeared with four ducks each. The birds had drowned and were hanging by their feet in their hands. Without saying a word or disturbing the remaining birds, we walked back to camp. On arrival, another woman brought some bark filled with clay. I'd seen her digging this some distance away while the men were hunting. She and the others smeared this gooey clay all over the feathers, about an inch thick, until the ducks looked like balls. They then sat them in the coals of the fire and left them for about an hour, turning occasionally."

He saw his father frown at him unbelieving at what he was listening to.

Sam gave him a nod and a smile and continued. "The clay had baked hard, and when broken open, the feathers all stuck in the clay. The birds were perfectly cooked in their own juices. We drank all the juices, not wasting a thing, except the feathers. I tried this myself sometime later and discovered just how difficult it was. Anyway, after some months, I had no idea of time, but I must have been with them for the best part of a year, if not longer, as I had arrived when it was cold, and it was when winter set in again that I got sick. I was really sick this time, and I was a problem, so they brought me to town by boat and left me at the hospital there. I was there for months, I think. In and out of consciousness. They gave up on me as they kept forgetting to bring me food, or if they did, I was too ill to eat it. Somehow, I didn't die. Eventually, I could sit up and even later stand, so I was discharged. I had nowhere to go, and I still wanted to die. I collapsed again under the rock where Bert Todd found me. He asked Anne if I could sleep in her shed. I think that was about September?"

Anne nodded.

"It was comparatively warm and dry and I had a stack of sacks and a blanket she had given me; I was in seventh heaven. I hadn't been warm for ages. Even in the aboriginal camp, they didn't have blankets. Anne gave me soup, a pastie and a blanket, and I slept, deep healing sleep. The next day she gave me more food, and I intended to leave her, I packed and left, but I was back again by that afternoon, grovelling to be allowed to sleep in her shed."

Annie turned his palm to her lips and kissed it.

"She allowed me back and brought me more food. I slept like a baby. Safe, warm, and fed. I'm not too proud to admit I cried; I sobbed. It was the first kindness from a white person that I had experienced for over a year and a half."

This time it was Lady Mari's turn to gasp back a sob.

All noticed but they stay quiet.

With an embarrassed, lopsided smile he started retelling his story again. "I tried to leave again the next day but came back and passed out again with tiredness that night. Only this time, I had a full stomach. By the third day, I managed to crawl to her garden. I'd done a bit the first day but this time I started weeding it. On my hands and knees, I could manage to move that much. Each meal she gave me, I gained strength, but I still wanted to just die. I'd given up. Then winter came, and I got sick again. The shed was cold, and as I was eating with her in the warm kitchen, I got a chill. Seeing I was ill, she brought me inside, and I slept in front of the kitchen fire on the settee. This time I knew I truly had met an angel. It was the first time I had a pillow and blanket for over nine years. She nursed me back to health again."

Lord James stifled a sob, as did Anne. Sam had never given her this much detail of those missing years.

"After some months, I'd noticed that her eyes were red and puffy from crying quite often, but I had no right to even ask why. She was still 'Miss White' to me. I did what I could to ease her burden of everyday life. We had discovered we could each read and that she even had some books. Our joy and delight was our reading together, for she had five wonderful books. There was The Diary of Samuel Pepys, John Donne, three Shakespeare's and the Bible. Back then, we rarely touched the Bible, that too came later, but the others we'd read together most nights, well, most of them. Sir Cecil, as you know, had taught her to read, and he had left her these books. Tim brought them with him when he came, and they were in the cottage waiting for her on her release. Oh, those evenings were a balm to my hurting soul. I had no idea what they meant to her, but as I said, I often saw her red eyes after she'd been crying. I wanted to hold her and comfort her but had no right to even touch her hand. Oh, how I wanted to give her some sort of emotional support and comfort. No, damn it, I desperately needed to hold her. Then one night we'd been reading, and as I read aloud from John Donne, I could feel her eyes burning into me." He paused and gently kissed the top of her head.

Anne turned with a murmur and laid her cheek against his chest, putting a hand on his heart. She knew what was coming and her boldness still embarrassed her.

"That night, out of the blue, she said, 'Why don't we get married?' Lady Mari, Father, I felt like I'd been kicked. All my wildest dreams of this had been just that... dreams. I had not even intentionally touched her hand. I could not say yes, even though my heart was bursting with joy. I knew I had to tell my story... but I couldn't. I was so ashamed of my conviction. I had no idea of hers either; I didn't care about that, but we could each have been axe murderers for all we knew. We each went to bed alone. Me, on the settee again, and her in her room. I could hear her crying. My heart hurt so very much." He wiped his thumb and finger across his eyes.

"The next day, we ignored the conversation from the night before and got on with our work, but then came nighttime. After dinner is when we normally did our reading. She gently placed the John Donne on the table, but I shook my head. 'Not tonight; I'm going to tell you my story,' I said, and so I did. Not as detailed as tonight, but enough for her to understand my shame. Then she revealed hers, again I wanted to hug her as she spoke. I did, however, take and caress her hand. My heart was beating a tattoo with just that touch, she returned it by taking my hand in hers. It was the first gentle touch I had had since my mother died when I was three. When she'd finished her story, we spoke briefly, and then I proposed this time."

"Go on, Sam, tell them everything," she said.

"Sure?" he asked quietly.

"We're their illegitimate children, and I slept with my mother's husband," she chuckled, "I think they'll cope. Yes, everything!"

"Okay," he kissed her hair again. "Well, she said yes. And I kissed her. Passionately, crushing her to me, something I'd wanted to do for some time. Oh, what a delight for me, but I intended to wait until marriage for anything more. However, that's not exactly what happened. She explained that she was so afraid that I'd leave her alone that she wanted us to marry so she'd not be alone again, she'd had enough, and it was nearly killing her. She'd not had someone in her life since Sir Cecil. It had even been longer for me. Ten years between, um, drinks, is well, hard to resist. Again, I drew her to me and kissed her. Passionately and almost drunk with her essence, I was nearly going to pick her up and... well, I pushed her gently away from me and went to get ready for bed alone. She went and changed with the same intention of sleeping alone, but at least with a smile on her lips. A person can only be alone for so long. Then the tears of loneliness came again, I could hear her sobs, and she came to me. When I saw her tears, I was gone. When she put out her hand to me, I knew she'd not be alone that night."

Anne's sob into his shoulder made him pause. He whispered, "I love you so very much." Then he caressed her cheek then he continued. "She said, 'I am so afraid I'll be alone again. I need to be needed, to be held and cherished. I need to be loved, even if it were just physical'."

Anne gazed at Sam, remembering those words and feelings. "Back then, I didn't know what love was; I'd never experienced it. Cec was kind, and I'd confused it with love, but what I felt for Sam crushed me, yet elated me too; I found it hard to breathe just thinking about if he left me. I could not bear that. I'd wished to die if he did that."

Sam's arms pulled her close to him. "I needed it too, my beloved. I couldn't believe you wanted me as just me, a convict, a rejected son and even a failed man. You have no idea how healing that was in itself." He bent and kissed her again.

A minute or so later, he continued their story. "The next day, we applied to get married, but being ex-convicts, it took time, some six weeks. Anyway, that night after our engagement, I went to settle again on the settee, I'd just pulled up my blankets, and the lamp was off. I became aware that she was standing next to me, again tear-stained and looking so sad. The firelight was silhouetting her body through her nightgown. I carried her back to bed, and we have never been apart since." He put his cheek on her soft grey-flecked hair of his beloved wife.

"There was no church in the town at the time, as the Sydney one had burnt down. We eventually married in the front room of our cottage that Tim had built for her. Our builder, Willy Knight, and the man who had found me that wet night, Bert Todd, were our witnesses. I was pleased and admittedly surprised she hadn't fallen pregnant in the weeks before we married. I admit from that first night, I put it out of my mind. By then, she was far too precious to me, but I had not acknowledged my feelings were love. When she did get pregnant, we were thankfully married. Danny was born twelve months after we married. I remember when she found out. I knew she'd been ill a few times, but we'd been given some kangaroo tail meat and if you overeat it, it can do that to you. It's very rich, so I didn't think much about it. We were often ill from eating something odd. Hygiene and cleanliness in the markets in Sydney is not that good. We didn't have much money for good food unless we grew it ourselves. On the third morning she again came in with a tear-stained face. She'd been ill again and suddenly realised why. Neither of us had thought about children. We both sort of presumed she couldn't have them, as she'd not fallen with Sir Cecil for the years, they were together, but admittedly neither of us had even thought about it."

"Ahh, about that…" said Lady Mari. "The boys and Ceccy caught mumps some months before Amelia was born, and Ceccy was in… um, great pain and swollen in his private area, for some time. He moved to London some three months after she was born. We did try again but, well, nothing happened, which for us was unusual. So, he stopped coming home. This was some six months before you were on the way, Anne. You could not have been his child, as we hadn't been together for over three months by then. I don't think he could father children after that. I certainly never fell again, and he tried hard enough in those three months. It's another reason I wasn't that worried about you, as I didn't think there would be any children."

"Oh, I didn't know," Anne said in amazement. What an odd conversation to have with one's mother.

"Well, Danny arrived, and during his birth, I had to assist the midwife, and that was an amazing experience, by the way. Every father should be able to do that. Anyway, it was taking too long to deliver with her lying down, and the midwife said to try the way the local aboriginal women gave birth, squatting. I won't go into too much detail, but I could not hold back whispering how much I loved her as she was delivering him. My own feelings had hit me like a wave when I thought that I could lose her. I suddenly realised what I felt for her was love. She was my life. I could not hold it in. She heard, but I was too scared to say more later. We let things float. If our marriage was no more than what it was, I knew I was still content with what we had. I loved her, and that was enough. I still could not work out how I could assist with bringing in money. She was exhausted working dawn to dusk, baking and selling her wares, and looking after Danny too. With Danny, it made it even worse as feeding him drained her energy even more. I did what I could, but it wasn't enough. Danny was a good baby, but I felt she was working too hard. Anyway, I thought about building an extension at the back of the cottage for Danny. He was still sleeping in a drawer on the floor of our room. So, I started drawing plans for an extension."

Annie nodded her agreement. That decision ultimately changed their lives.

Sam smiled, and said, "I met another man, a professional builder, who said they were good, and he paid me to draw pictures of his buildings. Finally, I was earning some real money. And I could do it from home and be on hand for her. I got paid 1/- per drawing. Funny, as the poor box I tried to steal didn't have that much in it. Anyhow, it was nearly a week's profit from her baking. Within a year, I earned £1 a month, and she was soon able to take things a bit easier. But I get ahead of myself a bit. When Josh, later he was Danny's father-in-law, hired me to do his drawings, other builders did too. On the day I had my first drawing accepted, I was over the moon. I'd also seen a change in Annie and saw the moods and feelings visible on her face. I'd watched as she'd fed Danny and saw the absolute adoration on her face for him. He was hers. Then I saw her looking at me; I saw far more than lust or contentment; I'd see the same look on her face as when she looked at Danny. So that night, I told her that I loved her and had for some time. As neither of us had experienced this unique feeling in our lives in any form, neither of us had realised what it felt like. I knew I could not live without her in my life, and when I thought I could lose her having Danny, I was shattered. It hit me, as I said, like I'd been kicked in the stomach, run over by a carriage, and thrown over a cliff all at once. I couldn't breathe; I needed to just be there, help her, touch her, and tell her of my feelings. Even though I was with her all the time, I could not bring myself to admit my feeling to her. I'd had enough rejection in my life. Well, as I had just finished the first plan, I was being paid to draw. I was on a high. Finally, I'd picked up the book we planned to read that evening, and it fell open at a poem we often skipped due to its, um, suggestive narrative. There were some of his poems we'd agree to skip due to, well, let's just say we'd mutually agreed to leave these out of the reading schedule, and this was one where he takes his mistress to bed. Well, Anne was my wife, but still, I was scared to admit how I felt, and I thought, damn it, I'm going to tell her. I read her the first bit of the poem, and I couldn't wait any longer. Then I told her that the poem was then going to be demonstrated. And then I told her that I loved her. I was so astounded when she told me that she too realised her own feelings for me were equally as strong. She'd heard me as I encouraged her during Danny's birth, and I think it made you think?" He looked down at her.

She nodded. "You're right; I had no idea what love was. With Cec, I felt cherished. I liked it, but I wasn't in love with him. I thought I was, but I was wrong. I didn't know that until I thought about how I felt for Sam. Without him, I didn't want to live either. I couldn't breathe when I thought about him not being in my life. Gutted and winded. That's why I cried all those nights ago."

Sam's thumb stroked her cheek. "Well, from then on, it sounds silly, but our happiness was complete, at least, so we thought. As you know our early life, we were both overwhelmed to be accepted for just being ourselves. Then Tim came and shattered our peace. Although I had told Anne most of my story, I'd not mentioned anything about titles or even this house. Hence she was unprepared when she saw it. I had just said it was big. Remember, Tim knew of me only as Sam Corbett. I had no idea until the next day he knew who I was. Tim had watched a game I'd played at Oxford. I had received an award as I scored four goals, but he knew me from school, where he was a senior. He recognised me, and the next morning he came privately and revealed he knew my real identity. He then told me of Nigel's death."

Lord James grinned. "I saw that game too, son! I was so proud of you and was frustrated too, as I could say nothing." Lord James looked at Sam with adoration written on his face. "I watched you collect the trophy, as proud as a parent could be."

Sam nodded thanks and smiled; he'd paused as he was still unsure about how he felt about Nigel's death. He shook his head, trying to scare the memory away. He drew Anne closer to him. "As I was arrested, the Earl threw at me, 'I'll disinherit you if it's the last thing I do.' I presumed he had, so I figured why stress her over something that would never happen, but I did tell her then. We still didn't mention it to Danny for ten more years. And we only did then as the solicitors had arrived and told me I was the Earl. I had no choice. We told him then, for I had the paperwork to what I'd hoped was to renounce the title, but it was only to break the Entail. Dan later told me I couldn't renounce the title even if I wished to. I was going to pass it directly to him. To say he was angry was an understatement. Livid is far more accurate. His vitriol was tangible."

He gave Annie a gentle caress. "As you know, he's an easy-going boy, and this was not like him. Anne made me pass over the letter from the Earl. I didn't want him to experience hate like that, but I didn't want to lose him because of it either, so I let him read it. The poor boy actually gagged, and soon he was on his knees begging my forgiveness. We three are very close, and remember none of us knew the relationship between the Earl and me. Danny came here ready to break the Entail too. Charlie and I had already agreed to sign it. They did so, and it was awaiting my signature on his return. I only held off because that day Vanessa told us of her pregnancy. A day later and this house would have been sold. Charlie didn't want it; neither did his sons. We were going to sell it and give away the money to charity. Vanessa went from the high to lows, emotionally, loving the attention and yet hating the pomp. However, we had no idea she was expecting; she only revealed that to Dan on her return; she knew and never said anything knowing that it would change Dan's mind. Now I look back; this explains much. Sadly, she died days after having Edmund. His birth, however, changed everything. Firstly, it cut Charlie out of the Entail documentation rights, so that paperwork was now obsolete, as because Eddie was underage, he was, of course, unable to sign them. By the time he gets to twenty-one, I'll probably be dead. So, the Entail stays in place."

Anne lifted her face to Sam.

He bent and kissed her gently. "So, against our will, we came back. We had to, for our grandson's rights and for our granddaughters' future. No matter how much we hated to come, we knew we had to. On the ship here, we met the Darling's. They were wonderful. We'd had no one to teach us anything about protocol or, well, anything over there. Um, there is no protocol for an ex-convict except to be subservient to all. We aimed to survive, and that's it. I remembered a bit from my childhood, but I honestly had forgotten much as I was only young. My best skill was hiding from the Earl and Watmore. What I knew I had the learning at school, as I was taught nothing here. I didn't understand why things were done and didn't ask for details, as when I was in the same room with the Earl, I learned to just keep silent. I just kept my head down and stayed out of his way as much as possible. It's when I found my haven here, my old library. But I knew that we had to return and face the music." He looked down to Anne. "That was when I found my secret library, love. You know the one with all the old books."

Anne nodded. The tiny old library was still a delight to them both. They would often sneak away and sit reading together. They would enjoy reading the prose and poetry as they had in Sydney.

"Onboard, the Darlings became good friends. We offered all we had, ourselves in friendship. They had to face their own music, but we didn't know that; it was some sort of case or inquiry. We didn't ask, still haven't, and they didn't share." He sighed, amazed that they had become friends. "I had refused to use my title even then, and so we became Anne and Sam, and they Eliza and Ralph." He took a deep breath. "I know we had told you bits and bobs over the past weeks, but I wanted you to know just what Anne means to me. Lady Mari, my pet name for her, has always been 'Anne joy'. I had, of course, no idea of who she was, nor it seems who I was." He looked at his father and smiled. "I just want you to know she is the reason I regained the will to live. I wanted to tell you the entire story uninterrupted."

Both Lady Mari and Lord James nodded.

"Oh, my dear son," said the Duke, "to know that you suffered so. If I'd known, I could have assisted. After you were arrested, I was out of the country for some time. First in France, then I had to see George Washington in his discussions on his Proclamation of Neutrality. I was part of the negotiating contingency. When I got back, Anthony Jenkins told me you'd just been arrested for theft. I found a friend of yours, Daniel Philpott, who'd visited you and he got some information for me. He would have headed back in to see you, but I pulled a few strings and got you out of that hell hole as fast as I could. I sent in some things to assist but heard later they never made it to you. So, sending money would have been out of the question. If I'd known before you'd been convicted, I could have sorted it all out, but by the time I found out, you were convicted and in gaol. I managed to get you put straight on the *Royal Admiral*, which was about to depart. I hoped that at least the diseases in the gaols like the gaol fever that abounded, wouldn't get you. Sam, if I were acknowledged as your father, I could and would have moved heaven and earth, but my hands were totally tied. Philip cut off all access to my information. Your mother was dead, and Anthony was my only source of access to you, and he'd already been threatened with dismissal if he was caught passing on information. He stilled though, so I needed him here as a sort of spy. I should have given him some money for you, though. I didn't think of that until it was too late. I had no idea that you were allowed none at all. I would have explained it somehow. I could have sent it anonymously to you at college. Though that in itself would have been dangerous as you may have thanked Philip, and then all would have come out. I sent out people to keep their eye on you, and I even sent a note to Mr West when I found out you were there. I paid him to hire you and not to put you in a chain gang. He was supposed to keep you safe." Lord James wiped his eyes.

"I was until I was released," Sam said. "Whatever it was, I just wanted to die. It wasn't really his fault we had little food, we were in drought."

Lord James broke in. "I felt so absolutely damned useless. Pardon my language, my dears, but I was so angry with Watmore. He knew I would've helped. I would even pay him a huge fee, if not an outright bribe, had I known. But he kept quiet about his involvement. He kept quiet for over forty years. It was when Danny arrived that day at Malvern Hall when Watmore boasted about what he'd done to Sam that I finally knew the truth. The man had Baptised you, and yet he did that to you. I stood beside Danny and supported him in a way I did with my other grandsons. I glared at Watmore, and he looked at me and just smiled, knowing I could say nothing in public. I just told him to leave, and surprisingly he did. I felt like decking the man. I believe Charlie told you that others turned their backs to him that day. That hurt him more than I could have done. Church attendance fell for that entire year after Danny left. When you came back last year and said what you did, I heard about it by that afternoon. I punched the air and cheered."

Lady Mari had sat silently through Sam's story. She knew what that kicked in the stomach feeling was like. She'd felt it often enough. When she was first raped at thirteen by her father, then first kissed Philip, their first liaison in the folly; then three months later, she found she was having his child. Each time she felt guilty. Philip was the first man she'd given herself to willingly. She was only twenty. At seventeen, she said she'd marry the first man who asked. She ended up asking her shy twenty-seven-year-old neighbour, Cecil, to marry her while they were on the hunt ride. His father was constantly badgering him to marry. She begged him, and he said yes. She knew that at least he was kind and gentle. She agreed to provide him with an heir or two. She would have agreed to anything to get her away from her father and his abuse.

She wiped her cheek with a lawn handkerchief. The memories were invading her thoughts, and she was unable to keep her emotions in check. She had told them far more than she had intended to, but it needed to be said for Anne to understand the horror she'd experience and what she would do to save Anne from being raped too. It wasn't as if her father was gentle. He enjoyed hurting and humiliating before he'd violate with whatever instrument he chose. Betsy knew; she too had been an innocent. He'd abused her so severely she was bedridden for a week. Her father thought it funny. She cast him out of the house that day, and he'd stayed away for years. When he died, she did not even allow a funeral.

Anne sat watching her mother's face. The emotions washing over her were obviously extreme. Their eyes met, and Anne read both love and pity in them. She had no idea what her mother's thoughts were but realised they were sad and causing her pain.

"Anna, my dearest love, do not think sadly for me. I am thinking back over hurts from my own childhood. I shall leave them unvoiced as they will not benefit you, and better still that they are now forgotten, as I will make new happy memories. Knowing what a beast I was brought up by and what he was like, I sacrificed you to save you from his vile actions. I will, however, tell you this. I do not know if you have heard of a thing called the 'Brotherhood of St. Francis of Wycombe' later called the 'The Hellfire Club', well Sir Francis Dashwood was a close friend of Father. Two of a kind, if you will. They went on the grand tour together. I'd hate to know what trouble they got up to over there. They used to take all sorts of lascivious and licentious pleasures, and raping innocents was just one of those. I heard rumours that some girls were even killed by this club, but I have no idea if they were involved in that. I think the word to sum up father would be a sadist. He took great pleasure in inflicting pain and delighted in the humiliation of the innocents. I do not wish to go into detail, for you do not need to know, but I'll give you the end of the story as it seems to be a time for clearing the air."

Annie started to move.

"No, no, stay there, girl. If you sit near me, I will be unable to speak." Her mother waved to her to stay with Sam. "Anna, when he died, I would not even give him a funeral. I got the minister to shove him in the crypt and told him no prayers were to be said. He deserved none. I would have no idea if he did as I requested. I doubt any were said, as the poor minister had to pick up the shattered pieces of the numerous girls' lives that Father had defiled, and I mean defiled. He also enjoyed cutting them with his knife. He did not do that to me, but Sarah bore scars as he cut a few times. Do you know I've not been asked once about him since he died? I feel for my second cousin, Percy, who inherited the title. It must be hard for him. I have only spoke to him once since he inherited. There was a fire soon after that and tragedy hit the family."

Anne was holding Sam's hand so tightly that he moved so he could get some circulation back, and he stroked the back of her hand to comfort her.

"Anna, please don't cry for me. Ceccy saved me. He was kind and gentle, as you know. But I never loved him. Philip was the love of my life, but he was married too. When I found out his Anne was also expecting,

Phil denied it was his, and the only person I could think of was you, James. I had wondered if she was meeting someone. I knew she'd go riding with Jenkins, but he was only fifteen. I didn't think it would be him. She hated Charlie's father with loathing, and Ceccy was in London. So that left you, James. Your father was dead by then, and you were nineteen or twenty as well, the same age as us, and a Duke. She finally confessed to me, and I to her." She turned again to Annie "James, Anne and I were all of an age. Philip was then twenty-seven, four years younger than Ceccy. As I said, Phil was a hypocrite. If Sam had been a girl, he might not have minded, but he was obsessed with Meldon Hall. Nigel was the apple of his eye. Not because he was his wife's but because he was legitimate. His hopes rested on him. When Nigel died, he was so angry. He came and saw me just after Nigel's funeral. I should add here that we had not actually stopped seeing each other after you were born Anna, we were just far more careful and discreet. As I said, he was the love of my life, but he was wrong about how he treated you Sam, and I told him so. That hurt me so much. We could have married after Ceccy died, as we were both free by then, but for some reason, it never happened. It's strange, but it never occurred to me before. I have a feeling Watmore had something to do with that too. He might have threatened to expose all if we had."

Lord James's head dropped. He said quietly, "He did. You hit the nail on the head there, Mari. After Danny's run-in with him at my place, I dug deeper. He'd take pleasure in offering Baptism for these poor innocents, normally in private. Then he'd bribe the parents. My Anne told me this in a letter years before, but I didn't believe it. I should have done. Philip was paying hush money to him monthly, and for years it went straight into Watmore's pocket. Sam, it may also have been a reason for him not to give you funds." He met Lady Mari's eyes. "My story is not so horrifying. I was bored when I first met Anne. I used to sit and watch her ride, admiring her fair beauty, and one day, she fell not far from where I was sitting. I rushed to her aide. To cut a long story short, I was nineteen at the time, sent down from Oxford for some stupid misdemeanour, and not old enough to head to London to have fun. I was a Duke and had no one to answer to as both my parents were dead. Though Anne became far more to me than just a bit of fun. I fell for her hard but did not touch her. I was horrified when she told me of her life here. From the day she told Philip she was carrying Nigel, he avoided her and her bedroom. Our affair started almost by accident when Nigel was six months old. I never meant to kiss her, but she tripped, and when she was in my arms, I could not resist." He fell silent, remembering the sweetness of that first innocent kiss. After some time, he continued."Nigel had not long been born, and nothing physical happened between us for almost a year. We'd kiss, but I had no intention of cuckolding my neighbour. By then, I was truly in love with her. Then one day, she arrived in tears flying into my arms. Philip had hit her for some stupid thing she had not even done. We ended up in our special secluded place in the mossy lined copse, and well, one thing led to another." James smiled to himself, thinking of that first time. "She was allowed to be accompanied by Anthony as he was only fifteen when we met. Philip trusted the lad. He would sit and keep watch for us, or leave us and exercise the horses. He saw how she was treated and would have done anything for her. Soon we met whenever we could. Anthony became our communication link. I'd wait in the same place daily or send notes if we couldn't. Anthony would exercise the horses daily, so it was easy for him to ride when he wished. We were by then so love and not at all careful, she fell pregnant with you Sam. Oh, even then, we enjoyed our liaisons. We continued to see each other until she was five months gone, then one day, Philip followed her. He caught us in an indelicate situation. He dragged her out of the thicket, and I never saw her again." James wiped a single tear from his cheek. "I regret none of it, Sam, for because of it, I have you. I only regret your suffering."

The four sat in the warm sunroom, each deep in thought with the raw and wounded emotions they each had coped with.

The sound of the tinkling laughs of the estate children echoed down the hallways.

Sam met his father's eyes. They were now smiling back at him.

Lord James coughed, then laughed a little. "So now, dearest children, we've aired our sorrows and dirty linens; we need to work out how to move forward. Your plans for the Hall are excellent, Sam, there is one area I think needs adding to a little. You are doing good things for the women and children, but I've heard of two young men, like Philip and I, who both lost our way when young. Charlie's Henry and his brother Tom need some resolute direction. Other young men, too, need to have their life of luxury removed from them. A good dose of reality is what they need. I would like us to put out heads together, perhaps with your wonderful Reverend Hugh, Tim, Nathan, and maybe others could get involved, even Charlie. With the moral happenings in London, the power of wealth is going to the heads of the young bucks and sending them off the narrow path of respectability. They are all so cashed up that they think they can do what they wish with women from any walk of life. They are forgetting their responsibility of their roles and ranks. Let me sleep on the idea, but I'd like to see something done for them too. This would be more of a one at a time situation. I'm stumped for how it would work."

Sam watched the pained look on his father's face. "Yes, that is another way we could assist. Let me know what you come up with."

Lady Mari chipped in, "I wonder, you know how they have finishing schools for young ladies; I was wondering about a three or six-months school for young peers. Letting them get to know the people behind the faces of the staff. That in itself may well be enough. Again, I'm not sure how it would quite work, but no harm in trying. Maybe if we speak to both Oxford and Cambridge Universities, they could be directed here when sent down rather than go to their homes. Almost like a conditional suspension."

James' eyes twinkled. "Perfect Mari I love it. I'm on the board at Cambridge University, so I shall suggest it next meeting."

Chapter 14   Pas de Deux
'The step of two' or 'Dance for two'

*T*he Baptism of James Samuel Daniel Corbett Garney occurred on Easter Day 1834.

That next week Hugh was in a quandary about the sermon topic and wondered what he should preach. He was sitting under a tree in the garden, his mind wandering; he saw Mrs Anne with Betsy and her mother, Lady Mari, surrounded by children. They had told him the whole story soon after they had known it. He'd also been consulted into the uses for the Hall. His mind was swirling with possible ideas.

There were now some twenty peer orphans living with the other children at the Hall. What a joyous, lively place it was. The children were all loved and happy. The Earl had officially made all the children his legal wards, and they were treated the same as his own grandchildren and the staff's children. They now all attended the new village school; Mr Sam had totally refurbished the old school and built a new hall for their use. He'd added a music room, supplied teachers, and encouraged all the adults in the village to attend reading lessons. Then he had stocked shelves with many books to use and a system for them to be borrowed.

Hugh smiled when he thought of the scores of disabled staff now employed at the Hall on the grounds and in the stables, and the volume of new faces seen as the trained staff were encouraged to move on to new positions so others could gain training.

Anthony was given a free hand with who to keep on permanently in the stables. The others were provided references and allowed to seek other positions, yet they all left well trained. The new outdoor and garden staff were fully qualified, yet they still took on new trainees, with the idea to place them in jobs elsewhere. This was something the injured soldiers and sailors could learn and do. The faces changed regularly as new soldiers and sailors completed training and moved on and others took their places.

Hugh took control of the young lads who had been sent down from various colleges and universities. First, he'd give them a morals lecture, and then Mr Sam took them in and showed them another side of life, including the consequences of their lust. He also pointed out the importance of their actions and the responsibilities associated with their positions.

These young men would come on condition their own parents were not told of their misdemeanours, and often they returned on holidays by choice. They nearly always returned changed men.

Hugh smiled when he thought of the volume of references that he wrote for the leaving staff. His were added to the Earl's ones, ensuring that the Domestic Bureau was in regular contact with Graham Long, the agent.

Lady Mari was tireless. At eighty-four, she was still deeply involved with their work. She often had company with her friend James seen with her on his arm. Having retired fully from Society, she said, "I am too busy to fritter away my time in a useless and wasteful way."

Hugh was thrilled when given a chance to first take up a parish and with the full support of the local peerage. When he heard of the previous incumbent, he found he had much un-teaching to do. He smiled to himself. Yes, the sermon this week would be on adoption and forgiveness. How apt! The reading for the day was doubting Thomas. He smiled again and, dipping his head, started to write.

Sunday morning, the church was again almost overflowing. The Family, as they now called themselves, took up the front three pews. The children all sat on the floor in front of the front pew. He'd not seen children so well behaved as these. Mostly, they sat still throughout the service. Occasionally there would be a wiggle, but no fights or pinching. The village children sat on the other side and took note of the Hall children's behaviour. They also were well behaved. Hugh gave a children's talk, and then the children went outside for fifteen minutes while he spoke to the adults. He watched as Miriam waited for all the children to follow her. He sighed; with them gone, he could concentrate. Yet, it was not the children who distracted his attention. The Sunday School, as he called it, allowed the adults to focus on his words. The children would have the story; usually, the Gospel, explained to them, and they got to draw a picture while listening.

Hugh waited until everyone settled. "Shalom – that means peace." He started his sermon. "Jesus probably used a similar greeting daily. Peace is what He wants for each of us; peace, joy, patience, love and understanding to name a few. God also wants us to trust Him. He wants us to come to him in faith and 'know' that He will forgive us; we only have to ask. So today, I shall concentrate on two words, forgiveness and adoption." He lifted his eyes from his notes. The sea of faces were all watching him.

"I'm going to combine the second reading and Gospel reading today as they are both written by John. The first part is from 1 John Chapter 5 verses 1 to 6, and the Gospel is from John Chapter 20 verses 19-31." Hugh spoke from not just his heart but knew that his flock were still hurting after the arrogant leadership they had experienced for so long.

Sam's eyes caught his. Sam knew those first three verses by heart.

"Whosoever believeth that Jesus is the Christ, is born of God. And every one that loveth him who begot, loveth him also who is born of him. In this, we know that we love the children of God: when we love God and keep his commandments."

Sam knew he was a child of God. Anne knew it too.

The Darlings had taken time to explain God, Jesus, and a new way of life to them. Sam had prayed with Ralph and asked for forgiveness for everything he could. He knew he'd been freed from those sins. After Anne and he had discovered their love, they had started reading the Bible daily. There was so much they didn't understand.

Ralph Darling opened their eyes to how to put what was written in the Bible into action. Although they still finished their days with the other five books, now accompanied by others, they started every morning with a Bible reading. It had taken time to learn the difference between religion and actual faith, but there was one.

Watmore had only taught religion; Hugh taught faith and forgiveness. The history of their births had nothing to do with how God saw them. They were both born innocent, as was every other child. Yet they paid the price of their parents' infidelity, and still, God had protected and brought them together to discover such a godly love for each other that they drew others to them to share it.

All the children sitting quietly on the floor some moments ago showed that.

The elderly lady sitting next to Anne, clinging to her other hand, showed that, and the Duke sitting in the pew across the aisle smiling at him also showed him that. Sam dragged his thoughts back to Hugh.

Sam caught the words, "...After Jesus' resurrection, He first appeared, not to a king, nor to a Roman, not to a Pharisee, nor an apostle, but to a repentant and forgiven prostitute. Mary of Magdala had followed

Jesus and was distraught when he died. However, he chose to show himself to her first. Not even to his own mother. Women were not often listened to in those days, yet they still had an important place in society. None of the apostles were women, yet she, Mary Magdalene, was chosen to be the very first eyewitness to his risen state…" Sam listened intently.

Hugh kept talking… "Mary asked for forgiveness and was granted it. Completely and absolutely, no questions asked. Totally wiped clean."

As Hugh spoke, Anne's thoughts reverted to her liaison with Cec. She'd never asked for forgiveness for that… nor for sleeping with Sam before they married. It had never occurred to her that she needed to do it. She caught her breath. Clinging to his hand, she bowed her head and asked for forgiveness to be washed clean and to start new, just like Mary had. They were coming up to thirty-five years of marriage. Since sitting listening to Hugh and his pure loving Faith, they had grown in knowledge and assurance of God's forgiveness. It's not that they hadn't believed in God; they had, but they had no understanding of forgiveness or even of the depth of His love for them.

Sam felt a teardrop splash onto his hand as it lay on Anne's lap. He looked at her and saw her face almost shining with joy. He gasped. He knew her so well he realised something had happened, something good. He stroked her hand with his thumb. More he could not do as they were in church.

Hugh was still speaking. Sam's mind had wandered again. Concentrating, he tuned back into Hugh's words as he said, "… and Thomas, he doubted, and he was talking to an eyewitness. Yet he doubted. It was not until Jesus spoke to him: *"Then he saith to Thomas: Put in thy finger hither, and see my hands, and bring hither thy hand, and put it into my side; and be not faithless, but believing. Thomas answered and said to him: My Lord, and my God. Jesus saith to him: Because thou hast seen me, Thomas, thou hast believed: blessed are they that have not seen, and have believed."*

"People, it's okay to doubt… if it leads you to question and change. For hopefully, that questioning is going to lead you to find out more about Him." He pointed heavenwards. "Thomas doubted, and he ended up going to India and teaching many others about God. Most of the others would have doubted, too; we know Peter certainly denied him. Every one of the apostles had to confess their doubts, sins and actions. Not one of us sitting here, from myself, My Lord Duke to young James in his mother's arms down there will live without doubt. And more importantly, every single one of us will one day stand before God for judgement, from the King to the street waifs and everyone in-between. Not one of us is exempt from standing before our Lord's judgement seat. We're told that in the book of Matthew, every word, every action must be answered for... You've heard that before... but, and this is the bit you need to listen to..."

Hugh fell silent; he'd wait. He wanted every eye and ear on him. He dropped his voice but still spoke loud enough for all to hear. "Every one of us is also given a way out, a free pass if you will. It will cost you nothing... but your life. Yes, God has sent his own son, Jesus, to bear our sins. He died for each and every one of us. Jesus took our sins, big and small. He, Jesus, bore the burden of our wrong-doings, and they were on Him when He died. The price for our sins." Hugh took a breath and said in a loud voice, "He, Jesus, PAID IN FULL! So, if we confess our sins and change our lives, then follow Him, that's it." He could still see the confusion on some faces. "Let me put it this way. What happens when you wipe chalk off a slate with a dry cloth? Come on, hands up..."

Anthony Jenkins put up his hand from the back of the church. "You can still see the words, sir."

"Yes, Anthony, you can still see the words. That's like mankind's version of forgiveness. We humans can forgive, but we don't forget. We bring those same sins up time, after time, after time, and time again. Sometimes to be brought up repeatedly and thrown in the face of the person who has asked for forgiveness. That's like the chalk wiped with a dry cloth." He heard a collective gasp but continued. "Okay, next question, George, you're a butcher. What happens if blood gets on your order slate? I saw it happen once, and you were spitting chips, to say the least."

George Smith stood and said loudly, "It totally obliterated my orders for the day, sir. Gone forever, and no matter what I tried, I could not get those words back."

"Exactly, George! And that was only a tiny bit of lamb's blood, wasn't it? Imagine what the blood of the Son of God, the Lamb of God, will do? You are all washed clean. Gone forever!"

A loud audible gasp echoed around the church.

Hugh heard it and smiled, Yeah! Now they were listening. He saw the children lining up to come back in. He wanted them to listen to this next bit, so he paused and invited them too. "Come and sit down. Children, you have timed it well. I have not finished, but I want you to hear this bit. Come, come."

When they had seated themselves and settled, he asked, "Now, do you know what adoption is?"

They had come in and sat as he spoke. Jo-Anne put up her hand, and Hugh nodded for her to answer. "Jo-Jo, can you tell us, please?"

She stood and said clearly. "It's where you don't grow in that person's tummy, you grow in their heart. It is like getting new brothers and sisters, like a gift. Just like all my new brothers and sisters." She waved her hand over the many children next to her. "They are my heart siblings, and I love them all just the same." She smiled and sat down.

"Oh, my dear Jo-Anne, exactly right. Jo-Jo, I could not have said it better. They grow in the heart. Well, we are all adopted. We are each adopted by God as his own children. Our earthly parentage doesn't matter because it's our Godly one that does."

Some sobs, a gasp or two, and sniffing were heard throughout the church.

"So dear friends, with our confession, our sins are wiped clean. From stealing a penny or two," Hugh's eyes fell on Sam; "to as bad as you can imagine, even to murder, no-one is beyond redemption. Yes, of course, there will be earthly consequences, but the Heavenly ones are our goal. We read of all the sins in the Bible; everyone can be forgiven; we just have to ask." He paused; every eye was on him, "Absolutely everything can be forgiven by God." He dropped his voice as though whispering but said for all to hear, "You just have to ask Him. We are already growing in God's heart. He is ready to adopt you. You just have to say YES to Him." Hugh pointed Heavenward.

Anne's face was still glowing. "That's me, Sam!" she said softly. "I'd not asked for forgiveness before. Now I feel clean."

On the other side of her, Lady Mari took her hand.

Anne looked at her face when she felt a teardrop on her hand too. Their eyes met, and Anne realised that she too was smiling widely. She, too, was forgiven.

Sam looked to his father; Lord James' head was in his hands as if in prayer, but he turned and winked at Sam when their eyes met across the aisle, both smiled. Both knew they, too, had been forgiven.

The service continued.

Holy Communion was celebrated, and as each person returned to their seats, Sam noticed that many of the faces were peaceful, quite a few were tear-stained, some glowing, one or two contrite.

Hugh said, "For our final hymn, we're going to sing one of my favourites, A Charles Wesley hymn. Some call it *And can it be*, I call it *Amazing Love* for that's what it is, God's amazing love for us. Ladies and gentlemen, please feel free to descant the hymn if you know it. Let us lift our voices to Him in joyful praise. Before we sing it with as much joy as possible, I'm going to read you the first and last verses. Think about the words as you belt them out loudly.

And can it be that I should gain
An interest in the Saviour's blood?
Died He for me, who caused His pain?
Hugh asked,"Did you get that bit?

"He, Jesus, died for me… and you and you and you…" Hugh punched his chest and pointed to his congregation.

who caused HIS pain
For me, who Him to death pursued?
Amazing love. how can it be
That Thou, my God, shouldst die for me?

And listen to the word of the last verse:-
No Condemnation now I dread;
Jesus, and all in Him, is mine.
Alive in Him, my living head,
And clothed in righteousness Divine,
Bold I approach the eternal throne,
And claim the crown, through Christ my own."

Hugh himself was croaky-throated after saying the words. "I want you each to know you can claim your eternal crown. Do not be afraid to ask Him. Now Mr Waddington, belt this one out loudly, please. Everyone, please be upstanding. Ready? Sing with gusto, and if anyone wishes to come and see me to know more, don't hesitate."

The organist did just as asked. He played the rousing hymn with great enjoyment on the new pipe organ that Sam had bought for the church with great joy and enthusiasm.

The harmony of voices rose and united; it seemed to almost lift the roof.

Tears of forgiveness streamed down Anne's cheeks.

Sam wasn't sure what to do, so he stood with her, just holding her hand. His eyes flicked over to Lady Mari next to her; she, too, was weeping. He sang the uplifting words of the hymn as he watched.

They sang *"And clothed in righteousness Divine,"* and Sam caught his breath, realising that yes, they were. All of them, himself included.

Anne's shining face lifted to meet his, "Sam, I feel I am clean."

He could see the joy on her face shining with delight; her tears were of happiness. He tucked her hand into the crook of his arm and led her outside. He could see she was clothed in the shining joy of forgiveness, as was Lady Mari. He could see that she, too, had been listening to the words of forgiveness.

Lady Mari took the Duke's arm and followed them out. He gave her fingers a gentle, caring squeeze. The rest of the family and children followed in an orderly fashion, each of the older children taking the hand of a younger one.

Danny brought up the rear of the family with baby James in one arm and Georgie in the other. The babe had slept through the entire service.

Sam and Anne both noticed the tear-stained faces of many of their friends and most of the girls brought from London. It seems they had all listened and that Hugh's words had hit home.

Sam said as much to Hugh as he exited. "Hugh, I knew you were the man I wanted here. If you look at the tear-stained faces that are exiting, but they were all smiling, you will know that your powerful sermon really hit home. We all need to be told about love, forgiveness, and acceptance, but this mob especially. You could have heard a pin drop today, Hugh. I won't say congratulations. I will, however, say, thank you."

"Thank you, Mr Sam; I feel blessed to be able to work with you, but can you stay back as I'd like a quick word, please."

Sam nodded, puzzled.

Anne walked up to Sam as he spoke. "I won't just shake your hand, Hugh. I'm going to give you a kiss. I'm twice your age, so no one will think more than it is. It's just a big thank you from me too. I was one with tears, too, Hugh; I feel washed clean. I've never felt this before." She went in and gave him a gentle kiss on his cheek after her hug.

Grinning at his wife, Sam moved them on so others could talk to him. They moved slightly away and turned so others could approach them too if they wished.

Lord James escorted Lady Mari to a bench seat circling a tree trunk. They sat knee to knee chatting quietly while watching the various family members.

Nathan and Phoebe approached. "Father, would you mind spending the day with Lady Mari? We've been invited to Tim's house for Sophie's birthday luncheon."

"You go off, son, I'll be content, and I'm sure well, looked after," the Duke replied, grinning. He'd not intended to go home with them anyway; however, he need not mention that now. Lord James had left some of his clothing in his suite at the Hall. Each visit, he brought more.

"Tim asked everyone in the family, but are to come around tomorrow on her actual birthday." Nathan loaded this wife and children into the carriage, and they waved as they headed off.

Once gone she said, "Oh, good, James, will you try that duet with me again today? I think it's time they heard it," Lady Mari asked with a slightly saucy grin on her lips.

"Absolutely, Mari, my dear, we are octogenarians; it's not as if we can get into trouble or anything." He chuckled. They watched as Nathan's carriage disappeared from view.

A large group of the staff decided not to catch the staff wagons back but to enjoy the sunshine, so they set off walking home across the fields.

Soon Hugh, Sam, Anne and the older couple were the only ones left. Betsy was sitting up on the driver's seat, waiting for Anthony.

Lord James and Lady Mari could hear Hugh's words float across the now quiet lawn. They desired to slowly dawdle to the carriage where Anthony was waiting to assist them in.

"I hope you didn't mind waiting, Mr Sam, but I wished to know if I have to ask permission from you too before getting engaged? I have not proposed yet, but I wish to," Hugh said nervously.

"Oh, Hugh, that is wonderful. No, of course, you don't, but having said that, I feel I should ask, and I think the question will be unnecessary but is she a believer?"

Hugh laughed. "Mr Sam, she is now. The reason I ask is that it's one of your wards. She's one of your London girls. It's Miriam Lock. She'd not been forced to degrade herself as you saved her in time, and I'm not sure what the Bishop will say if he finds out about her near fall."

"Well, he won't hear from me," said Anne.

"Nor from me," added Sam. "And Hugh, I'll also write her a character reference just in case. I'll say she's been our guest for some months and has become a good friend, which by the way, she has. I think I will legally make her our ward too, she's still underage and it will give her a status of sorts. Then he'll have no issue, will he? She's a lovely lass. I so wish we could save them all before they are forced into such pitiful state."

Hugh looked shy. "To say I'm scared is somewhat of an understatement, sir, but I find I can't get her out of my mind, and I get distracted when I know she is in church, so much so that I have asked her to sit out of sight during my sermons. She's started taking the children out, and that helps." He blushed delightfully. "I shouldn't really admit that after such a sermon, should I?"

Sam chuckled. "Oh, Hugh, come for luncheon. Ask her afterwards." Sam gave him a gentle slap on his back. "Again, I won't say congratulations just yet. I'll save that for later. You're not a Curate anymore, so do you have to run it by a Bishop?"

"Probably not, but I will. Got to look to do right; otherwise, I'm not practising what I preach. I'm not sure what I'd do if the Bishop says no." He shrugged. "I'll not cross that bridge, sir. I'd love to come for luncheon if I may."

Sam nodded and ushered Anne to the waiting carriage. The Duke and Lady Mari were already inside.

"Home, thanks, Anthony." Sam smiled at his elderly groom. He rarely got to drive a coach, but Sundays were special.

Betsy gave Sam an extra big grin.

Anthony loved going to church, and this way, he would combine his two loves, horses and Jesus; he wasn't quite sure which he loved more. He always said Jesus when asked, but he smiled to himself, knowing his passion for the beautiful creatures he'd spent his life caring for. He could certainly add the four people in the carriage as very special, and especially the one sitting next to him. He knew they were all dear to his heart. They were his only family. He'd not yet let on that he too was the illegitimate son of a peer, well more than a peer, his father had been a Royal Duke. He had a feeling Mari had guessed.

In the carriage the conversation had been overheard. "Well, that is a surprise," said the Duke. He had Lady Mari's arm still tucked in his elbow; he was caressing her hand with his thumb.

"She's a sweet girl and will make a wonderful minister's wife. She's very caring. She's nearly always first in to assist when someone's sick. Yes, she'll do for Hugh." Mari felt James squeeze her hand. She looked up at him and smiled.

~

They arrived back at the Hall before the walking staff, so they went up and changed out of their church clothes.

James waited in the corridor for Mari and was about to walk her down the stairs. "I shouldn't have waited, should I?" He chuckled. "I think we're safe enough at over eighty, though. Shouldn't start too many wild rumours."

"Oh, James, behave yourself," She smiled mischievously, "About the most mischief we can get up to is to sneak off and practise our duet. I do so want to surprise them. Do you think we can do it today? Do you think we're ready?"

"Sure about that, Mari?" He caught a surprised look and winked at her. He continued seriously, "Yes, I think we're ready; after Hugh takes Miriam for a walk, I've told Betsy to make herself scarce. Did you know she's been walking out with Anthony? So, she won't need much persuading to take some time off." James grinned. "You might yet get a groom as a brother-in-law."

"There's more to Anthony than you know, James." She gave a very nervous chuckle. "I feel as nervous as a schoolgirl."

"Here's something to make you a little more settled. I'm going to kiss you, Mari. I've wanted to for some weeks, do you mind? For I find that my heart is not as frozen as I had thought."

"No," she almost whispered. "Not at all, for mine is in the same condition, James."

Lord James stopped in a darkened section of the corridor and was about to draw her into his arms when they heard the running footsteps of the children approaching. "Darn, later." He lifted her chin and gave her a quick peck on her lips instead.

She laughed.

The family had a Sunday luncheon in the vast formal dining room. Sam had stripped the valuable ornaments from the room, as twenty-something children were not all that careful. The luncheon room was filled with laughter.

Anne had refused to sit so far from Sam at the foot of the vast formal dining table. She sat next to him at the head of the table. The Duke sat next to him and Lady Mari next to her. Everyone else sat where they wished.

Sam asked Hugh to say, 'Thanks to God' before they ate.

Hugh was sitting near the foot of the long table. The end seat was empty as Sam said that is the Jesus seat. A vacant place was set at every meal. Not always at the foot, but an extra place was laid at every meal. Hugh stood, everyone joined hands, and bowed his head, gave a thanksgiving prayer for the food, and then sat down quickly.

All had fallen silent and stayed so.

Miriam was sitting directly opposite him. For some reason, no one had started talking after the prayer. He knew he would not be able to concentrate with her so close. He stood up again walked around the table to her side. He fell to one knee and proposed in front of the amazed family group.

She giggled and nodded. "Yes, Hughie, I will, absolutely I certainly will." She bent to kiss him in front of everyone, although embarrassed, he returned her light caress with more pressure than was proper.

A cheer rose from around the table.

Hugh blushed and then pulled her to her feet, drew her into his arms and kissed her again. Only this time with all his heart. Grinning broadly, he shooed the child sitting next to her to his old seat on the other side of the table and sat down next to her.

The Duke was chuckling then said, "Bravo, lad. Show 'em how it's done."

With that, the luncheon continued. The babble of conversation reverberated around the room.

Children giggling at the kiss made Hugh blush again. He reached under the tablecloth and took Miriam's hand. "Sorry, I had it all planned differently."

"Oh, Hughie, I don't care; this way, I get to share it with my new adopted family. It will mean you are part of them now too," she said sweetly.

"Oh, yes, I suppose so. I'm still knocked sideways by you, sweetheart. I feel I have put you on the spot somewhat. We still have to get the Bishop's permission, but Mr Sam will send a character reference with us. He said he's going to legally make you his ward if you're happy to do that?" he whispered softly. Hugh met Sam's smiling eyes, dropped his own, then raised them again, blushing and grinning.

"Hughie, I would have said, yes whenever you asked me." She grinned and whispered, "I'd turn somersaults in the Cathedral aisle if it means I can marry you."

Hugh grinned again. "Um, that won't be required, love."

Luncheon over, the family group broke up. Hugh and Miriam headed out for a walk in the gardens; they invited all the children to go with them. They would make the best chaperones.

Betsy pleaded tiredness, but Lord James knew she was going to see Anthony.

Danny and Georgie also retired for a rest, as little James had been awake a few times through the night. He slept in the room adjoining theirs rather than in the distant nursery.

Anne and Sam intended to have an afternoon rest too, but Lady Mari had asked a favour. "Dears, could you possibly join us in the music room?"

"Yes, Mother, of course," Anne looked puzzled. After the masses had disappeared, the four were left sitting quietly at the table.

The Duke lay back in his chair. He watched his son and daughter-in-law's faces. "We have a surprise for you. We wrote and have been practising a piano piece for you two. We thought you may like to hear it." The smirk on his father's face, Sam had learned over the last months, meant mischief of some kind. He loved it.

Lady Mari was grinning mischievously. Something was definitely in the wind.

The four ambled along to the music room. The heavy royal blue velvet curtains had been thrown back, and all the French windows stood wide open. The room had been hung with many mirrors, reflecting the sun, making the room look magical.

Sam and Anne gasped as they entered through the double white doors. The brand new black grand piano that Sam had bought for Lady Mari sat in the corner of the room with the sunshine hitting the music stand. He'd heard the lively tunes emanating from the room over the months. Sometimes Anne and he had sat outside the room listening to her pure enjoyment of the instrument. Sometimes they danced. They had been caught dancing to the music more than once.

"Sam, both of us have dabbled at writing a tune or two, and we have put together a little wedding anniversary treat for you both. Thirty-five years we believe."

Lord James sat on the long piano seat, laying his whale tooth walking stick on the ground beside him, and Sam handed Lady Mari in next to him. She then shooed Sam away from the instrument. "Go do what you two do best, my dears." She waved her hand for them to step away. "We've called this *Danse d'amour*, or the dance of love."

Sam did, taking Anne into the middle of the room. He heard James whisper, "Ready?" And then, "On the count of three," the tinkling sounds of the opening bars of music started.

While Sam and Anne stood waiting for the melody. Sam bent and gently brushed Anne's lips with a kiss. "Have I told you how much I love you today?"

"No," Anne's reply was to reach up and kiss him.

Lord James joined in with the base notes of the introduction, then Sam realised that the tune was in 3/4 time; his face lit up, and he took Anne into his arms and drew her close for the waltz. "Join me for the dance of love, my sweet," he whispered into her ear. As the hauntingly lovely music floated in the air, they danced.

The pair at the piano lifted their eyes to their children, obviously still so much in love after thirty-five years of marriage. Both now oblivious to the watching eyes of their parents, they kept dancing.

"I told you they'd love it," James whispered to Mari.

He bent and gave her a quick kiss without missing a note.

They played on unnoticed by their children.

Sam had drawn Anne closer, into more of an embrace than a waltz hold. Both were consumed with the melody of love the music portrayed.

Anne's eyes were fixed to Sam's. Tears welled and trailed down her cheeks.

Sam knew they were from happiness, but they stirred his heart. Sam, too, was overwhelmed with the beauty of the music and the emotions it provoked. As they twirled around the sun-drenched room, he lowered his head and drew her into a passionate and stirring kiss. The world around them fell away, and they were transported to a place of peace and contentment. He twirled her out through the open verandah doors of the glorious room but still in sight of the piano. Neither were even aware the music itself had stopped as their kiss deepened.

Anne was first to draw back. She opened her eyes, finally realising the music had stopped. "Sam, look," she whispered and nodded towards the piano. Their parents sat entwined in each other's arms.

James had lowered his lips to Mari's, and she was, as she said to them later, satisfactorily kissed.

Anne drew Sam further along the terrace to leave their parents alone with the echoes of the lovely music still in their hearts.

All the pain of their past lives were now both forgotten and forgiven. The music of life would lead them to joy, for all were now dancing to the same tune, one of forgiveness and a new life.

Chapter 15 Epilogue Will You Dance?
1835

A select group stood in the chapel at Meldon Hall. They were Sam and Annie, Earl and Countess of Meldon; Danny and Georgie, Viscount and Viscountess of Clarestow; Johnathan and Phoebe, The Marquess and Marquisette of Roxborough; James, Duke of Malvern and Lady Marianna Broome-Hall. The final member of the group was the Rev Hugh Williams.

Hugh stood facing the group, and two stood in front of him. One was dressed in a stunning cream gown and had a small veil over her face. Beside her stood a debonaire gentleman, and she clung tightly to his arm.

Hugh began the words of the marriage service. "Dearly beloved …"

The vows repeated, and the promises made, the newly married couple turned to each other and the groom lifted the lace veil to look down on her glowing face. He saw the face of a beautiful twenty-year-old girl he had known so long ago. He bent and kissed her with the pent-up passion he'd kept bottled for so long.

Her arms reached up and entwined around his neck. She saw him as he was when he too was only twenty.

Finally, they turned and faced the family. The two grinning and delightfully happy people had finally found and married the final loves of their lives. They could have been a couple of any age from the back, rather than the octogenarians they were. They turned and the joy was visible on their softly wrinkled faces.

The smiling wrinkled blue eyes of the bride met those of her daughter, and she winked. The groom's brown eyes met those of both his sons, and he smiled lovingly at them both.

The groom leaned on his whale tooth walking stick as he escorted his bride down the aisle.

Danny was staring unbelievably at the bridal couple in front of him. It had finally occurred to him; his grandparents and they had just married each other. His maternal grandmother was now the Duchess of Malvern. A slow smile spread over his face.

Georgie took his hand and squeezed it gently. She would have loved to have had her father invited but knew that if they were to keep the wedding quiet, they had to keep it just *en-family*. Their own marriage was the last one celebrated; two more were coming up. Her brother Robbie was also to finally marry. He'd fallen in love with a mystery lady some eleven years before and had lost her. He was now going to marry his best friend's sister, Amelia. The last marriage planned was the Reverend Hugh Williams himself, just a month later. Reverend Hector James was coming from Maidstone to perform that ceremony. Rev Hector James would stay for a fortnight while Hugh took Miriam for a honeymoon. His nephew, another Hugh, was coming from Theological college and would hold Morning Prayer services for the two weeks Hector was away from Maidstone Parish. Sam had arranged accommodation for Hugh and Miriam in Brighton.

Georgie looked lovingly at her husband; she also had to find the right time to tell Danny he was to be a father again.

The dance of life played on …

It took time to write a long overdue letter, but Sam eventually wrote to Major Tom Turner and permitted life tenancy for the man who had cared for him all those lonely years.

Earlier that year Ned Grace had returned to England to take up his own title. Sam invited him to seek his assistance. Together, these second sons would change the way the poor and unloved were treated. It was time to pay back some of the good he had been given unaware throughout his life, but Sam was determined to do that.

Meldon Hall
West Sussex
15 December 1842

Major Thomas Turner
Rock Cottage
Sydney New South Wales

Dear Tom,

I should have written well before this, but life seemed to get in the way. It's getting on for ten years since we left, and I find that this is yet the most challenging letter to write. After many discussions over what to do with our house in Sydney, we have decided to keep it for the moment. We are happy for you to live there for as long as you wish... but the rent will drop to a peppercorn 1/- a year. This is just to protect it legally should our grandchildren ever wish to emigrate. This may happen in years to come, and if so, it would be lovely for them to have something of ours.

Danny and Georgina have six children of their own, two boys and four girls. With Danny and Vanessa's children, our ten grandchildren have been joined by forty other peer orphans over the years. Most we have taken in as our wards. A few have already married and have made good homes for themselves, and some have moved on to other positions in life. Rob's father, Sir Tim, still holds the reins at Broome-Hall Manor.

Tom, I have had to speak at Lords on the proposed changes of the Bastardy Act. Can you believe that I have now spoken in the House of Lords about the plight of the innocents? So, I have to employ this tactic when summonsed to London for my duty at Lords. Ned took my advice to heart. You saw how I was treated over there when they found who I was. (Can you hear me groan?). Tom, here it's worse, only in reverse, I am shunned due to my convict background. This suits me well. Although many still grovel for financial hand-outs if they see me.

I want to thank you for keeping your eyes on me, on us both, actually, and for your care and compassion. I thought I had gone through my life uncared for and that in itself is a great tragedy, for nothing is more unbearable than to be rejected, particularly by those who should have cared for you. So, I say, 'thank you' from the bottom of my heart.

I have written to the agent cum accountant in Fraser Findlay's office and have let them know my desires re-rent. If you wish someone to move into the cottage or if you want to move there yourself and move someone into the house, he has my authority to discuss these things with you; it is at your call. Take this letter as confirmation if you so wish. Treat the place as your own, up to a point. He has access to ample funds for repairs, and I'd like both buildings to be kept in good *condition, so do not skimp on those, please. Even do some extensions if you wish.*

Tom, my years there with Anne were happy ones, and we often talk about those days. I find it's hard to believe that Anne and I are now sixty-nine, and we both turn seventy next year. Danny will turn forty next spring. Our family here is very dear to us. The Duke of Malvern, known to us all here as Lord James, and Lady Mari, have brightened our lives. Did I mention he married Lady Mari Broome-Hall, and they have moved in here with us? They married about six or seven years ago now. The Duke handed his Estate over to his son Nathan, and the elderly couple are living in retirement with us. They are now aged ninety-one and are getting frail in body but not in mind. They make us laugh frequently. We are a very happy household. They both love helping with the children and so after they married, I suggested that they live here instead of at his Castle. He jumped at the chance, and so they made their home here with us. Lady Mari is, as you know, Sir Cecil's widow, the benefactor of the cottage to Anne. She is related to Anne. It is a delight to share our home with them and anyone else who needs a place. Our staff training school brings us in contact with people from all walks of life, and these two dear souls have taken it upon themselves to instil manners, deportment, and life skills to the less fortunate. They are still spry and still teach dancing, piano, grooming and cleanliness. They wrote us a beautiful duet for our thirty-fifth wedding anniversary, and each year since then, they have added to their repertoire. We four dance together often. Another delightful person who has come to live with us is Annie's Aunt, Betsy White. She too married late in life, and she and her husband, Anthony Jenkins, are integral to our work here. They also decided to make their home with us. Anthony is another with a history of peers as parents, but he will not let on who they are. He jokingly said his surname should have been Fitz prefix, and not Jenkins, but he kept his mother's name, so he out-ranks us all. More he would not say. Anthony is a whiz with horses and has much to teach anyone who will listen to him.

All the new staff are taught to read and write, but few are here for more than six months before the Domestic Bureau in London seeks their skills. It seems that word had spread that our staff trainees are polite and well behaved, causing their new employer's little trouble. We tell the Bureau that if they get any enquiries from dubious households, or where they know issues to have previously occurred, that the Bureau should look elsewhere. Our people have had enough trauma in their lives to have to deal with unscrupulous employers. Each staff member knows that they will be welcomed back with open arms if a position is untenable. This gives them the security of a home base. The hardest to place are those with severe burns. We had a case where four grooms were caught in a stable fire, and how they survived, I have no idea. Their skin looks as though it just melted from their faces. Amelia's brother, Jimmy has taken them on permanently, along with their families. They get to stay together, and *their wives are all friends. If people only knew how healing a little care was, they would do more for others.*

Tom, you know how massive this place is. I used to hide in many empty rooms as a small boy, but I found some rooms I still have not been into. I thought you would be interested to hear that Anne and I were wandering through the old rooms in the old wing during one particularly wet week, and we found ourselves in an unfamiliar part in the attic rooms of the original West Wing. We found a room stuffed full of suits of armour. We are at over one hundred suits and still sorting. They were just dumped in piles. Not something most houses would have. I chuckled, remembering one of the last conversations I had with you about such a thing. I have set about reassembling them, and the staff and children are having great fun polishing them up.

I must away as I hear the children released from their classes. There are now over fifty of the little darlings; mind you, ten belong to Danny. Edmund is the image of his father; you would not know him from the tiny babe he was. Young James is a mini version of his older half-brother. Then there is little Timothy Samuel. He's four and has me twisted around his chubby fingers.

Victor and Thea, our Butler and Housekeeper, have three children, and seven more belong to other staff members. All the children are back here as the village's new school is not yet completed. We are building a brand-new school in town as the other one burned down about six months ago. Only the music room and library were spared. This has allowed me to start with a clean slab and build a fabulous facility for the community. All paid for with the Earl's money, how he would have hated that! All the Hall children will be attending there to encourage the village children to go too. I want all children in the village up to the age of twelve to attend school regularly and learn to read and write and learn other subjects. I feel that education will open new avenues for them. Probably not here, in mother-England, but in the colony. All things are possible as the classes are much more blurred over there. Eliza Darling will present Jo-Jo next year, so life goes on...

Oh, Tom, I miss the warm climate. It's so cold here, and the damp simply permeates the soul. It's December – it should be HOT, not snowing.

I really must be away. Enjoy our house while you may. I will give at least six months' notice should we ever need it.

Again, our thanks. Anne sends her regards and gratitude too.

I so wish I was just Sam Corbett again...

Samuel Corbett Garney
Reluctant Sixth Earl of Meldon

Author's note on the manuscript
Mum's original plan for the book…

Sheila Hunter, Mum, penned 36k of this story, but in her original version, she killed Annie with a heart attack, had Sam sign the entail release with Charles and Danny, and then Danny ran away disgusted with his parents. They never saw him again.

I didn't like that finish, and it was why she never completed writing this story; she didn't like it either.

So, I deleted the last chapter, modified the one before and rewrote it to have a happy ending.

Mum intended to tell the story of the house, which was titled, 'The House.'

I have continued the house's history in my later books to honour mum. Amelia Macdonald's sons and other family members come to live there. It gets mentioned often until the building is sold towards the end of the 1800s.

Therefore of the 110k words in the book, the first 30k are hers. I hope you enjoyed the story and could not pick where I started writing.

Sara Powter

The story continues in the rest of the Unlikely Convict Ladies Trilogy…
Read Robbie and Amelia's story in
Amelia's Tears
Paperback   ISBN: 9780645110739
Ebook   ISBN: 9780645110746
Hard Cover ISBN 9798420617953

https://amazon.com/dp/0645110736
https://amazon.com/dp/B09SS855BR

PLUS
Ned Grace is a frequent character in The Lockleys of Parramatta series, and his background and future will be revealed in many of my other books. Ned is modelled on a friend, who, although not titled, is as good and faithful as the character in my books.
And…
If you sign up for my newsletter, there is a FREE Ned Grace Story available from June 2024 when you sign up to my Newsletter. (QR on the last page)

Characters

Annie White b 1773 affair 1790, convicted 1792, served 7 years free 1797 bakery.
Annabella Phillipa Joy arrived on the *Pitt* as a convict in 1792
m Oct 1802 **Samuel** James Corbett Garney (Lord Garney/Viscount Clarestow then 6th
Earl Meldon) Meldon Hall-mother Anne Corbett – **Sam** arr on the *Royal Admiral* 1792
#1 **Daniel** James Corbett Garney b Nov 1803 Sydney
m1 Jan 1822 **Vanessa** Comfrey
      #1 **Jo**-Anne (Jo-Jo) b Sept 1822
      #2 **Lucy**-Anne b 1825
      #3 **Mary-Anne** b 1827
      #4 **Edmund** Daniel James b 29th May 1831
m2 2 July 1833 **Georgina** Styles – 6 children 2 boys 4 girls
      #1 **James** Samuel Daniel Garney b March 1834 West Sussex
      #2 Georgina Anne
      #3 Adelaide Margaret (**Meg**) m **Bobby** Pittford
      #4 **Timothy Samuel** (Military)
      #5 Sophia
      #6 Christine

Annie's friends in Sydney

Bert Todd - delivers wood.
Willy Knight – the builder, married 6 kids – son is the delivery boy
Mrs **Beccy** Frame - father is Bill Sanders
Fraser Finley – financial advisor/agent
Mrs Peg Tremaine – Annie's assigned 'owner'
Mrs Pitt – the midwife
Josh Comfrey – 3 daughters – the youngest, Vanessa Comfrey. m Danny Corbett

Sir **Cecil** Broome-Hall (sons Albert & Henry) b 1742
Lady **Marianne** BH nee White - Lady Mari b 1752 (Annie's mother)
   (Daug of a Duke of Cheatham)   (sons Albert & Henry, daug Amelia Elizabeth -
   Elspeth)
   Maid friend **Betsy** b 1769 (mother Sarah b 1753)
   Cec's Nephew -Master **Timothy** Styles, now Sir Timothy Broome-Hall m to **Sophie** 6
kids
      #1 **Robert b 1803** m 1835 **Amelia** Black nee Westaweller   3 children
   #2 Timothy #3 Sophia #4 Adam #5 Victoria #6 **Georgina b1814** m 1834 **Danny**
m2 1835 **James** Malvern both aged 83
James, Duke of Malvern from Malvern Hall (Lord James) b 1752
        m 1778 **Adelaide** d 1823
            #1 Johnathan (**Nathan**) -Marquess Roxborough b 1778
                Grandson James Douglas (**JD**) b 1803
            #2 Grace b 1780
        m 1835 **Mari**anna Broome-Hall b 1752 aged 83

Lord **Philip** Garney – Fifth Earl Meldon 1746 d 1830 (Sam's stepdad)
m 1769 Lady **Anne** Corbett b 1752
   1 **Nigel** Died as Viscount Clarestow 1770 d 1820
      2 **Samuel** James Corbett Garney b July 1773
Charlie Garney – Sam's cousin – married to **Alice** Chambers lives at '*Oakwood Park*'
      6 kids – **Henry** b '08; Samuel Thomas (**Tom**) b '10;
      Frances b '12; Caroline b '14; Richard b 17; AliceMay b '20

Rev Watmore – Clergyman who accused Sam of theft
Rev Hugh Williams – New minister m **Miriam** Lock – from London

Ned Grace, later Duke of Gracemere b 1799 d 1870
<u>**Meldon Hall staff**</u>
Nursery Maids Abigail (Abby) and Mary
Victor Jamison, their butler – m Thea
Mrs Dorothy (**Thea**) Murchison, the Housekeeper
Anthony Jenkins – head groom/Stable Manager m Betsy White
Graham Long – Estate Manager and agent – son of Maxwell
Miriam Lock m **Hugh Williams**

<u>**Children were taken in**</u>
Sally, aged 5 in 1833
6 months later – 12 children and a school in Nth wing – 20 in all. By 1835;
40 at the end – 1842

<u>**Real people**</u>
Governor **Ralph** and **Eliza** Darling – on the '*Hooghly* 10/1831'
Ann Dumaresq was a devout philanthropist, Eliza Darling's mother
The Hellfire Club and Francis Dashwood and his cronies

Bibliography

Victorian Dance Pict
https://dancebetternow.typepad.com/blog/2016/11/how-to-tell-if-a-lady-wants-to-dance.html

Convict woman drawing
https://tradecoastcentralheritagepark.com.au/convict-womens-prison-and-factory/#prison

Sam Corbett pict – actually John Batman
John Batman drawing, Tasmanian Archives and Heritage Office - public domain

Chap 3 Slab hut drawing
A slab hut depicted in 'Mr. Birch's old hut: Seven Hills Estate.'
(State Library of Victoria, H88.21/73, drawing by Charles Norton)

Chap 4 house
https://sydneylivingmuseums.com.au/convict-sydney/what-was-convict-assignment#gallery-1

Chap 8 – Stowe house engraving
https://en.wikipedia.org/wiki/Stowe_House#/media/File:Stowe_House_-_fachada_sul_(1829).jpg

Ralph Darling History
https://adb.anu.edu.au/biography/darling-sir-ralph-1956
Departure – https://en.wikipedia.org/wiki/Ralph_Darling

Other drawings used are Royalty-Free - Public Domain.

If you loved this book, these are similar.
(All are stand-alone stories)
A First Fleet Convict Story 1788
A First Fleet story with the descriptions taken directly from the Journal of Doctor Arthur Bowes Smith who was the doctor on board the Lady Penrhyn.

Gentle Annie Soames
Her dreams lead to unexpected outcomes. An Australian First Fleet story.

Annie Soames is a girl beloved by the community but not afraid to voice her desires. That leads to trouble, illicit love, and a world turned upside down.

Oliver Quilpie, the recently married Marquess, discovers his arranged union is not to his taste; he is drawn to his wife's companion. Unfortunately, he is unable to keep his hands off her. For revenge, Annie mimics her every move while riding but is dressed as a highwayman. However, she had now fallen in love with him. This action finally leads to her arrest and transportation to a faraway land.

After some years, Oliver's wife dies, and his thoughts turn to Annie. He seeks to find her, but she has vanished. He is horrified to discover she was transported to New South Wales as a convict on the *Lady Penrhyn.* He follows with a shipload of supplies on the *Kitty.* Will Annie want to see him?

ISBN 9780645441574   ISBN ebook 9781923097063   LP ISBN 978-1923097346
July 2024

The Hunter to Macquarie Collection 1795-1822
When Upon Life's Billows
Sydney 1795-1821 - Governor John Hunter

Captain John Hunter was born to a life at sea. The wind blows where no man knows, and John is caught up in the tempest. Although wrecking his ship, the *HMS Sirius*, in 1790, he became the second governor of the rough and filthy penal settlement of New South Wales. He always seems to be in the wrong place at the wrong time, trusting the wrong people.

Helena Rosedale is not a typical female convict. She fights tooth and nail to stop the men from abusing her. She gains the name of Helena the Hellcat.

Crispin Milroy is alone in the world and one of the new governor's security detail. Can he win the fair lady's heart? Life in 1795 in Sydney Cove is raw at best. Food is scarce, and disease often ravages the settlement. Life throws everything except death at these three, yet somehow, they survive. Why does John trust this young couple when others betray him?

What trials must Helena and Crispin endure to make their new lives in this raw town bearable? How can John ease their path?

ISBN: 9780645783339   ebook ISBN: 9780645783346
Coming 2025

Saddler's Song
London 1790s to Parramatta 1840s

George Ellis is a tanner's son living on the outskirts of London. When disease takes his family. Alone and hurting, he seeks to find a new life for himself. Hearing from a friend about the possibility of setting up a business in New South Wales, he sells up and leaves all he knows. His beloved violin is his most valuable item, and his talent for making beautiful music is hidden from all but a few.

Ben Parker is a saddler, like George; he is also alone in the world. Ben also sells up to move to the new colony. The two young men meet and combine their skills to start afresh in a new world. During the journey out, George's skill as a violinist is revealed. On arrival, they find accommodation with a family with many lovely daughters. Two of these girls steal their hearts, but how will the business survive in an animal-starved land with limited access to leather? What is the saddler's song?

ISBN : 9780645783353   eISBN: 9780645783360
Coming 2025

Tuppence to Pass
London 1800s to Parramatta 1820s - Governor Lachlan Macquarie

Josh Callan is a London lad who makes the best of the life that has been dealt to him. Stealing from the man who killed his father gives the family a change of direction. Josh is arrested, but the judge belittles him, saying he's not worth tuppence. He is transported to the penal colony of Sydney as a convict just as **Governor Macquarie's** term starts. He proves his worth and falls on his feet, becoming the governor's groom and confidante.

Life in the Colonial town opens opportunities they could never have dreamed about in England, but can Josh find his niche?

Where will this strange friendship take Josh and his family?

ISBN : 9781923097070   eISBN: 9781923097087
Coming 2025

His Majesty's Pageboy
London to Emu Plains, Australia, in the 1800s

Jack **Turner** was born into a life of pomp and privilege that was not rightfully his. He was brought to the royal court for his own protection. By age ten, he was King George the Third's pageboy and known as Lord John. For years, Jack roils against society's immorality and people's shallowness; then, he meets an unspoiled young girl amongst the mire of humanity whose purity stands out. He is unable to pursue her before his life hits a wall.

Martha Alexander is the daughter of a wealthy shipping merchant. She has been presented to London's second tier of society, where she meets the young man of her dreams. She is expected to marry well, and Lord John sets her heart fluttering. However, her father's drinking shatters her future. He was made to sign all his possessions away while drunk, unknowingly including his daughter. Refusing a forced marriage changes her life. How do these two end up as convicts in Australia?

Paperback ISBN 9781923097308   eISBN 978192309792

Coming 2026

Fist Full of Holey Dollars
Sydney Cove 1810+

Captain **Rudi Greenwood** is a lonely man stuck in a job with no purpose in a land where alcohol is currency and rules are often overlooked in the pursuit of wealth.

Bethany Edwards is a bereaved woman carrying her dead husband's child. Rudi's attraction to the beautiful widow forces him to rethink his attitude and consider someone else. She turns to Rudi for help and support, but is that all she feels?

When **Governor Lachlan Macquarie** asks Rudi for help improving the roads, a casual remark changes Rudi's life and impacts the entire colony. To address the alcohol problem, he suggests a new currency be created.

With Bethany by his side, will he take up the challenge the governor offers him? What does he do that makes him hated by the exclusives and free settlers in the colony?

Paperback ISBN 9781923097407   eISBN 9781923097414

Coming 2026

Far From the Whispering Sheoaks
Set in Australia in the 1817+

Fanny Little was in the wrong place doing something she thought was legal. Her actions saw her arrested, tried, and banished. She was assigned from the female prison to ex-soldier Gordon McKenzie and soon found herself in a despicable and humiliating situation of being sold in the public marketplace.

Phil Bentley is a man running from his jealous uncle, and he finds solace in a secluded farm half a world away. With the community on their side, can Phil save Fanny from Gordon's vile abuse? Why is their relationship destined to court controversy? And who is Jas? Why does Gordon wish to harm the child? Will they ever escape the shadows that are chasing them?

Paperback ISBN 9781923097315   eISBN9781923097322

Coming 2026

Bound Down in Iron Chains
Set in Australia in the 1818+

Howard Marlow is a studious and honest London bookkeeper. When he is asked to help a friend's brother do his bookwork, he unknowingly helps a crime gang. He is arrested, convicted, and transported. On arrival, Howard is assigned to the boy's orphanage with a possibly crooked soldier in charge. He is asked to use his skills to decipher the bookkeeping entries that make no sense. He discovers his love for the affection-starved boys at the orphanage.

Naomi Buckingham, a convict girl, is thrust into the harsh reality of the orphanage alongside Howard. She is assigned to the orphanage, but it is far from the refuge she had hoped for as the supervisor is a man who harbours no respect for women. With no one to rely on but the new accountant, she grapples with the question of trust.

Naomi is the key to breaking the bookkeeping code, cracking the case wide open. Can Howard use his brains to save them both? How do they become involved with some of the worst criminals in the New South Wales penal colony?

Paperback ISBN 9781923097353   eISBN9781923097360

Coming 2026

Dancing to Her Own Tune

Co-authored by Sheila Hunter and Sara Powter

Sydney 1790s to England 1830s

Annie White is released after serving seven years as a convict in Sydney. She gets a visitor who, with his help, she can start a baking business. She is then asked to assist another sick man, **Sam** Corbett. Annie nurses him back to health, and a relationship develops. They settle into a life together, barely making ends meet; she realises she's expecting a child. Sam has his past laid bare and must adjust to the revelations. They both must face their accusers and find that the answers to their questions are not what they thought. Their life experiences seem to cling to them, and unable to shake them off, they end up back in England. They must face their ghosts and discover they are not who they think they are. How can they turn their anger and spite into love and forgiveness? The Dance of Life goes on.

ISBN 9780645110715   ISBN9780645110722

Long-listed in the Historical Fiction Company Competition 2022

Amelia's Tears

Parramatta 1828 – England 1840s

Amelia Westaweller awaits her assignment in the Parramatta Female Prison. Forced to leave the relative safety of gaol, she is assigned and now faces her worst nightmare. A foul man claims her and makes her life a living hell. Then, her world goes black. A glimmer of hope arises when she hears from her brother, Jim, who has enlisted a friend to help her. She writes to Jim, pouring out her heart and telling him of the horrors of her new life. He encourages her to stay firm in her faith. All she can do is pray. When Major **Ned** Grace, her brother's friend, enters her life in Parramatta, he starts to ease her path. Things have changed, as now she has a child in tow. How can Amelia forge a new life for herself? What man could want her with her background and a child at her side? Who is the gentleman who turns her tears of sadness into tears of great joy?

ISBN: 9780645110739   eISBN: 978-0-6451107-4-6   Hard Cover ISBN 979-842061-7953

A Lady in Irons

England 1800s - Parramatta 1808+

Katy Harrington is mourning the death of her husband after he died in a shooting accident. Barely coping, she awaits the birth of their child. If it's a girl, she must hand the family home to her husband's brother. The day after giving birth to a daughter, she and her daughter are left on the side of a road. She collapses and is found by someone she thought had died in a fire ten years before. **Perry White**, badly scarred himself, nurses her back to health. They marry and move in with her widowed friend, Mary.
After some years, she discovers her husband and friend in each other's arms. Now living in a love triangle, she flees. Grasping the only straw available, she intentionally gets arrested and is sent to a colony far away. By doing this, her marriage can be annulled.
What happens in the Colony is different from what she expects. Governor Macquarie comes to her rescue, but what of Perry and her children?

ISBN: 9780645110784   eISBN:9780645441505

NO MORE, MY Love

Hunter Valley, NSW 1820s

Jess Elkin is distraught when tragedy ravages her family. She becomes the victim of a carriage accident and is nursed back to health by the driver, **Marcus Ryan**. Marcus was not expecting to fall in love. Yet, when Jess's fortunes suddenly turn for the worse, Marcus must decide how far he will go to pursue her. As time passes in Newcastle, Australia, Marcus must take a business trip and is taken by pirates. Jess is left wondering if her will keep his promise to return to her... Will she ever see him alive again?

ISBN: 9780645441536   eISBN 9780645441581

Long-listed in the Historical Fiction Company Competition 2023

The Vine Weaver
Hawkesbury River area 1820s+
New Beginnings and Old Threats

In the 1820s, Australia, **Joel and Hetty Walker** live on a secluded farm on the Hawkesbury River, which becomes a healing haven for the protection of young convict women. A series of events brings **Fran Rea** to Hetty's attention, and she is taken to the farm. Fran and Hetty develop a cottage industry under the compassionate eye of farmhand **Hector Macdougal;** Hector's loving words change lives. It is to him that Fran turns when threatened. The vines now must draw them close to survive the future revelations, and of those, there are many.

ISBN: 9780645441512   eISBN: 9780645441529

Long-listed in the Historical Fiction Company Competition 2023

https://amazon.com/dp/0645441511   https://amazon.com/dp/B0C6Z552Y2

The story continues in Scotch at The Rocks…

Scotch at The Rocks
Glasgow, Scotland, early 1800s to The Rocks, Sydney 1830s

Orphaned children Brodie Stewart and Heather Anderson live on Glasgow's streets. Although hungry, somehow they survive and keep out of trouble. Heather finds a job and looks to be settled; things go pear-shaped for them both. Eventually, they marry by declaration, yet even that gets messed up, and they are both arrested soon after they make their vow. In 1838, they were transported to Sydney as convicts. Heather arrives within weeks of Brodie, and they are assigned close to each other. They are now living on the docklands in Sydney, called The Rocks. They now have to forge a new life halfway across the world from their homeland.

Adventures abound, and Brodie gets press-ganged. While he's away, Heather's life changes and soon, she's officially selling Scotch Whisky at a shop in The Rocks.

You can take a Scot out of Scotland, but where did the Scotch come from?

ISBN 9780645441550 ebook 9781923097001 Large Print 9781923097254

Waiting at the Sliprails
The Bathurst Road 1830s
A Convict's Tale

Bea Dawes's term of conviction nears an end, and she has few options other than marriage to a stranger or going on the street.

Jack Barnes, the hired drover, wants a wife. Bea accepts his offer; then, she discovers that he could be gone for months, leaving her alone with **Billy and Netty**, part of the tribe of an Aboriginal tribe who live on his secluded farm. Bea learns to love her husband and also this wonderful aboriginal couple. Drought ravages the farm, and Jack must hit the long paddock with the flock. In his absence, a visitor arrives, threatening to destroy everything she has worked so hard for. Can Bea touch her heart? Can she cope? Will the drought ever end? And when will Jack return?

ISBN: 9780645441543   eISBN: 9781923097032

Winner of the Spring 2024 Pencraft Award for Christian Historical Fiction

Convict Shadows of the Past
Two Jennifers, two hundred years apart

Jenny Kellow is eight years old when she learns of her convict family history. Then discovers that she was named after a convict from nearly two hundred years ago. Her grandfather's stories inspire her to dig deeper into her ancestors' convict past. From her grandfather, she hears stories of bushrangers, convicts, and life in the infant colony of Parramatta. She sets about retracing the footsteps of her convict great-great-great-grandmother to honour her. Jenny's search starts with microfiche back in the 60s, and she learns about the small tin mining town in Cornwall and the production of a cheese that sets London afire. She discovers her ancestor, **Jennifer Kellow,** has brought these cheese-making skills to Parramatta, where she taught others her craft. Echoes of the past can still be heard if you know where to listen.

Who was the first Jennifer, and what does she have to do with cheese? Why is she so elusive? Did Jenny's ancestor, Jennifer, ever see those two small crosses carved into the bricks of the Female Factory? Would Jenny ever find out her ancestor's story?

ISBN: 9780645783315   ISBN ebook 9780645783322

A NaNoWriMo 2022 book winner

January 2024

In Defence of Her Honour

London 1800s to Parramatta 1819

Will the real man of quality please stand up?

Bill Miller was raised and educated with the sons of the family. The youngest, Bert Edison-Browne, had been his best friend. However, jealousy intervenes when Bill's excellent schoolwork curtails their friendship. He wins a scholarship and enters Oxford University. When Bill's father dies unexpectedly, Bert insists that Bill take over as butler, but it's more to oppress him. Bert's jealousy grows and festers. Now looking for a way to rid themselves of their new butler. A ruckus ensues, and Bill is arrested for assaulting Bert.

Molly Ross is the housekeeper's daughter, and she will vouch for him. It's too late; Bill has been arrested and is soon sentenced to be transported. With Bill gone, Molly now fights to defend herself from Bert. After hitting him with a pan, she, too, is arrested and sent to Sydney. Bill and Molly arrive with letters of introduction and compensation from Bert's father. Soon, they will be running the best inn in Parramatta with an endorsement from the governor.

ISBN 9780645441567   ISBN ebook 9781923097049

I Can't Stop Tomorrow

Irish Famine 1840s to Avoca Beach, Australia

Escaping bigotry and prejudice in Ireland, the O'Shane family lives on a secluded farm on the west coast of Ireland. The potato blight soon decimates their farm. It's always darkest before dawn, and the two remaining girls cling to the hope of a new life. With the kindness of strangers, the eldest girls, **Clare** and **Kerry O'Shane**, head to their cousin, Sal Lockley, in Parramatta, Australia. A new, wonderful life awaits them both. **Shéamus Connor** is the annoying teenage boy who reluctantly draws Clare's affection. However, living in a convict town means ruffians abound.

John Moore is a bad-tempered and troubled Irishman who is content to live alone on another secluded farm until he discovers Clare and two other lads need rescuing.

Can John protect her from the pain inflicted by an evil world?

Can Shéamus find his lost love who has fled?

ISBN: 9780645441598   ISBN ebook 9781923097056

Madeline's Boy

England 1830s to New South Wales 1840

A red-coat soldier's tale.

All is not straightforward when money and titles are involved.

Orphaned, afraid and on the run, Chip must Flee.

Madeline was his mother's best friend. Maddie now needs to keep her charge safe and alive. She must give up her life to protect the boy she has loved since birth.

Months after Chip's parents' demise, Maddie sets out to deliver Chip to his Uncle Humphrey, who lives in Sydney. Through him, she meets Chip's friend Tim, who falls for Maddie— but will they find happiness?

The menacing presence soon finds Chip, and Maddie needs to hide him again. They are moved from hidden farms to secret valleys, ending up in an aboriginal encampment.

Can Tim find a way to be with Maddie? And if so… Will Chip ever be safe?

ISBN: 9780645783308   ISBN ebook 9781923097094

Nov 2024

https://mybook.to/MadelinesBoy

Jam or Marmalade for Tea

England 1820s to New South Wales 1825 (Governor Brisbane Era)

Martha Hamilton is the eldest of four orphans struggling to survive on their own. Caught stealing, she is tried, convicted, and transported to New South Wales. With her family gone, she becomes despondent. Life holds no meaning for her, and the ocean waves look inviting.

Captain Guy Manning is a frustrated and injured redcoat soldier returning to Sydney to take up a new assignment. He notices Martha trying to jump overboard and rescues her. How do two cats bring them together?

A convict ship is no place for romance, and she's far too young anyway, isn't she?

Can Guy save her and forge a life together for them? What connections does he have to try and save her siblings? Why is marmalade important for their future?

Paperback ISBN 9781923097933   eISBN9781923097285

A NaNoWriMo 2023 book winner

Jan 2025

Unshackled Lives
Set in England & Australia in the 1800s
Australian historical fiction of early colonial days

Ned Lockley is the second of four sons of the Duke and Duchess of Gracemere. As his mother's favourite, his childhood years were blissful, but he needs to grow up and quickly.
A whirlwind romance is followed by a loved one's betrayal. The following emotional turmoil is hard for Ned to cope with, especially amid a collapsing, immoral society.
Ned can't stay as even his family is falling apart. His mother's words to remain true to himself and his faith make him leave everything he knows. How does Ned end up in New South Wales in charge of placing female convicts? Will he ever find happiness or discover who Charles is?

ISBN 9781923097377   eISBN 9781923097384   LP ISBN: 9781923097391

A 100-year, six-part Australian Colonial series
The Lockleys of Parramatta 1800-1900

Hands upon the Anvil
A blacksmith's life and love are more than work
Parramatta 1830s

Eddie Lockley's parents were transported for their crimes. Can a steadfast lad rise above his origins and guide others to succeed in a land of opportunity?
Ten-year-old Eddie longs to help his mum and dad. Living in a convict town with his family, the keen youngster has been working with the local blacksmith since his sixth birthday. But when a lieutenant doesn't stop abusing his older brother, the young boy yearns for the day when he can stand up and end the torment. Though he's thrilled when his mentor offers to send him off to learn his letters, Eddie fears he won't be around to watch his sibling's back. But as he takes on the biggest adventure of his life, the brave believer soon discovers God is looking out for everyone he loves. Does this young man in the making have what it takes to change everything for the better?

ISBN 9780994578235 Ebook ISBN 978-0-9945782-5-9 Hardcover 9798496177368

https://mybook.to/HandsUponTheAnvil

Out Where The Brolgas Dance
Gold is found, and so is love
Parramatta 1840s
How can a question change so many people?

It's the 1840s, and discoveries across the Blue Mountains continue. Major Mitchell's new road is complete, and towns are planned and being built. Abundant land is available for those who want it. Eighteen-year-old **William "Wills" Lockley** has laid a solid foundation for a respectable career as a blacksmith, but the Lockley lust for adventure flows deeply within his veins. He dreads the monotony of work at the blacksmith's forge and yearns for adventure in a new frontier. Wills meets six Englishmen (*Coping with what is now known as PTSD*) who have the means to make his dreams come true. What they discover changes the Colony and their lives forever. Gold fever ensues. While in the West, Wills must deal with an uncertain romance. Does Cathy even want him?

ISBN 9780994578242 Ebook ISBN 978-0-9945782-6-6 Hardcover ISBN 9798755445504
LP ISBN 9781923097155

https://mybook.to/OutWhereTheBrolgas

Diamonds in the Dirt
Diamonds, love and money... but there is much more to life.
Parramatta 1850s

Luke Lockley, the youngest Lockley son, has completed University, and his life has no direction. No job, no money, and no love. Desperately alone, he prays for guidance. How can Luke trust that God has a plan for him if he can't even find a job? He does the only thing he can ... he prays. Within a week, life has changed ... oh, how it has changed as his brother Wills turns up with a suggestion. Would Luke be interested in joining the expedition with John Evans? **Reverend William Clarke** needs assistance on a Government Mineral Survey. The challenge, adventure and finds are life-changing for many. However, it gives Luke meaning, purpose and direction. The condition of his heart problems also takes a turn. Can he walk away? Will she wait for him?

ISBN:9780994578273 Ebook ISBN: 978-0-9945782-8-0 Hard cover ISBN 979-8788011141

https://mybook.to/DiamondsintheDirt

The Earl's Shadow
Who or what is the 'shadow'? How does it affect so many?
Parramatta 1860s

Charles Lockley is the Earl of Coxheath. He spent his youth as a convict in Parramatta and had no idea he was an Earl. He had minimal education and few social skills. His eldest son, **Charlie,** is no different.

Now faced with his own mortality, Charles has to work out how to live the remainder of his life after a near-death experience. He is called to step way out of his comfort zone in London. His action will change the world for many. The echoes from the past still haunt Charlie. London is calling the family, and they can't postpone the trip. How does the Cobb and Co. coach driver **Jim Leslie** fit in? And precisely what is *'The Earl's Shadow'* that he speaks about? What happens if the 'Shadow' is gone?

ISBN: 9780645110708 Ebook ISBN 978-0-9945782-9-7
Released June 2022
https://mybook.to/TheEarlsShadow

Once a Jolly Swagman
An old black Billy Can contain the secrets of an incredible life
An Australian Historical Novel
Set in 1870s Parramatta and Kent, UK

Rick Lockley, battling his family's expectations, runs away to find himself. **Jack,** a jolly swagman, takes him under his care. Even after years together, Rick knows little about the old man.

On his death, Jack leaves Rick his precious billy can; the contents reveal Jack's identity. Stunned, Rick must travel to England to finalise Jack's wishes. There, he uncovers Jack's life of love, betrayal and a link to his own family. Rick also discovers there is much more to learn about this enigmatic man.

ISBN 9780645110753   Ebook ISBN 978-0-6451107-6-0
Released Sept 2022
https://mybook.to/OnceaJollySwagman

Jonty's Journey
Gems, Love, Artists and a Golden Lion
Australia and South Africa 1880-1902

Sydney Jeweller Jonty Evans' passion for gems takes him to Africa at a volatile time. He finds the diamonds he wants and is given a lion cub. Jonty is all but kidnapped. His experiences in the Transvaal plunge him into questioning everything he knows of life. Soon, nightmares haunt him. (Now known as PTSD.) On return home, he nearly messes up his love life with **Lottie** before it even starts, and he struggles to settle. Lottie's father, **Luke** Lockley from Parramatta, takes him in hand and points him to someone who can help.

Jonty is then recalled to Africa as a liaison and reconnects with his lion, Chimbu, when he saves the life of his security detail. His life journey introduces him to the most amazing Heidelberg artists, politicians, poets, rebels, and the scapegoat soldier Harry Breaker Morant. Can Jonty bury the past and regain the peace he's lost?

ISBN 9780645110777 HC ISBN 9781923097124   Ebook ISBN: 978-0-6451107-9-1
Released Feb 2023
https://mybook.to/JontysJourney

242

Co-Winner of 1999 NSW Senior Citizen of the Year, In the Year of the Senior Citizen

Mattie

The Story of an Australian Convict Child
An Australian Historical Story inspired by real Life.

An orphaned child, Mattie is convicted of petty theft, sentenced to seven years, and sent to Australia. She meets another convict woman who, at her death, gives Mattie a chance for a new life. She makes the most of everything that comes her way, earning her freedom, falling in love, marrying, and becoming a mother. But life is not kind to her.

She meets bushrangers, moves to the gold fields in Bathurst, and starts a store. Yet she is the kind of woman who made Australia what it is today. Can she survive alone in a man's world? A remarkable woman who breaks down all her barriers.

(Mattie's story continues in The Lockleys of Parramatta - bk 4 & 6)

ISBN 9781503252370 & ebook AISN B00TTEDBTO

(The story continues in The Earl's Shadow & Once a Jolly Swagman)
Released 2015

https://mybook.to/Mattie_sh

Ricky

A boy in Colonial Australia

Ricky English and his mother immigrated from England to join his father in the new Colony of Sydney. Upon arrival, there was no sign of his father. Ricky's mum uses the tiny amount of money they brought to get lodgings in a run-down building. Things go from bad to worse when his mother dies; he is thrown out of the rooms, and the caretakers confiscate all their possessions.

Ricky lives on the streets of Sydney Town as a street waif. Ricky finds safe places to sleep and befriends freed convicts who can help him survive. One day, he encounters a lost child and helps reunite her with her family. These people try to help him, but he insists on doing things his way because of his stubbornness. However, he has found a mentor and confidante. The story follows him through his life. He survives and turns his life around, helping others along the way. **(Will's story continues in Jonty's Journey)**

Paperback ISBN 9780994578211 Kindle ASIN: B00MLYN6IG
Released 2014

https://mybook.to/Ricky_sh

The Heather to The Hawkesbury

Four Scottish families brave a new life in a strange land.

Mary Macdonald and husband **Murd** and family; her brother **Fergus** MacKenzie; sister-in-law **Caro** MacLeod; cousin **Alex** Fraser and all their families who have had to emigrate from the Isle of Skye during the "Clearances."

The story follows the four families from Scotland on the ship out to the NSW colony in the 1850s. Mary does not cope with the changes and losses that occur in the first months in the colony. The other women in the family rely on her, and she nearly crumbles. The families struggle together through accidents, losses, trials, floods, and hard work and forge a strong bond with their new country. Trials, tribulations and triumphs see the four families make a firm mark in their new homeland. The immigrants from Scotland helped make Australia what it is today.

ISBN 978994578228   ebook AISN B01A21JYWQ   Large Print ISBN1533473641
Available on Amazon/Kindle & Large Print
Released 2016

https://mybook.to/TheHeathertTHawkesbury

Sara's Author Bio

Sheila Hunter and Sara Powter were a passionate mother-and-daughter team of amateur genealogists. While working together on their family tree, Sheila and Sara made many captivating discoveries. The greatest of these was finding four convicts, and these four had very different perspectives. They were sent to Australia from 1792 to 1814 during the height of Convict transportation. Before her *passing* in 2002, Sheila adapted some of these histories into enchanting stories, her Australian Colonial Trilogy. Sara later had these published. A fourth she left unfinished, and this inspired her to finish it. However, before she did, **The Lockleys of Parramatta** were created. The first two in the series were completed before she completed '**Dancing to Her Own Tune**' for her mother. (*Sheila wrote the first 30k words*)

Vividly living through the Colonial Era, these books delve further into the theme of overcoming adversity in Colonial Australia and how it developed, the demise of the Convict system and the discovery of mineral wealth.

Sara intricately weaves accurate, archival data and a charming narrative to create a series of tales of faith, love, loss, and redemption.

And so, two hundred years after her family arrived in Australia, Sara continues the Australian Colonial stories started in **Lockleys of Parramatta,** followed by the **Unlikely Convict Ladies** Trilogy. **The Hunter to Macquarie Collection** and **The Convict Birthstain Collection** are all stand-alone novels. More Historical Fiction books are to follow… as they are already in the editors' queue.

See Sara's web page to keep up to date with more stories.
With an online store available for a signed copy of Sara's books.
www.sarapowter.com.au   (*Australian Postage only*)

Amazon Aus QR

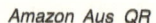

Feel free to email me at
saragpowter@gmail.com

BOOK BUB
https://partners.bookbub.com/authors/6273615/edit

FACEBOOK https://www.facebook.com/profile.php?id=100063887262514

Do you want the book *UNSHACKLED LIVES for FREE?*
Download from Book Funnel after you sign up.

FREE Newsletter signup
From my web page.

Sheila Hunter's Biography

Sheila Hunter was passionate about her family and loved to research their history. Her father, Murdoch, was the grandson of Scottish immigrants, and he was both born and brought up on the Victorian goldfields, as was her mother. These stories are gleaned from a mix of her husbands and her Scottish families and their settlement and contribution to our country.

Sheila's husband's family were also from Scotland (McLeans) and came out as described in the book, but they were of the illiterate class (speaking only Gaelic) from the Isle of Mull. Life was hard for them, and they were helped to learn and settle in the new colony by John (Dunmore) Lang and his wife. They were taught to cut trees, farm, milk cows, and make cheese, and they learnt with gusto, turning these skills into what later became **Norco Dairy Co-Op** in Northern New South Wales.

Sheila was born in New Zealand to Australian parents Murdoch and Mabel McDonald (or Macdonald as they were known before they went to NZ) and moved back to Melbourne, Australia, with her family when Sheila was a child. She was a nurse by training but an adventurer in her life! A wife and mother, she was a great storyteller, often making up very long stories for her children and grandchildren. They would listen, entranced by the stories of her telling. Often, these whiled away many hours of travel in the car while travelling Australia.

In 1999, Sheila was awarded one of twenty Federal Recipients of the **Year of the Senior Citizen Awards.** She was an amazing woman! Life was tough growing up during WW2 in a single-parent family (her dad had returned to his children in New Zealand). They lived near the docks in Melbourne in a family Service Station. Sheila went to school during the day and worked in the Service Station after school, at weekends and nights. During this time, she won a full 'Cello scholarship to Melbourne's conservatory, but it was during the war and on arriving home one day, she discovered that her mother had sold her 'Cello to help pay the household bills. Life was hard!

On leaving school, she enrolled in Nursing only to be the butt of jokes from her family, but she not only succeeded but excelled at this caring role, ending up as acting Matron of 'Roma' Private Hospital in East Gosford NSW. Sheila married Norman M. Hunter in 1955 and lived in Avoca Beach all their married life. They had two children. Norman and Sheila were a well-known couple on the Central Coast NSW, with Norman a renowned Real Estate Agent who also built, owned and operated Avoca Beach Picture Theatre in Avoca Beach, as well as amassing a fantastic Natural History Collection that was known and studied worldwide and together they were part of many groups and associations in the area.

It was soon after their marriage that they faced the loss of Norman's orchard on the Nepean River at Birds Eye Corner, Castlereagh, due to dust from the Gravel pit from the next-door farm at Castlereagh, near Penrith NSW. This same orchard was the first farm in the area in 1801 at *'Jacksons' Ford'* or *'Birds Eye Corner'* at Castlereagh (known in the book as *Riverbend*).

In 2000, her beloved husband and fellow adventurer, Norman, died from Dementia, and she, unfortunately, followed only two years later from Cancer.

I have endeavoured to continue the stories of some of her beloved characters in some of my books.

Shelia Hunter, my wonderful, inspirational mother, died in 2002

Sara

www.ingramcontent.com/pod-product-compliance
Lightning Source LLC
Chambersburg PA
CBHW031945240626
47153CB00003B/867